MYTHS AND FOLK STORIES OF
BRITAIN AND IRELAND

KENNETH M^CLEISH

MYTHS

AND

FOLK STORIES

OF

BRITAIN AND

IRELAND

LONGMAN

For
ROBERT YEATMAN

McLeish, Kenneth
  Myths and folk stories of Britain and
  Ireland.
  1. Tales — Great Britain   2. Legends
  — Great Britain   3. Tales — Ireland
  4. Legends — Ireland
  I. Title.
  398.2'0941   GR141
  ISBN 0-582-23599-5

LONGMAN GROUP UK LIMITED
Longman House, Burnt Mill, Harlow, Essex CM20 2JE, England
and Associated Companies throughout the world.

First published 1986

Set in 11/13 Linotron Palatino

Printed in Great Britain by Butler & Tanner Ltd, Frome, Somerset

CONTENTS

v

CONTENTS

INTRODUCTION

The stories

Most of the stories in this book were first told in the Dark Ages, between the fourth century A.D., when the Romans abandoned Britain, and the eleventh century A.D., when the Normans came. Their main purpose was entertainment: in times when reading and writing were rare, bards, jesters and tale-tellers were welcome everywhere, and listening to stories was a pastime enjoyed by everyone.

The heroes and heroines of most of the stories were ordinary mortals, either lords and ladies or plain folk leading simple lives. But their adventures were far from ordinary. Their world was full of giants, dragons, witches, goblins and shape-changers, and magic was vital to everyone, from blacksmiths and washerwomen to warlords like Beowulf, Cuchulain and Lancelot. As well as enjoying the supernatural, people liked their stories to include real people and places, and the story-tellers obliged by setting their accounts in actual towns like York or Caerleon, and by incorporating such historical characters as Julius Caesar or Joseph of Arimathea.

Nonetheless, no one for a moment believed that any of these tales were true. The Brittany or Camelot they mention are as fantastical as Lionesse or the waterfall that rims the world; Julius Caesar fights side by side with giants; people live for four or five hundred years, with little concern for what 'true' history might say. The stories give a kind of alternative, invented account of the British Isles, located not in real time and space but in the imagination. There are no time-charts or maps to them: magic needs no such boundaries.

Later accounts

Over the centuries, many writers have tried to make ordered sense out of these random tales. The King Arthur stories, in particular, attracted the attention of Christian writers who reworked them in Christian terms, setting Masses and chapels side by side with the original myths' giants, wizards and shape-changers without any feeling of unlikeliness. Would-be historians quarried the tales for early kings and queens, and linked them to what they already knew of other nations' history – which is why Old King Cole makes alliances with the Romans, or Galahad travels through the same heathen lands as the historical crusader-knights. Other stories, by contrast, and particularly those from Wales, Ireland and Scotland, keep to pre-Christian, Celtic roots, and their events move in a disordered, timeless blur, the poetry of dreams.

The present book, like its companion-volume of Greek myths *Children of the Gods*, sets out to tell the basic stories straight through without interruption, disentangling them as much as possible from later, more 'logical' or 'ordered' accounts. To expand, explore and explain where necessary, we have put other stories, alternative versions, notes, lists and family trees in a separate section at the end of the main text. A star * in the text means that there is more information in this section. A dagger † refers to a family tree. On pages 257–259 are some suggestions for further reading, a guide to some of the more striking later uses to which these stories have been put.

Acknowledgements

Kenneth McLeish's versions of *The Bogles and the Moon* (Chapter 19), *Dougal and the Wizard-King* (Chapter 20) and *Kathleen* (Chapter 21) appeared, in a slightly different form, in his *Tales of the British Isles* (Ginn, 1984), and we are grateful for permission to use them here. The story of *Assipattle* (Chapter 20) is retold from an oral account in *The Folklore of Orkney and Shetland* by E. Marwick (Batsford 1975). The author thanks Valerie McLeish for help and encouragement during the writing of the book and for compiling the index; he is also grateful to Anne Nash for typing it. Author and publisher acknowledge the financial assistance of the Arts Council of Great Britain.

How to pronounce the names

Most names are pronounced exactly as they look. The pronunciations of the commoner Welsh and Gaelic names are shown below:

Arawn	/arown/
Blodeuedd	/blodie-eth/
Cearnach	/kyahnakh/
Celtchair	/kyeltkhieə/
Conchubhar	/kawnkhoohah/
Cuailgne	/koohlyə/
Cuchulain	/kahoohlin/
Culhwch	/kilhoohkh/
Eoghan	/ohn/
Feirceirtne	/feəkeərtnə/
Gilvaethwy	/gilviethwee/
Goreu	/gawrie/
Gwawl	/gwowl/
Gwrhyr	/goohriər/
Laoghaire	/llyərə/
Leoghaire	/llyawərə/
Lleu	/llay/
Lughaidh	/lloohee/
Mallolwych	/mallawlwikh/
Manawydan	/manawidan/
Niwl	/nyoohl/
Pwyll	/poohill/
Wrnach	/oohrnakh/

KEY

			ie	as in	bite	kh	as in	loch	
			o	as in	pot	l	as in	led	
a	as in	bad	oh	as in	note	ll	as in	Llandudno (Welsh l)	
ah	as in	father	ooh	as in	boot	m	as in	man	
aw	as in	saw	ow	as in	now	n	as in	sun	
ay	as in	make	b	as in	bad	p	as in	pot	
e	as in	bed	d	as in	day	r	as in	red	
ee	as in	sheep	f	as in	few	th	as in	thing	
eə	as in	there	g	as in	good	v	as in	view	
ə	as in	about	h	as in	hot	w	as in	wet	
i	as in	ship	k	as in	king	y	as in	yet	

BEGINNINGS

1

GIANTS

Albion

The boldest of all the giants, in all parts of the world, was Albion. He was king of a small triangular island in the northern sea, and every one of its inhabitants, giants, mortals, trolls and elves, paid him homage. The island was pleasant and fertile: its woods were full of deer, its rivers teemed with fish, cattle browsed in its meadows and its moors were shaggy with sheep. It was a peaceful place, and its people lived in plenty and content. Only Albion was restless. He knew a secret hidden from his followers: there was a world outside their island, and what seemed a paradise was really a prison. They were trapped, prisoners of the gods, and their gaoler was Hercules.

In the first years of the world, many centuries before, there had been peace and harmony among all its inhabitants. But as the years passed, squabbles and border-wars began. The fiercest of all were between the earth-born giants and the sky-born gods. The gods coveted the forests and valleys where the giants made their homes; the giants envied the gods their cloud-palaces. For centuries hatred festered between them; but their power was equal and neither side could outmatch the other. In the end the giants decided to band together and destroy the gods in a single, devastating assault. They built a stone-pile as high as heaven, clambered up it and began tearing down the gods' battlements and lobbing hills inside like pebbles, to crush the gods. The gods fought them off with stones from the battlements, beams from the castle roof, enormous ladles and cauldrons from the kitchens. But they were outnumbered, and would have lost the battle if Hercules, the strongest mortal in the world, had not climbed the stone-pile to rescue them. He carried a club made from a ripped-up tree, a bow and a quiverful of arrows that never missed. One by one he toppled the giants from the stone-pile; when they crashed from heaven to earth and the breath was knocked out of them, he scrambled after them and clubbed them dead*.

So the giants' army was defeated, and their corpses lay strewn across the countryside. The survivors gathered their families and stumbled into exile, while the gods jeered at them. But the gods' jeering soon turned to fury: they found that the giants had stolen the golden apples* that guarded the gods' immortality. Desperate, they mounted their wind-horses and galloped after them – in vain, for the giants had slipped away to the northernmost countries of the world, and kept themselves and the golden apples well out of sight. The gods gave Hercules the task of tracking them down, rebuilt their castle walls and went back to their old lives of feasting and enjoyment. But without immortality they knew that one day, far in the future, their power would end and their glory would pass from the world forever.

As for the giants, they had the apples and they had everlasting life*. They leapt and pranced for joy, and their dancing shook the earth. They made peace-treaties with the trolls and forest-spirits of their new northern homes, and settled there. But their fear of prowling Hercules made them wary, and they developed a skill close to invisibility, and have used it ever since. If danger threatens or if strangers approach who might be stronger than themselves, they stand stock-still, hardly breathing, and the strangers mistake them for trees or hills and pass harmlessly on their way.

All this was what Albion remembered; this was what made him restless. He thought it absurd that a giant-king, an immortal like himself, should have to skulk in a backwater of the world for fear of Hercules, a puny mortal half his size. He planned to travel south, ambush Hercules and kill him; after that, Albion would collect a second giant-army, build a second stone-pile, besiege the sky-castle and unseat the gods.

Albion began striding the length and breadth of his kingdom, practising his wrestling-skills on deer, cattle, wolves and bears. At last his spies brought word that Hercules had been sighted, striding west to attack giant Geryon*. Albion leapt from the southernmost cliffs of his kingdom, splashed across the sea to the mainland and made his way south. He planned to lie in ambush for Hercules in a mountain-range called the Pyrenees, jump out on him and throttle him. Unfortunately Hercules, who was well used to giants' ways, realised what was happening, crept up behind Albion and battered out his brains before

2

he could lift a hand to defend himself.

Hercules left Albion's carcase to rot where it lay and passed on his way to deal with Geryon. He had no idea who Albion was or where he came from: he thought him just another giant, and killing him just another morning's work. But to the people of Albion's kingdom, their lord's death was a tragedy. They crept south, hiding carefully from Hercules, gave Albion's body a royal funeral, and honoured his memory by naming their island after him.

Brutus

The death of their king destroyed all ambition in the giants of Albion. They kept to their peaceful island, seldom venturing past the cliffs and seas which guarded it from the mainland. They tended their animals and grew their crops, cut off from the world and content to be so*. Their isolation lasted for centuries: even the apples of immortality were forgotten, and gathered dust in a forest cave*.

While Albion stagnated, the rest of the world changed fast. Its rulers had once been gods, spirits, nymphs, elves and other supernatural creatures; now human beings ruled. They peopled every continent, sailed ships on every sea, and filled the sky with a buzz of words that rose to heaven and beat on the gods' ears as waves beat on the shore. Some of the words were peaceful: prayers, songs, stories and endless, affable gossip. But from time to time peacefulness curdled into violence, and the noise was all of war: battle-cries, victory-cheers, funeral-laments and the snarling of politicians.

The fiercest human war of all was fought between the peoples of Greece and Troy. It began when Paris, a Trojan prince, kidnapped the Greek princess Helen, and the Greeks sent an army to win her back. For ten years they besieged Troy, and the fighting was so fierce, and so evenly matched, that the gods gave up all their other entertainments and ran to watch. In the end the Greeks used the trick of the Wooden Horse*, slipped armed men into Troy and captured it. They slaughtered every Trojan who resisted, crammed the rest into cargo-ships and took them home as slaves. Only a handful of Trojans escaped. Prince Antenor led a column of refugees overland to Gaul, and settled there; Prince Helenus led his followers westwards, and hid where no Greeks would ever think of looking for him, in the heart of Greece itself; Prince Aeneas, son of the goddess Venus, sailed south to Italy*, married Princess Lavinia and founded the Roman race.

In due course (since all human beings, even goddesses' sons, are mortal) Aeneas died and his son Ascanius became king. By this time Ascanius was already an old man, and his son Silvius was a grown-up prince with a group of followers all his own. He was wild and headstrong, far beyond Ascanius' control, and he and his followers racketed all over Italy, drinking, gambling, rioting and doing exactly as they pleased. In the end, Silvius made love with his own cousin and made her pregnant, and the royal soothsayers told King Ascanius that the child would cause the deaths of his father and mother, would wander the world in exile till he settled in a far country, and would establish a kingdom greater than any the world had ever seen. Sure enough, when the time came for the child to be born, his mother lay three days in labour and died of it. Her servants called the baby Brutus* and gave him to nannies to bring up. He grew up strong and fearless, and when he was big enough to sit astride a horse he became one of his father's wildest and most riotous followers. On his fifteenth birthday he went hunting with his father, accompanied only by the beaters whose job was to drive game towards them. The beaters disturbed a stag, and Brutus set arrow to bow and fired. At the exact moment when the arrow left his bow, the stag leapt sideways and Brutus' arrow stabbed his father's heart and killed him.

So the first part of the soothsayers' prophecy came true, and King Ascanius saw to the second part by banishing Brutus from Italy. Brutus, saddened and sobered by his father's death, begged a boat, a sword and a single servant, and sailed with heavy heart to Greece. Here he was astonished to find a tribe of outlaws living in the woods, and even more astonished to hear their language: not Greek but Trojan like his own. They were the descendants of the Trojan refugees Helenus had led to Greece after the fall of Troy, and of runaway Trojan slaves who preferred life in hiding to serving cruel Greek masters. When these people heard who Brutus was, they elected him their leader and begged him to take them far away from Greece. What could Brutus do? He had no ships, no money and no power; his people's only weapons were kitchen-knives, pitchforks and the puny bows and clubs they had cut for themselves in the woods. They would be no match for well-trained, well-armed Greek soldiers.

Instead of weakness, Brutus decided on a pretence of strength. He sent a letter to Pandrasos, king of the Greeks, telling him where the Trojans were and demanding either land to cultivate in peace or ships, money and freedom to sail wherever in the world he chose. Pandrasos replied to this letter exactly as Brutus supposed he would, by sending an army – and the Trojans tricked them into the woods, half a dozen at a time, killed them and stole their weapons. In the end Brutus led a party of men into the Greek camp at night, and kidnapped Pandrasos from under his sevants' noses. Pandrasos stood shivering in his nightshirt, surrounded by Trojans; the moonlight glinted on their knives, and Brutus said, 'Now will you agree to our demands? Give us ships, food, money, freedom to sail – and your own daughter Imogen as queen.'

Grinding his teeth, Pandrasos agreed. Hercules carried the proclamation round his kingdom – and so many Trojans came flocking from the woods that a fleet of 324 ships was needed to carry them all from Greece. While the Trojans began loading food, water and weapons, and Pandrasos gave each of them a present of gold or silver according to rank, Brutus and Imogen were married. The Trojans embarked and the fleet set sail; Imogen stood on the deck of Brutus' ship, gazing back at Greece with tear-filled eyes. On shore, however, Pandrasos and his people laughed with joy to see their troublesome enemies leave at last, and their whoops of satisfaction filled the sky.

Corin

All that day, the next night and the day after, the Trojans sailed through calm seas with the wind behind them. At evening they beached on a small island and went ashore. The island had wide roads and well-tilled fields, and the smoke from a thousand cooking-fires rose from its farms and villages. There were geese and chickens in the yards, and sheep and goats in the byres, crying to be milked. But for all these signs of habitation, the Trojans found not a single living soul – and when they climbed to the main town of the island, they found its streets clogged with corpses, its water-cisterns foul with blood and its air greasy with the stench of death. Pirates had visited it that very morning, slaughtered the inhabitants, looted their property and carried their children away to slavery.

Sickened and sorrowful, the Trojans wandered through the echoing streets, peering into empty houses and stepping over the gaping bodies of the dead. They were reminded of their own city, Troy, on the night the Greeks captured it. Was it a sign from the gods? Was this the new home the Trojans had fought so hard and sailed so far to find?

To fill his people's minds, Brutus set them to burying the dead, slaughtering animals and gathering wood for cooking-fires. While they prepared a sombre, heavy-hearted meal, he walked alone through the dark streets of the town, to the temple at its heart. It was sacred to the moon-goddess, and he made offerings of corn, blood and wine, prayed to her for guidance and lay down in the yard to sleep. In the dead of night the goddess herself visited him, a gigantic figure in glittering silver robes. She told him that the island was not the Trojans' new home, that they were in immediate danger from the pirates, and that they should sail west through the Pillars of Hercules*, north along the lip of the waterfall that girds the earth, and on till they found an island inhabited by giants: here they were to settle, and they would build their new kingdom.

As soon as it was dawn, Brutus ran to the seashore, roused his people and hurried them back on board ship. Muttering and grumbling, they bent to the oars. Why should they leave a well-stocked, fertile land for the miseries of open sea? All it needed was one sharp glance from Neptune, god of the sea, one storm, and they would be tipped over the rim of the world and drowned. There would have been mutiny if the lookout had not seen, far behind them but closing fast, the fleet of pirate-ships, their sails fat in the breeze and their weapons glinting in the sun. All Trojan muttering ceased; they hurled on all the sail they had and stirred the sea to foam as they rowed desperately for the Pillars of Hercules.

The Pillars were like stone jaws gaping to drink the sea. The channel between them was white with foam; waves hurled themselves at the rocks on either side; spray hung like fog. The Trojans heard the pirates shouting in alarm behind them, and saw them wheel their ships and give up the chase; they felt the current snatch their keels and toss them through the straits; they cowered as the rock-walls loomed on either side; then they were through, bobbing like twigs in a stream.

For the rest of that day and all the next night they rowed wearily northwards. In the mists to their left they could hear the rumble of the waterfall at the rim of the world; from time to time in the darkness they heard howls and shrieks which they took to be ghosts' wailing or the singing of sea-witches who hunt for human souls. In the morning, worn out with terror and with rowing, they beached the ships and splashed to land. They flung themselves on the pebbles in rows like herrings, and fell into exhausted sleep. They would have lain there till evening, a whole army snoring in the shallows, if Brutus had not suddenly sensed a shadow across his face, and leapt up with a cry which snatched the others from sleep and sent them fumbling for their swords. Standing over him, blocking the sun, was a man three metres high, dressed in fawnskins and brandishing a club made from a torn-up tree.

'It's Hercules!' the Trojans wailed, dropping their swords and clutching each other in panic. 'What hope is left for us now?'

But instead of battering Brutus dead, the stranger gave a bellow of delight, threw down his club and hugged him like a long-lost friend. It was not Hercules, but his son Corin (whom he fathered on a local girl on his way to deal with the giant Geryon); Corin was the king of the area, and his people were descendants of the refugees who had years before followed Antenor from blazing Troy; they were distant cousins of Brutus' own followers and now fell on their necks and welcomed them. There was feasting and dancing for days, and much love-making between Brutus' young men and the girls of Corin's tribe. But even this welcoming spot was not the Trojans' new homeland. There were too many people for the countryside to support, and the mountain-tribes inland were many and hostile. In the end Brutus called the people together and offered them a choice. All who wanted could stay where they were, settling the countryside and defending themselves against the mountain-people as best they could; the others would go back on board ship, and he and Corin would lead them north again to unknown lands, to the fertile island the moon-goddess had promised them.

So they divided, with many tears. The settlers began building walled towns and castles to keep out the mountain-people*, and Brutus, Corin and their followers sailed north. They travelled for days, following the coastline and landing each night for food and rest. Whenever their spirits flagged, Brutus encouraged them by reminding them of the moon-goddess' prophecy, and Corin took a hand at the oars, rowing as strongly as three ordinary men, and telling uproarious tales of the giants he had wrestled (for he hated them and hunted them as fiercely as his father Hercules had done). On the whole voyage they were attacked only once, by a tribe of Gauls led by King Goffar; the Gauls outnumbered the Trojans ten to one, and would have finished them off if Corin had not run berserk across the battlefield, swinging a two-handed axe and splitting enemies like firewood. After this adventure they left the mainland coast behind, crossed a stretch of wind-blown stormy sea, and came at last to the place the moon-goddess had promised them, the island of Albion with its white cliffs gleaming in the sun.

At first, when the Trojans landed in Albion, they thought it another deserted island, like the pirate-plundered place they'd visited before. But in the weeks that followed, as they built houses and began ploughing the land for fields, they discovered that they were not alone. There were giants in the woods and hills, and although they kept well out of sight and never made a full-scale attack, they reached out of hiding whenever they could, snatched cattle and people and crunched their bones. This went on until Corin surrounded the whole area with giant-traps, deep holes in the ground camouflaged with branches. The giants were too slow-witted to step over them, and every time one was caught Corin hauled him out of the hole and throttled him. Finally, the leader of the giants, a four-metre, two-headed monster called Gogmagog, gathered a score of his bravest followers and came lolloping out of hiding in the trees to attack, swinging a firtree-club and hallooing till the hillsides rang. The Trojans were unarmed and helpless, and the giants captured many of them and squeezed their lives. But then Brutus and his men began tangling the giants' legs in hunting-nets, and as soon as each giant crashed to the ground Corin put his hands round his throat and strangled him. Finally only Gogmagog was left, and Corin threw down his weapons and roared at him to settle the battle by a wrestling-match. They circled each other, tall as saplings, looking for an opening. Suddenly Gogmagog sprang on to Corin's back, wrapped his arms round him from behind and began snapping his ribs like twigs. Gasping with pain, Corin used all his strength to lift Gogmagog clear of the ground, staggered to the cliff-edge and tipped him over. Gogmagog shattered like a stone on the rocks below*.

Gogmagog's death ended the giants' resistance, and the settlers were left at last in peace. Corin's followers made their home in the westernmost corner of the island, and called it Corinwall, or Cornwall, after him. Brutus' followers, calling themselves Brutons, or Britons, after him, spread across the southern part of Albion. As for the giants, they retreated even deeper than before into the woods and gullies, and have stayed in hiding ever since.

2

KINGS AND QUEENS

Brain-sickness

Brutus ruled Britain for twenty-three years, and when he died the island passed to his sons Locrin, Albanact and Camber. Locrin ruled his father's old kingdom in the south; Albanact ruled the north of the island, and called it Albany after himself; Camber ruled the west, and called it Cambria. There was no argument between them. But far away in Germany, across the eastern sea, King Humbert had long been looking at Britain with greedy eyes, and now he gathered an invasion-fleet and swept into Albany, killing Albanact and forcing his people to scatter south for help. Locrin's and Camber's army met the Germans in pitched battle beside a wide river in the north. The British outnumbered Humbert's forces and easily routed them, and Humbert himself hid in a rowing-boat, hoping to slip down the river unnoticed and escape. But the river was tidal, and the tide was on the flood: he sank and drowned, giving his name to the river (the Humber) for evermore. Next morning Camber and Locrin went to inspect the German captives – and Locrin fell headlong in love with one of them, Humbert's daughter Estreldis.

To say the least, this was unfortunate. Locrin was due to marry someone else, Gwendolen, daughter of King Corin of Cornwall, and although Corin was by now aged, a husk of his former self, he still had the strength of three ordinary men, and an army to back any claim he cared to make. The choice was impossible, and Locrin agonised over it for weeks. Finally he decided. He married Gwendolen and made her his queen, and for his German princess Estreldis he dug an underground room, by the moon-goddess' temple in his capital city, and furnished it like a palace. He visited Estreldis each day for seven years (pretending to Gwendolen that he was sacrificing to the goddess), and at the end of that time both Gwendolen and Estreldis were pregnant. They bore children on the same day, Gwendolen a son called Maddan and Estreldis a daughter called Hebren. Hebren stayed hidden underground with her mother; Maddan went to his grandfather Corin to learn horse-riding, wrestling, archery and other princely skills. So the children grew up, and on the day when they were both sixteen, the aged Corin unexpectedly died, and Gwendolen went to Cornwall for his funeral. At once Locrin fetched Estreldis and Hebren out of their underground room and proclaimed that he was divorcing Gwendolen and making Estreldis his queen, that very day. Furious, Gwendolen gathered a Cornish army and led it against Locrin's forces, galloping on a white horse at the head of it with her father Corin's bow and arrows in her hands. The armies met and fought, and before the day was far advanced Gwendolen set arrow to bow and shot Locrin dead. She proclaimed herself queen of all Locrin's lands, buried Estreldis alive, and threw Hebren to drown in the wide river which separates the kingdoms of Cornwall and Cambria. (It is still called the Hebren, or Severn, after her.)

Locrin's treatment of Gwendolen, and Gwendolen's even more savage treatment of Estreldis and Hebren, were the first signs of a brain-sickness which infected generation after generation of Britain's kings and queens. Sometimes it lay hidden, and the rulers were noble and kind; at other times it raged in them like plague, driving them to acts of cruelty or insanity like none seen on earth before. Gwendolen's grandchild Mempric murdered his own brother to snatch the throne, then scandalised everyone by marrying not a princess or other young woman but a handsome boy; wolves ripped him to shreds one day on a hunting trip. His descendant Bladud was was even crazier: he rejected the moon-goddess and instead worshipped Sul, a witch from the underworld who bubbled to the surface in boiling sulphur-springs*. He experimented with spells and magic potions, and the end of his reign came when he decided one day that he could fly, leapt off his palace roof flapping his arms and muttering spells, and crashed.

King Leir

After Bladud, it seemed at first as if the brain-fever had abated. His son Leir was one of Britain's sanest and best-loved kings. But Leir's reign dragged on for sixty years, until there was hardly anyone alive who could remember the start of it. As he grew older, the brains curdled in his skull, and he alternated between arrogance (the rags of his former majesty) and drooling, self-pitying senility. He had three grown-up daughters, Goneril, Regan and Cordeil, and one day decided they were ripe for marriage and sent for them. 'I intend to divide my kingdom between you,' he said. 'But first, I demand to know how much you love me. Answer in turn. First, Goneril.'

'I love you more than my own self,' said Goneril.

'A third of my kingdom is yours. Regan?'

'I love you more than anyone else on earth,' said Regan.

'A third of my kingdom is yours. Cordeil?'

'Father, how can I answer? I love you as much as any father deserves,' said Cordeil.

This answer threw Leir into a fury. He divided Cordeil's third of the kingdom between her sisters, and banished her to Gaul where she married Aganip, king of the Franks. Goneril married the king of Albany and Regan married the king of Cornwall; it was agreed that they should entertain Leir and his followers, one month each in turn. But Leir was old and petulant. He took four hundred followers to Goneril's castle, and he and they lorded it over her husband and insulted her servants till she could bear no more of it. 'Father,' she said, 'you must go to Regan now – and when you next come here, leave all but two hundred followers behind.' Furious, Leir set off with his followers to Cornwall. But Goneril sent riders to warn her sister, and Leir found Regan's castle barred against him, and she refused to let him in unless he dismissed all but a hundred of his followers. Backwards and forwards he went between his daughters, and the end of it was that he was left with no followers at all but his jester, a wild-eyed old man as crazy as himself. They wandered together in the forests and on the bleak moors, and Leir in his madness raged at the weather and shook his fists at the storm. Winter was coming, and the jester knew that they could not survive it unless one of Leir's daughters took pity on them. He shipped his babbling master across the sea to Gaul, and Leir threw himself on Cordeil's mercy. She pitied him, and rage at the way her sisters had treated him set hatred blazing in her mind. She stormed to Britain with a warfleet, conquered the combined armies of Goneril and Regan, executed them both and restored her father to his throne. He ruled peacefully for three more years until his death, when Cordeil succeeded him*.

As soon as Cordeil became queen, the family madness descended into her nephews (Goneril's and Regan's sons) and sent them rampaging across the countryside like maddened cattle. They fought each other; they fought the farmers and townsfolk; they fought the armies Cordeil sent to capture them. In the end she was filled with such despair that she hanged herself, and the two young men divided her kingdom between them. Even then their arguing continued, and the royal madness took a new form still: hatred between brothers. For generations every pair of princes bickered and brawled, and in the end two squabbling brothers and their mother brought the dynasty of Brutus and Corin to a dismal end. Ferrec and Porrec, the sons of King Gorboduc, fought from the moment they were born, and when he died raised armies and made war on one another to win the throne. Porrec killed Ferrec – and madness welled up in the mind of their mother Judon, so that she crept into Porrec's bedroom and tore him limb from limb. Civil war followed, with bloodshed and misery on every side; in the end King Cloten of Cornwall seized control and a new dynasty of British rulers, untainted by madness, at last began.

Britons and Romans

While Cordeil was queen of Britain, two twin brothers, Romulus and Remus, founded the city of Rome in far-off Italy*. Until that day the peoples of Britain and Italy (who shared an ancestor, Trojan Aeneas) had been good friends. In the time of King Ebrauc of Britain, the Britons had even helped the Italians repopulate their country: there were no Italian women, and the Italian race would have died out if Ebrauc had not sent his own thirty daughters to marry Italian noblemen and fill the land with babies.

As soon as Rome was founded, however, all friendship came to a sudden end. Romulus and Remus were sons of Mars the war-god, and their fiery character passed from them to the people of their city. The Romans were interested in conquest, not friendship: when they wanted something they took it, with no apologies and no regrets. And what they wanted was tin from Cornwall and silver and gold from Cambria. At first they made trade-agreements; but as the years passed and their power grew, it was obvious that they would soon turn to war instead. Their growth was checked just once, when the British princes Belin and Brenn* took an army to Italy, sacked the city of Rome and burned it; but the Romans soon recovered, and ever afterwards, as well as coveting Welsh and Cornish metal-mines, they regarded the Britons as dangerous enemies and planned to make them slaves.

In the reign of King Casbellaun of Britain, a Roman prince called Julius Caesar wrote to the Britons offering them the choice of alliance (and paying taxes to Rome) or slavery. Casbellaun wrote back that the Britons had a third choice of their own, and preferred it: freedom – and when Caesar furiously invaded, the British routed his armies and sent them whimpering back to their ships. Britain would never have fallen, if Casbellaun had not quarrelled with one of his most powerful supporters, Androgeus, and so split the British against themselves. Caesar took his chance, and with Androgeus' help trapped Casbellaun's soldiers on a hilltop and starved them into surrender. Casbellaun had to agree to accept alliance with Rome, and to hand over taxes of fifteen times his own weight in silver every year. He sent his nephew Cunobelin* to be educated in Rome, and when Cunobelin grew up and became king of Britain, he began a friendship between Rome and Britain which lasted for sixteen generations, till barbarians from the east destroyed the city of Rome itself.

The plundering of Britain

The link between Britain and the Romans lasted for four hundred years*. The Britons paid taxes to Rome, and in return the Romans built roads, castles and towns in Britain, taught the people efficient ways of farming and sent legions to protect them against Picts from Albany, barbarians from Hibernia and Cambria, brigands from Gwent and Geats and Saxons from across the sea. Above all, they gave Britain the religion of Jesus Christ: they built churches and abbeys, and sent priests to teach the Gospel. The first Christian Roman emperor, Constantine, was born in Britain; his grandfather was old King Coel*.

To the people of Britain, their island was a Garden of Eden, a peaceful paradise far from the turmoil of the world. It would have surprised them to know that the Romans regarded it as a remote, chilly place, blanketed by drizzle and filled with people too spineless to defend themselves. The Romans put up with Britain's hardships for the sake of its tin, gold, leather, corn and slaves; but as soon as barbarian armies began attacking Rome itself, they pulled their legions home and left the British people to learn warskills or surrender to the invaders, whichever they preferred.

As soon as the Romans were gone Britain's enemies fell on it like wolves on a sheepfold. Saxon fleets harassed the coast, and Picts and Cambrians plundered the border-towns. For a time, under the strong rule of King Octavius of Gwent, the British held them back; but Octavius was an old man, and as the years passed his hands grew too shaky to hold a warspear and his mind too senile to concentrate on state affairs. He planned to pass royal power to his only child, a daughter, and to the man she married – and he hoped for a war-chief who would win the respect of every noble in the land. But two princes, not one, came forward for the princess' hand. Their names were Conan and Maximian, and they began by fighting it out like dogs; then they decided that the British throne was hardly worth dying for, and that if they joined forces they would find richer pickings somewhere else. They made a truce; Maximian married the bewildered princess, and as soon as the crown and the British army were his he abandoned her forever, and he, Conan and their armies sailed to mainland Gaul and invaded the rich country of Armorica. Armorica was a land of farmers, not soldiers; its people were so unhandy at fighting that they held their spears the wrong way round, dropped their swords on their toes and finally turned and ran whenever soldiers came in sight; they fell into British hands as ripe apples fall from trees. As soon as the fighting was done, Maximian led his army south to attack the Romans, and Conan crowned himself king of Armorica and renamed it Brittany*. He decided to fill it with settlers who were British through and through, and sent messengers to Britain welcoming anyone who cared to come.

The Saxons, Picts, Cambrians and other barbarians watched with glee as fleet after fleet set sail from Britain to Brittany, gradually emptying Britain of fighting men – and as soon as there was no one left to defend it but women, children, priests and nuns, they swarmed to attack. Britain was like a rich carcase in a field, and for fifty years plunderers fell on it and gorged themselves. They burned the farms and sacked the towns; they cut the throats of every male they found, raped the women and battered out children's brains before their mother's eyes. Above all, they smashed the churches, defiled the altars and crucified the priests. What could the Britons do? They were too few to defend themselves and too scared of plunderers to work the land: if there had not been fish in the rivers and game in the woods, they would have starved. As each generation of children grew up, their elders tried to persuade them to stay and make a stand; they failed each time, and shiploads of refugees abandoned Britain for

14

Brittany, Germany, Italy and the lands beyond, leaving their country wallowing like a dying whale in the cold northern sea.

Constantinus

At last the few British survivors could stand no more of it. They provisioned a boat with fresh water and salted herring, put an old priest called Guithelin into it and told him to go to King Aldroen of Brittany (Conan's great-grandson) and offer him Britain as a gift, if only he would come with an army to defend it. Guithelin's monks rowed him to Brittany, and he faithfully delivered the message. Aldroen was delighted with the offer – not for himself (for why should he give up a rich, settled country for an underpopulated land harassed by enemies?), but for his ambitious brother Constantinus. Constantinus badly needed a kingdom of his own, and Aldroen thought the British offer an ideal way of getting rid of him; he gave him two thousand men and a fleet of ships, and rubbed his hands with satisfaction to see them sail. Constantinus landed at Totnes in Devon, and the Britons ran to welcome him, waving their arms and filling the sky with thin, starved cries. Guithelin crowned Constantinus king of Britain, and gave him his own god-daughter as queen.

It was one thing to be crowned king, and another to make Britain fit to rule. Constantinus and his soldiers spent their lives marching from one end of the kingdom to the other, fighting bloodthirsty battles against ruthless barbarians. The threat of death was constant; there was no security, and as soon as each of the king's three sons was born, Constantinus sent him deep into the countryside to be brought up in safety. Constans (the eldest) went to an abbey at Winchester, where he trained to be a monk; his brothers Aurelius and Uther went to Guithelin, who taught them the arts of government.

So the years passed, and gradually, thanks to Constantinus' leadership, the British people's confidence returned and they began to rebuild their towns and gather up the rags of their former lives. They were full of gratitude to Constantinus, and eager to honour him – and the more they fawned on him the more the native British chiefs began to plot against him. Jealous of his royal authority, and terrified in case he handed the kingdom on to his sons and established a dynasty – a foreigner, a stranger from overseas! – they skulked in their castles

15

planning his downfall, until one day, when the princes Aurelius and Uther were hardly ten years old, an assassin dragged Constantinus behind a hedge in his own castle garden and cut his throat.

3

VORTIGERN

Pulling the strings

The man who murdered Constantinus was Vortigern, prince of Gwent. He wiped his knife and put it away, then staggered round the hedge shouting for the guards. He said that a gang of murderers had held him helpless while they killed the king, then clubbed him unconscious and made their getaway. Everyone believed his story and admired his bravery. They would have crowned him king that very morning if he had not cunningly pointed out that there were three royal princes ahead of him, even if two of them were children and the third was an apprentice monk. Next, he galloped to Winchester and asked to see Constans, the dead king's heir. Constans was nineteen; he was weak-willed, foppish and foolish, and Vortigern easily persuaded him that it would be far more fun to be king than to spend his life hoeing cabbages and muttering prayers. Constans let his hair grow long enough to cover his tonsure and support a crown, and changed his monk's brown-sacking clothes for royal velvet; not long afterwards Vortigern escorted him to London and watched with a secret smile as the people crowned him king.

Constans loved being king. He spent his days hunting, hawking, galloping round his estates on a pearl-white charger, flirting with palace ladies and enjoying gargantuan banquets of peacocks, sucking-pigs, roast swans, marzipan and honey-ice, while musicians sang, tumblers danced and jesters told riddles and showed him conjuring tricks. The one thing he hated was government, and he gladly left that to Vortigern, signing every document put in front of him and answering 'Yes if you like' to every question he was asked. In short, he was a gorgeous, sawdust-headed puppet, and Vortigern pulled his strings. The British chiefs and nobles who had muttered against King Constantinus fretted even harder than before – but what could they do to stop Vortigern? He surrounded himself with armed guards, and kept a rabble of Pictish soldiers loyal to him (by giving them strong drink and cash, the two things they loved best in the world); people who spoke out against him disappeared soon afterwards, and their mutilated bodies were found in the castle pond. Even when Vortigern's Picts burst into King Constans' bedroom one night in a drunken orgy, slit his throat and placed the crown on Vortigern's head, none of the nobles dared interfere. They took the princes Aurelius and Uther to Brittany for safety, and sat there in exile waiting for Vortigern's old age and death, the only possible end they could think of to his tyranny.

Hengist and Renwein

In the end Vortigern was overthrown not by old age, disease or rebellion, but because he came up against a trickster even cleverer than himself. One May morning, three Saxon longships beached in Kent and their crews disembarked and marched to Vortigern's castle in Canterbury. They were tall, broad-shouldered warriors with blue eyes and braided blond hair, and their leaders were Hengist and his brother Horsa. They swaggered into the castle and bowed like a troupe of actors before the king. 'Lord Vortigern,' said Hengist, 'we throw ourselves and our weapons at your feet. We are Saxons from Germany, and we have been banished from our own country. We have sworn by Odin the war-god to give our fighting-skills and loyalty to any prince who welcomes us – and it is for you, now, to decide if we stay here or go back to our ships and leave in peace.'

'Odin the war-god?' said Vortigern. 'Not Christ?'

'No,' said Hengist, and at the name of Christ his followers growled and rattled their weapons. Vortigern decided that he was dealing with mindless savages, and thought he had nothing to fear from them. He appointed them as his royal bodyguard in place of the Picts (whom he had piously beheaded for Constans' murder) and gave them castles and land in Lincolnshire, in the fen-country: he hoped that draining marshes and farming muddy fields would use up all their energy, and leave them no time to threaten the peace of Britain or his own security.

But Hengist knew the power of false smiles and cunning words just as well as Vortigern, and trapped him in exactly the same web of cunning as Vortigern had used against Constans long before. 'My lord,' he said humbly, 'give me permission to build a castle in Lincolnshire, as large as can be encircled by a single leather thong, and let me invite more of my followers from Germany, enough to fill it.' Vortigern, thinking that leather thongs were short, and calculating that any castle encircled by one would be tiny and hold only a handful of soldiers, gladly gave permission. At once Hengist slaughtered the largest bull in Lincolnshire, and set his butchers the task of slicing the hide into a continuous thong as thin as a woollen thread and over a kilometre long. He used it to measure out the land for a castle, and when the castle was built he brought from Germany eighteen long-ships filled with warriors, and with them his daughter, the witch Renwein. Pretending loyalty to Vortigern, he offered him Renwein's hand in marriage, and asked nothing in return but power over the county of Kent (including Vortigern's own castle in Canterbury). At first Vortigern hesitated; but then Renwein smiled witch-smiles at him, eagerness to make love with her drove out every other thought and he agreed to everything Hengist asked. Vortigern's existing wife fell mysteriously sick and died, and the wedding took place soon after-wards. When it was over, Hengist went to Vortigern with another cunning suggestion. 'My lord,' he said, 'those Picts you executed for murdering the old king – what if their kinsmen bring an army south to slit your own throat in revenge? Invite my son Orca from Germany, with ten shiploads of men; give him the countryside round the Humber to rule. No one here covets such barren, empty land, and Orca and his men will be a wall of flesh for you against the Picts.' Once again Vortigern hesitated; once again Renwein smiled her smiles at him; once again his will turned to water and he agreed.

At this point the British people began to panic. Everywhere they went the countryside was filling with armed Saxons. Where would it end? Were they to be nothing but slaves in their own country, ruled by a criminal and his wife, a witch? They left Vortigern to his Saxons and set up his son Vortimer as rival king of Britain. Vortimer gathered an army of British bowmen, and strengthened it with Vortigern's blood-thirsty enemies the Picts, till the Saxons were no match for him at all. He defeated them in four bloody battles (in one of which Horsa, Hengist's brother, was killed), and sent Hengist and his warriors bruised and bandaged home to Germany. Then he passed a law handing back to the Britons all the land the Saxons had stolen, went triumphantly south to visit his father Vortigern and stepmother Renwein – and foolishly drank a toast to his own success from a wine-cup handed him by Renwein. His death was lingering and painful. Renwein buried his body in a secret grave at night, put her husband Vortigern back on the throne and sent word to Hengist that it was safe to return and claim the kingdom. The Saxons came in a fleet of longships, and Vortigern, terrified that they meant to exact bloody vengeance for his son's victories, hastily invited them to a peace-conference at Avebury, and specified that no man was to carry arms. The British chiefs left their weapons at the door and went inside in nothing but their finery; the Saxons hid daggers in their boots, and at a sign from Hengist leapt on the Britons and cut their throats. Four hundred British chiefs were murdered – and Vortigern saved his own skin only by falling on his knees and granting Hengist everything he cared to demand, except only the kingship which Vortigern kept for himself.

But whoever had the name of king, the Saxons ruled, and they celebrated their victory by pillaging everything in sight. The Picts flocked gleefully south to share the plundering; British law was dead, and Vortigern fled to Cambria and barricaded himself in a castle in the most trackless corner of the country he could find.

Vortigern's tower

But however trackless the country, and however cunningly he hid himself, Vortigern knew that one day the Saxons would hunt him down. They were quartering the countryside, alert as hunting-dogs; with every burnt farmhouse, every throat-slit peasant, they came one step nearer to finding him. He sat in the hall of his castle in Cambria, his face grey with fear and his royal robes sagging round him like a tent, and begged his wise men for advice. 'Build a tower,' they answered. 'A doorless, windowless tower on the peak of Mount Erith. No sword or arrow will hurt you there.'

Vortigern leapt to work. He summoned every stone-mason in Cambria, and sent a long line of workmen, with pickaxes, shovels and cement-buckets, plodding up the slopes of Mount Erith. On the first day they cleared a site for the tower-base, and marked it out with foundation-stones; next morning, they found the stones vanished and the ground tumbled and broken as before. They worked for a second day preparing the site, and in the night their work disappeared just as before. They laid it out a third time, and this time set guards; next morning the ground was rubble-littered as before, and the guards were ashen-faced and gibbering. In the night, they said, the mountain had shaken itself like a waking animal, and the ground had gaped like a gullet and gulped the stones.

Vortigern was beside himself. Was even the earth against him? Shivering, he picked his way with his wise men to the boulder-strewn summit and asked their advice. They told him that the mountain was bewitched, and that the only way to break the spell was to mix the tower's cement not with water but with the blood of a shape-changer, a child of air*. This filled Vortigern with even more despair. Cambria was full of wonders and supernatural beings, but no word had ever reached him of shape-changers. In the end, however, he found one himself, at home in his own castle yard. He was walking forlornly one day in the rose-garden, when he heard two children's voices squabbling behind a hedge. One was a girl's voice, high and clear; the other was husky and breaking, the voice of a half-grown youth. As he listened, Vortigern heard a shout and the sound of a slap, and he ran round the hedge to stop the fight. There was no one there but a boy of about fourteen, sitting on the grass and chuckling to himself. 'Who are you?' Vortigern asked. 'And where are that young man and the girl he was bullying?'

'My name is Merlin,' said the boy. 'There's no one here but me. I am the others.' And while Vortigern blinked in amazement, the boy turned into a young girl and curtseyed, turned into a young man and bowed, and then turned back to his own self, sitting on his heels in the grass and laughing.

A shape-changer! Vortigern shouted for his soldiers, and ran to grab Merlin's arm before he could turn into an insect and fly away, or into a trickle of water and vanish into the ground. Without once letting go of him – for a tight grip is the only way to hinder a shape-changer's magic – a pair of soldiers carried him to the summit of Mount Erith, and Vortigern's wise men followed with spell-books and butchers' knives. All the way up the mountain, Vortigern's Christian conscience kept nagging him. Should Merlin, supernatural being or not, not be given a chance to make his peace with God before he died? Accordingly, when they reached the summit, he made them all stand in a huddle in the mist while he explained to Merlin what was happening. To his amazement Merlin shouted with laughter, shaking and wriggling while the soldiers struggled to keep hold of him. 'A spell!' he spluttered. 'A spell – on a whole mountainside? My lord, spill the blood of these fake wise men, and let me live. I'll show you why the ground shakes. Dig down, here under our feet, and you'll find a pool of water and an underground cave. That's what eats the stones.'

The wise men scoffed, but Vortigern ordered his workmen to shift the rocks and dig. At first there was dry earth, then clay, then ooze, and finally they broke into a muddy cave half full of water and clogged with rubble. 'Drain it,' said Merlin. 'In the ground underneath are two dragons, sleeping; every time they toss in their dreams, the earth heaves and the mountain splits.' When they heard the word 'dragon' all Vortigern's workmen turned tail and ran, so Vortigern snapped his fingers at the wise men to drain the pool. White-faced, slipping and sliding, they scrambled over the muddy lip of the hole, formed a bucket-chain and began to bail. By mid-morning they had reached bottom: a rock-floor strewn with stones and puddled with mud. The wise men scrambled out and they, Vortigern and the soldiers peered over the hole's edge, timid as rabbits. Nothing happened, for minutes on end – and then, just as Vortigern was lifting his arm to give the signal for Merlin's execution, the earth roared like a bull, the cave-floor split apart and two dragons* billowed out of the ground as tall as houses, hissing and flapping leathery wings the size of sails. One was white, the other red; they soared into the air, and Vortigern, the wise men and everyone but Merlin and the terrified soldiers who were guarding him fell on their faces in the mud and hid their eyes. The dragons clashed their fangs and scythed the air; their fire-breath charred the ground, till solid rock bubbled like toasted cheese; then, after swooping in formation three times round the mountain-top, they spiralled into the clouds and disappeared*.

Vortigern's wise men scrambled up and began picking mud from their faces and their hair. Vortigern went angrily to Merlin. 'What does it mean?' he said. 'Explain it!'

'It means your death,' answered Merlin. 'The dragons are Aurelius and Uther, brothers of King Constans whom you created and you destroyed. They have grown up into warrior-princes; they will fight you for the British throne, and they will char you dead with fire.'

So saying he wriggled free of the dumb-struck soldiers, changed into a magpie before their eyes and flew away. Vortigern was terrified. His wise men tried to soothe him. 'It can't be true,' they said. 'He's a beardless boy – what can he know of the future? Finish the tower: you'll be safe inside.' Trembling, Vortigern gave orders for the dragon-hole to be filled in and the tower built on top of it – and soon afterwards

Aurelius and Uther swept from Brittany in a warfleet, cornered Vortigern in his tower and set fire to it. The flames licked up the solid stone like straw, and when the fire died down and Aurelius' soldiers picked over the embers, nothing was left of Vortigern but a handful of greasy ash on the black, charred ground.

Renwein's revenge

So Vortigern's futile and treacherous reign ended, and Aurelius, prince of the true royal house, became king instead. His kingdom was in tatters. The churches lay burnt and plundered, their altars desecrated and their doors flapping in the wind. The towns were smouldering ruins, with terrified people peeping from the rubble at passers-by in case they were Saxons or rampaging Picts. The roads were pitted and potholed, strewn with corpses; brigands lurked in the woods, waiting to jump out on strangers and slit their throats. It took Aurelius five years to put an end to it. He cleared the roads, rebuilt houses and churches, set up magistrates in every town and re-established the king's peace and the rule of law*. For a time the Saxons resisted, but then Aurelius captured Hengist and beheaded him, and that shook the fight from them. The British army funnelled them north to the Humber (where they jumped into boats and scrambled home to Germany) or further still to the moors of Northumberland and the trackless forests of Albany (where wolves and ogres lived, and no humans but the Picts ever made their homes): they vanished from Britain, for a time, as spilled water vanishes into sand.

As for Renwein, Vortigern's Saxon queen, she lived on for a time in her fortress near Canterbury, surrounded by loyal soldiers and by her witch's bodyguard of goblins and devils. At first (since witches have the power to withstand passing time) she never aged, but seemed as young and beautiful as when she first infatuated Vortigern. But as Saxon power in Britain crumbled, her looks crumbled with it, until she turned into the old crone she really was: her hair straggled, the flesh hung from her bones, her voice was a cackle and her wits were wild. In the end she and her foul followers fled from Britain forever – and in the last moment before she disappeared she sent for Ambron, the wiliest human in her court, and handed him a glass poison-phial. 'Use it when you can. Kill Aurelius!' she hissed and vanished.

Ambron waited for a year, living like a tramp in the woods and biding his time. Then word came that King Aurelius was lying sick in his royal castle at Winchester, with a disease none of his doctors knew how to cure. Ambron dressed himself in velvet clothes and galloped pell-mell to Winchester, where he claimed to be a doctor newly back from the Holy Land, with a phial in his saddle-bag of the fabulous panacea, the medicine which would cure every disease known on earth. Aurelius drank the potion and snuggled down in bed to give it time to work. But instead of curing him, the poison turned the blood in his veins to putty and killed him. So Renwein took her revenge on Aurelius for killing her husband Vortigern, and the wheel of murder moved on one more turn*. As for the traitor Ambron, he melted into the crowd in the castle hall and was never seen again.

STORIES OF CAMELOT

4

ARTHUR

Uther Pendragon

At sunset on the day King Aurelius died, a fireball streaked across the sky over Cambria, where his brother Uther was fighting the barbarians. At first it was like a golden ball tossed up by some giant beyond the hills, but as it flew through the air it took on dragon's shape: its eyes were flames, its body was embers, its tail was smoke. Uther's soldiers cowered and covered their eyes as the fireball divided above them; a single shaft flew over Britain and Brittany, and a scatter of seven smaller lights hissed into the Irish Sea and disappeared*.

While his army cringed and moaned, Uther asked Merlin what the fireball meant. Merlin answered that the dragon was Uther himself, the new king of Britain; the light-shafts were Uther's children and grandchildren, the bright shaft his son Arthur, who would rule Britain and Brittany after him, and the seven smaller lights his grandchildren, who would rule the west. As soon as he heard this explanation, Uther hurried back to Winchester, gave his brother Aurelius a glittering royal funeral and buried him in the centre of the Giants' Ring at Avebury. Then, to fix Merlin's dragon-prophecy forever in people's minds, he gave himself the surname Pendragon ('dragon-head') and declared it a royal name, to be used only by himself and his descendants. He ordered the royal jewellers to make a pair of golden dragons, put one in Winchester Abbey in his brother's memory and kept the other for himself, to be carried gleaming before him when he went to war.

The Easter after he was crowned, Uther invited all the lesser kings of Britain and their wives to a week-long feast. Among the guests were Gorlois, king of Cornwall, and his wife Ygern – and Uther fell passionately in love with Ygern and made up his mind to make love with her. He courted her for days: he rode with her, sat with her, passed her banquet-titbits, and flirted with her till everyone guessed what was in his mind and even Gorlois grew suspicious. At last Gorlois intercepted a message from Uther asking Ygern to go to bed with him, and he stormed back to Cornwall, locked Ygern in a siege-proof tower at Tintagel, settled himself and his men in his own royal castle, Dameliock*, and challenged Uther to do his worst. Uther sent a herald, ordering Gorlois to bring Ygern back at once or else to stuff his larders and stock his fishponds for a siege to the death; when there was no reply he sent an army, trundling battering-rams, ballistas, fire-bows and huge siege-towers*; finally he came himself with his servants, made camp just out of Gorlois' arrow-range and settled down to starve him out. But Gorlois had taken the herald's advice and crammed his larders; Uther had to buy provisions from the peasants round about, and they were loyal to Gorlois and offered him nothing but scrawny cattle and mouldy corn. Uther sat in the drizzle day after day, willing Gorlois to surrender and pining for Ygern. After six weeks of it he sent for Merlin, and asked if there was no magic way of getting what he wanted. 'It's simple,' Merlin answered. 'Every night at midnight, Gorlois slips out of a secret door at the back of the castle, gallops on a fast black horse to Tintagel and spends the night with his wife. Tonight he'll arrive as usual – except that he'll be two hours early, and he'll be you, disguised.'

The plan worked perfectly. At ten o'clock, in the dark hour before moonrise, Merlin gave Uther a potion which changed his appearance and made him seem Gorlois' identical twin; Uther galloped on a black horse to Tintagel and he and Ygern made love all night; it was in that love-making that Arthur, the future king of Britain, was conceived. Meanwhile, as soon as Uther left camp, Merlin sent word to Gorlois that the king had given up the siege and gone home. Gorlois sallied out of Castle Dameliock with his soldiers, expecting to find Uther's camp ripe for capturing, and so fell into Merlin's trap and was killed. Next morning, Uther slipped out of Tintagel and resumed his own appearance – and the next thing Ygern heard was messengers hammering on the door with news that her husband Gorlois was dead. She mourned for forty days, as a good Christian should; but as soon as the mourning was done Uther married her and made her his queen, and on the wedding-night told her everything that had happened, and that the baby growing in her womb was not Gorlois' but his.

So the trick was played, and Uther was well satisfied. In the spring of the following year his son Arthur* was born, and a year after that his daughter Morgaus*. The Pendragon dynasty was established, and the kingdom of Britain seemed secure. But its security was founded on evil acts (Merlin's disguising of Uther, and his tricking of Gorlois), and evil acts in the end exact their penalty. While Uther ruled Britain in what he thought was prosperity, in Germany the Saxons were re-arming and building an invasion-fleet. They sailed to Albany, made alliance with the Picts and poured south, sacking every city loyal to Uther and slaughtering its inhabitants. Each time the British army challenged them they melted into the woods and disappeared; as soon as the soldiers left they re-emerged and went on pillaging. One by one the local British kings joined them or were killed by them; there was no stopping them. In the end Uther began to fear for the safety of his children, and did as his father Constantinus had done before him: he sent Morgaus and Arthur for safe-keeping to the countryside. Morgaus went to a nunnery, where she learned reading, writing and the skills of house-keeping and herb-lore; Arthur went to Ector, king of Gwent, and learned the skills of riding, hunting, fighting and ruling alongside Ector's own son Kay*. Meanwhile, Uther spent his summers campaigning against the Saxons and his winters recovering at one or other of his castles in the south. For several years he held the Saxons at bay, but then one winter he caught a fever, and while he lay sick in London the enemy overran the countryside as far south as St Albans, where they gathered their hordes in preparation for a pitched battle which would make Britain theirs once and for all. Without Uther, his soldiers had no heart for fighting; in the end he dragged himself from his sickbed, travelled to St Albans on a litter between two horses, and ordered his men to attack the town with the same siege-weapons as he had used against Castle Dameliock. When the Saxons saw the huge siege-towers advancing against their walls they surged out of the town in panic, and Uther's soldiers fell on them and cut them down. Uther watched the slaughter from his sickbed; the heat of the day and the excitement of battle inflamed his blood, and before the day ended his soldiers' triumph-cries turned to howls of grief at the news that their king was dead*.

The sword in the stone

Uther was buried with pomp and ceremony – and before he was snug in his grave his nobles began squabbling for the crown. Britain was full of chiefs, each with a castle and a band of loyal followers. Each coveted royal power, none was strong enough to dominate the others, and they jostled and argued like children queuing for a treat. At last Merlin told Bishop Brice a way to end it. 'Send to all the noblemen,' he said, 'and invite them to celebrate Christmas here in your cathedral. Tell them that just as Jesus was born on Christmas Day to be king of the whole world, so, by a miracle, he will show us at Christmastime the rightful king of Britain.'

Neither Bishop Brice nor the nobles, when their invitations arrived, believed a word of it. Nonetheless, at the end of December everyone went to London to see what would happen, and the streets were full of horses, wagons, men-at-arms, bishops, monks, nuns, lords and ladies in their finery and ordinary people gaping at the show. In the days before Christmas nothing extraordinary happened, and people began to scoff at Merlin's prophecy and would have burned him for blasphemy if he had been there to burn. But he was nowhere to be seen, and they grumblingly decided to make the best of it, celebrate Christmas, and then go home and take up their squabbling where they'd left off.

On Christmas Eve everyone crowded into the cathedral for Midnight Mass. They clustered round fire-baskets, shuffling their feet and blowing their fingers against the cold: lords, priests and commoners all watching reverently as Bishop Brice and his servants celebrated Mass. Among them were all the warlords ambitious for kingship – and to one side, in a group beside a pillar, stood Ector of Gwent and his grown sons Kay and Arthur.

When Mass was over and the cathedral bells began pealing news of Christ's birth across the town, the worshippers hurried outside. And there, in the centre of the cathedral green, they found a lump of stone as big as a farm-cart. It was smooth and flat, not fissured like other stones; stuck into it was a glittering warsword, and on the blade, in letters of fire, was written 'This sword is Excalibur, the Hungry One, and whoever pulls it from the stone is Britain's rightful king.' The young nobles gathered round the stone in a scornful group. 'Is this all?' they asked. 'Is this Merlin's miracle? Any fool can stick a sword in a stone – and it hardly needs superhuman powers to pull it out again.' They began giving the sword-hilt experimental tugs to see how loose it was. Then, one after another, they tried to pull it out. Some banged it sideways to loosen it; some levered it; some picked with daggers at the place where it joined the stone; some braced their feet and tugged till the veins knotted on their foreheads; two even pulled at it together, announcing that if they freed it they would share the kingdom. At last, when all had tried and failed, Bishop Brice ordered that the sword and the stone should be covered by a tent and guarded, and that anyone who liked was welcome to try and free the sword. If no one had succeeded by New Year's Day there would be a tournament, and the winner would be crowned king.

In the next few days, many young men went to the tent to try their luck. Some swaggered in openly, in noisy groups; others went privately, to keep their efforts to themselves; others took wise men and magic-books, to charm the sword from the stone with spells. But at the end of a week Excalibur was still stuck fast, and everyone forgot it and turned their attention to the tournament. Ector had decided that he was too old for jousting, and Arthur was too young: the family fighting was to be done by Kay, and if he won his father and brother would gladly bow to him as king. Kay had never taken part in a tournament before, and spent his time swaggering about in his helmet, trotting his warhorse up and down and brandishing his sword. While he was doing this, on the very morning of the tournament, swinging the warsword round his head, he accidentally jarred it on a tree-branch and the blade splintered to pieces, leaving him nothing but the broken stump.

'Never mind,' said Arthur. 'I'll find you another.'

But that was easier said than done. No one else in London was eager to lend Kay a sword in case it, too, ended up in pieces; armourers and blacksmiths were too busy to make a brand-new sword, or said it would take days. Arthur spent the morning searching, and was walking back disconsolately to tell Kay he had failed, when he suddenly remembered the sword in the stone on the cathedral green. Until then, he had thought himself too young for it, but now he thought, 'It's not impossible. What harm can it do to try?'

The soldiers guarding the tent were not keen to let a fifteen-year-old boy inside. But their orders were that anyone who liked was to be allowed to try, and they grumblingly opened the flap and let Arthur pass. Remembering how everyone else had struggled to free Excalibur, he put both hands to it, braced his feet against the stone and tugged. To his amazement the sword slid out of the stone as a knife leaves butter, and he fell in a heap on his back. He thrust the sword back into the stone and this time pulled it out one-handed. Then, while the men-at-arms ran to tell Bishop Brice what had happened, he put the sword

31

over his shoulder and took it to his brother Kay. Kay ran to Ector (who was eating lunch), waved the sword and shouted, 'Look, father! Excalibur! The sword from the stone!'

'How did you come by it?' said Ector.

'Arthur gave me it,' said Kay.

'Arthur?' shouted the young men, slapping their thighs and making a joke of it. 'A child, a yokel from the backwoods – how can he have succeeded when every one of us has failed?' Instead of answering, Ector took them to the cathedral green and there, before their eyes, made Arthur stick Excalibur in the stone and pull it out, time and again till they were all convinced. Then he told them how Arthur was not his own son at all, but the child Uther Pendragon had given him for safekeeping long ago. One by one the nobles knelt and accepted Arthur as their king. But for all their fine words, their hearts were dark. Even if Arthur was Uther Pendragon's son, even if he had passed the trial of the magic sword, he was still no more than a half-grown boy, and they saw no reason to let him lord it over them*.

The Round Table

Before Arthur's reign was two years old, the British lords' scorn for him turned to hate. Six months after he pulled the sword from the stone he was crowned king in London, and invited every king, queen, lord and lady in Britain to a coronation feast. Among the guests were King Lot of Orkney and his young wife, and as the feasting, hunting and dancing went on it was clear that the queen's beauty had caught King Arthur's eye, just as his mother Ygern had fascinated King Uther many years before. She was a year or so younger than he was, but was so like him in appearance, as close as his reflection in a mirror, that people might have taken them for twins. She was as much in love with him as he was with her, and the end of it was that they made love with each other and she went home to Orkney pregnant with Arthur's child. Not long afterwards, Arthur began suffering abominable nightmares: he dreamed that demons were swarming over Britain, tearing it apart, and when the royal dragon confronted them they turned their fangs on it and all but ripped it dead. He asked Merlin to explain, and the explanation horrified him even more than the dream itself. The demons were the eleven kings of Britain, Merlin said, and their fury at the royal dragon (Arthur) was caused by his love-making with the queen of Orkney. What he had done was worse than adultery: she was no ordinary girl, but his own sister Morgaus who had been sent away long ago to be brought up by nuns. She would bear him a son, a brother-son, and when the child grew up he would take arms against Arthur and spill his blood. So Merlin explained the dream. For nine months Arthur fretted over what to do, till his servants asked each other anxiously if he had lost his mind; his anguish lasted until Mayday, when Morgaus gave birth to a baby boy and called him Mordred. Arthur decided that the only way to cheat the prophecy was to kill the child – and to prevent anyone discovering the secret of Mordred's birth he issued a decree saying that a witch had cursed all the royal children born that year on Mayday, and they were to be rounded up and drowned. None of the eleven royal families in Britain escaped: one by one, tearfully, the queens handed over their babies to Arthur's soldiers, while the kings looked on and ground their teeth. A boatload of screaming children was cast adrift in the sea; days later it smashed to pieces on the rocks, and all the babies but one were drowned. Only Mordred escaped: a fisherman who knew knothing of the prophecy rescued him and took him safely to his mother's arms in Orkney.

For months afterwards, the fathers and mothers of the dead children seethed against Arthur and plotted ways to kill him. He was the king, protected by loyal soldiers and by Merlin's magic; even so, they hoped to slip in on him unawares and cut his throat. They thought their chance had come when Arthur gathered an army to fight the Saxons at Mount Badon, and camped for the night in a nearby forest. The eleven kings arrived with soldiers, claiming they had come to fight the Saxons, and set up camp in a circle round Arthur's tent. Their plan was to creep out at dead of night and murder him; but word of it reached Merlin's ears, and at the pre-arranged hour, in the darkness just before dawn, all the kings' tents fell on top of them and held them squirming in the mud till morning. They picked themselves up, filthy and furious, and went to breakfast – and the first thing they saw was Arthur, striding alone down the hill in glittering armour, with the gold Pendragon emblem on his helmet and Excalibur bloodthirsty in his hand. He walked straight for the Saxon battle-line, and before the Saxons could collect their wits he was swinging Excalibur and scything them. The Saxons fell back in panic, and the eleven kings and their followers, forgetting their hatred of Arthur, surged to support him. In a single hour the Saxon army was cut to shreds; Arthur and Excalibur alone killed four hundred and seventy men*.

Arthur's battle-bravery convinced many of the kings to swallow their hatred and accept him as king – and soon after the battle Merlin suggested a plan which won the others' hearts. He told Arthur to build a round table and set it up in the council-room of his royal castle at Camelot*. It was modelled on the table used by Jesus and his disciples at the Last Supper, and there were places for Arthur himself and for each of the eleven kings. The table was the meeting-place for the high counsellors of Britain, and because it was round all of them were equal and none had greater or lesser honour than his neighbour. The kings served Arthur loyally from that day on, and the memory of their murdered children faded from their minds*.

The wooing of Guinever

Once the kings were loyal, Arthur turned his mind to his own happiness, and began looking for a wife. The woman he chose was Guinever, daughter of King Leodegran*, and he set off to her father's castle, accompanied by Merlin and thirty-eight followers, to ask for her hand. They travelled disguised as simple soldiers and with Arthur's Pendragon helmet packed in a saddle-bag, and were surprised to find the countryside round Leodegran's castle seething with armed men. There were brigands from Wales, Picts from Albany, and giants from Hibernia blundering among the humans like beetles keeping step with ants. Arthur and his men pulled their cloaks across their faces, set spurs to their horses and galloped to Leodegran's castle for safety. Inside they found Guinever and the other women locked securely in the centre tower, and Leodegran and his men scurrying about the courtyard, gathering spears and arrows, sharpening their swords and nerving themselves for a deadly siege. There was no time to find out who Arthur was or to ask his business: Leodegran said that the heathens were massing for a dawn attack, allotted Arthur and his men a section of the wall and told them to guard it with their lives.

The battlements were cold and cramped, and long before daylight Merlin had had his fill of them. He went to the gate-guards and demanded that they open up and let him out, and when the guards refused he took the gates in his two hands, lifted them bodily from their hinges, bolts, bars, beams and all, threw a mist-cloud round Arthur and the thirty-eight soldiers, sent them charging against the heathens, and replaced the gates snug in their sockets as if they had never been moved. The heathens heard hooves and warcries advancing against them, but could see nothing except a cloud of mist; then Arthur unsheathed his sword in the rising sun and put on his Pendragon-helmet, gold rays streamed from him like spears and Excalibur glittered in his hand. He galloped round the battlefield sowing death, and Merlin lifted the magic mist to let the heathens see just who had come to fight. Leodegran's men threw open the castle gates and surged to the attack.

The battle lasted all day. Each of Arthur's men was like a jampot, and the heathens buzzed round them like wasps. The Picts gouged, slashed and jabbed; the Saxons swung their axes, yelling battle-cries; the giants bit and crushed; the air was raw with death-screams and triumph-shouts. On their side, Leodegran's men fought grimly and silently; Merlin trotted round the battlefield on his pony, scattering blindness on the enemy; from her tower window Guinever watched the fighting below, and each time she saw the glint of Excalibur or the golden Pendragon-glow, her heart beat faster and she knew that she was in love with Arthur. At last the battle ended: Arthur sliced off the head of Safiran, the enemy leader, and the heathens ran wailing for the woods. Of the vast throng who had seethed round Leodegran's castle walls, only a few dozen were still alive to tell of it; a crows'-feast of corpses littered the fields and choked the streams, and when Leodegran knelt before King Arthur and offered him victory-thanks, loyal homage and his daughter's hand in marriage, they were both so sopping with heathen blood that it was like two butchers embracing in a slaughterhouse.

The wedding-feast at Caerleon

This was Arthur's wooing of Guinever*: a matter of magic, blood and death – and as soon as their wedding-day was settled, he decided to hold a glittering celebration before all his subjects and his allies. The place he chose for it was Caerleon, a town beside the River Usk in Gwent. The river was navigable all the way from the Severn: visiting kings and queens would be able to sail to their lodgings in the centre of Caerleon without setting foot on land. On one side of the river were woods and water-meadows, and beside them Arthur ordered palaces to be built for his guests, with red roof-tiles and gold-painted gables whose magnificence was equalled only by the Pope's palaces in Rome. On the other river-bank were two fine churches, a nunnery dedicated to St Julian the Martyr and a cathedral with an archbishop, a library of books and a whole convocation of monks and friars. There was even a university, staffed by two hundred astrologers, who studied the movement of the stars and predicted the most propitious day for Arthur's and Guinever's wedding-festival.

So the town was made ready, and the archbishops, bishops, monks and nuns began practising their anthems. Invitations were sent out, and before long fleets of royal barges began sailing upriver, stately as swans, bringing guests from every kingdom in Britain, Brittany and the lands beyond*. On the wedding-morning (the day after the holy festival of Whitsun), the royal guests all took their places in the cathedral, and the archbishops and other dignitaries went to fetch forth the king and queen. While bells pealed and the people cheered, they led Arthur and Guinever in twin processions through the town. On Arthur's right and left walked an archbishop, as custom was; in front walked the kings of Cornwall, Albany, Cambria and Gwent, each bearing a golden sword; behind was a choir of priests and boys, swinging incense-pots and singing hymns. A second procession brought Guinever. Two bishops led her by the hands, and four queens walked in front of her carrying doves of peace; her choir was of nuns, and her followers were married women from all classes of society, high and low.

Arthur and Guinever took their places on carved oak thrones, and the archbishops and bishops placed royal crowns on their heads. Then the chanting and singing of the wedding-ceremony began, and the sound was so magnificent that many townspeople ran wildly about the streets all day as if they were drunk on it. In the evening Arthur and Guinever changed their wedding-robes and crowns for lighter clothes, and led their guests to a royal feast: the food was served by Arthur's foster-brother Kay and a thousand princes dressed in ermine, and Bediver and a thousand princes dressed in miniver poured the wine. They spent the next few days in hunting, dancing and merry-making; every morning the young men held archery-competitions beside the river, and their elders watched from the palace windows and cheered them on*.

Arthur and the Romans

While the wedding-celebrations at Caerleon were at their height, a Roman warship sailed upriver unexpectedly and anchored in the town. On board were sixty senators, greybeards with purple-fringed togas and silver staffs, and they handed Arthur an insolent letter from Leo, emperor of Rome, who had not been invited to the festival. He began by calling Arthur an upstart and a tyrant, went on to demand the taxes the British people had not paid for fifty years, and ended by threatening, unless Arthur brought the money to Rome in person three months from that date, to send invading legions and force Arthur's people to pay a terrible blood-price for their leader's disrespect. This letter threw Arthur's followers into turmoil. The hot-headed young men of the Round Table wanted to kill the sixty senators then and there and send their heads back to Leo in bags like cabbages; his soberer followers wrung their hands and asked how they could possibly defend themselves against Roman legions, the most vicious fighters in the world; most of the lords, however, agreed with King Cador of Cornwall, who licked his lips with pleasure and said that war was just what Arthur's armies needed, as the last few months of peace had left them slack-muscled and undisciplined. Before the wedding-celebrations were over every one of Arthur's royal guests had promised soldiers to help him beat the Romans, and he sent the sixty senators back to Rome with a letter telling Leo to expect him in August not creeping like a criminal but galloping at the head of his armies with fire and sword. He left Britain in the care of Guinever, gathered his troops and sailed for Brittany.

In public, before his people, Arthur kept up a show of confidence. But in private, lying in his cabin as the ship bucked its way to Brittany, he shook with doubt. He had a brave army, thousands of unflinching men led by the warrior-lords of his own Round Table; but the Romans outnumbered them ten to one, their soldiers came from Arabia, Asia, Africa, Persia, Egypt and India, and they were led by Lucius Hiberius, the cunningest general of all those times, who had never been beaten in battle and would, it was said, have outmatched Julius Caesar himself if it had ever come to war. Above all, the Romans had in their service fifty giants, so huge that they kicked aside horses like kittens and rode on elephants, and with hide thick enough to blunt any mortal spear or sword. Arthur tossed and turned wondering if he was right to lead his people against such fearful odds – and in the middle of his

37

pondering he fell asleep and dreamed a prophetic dream. On one side, swooping from the western sky, was a dragon: its scales were azure-blue, its fangs and claws were gold and fire poured from its jaws and lit the sea. On the other side, from the east, padded a grim black bear: its feet were on land and its head pierced the sky; its eyes were lightning and its paws were thunderclouds. The dragon dived, hissing fire, and the bear snatched it by one wing and began squeezing the breath from it. But the dragon's breath was fire, and the flames set the bear's fur ablaze and sent it crashing to the ground, where it burned to ashes. The dragon flapped into the sky and disappeared, and Arthur knew that it was his own Pendragon emblem, and that his dream meant victory*.

The army had no sooner disembarked and was pitching camp than messengers galloped up with news of the enemy. The Roman legions, led by Lucius Hiberius and the fifty giants, had made their way across the whole of France to ambush them, scattering defenders as men swat flies. They were even now sleeping in the fields round Rouen, gathering their strength for a surprise attack next morning. When Arthur's younger followers (led by Kay and Bediver) heard this, they were hot to attack the Romans immediately and catch them still blurred with sleep. But Arthur made a far more cunning plan. He sent two lords secretly ahead to set up an ambush of their own in the woods, grouping their men in two long pincers round the enemy. Then he told Kay and Bediver to ride as noisily as they could into the heart of the Roman camp, blowing bugles and hallooing. They reined in their horses where Lucius and his officers were asleep, and the Romans stumbled out of their tents, rubbing their eyes, to see what all the noise was about. 'Lucius Hiberius,' said Kay, repeating the exact words Arthur had given him, 'you and your men are trespassing. This is British territory, and King Arthur and his army are sworn to protect it. Not only that, but Arthur is the rightful emperor of Rome, a descendant of King Constantinus, and as your true commander he orders you either to lay down your arms and surrender, or else to fight to the death for what you claim is yours.'

When he heard these words, one of Lucius' officers called Gaius threw his head back and laughed out loud. 'Just listen to him!' he said. 'What a turkey-cock! What makes these pipsqueak Britons think that they can challenge the world and win?'

Those were the last words he ever spoke, for before they were out of his mouth Kay sliced off his head and kicked it aside like a football.

Then he and Bediver wheeled their horses and galloped away. The furious Romans ran for their weapons and pelted after them – and this, too, was exactly according to Arthur's plan, for Kay and Bediver led the enemy uphill into the woods, and the waiting lords closed the pincers of their ambush and began funnelling them to their deaths as fishermen funnel fish. The Romans were taken by surprise, and were battling an enemy whose numbers none of them knew; thousands were cut to rags among the trees, or fell from their horses and were kicked to death. Kay and Bediver galloped everywhere among the combatants, and each time a man was killed Kay shouted 'There! Tell Gaius in hell that *this* is how pipsqueak Britons boast!'

It would have been a short battle and a British triumph if Lucius had not rushed back to camp at this point and pummelled his fifty giants awake. They were used to leading the legions, not following them, and at first they lurched up the hill like bewildered cattle, too dull-witted to work out what was happening or even to decide between friend and enemy. But then their leader Galapas stirred their blood-lust with roars and blows and they surged into the fighting and began snapping Arthur's soldiers' necks like celery-stalks. There was no facing them: arrows, spears and swords were as useless as matchsticks against their hide, and they were so tall that their only vulnerable parts, their eyes, were high out of reach. Then Arthur leapt from his horse, ran up behind Galapas, slashed through the tendons of his legs with Excalibur and sent him sprawling on the ground. 'Look!' he shouted. 'On the ground, they're no bigger than any other fallen enemy!' One by one he toppled the giants with Excalibur (whose blade, forged in the magic island of Avalon, made short work even of giants' hide), and as soon as they were on the ground his soldiers swarmed on them like ants, poked out their eyes and bundled them down to hell. When they were all dealt with, Arthur ran after Lucius Hiberius himself, and with a single blow of Excalibur split him from helmet-plumes to navel. The general's life flew away to hell, and with it flew all Roman eagerness to fight.

The battle was over. Arthur set the enemy prisoners to burying the bodies, and ordered his priests to sing Masses for the dead men's souls. The giants' carcases were piled in heaps and burned. Arthur took the corpses of Lucius Hiberius and fifty-nine of his noblest officers (so making sixty altogether, the same number as the senators who had brought the emperor's insolent letter to him at Caerleon), embalmed them with spices and unguents, laid them in coffins and sent them in a

39

line of wagons back to Rome, with a message to the emperor that this was all the tax the British intended to pay, and that they would pay the same amount any time he cared to ask.

There was weeping and mourning after the battle, for many brave soldiers had died in the fighting, including Arthur's old foster-father Ector, apple of his heart. But that day's work ended the Roman threat forever, and from then onwards Arthur was left to rule without interference: ambitious warlords everywhere respected him and turned their harassment somewhere else*†.

5

GAWAIN

Young Gawain

Gawain was Arthur's nephew, the son of his sister Morgaus and her husband Lot, king of Orkney. Morgaus' children were divided between light and darkness: two of her sons (Mordred, whom she bore out of incest with her brother Arthur himself, and Agravain, whom she bore to Lot) belonged to darkness, and were destined to cause suffering and destruction; Gawain, Gaheris and Gareth belonged to light. Even so, in Gawain's own character, light and dark were endlessly at war. His strength waxed and waned with the sun each day: he was feeblest at dawn when the sun was cold, and grew with it in vigour and dazzle to a noonday peak, only to decline again to feebleness as dusk approached. When his mood was sunny, he was charming, fearless and hot to flirt with every girl he met; when his mood was dark, he brooded like a thundercloud.

When Gawain was seventeen, he left Orkney and rode south with his brothers Agravain and Gaheris to join King Arthur's court. The three young men spent all summer on the journey, with never a care for the giants, trolls and savages who infested the Northern Lands; their youngest brother Gareth trotted behind them on a pony, out of sight. He was fourteen, too young for fighting; but he slipped away when his brothers left home, and followed them, as fearless as they were. Gawain, Agravain and Gaheris at last reached Camelot, and Arthur made them welcome and gave them places at the Round Table. As for Gareth, he disguised himself as a scullion, took a job in the royal kitchens and worked there for a year, unnoticed by everyone except Kay, controller of the royal household, who nicknamed him Handy on account of his clumsy way with pots and pans*.

Gawain's bravery (at least in the morning of his life) soon made him one of Arthur's most trusted followers. If anyone was needed to rush headlong into battle, or to fight without hesitation for his own or the king's honour, Gawain was sure to volunteer. His charm made him irresistible to the court ladies, too, and he was an especial favourite of Queen Guinever. One day he, Arthur and Guinever went deer-hunting in the forest, and all morning the woods rang with the sound of hunting-horns, the shouts of beaters driving the game, the barking of dogs and the crackling of branches underfoot. But for all their efforts they caught nothing, and by mid-day Guinever was exhausted. She begged Arthur and the others to carry on the hunt by themselves, and leave her to rest, and Gawain politely offered to stay with her and protect her. The place they chose was a clearing in the wood beside a wide, deep lake called Tarn Wadeling, whose water was so still and cold that even now, when the sun was at its highest overhead, mist lay on it and the air was dank and cold. Guinever shivered as Gawain helped her from her horse and spread a cloak over a mossy log for her to sit on; then suddenly the sky blackened as if a giant's hand had snuffed the sun, and Guinever stared at the Tarn and began to scream and scream. Gliding across the water was the figure of an old woman in grey grave-wrappings, and her clothes, her body and her crown coiled like smoke-wisps, transparent in the breeze. Gawain splashed into the lake, held out his sword with the hilt uppermost to form a cross, and challenged the ghost. 'No further!' he said. 'Say who you are and what you want.'

'I'm King Leodegran's widow, Guinever's mother,' said the ghost. 'When I was alive I made a holy vow, and broke it – and now I'm condemned to wander the world in anguish, until land-sacrifice is made and a million Masses are said and sung for my immortal soul.'

'What land-sacrifice?' said Gawain. But the ghost melted into the mist without another word, and the cloud lifted, the sun shone and the birds sang as if it had never existed. The whole thing was a mystery, and there was no solving it – at least until Arthur and his men came back from hunting, bowed down with game. They took Guinever (still trembling with terror) into their safe-keeping, and Arthur decreed a banquet that evening to restore her spirits and to celebrate the day's successful hunt. Then, when the feasting was at its height and the hall rang with laughter and the clatter of cups and knives, there was a hammering on the door and Galeron, King of Galloway, burst into the hall.

'Arthur,' he said, 'you've wronged me, and I demand vengeance.'

'What wrong have I done you?' asked Arthur, and his young men growled and shifted in their seats.

'You gave Gawain land in Galloway that belongs to me. I demand that he surrender it now, or fight me for it in the morning as soon as the sun is up.'

Land-sacrifice! Everyone looked at Gawain, but it was evening, not morning, and his strength had ebbed. 'No surrender,' said Arthur. 'The fight will take place tomorrow, not at sunrise but at noon.'

So Galeron and Gawain fought next day. Gawain was in his full noonday strength, and could easily have killed Galeron. But the coming of the sun had also brought back his good temper, and long before the fighting grew dangerous he threw down his sword and said, 'My lord, I submit. If the land is truly yours, take it. All I ask in return is that you pay for a million Masses for the soul's rest of the mother of my lady, Queen Guinever.' In the whole court, only Guinever knew what Gawain meant by this surrender: Arthur, his nobles, and most especially Galeron frowned as they tried to make sense of it. But in the end Galeron agreed to the price, the land once more became his property, the million Masses were said and sung, and the ghost of Queen Guinever's mother was never seen beside Tarn Wadeling, or anywhere else, again*.

In the same way, thanks to his blend of politeness and bravery, Gawain once persuaded two of the fiercest giants in Italy, Spinagros and Golagros, to offer Arthur loyalty. The king's party was on pilgrimage to the Holy Land, and they were riding through Italy when they were caught in a storm. In the pouring rain Arthur, Gawain and Kay were separated from the others and wandered from the road into trackless moorland. They came to a watchtower high on the moors, and from inside came the smell of roasting meat. Kay dismounted and went in, and found a dwarf squatting on the floor roasting thrushes on a spit. He was so hungry and thought the dwarf so puny that he forgot good manners, snatched the spit without a by-your-leave and ate the nearest thrush in a single bite. The dwarf began squealing, a door at the back of the tower was flung open, and Giant Spinagros appeared, roaring with fury. He banged Kay on the head so hard that he sent him staggering, and at once Gawain dismounted and ran into the tower. But instead of attacking Spinagros he knelt before him, begged his pardon for Kay's rudeness, and so charmed him that he not only invited the three of them inside and gave them supper, but agreed to ride with them next morning and show them the path out of the moor. As they rode along

43

they saw another tower in the distance, and Spinagros said that it belonged to Giant Golagros, lord of those parts, a monster so fierce that he had never been beaten in a thousand years. 'Leave him to me,' said Gawain. It was early morning, and his strength was small; but he trotted to the tower door and asked Golagros, with great politeness, to offer King Arthur of Britain the homage he deserved. Golagros answered by climbing the tower and throwing rocks. For two hours, while the sun climbed the sky, Gawain scampered about dodging them; then he burst down the door and challenged Golagros to a duel. They fought with clubs, swords, boulders, pitchforks and lumps of wood, and at last Golagros realised that Gawain was more than a match for him. 'What shall I do?' he wailed. 'It's prophesied that If I'm ever beaten in battle, my strength will vanish and I'll die.' 'It's easy,' answered Gawain. 'Before you're beaten, let's shake hands and call this fight a draw.' So they did, and Golagros welcomed Arthur and Kay and made a feast in their honour. He offered to become Arthur's servant, and to travel with him to the Holy Land; but Arthur (who was no friend of giants, however loyal) smilingly refused, and he, Kay and Gawain rejoined their men and travelled on to the Holy Land.

Only one thing could make Gawain forget his manners, and that was the sight of a pretty girl. Sometimes he fell head over heels in love so quickly that he found himself in deadly danger, and had to rely on quick wits and fighting-skill to save his life. Once, when he was riding alone through unknown countryside, he came across a young lady picnicking in a meadow with her maids. He gave a whoop which sent the maids scurrying, and he and the lady spent the afternoon picnicking and talking, until they were so smitten with each other's charm that they threw off their clothes and began making love. The terrified maids, meanwhile, had run to fetch the lady's father and brothers, and they came galloping to the rescue with spears and swords. Gawain was stark naked; he snatched up a sword and was soon trying to fend off three well-armed, furious men. It was near evening, and his strength was weakened both by the setting sun and by his love-making with the lady. He would have been hacked to pieces if the lady, naked as she was, had not thrown herself on her father's and brothers' mercy, crying that she was as much to blame as he was and that they should kill her first. Roaring with rage, her father snatched her up on his horse and galloped away with his sons behind him. As soon as they were gone, Gawain hurled on his clothes, jumped on to his horse, and took care never to visit those parts again*.

Ragnell

Not long after this adventure, King Arthur went on pilgrimage to York, to visit the birthplace of his ancestor Constantinus, and on the way stopped to hunt in the forests of Cannock Chase. The woods were well-stocked with game, but they were trackless and wild, and neither Arthur nor his nobles had ever hunted there before. In the afternoon a thunderstorm blew up from nowhere, and a sudden flare of lightning made Arthur's horse rear and bolt. It galloped pell-mell through the trees, while leaves flailed his face and branches snatched at his clothes, and by the time he controlled its panic he was lost in featureless heathland in the middle of the forest, and was forced to beg a night's lodging in the only shelter he could find, the castle-tower of Gromer-somer Joure. Gromersomer Joure was a robber-baron, and it was his custom to give travellers a lavish welcome, but next morning, if they failed to answer the riddle he set them, to murder them and spike their heads on his castle walls. The question he asked Arthur was, 'What do women want most in all the world?', and in deference to Arthur's royalty he gave him a year and a day to find the answer, only making him promise to return even if it meant his death.

If Merlin had still been at Arthur's court, the riddle would have been answered as soon as asked. But Merlin had long been a prisoner of the Lady of the Lake, and Arthur was forced to ask advice from the best men could find. He began with the Archbishop of York (who answered 'The Kingdom of God'), and spent the next months anxiously collecting replies from every lord and priest in the country, while his secretaries wrote them down in a parchment book. The answers ranged from 'fine clothes' to 'a noble husband' and 'happiness'. But the more answers Arthur heard, and the fatter his secretaries' book became, he more dissatisfied he felt. (In all this time, it never occurred to him to do the obvious thing and ask women themselves, and so every answer was framed, like the question itself, from the male point of view.) Then, one day as he was riding disconsolately home after travelling forty kilo-metres to consult a cave-dwelling hermit (who gave him the answer 'Fire in the hearth, food in the belly, a baby in the womb'), he dismounted to open a gate in a wall, and almost fell over an aged peasant woman in tattered, filthy clothes. Her face was covered in warts; her skin was flabby and one eye had sunk into her cheek, leaving a down-tugged, purple crater in her face.

Arthur shuddered, and felt for a coin to give her before opening the

45

gate and hurrying on his way. But she plucked his sleeve and said, 'Arthur! Ask me the answer to the riddle: only I can tell you true.'

'What is the answer, granny?'

'First agree to the price. If I tell you the answer true, you must give me the noblest young man in your court to be my husband.'

'Gawain?'

'Gawain.'

Arthur thought, 'There's no harm in it. How could a withered old hag give me the true answer, when so many wise and holy men have failed?' Aloud he said, 'If your answer proves true, and if Gawain agrees to marry you, I promise. What is it that women most want in all the world?'

'Their own way,' cackled the crone and disappeared.

When the year and day were over, Arthur went back to Gromersomer Joure's castle, with two servants clutching the enormous book of answers. He began to read the answers to Gromersomer Joure, and at each one the robber-baron threw back his head and roared, 'Wrong, King Arthur! Prepare to die!' But when Arthur came to the last page and read out the old woman's answer, Gromersomer Joure stamped to his feet, bellowing with fury, and roared, 'Their own way! Their own way! Only Ragnell can have told you this. My own sister has betrayed me, and one day I'll take revenge!' He and his castle disappeared like leaves in the wind, leaving Arthur wondering how to tell Gawain that he was promised to the ugliest hag in Britain.

To his surprise, Gawain took the news cheerfully and not angrily. He sent his servants to find Ragnell, and the court women bathed her, trimmed her bristly hair and dressed her in lace petticoats and a silken wedding-gown. Gawain silenced the other young lords of Camelot (who were full of thigh-slapping, ribald jokes about how Gawain the Heartbreaker had ploughed his last furrow, and how warty, toothless Rag Nell was the ideal wife for him) by treating Ragnell, throughout the wedding-ceremony and the banquet which followed it, with the courtesy due to a queen rather than as a peasant from the fields. After the banquet, Ragnell's maids led her to the bridal chamber and readied her for bed (taking care not to touch her warts); at last Gawain said goodnight to his companions, undressed and slipped into bed beside her in his nightshirt. 'My lord,' she whispered, while the air hissed and whistled through her teeth, 'kiss me, and I'll be your loyal wife forever.'

Gawain was revolted by the feel of her bony body in his arms. But he nevertheless bent to kiss her, as an honourable husband should – and as soon as his lips met hers she changed from a stunted crone to a beautiful, smiling girl. 'Thank you, my lord,' she said in a honey-echo of Ragnell's wheeze. 'Your unselfishness has freed me from half the spell of ugliness my brother cursed me with. Now you must choose. Would you prefer me ugly by day and beautiful by night, or the other way round?'

Gawain lay back, thinking. Would he prefer her beautiful in the daytime, in front of all the other young men of Camelot, or beautiful at night, naked in bed for him alone? Then he thought, 'Both solutions are selfish. Ragnell herself has told me what to answer,' and he turned and said, 'My lady, the choice is yours: in this as in all other things between us, you must have your own way.' This answer broke the rest of the enchantment, and from that moment onwards Ragnell was as beautiful by day as she was by night, and everyone envied Gawain the wife good fortune and good manners had won him.*

The challenge

Every year at the time of Christmas and New Year, Arthur gathered all his nobles in Camelot for a fifteen-day celebration. The lords and ladies began each day in chapel, praying and listening to anthems sung by rich-robed choirs; the young men spent their mornings in contests of riding, archery and swordsmanship, while their wives and elders cheered them on; they passed every afternoon in dancing and every evening in banqueting, while minstrels sang love-songs, tumblers and jesters entertained, and a never-ending line of servants filled the wine-cups and loaded the tables with meat, fish, cakes and fruit of every kind. All through this season, it was Arthur's custom not to sit down himself to the feast until he had heard a tale, or seen a sight, of wonderment, fit to be talked of for years to come – and just such an event took place on the evening of New Year's Day. The dancing and present-giving were over, and the lords and ladies were gathering for supper. King Arthur personally greeted each new arrival, strolling among them and making affable conversation as they took their seats. Guinever was enthroned at the high table on the dais, with Gawain on her right and Agravain on her left, and the others took their places as their rank demanded, until only Arthur's seat was empty. The trumpets blazed a fanfare, and to a din of drumming and piping servants crowded in with food and wine.

Everyone had been served, and people were lifting cups to their lips or taking the first morsels of food, when there was a new, discordant fanfare from the castle yard, and an unseen force pushed the doors so that they burst their bolts and crashed open against the walls. There was a clatter of hooves, and a single figure rode into the hall on a warhorse, drawing every eye and hushing every tongue. The horse-man was as tall as two ordinary men, and his horse was suitably gigantic; both he and it were green from head to toe. The rider wore green velvet, sewn with emeralds; his beard and hair were green, and his hair covered his arms and shoulders like a living cape; his horse's green skin was oiled and polished, and its mane was plaited with gold thread; in his right hand he carried a holly-branch, and in his left hand a green axe, sharp as a razor and tall as a tree.

The green man rode to the edge of the royal dais, swept his eyes along the line of banqueters, then pointed his holly at Arthur's empty throne and asked, in a voice which rattled the rafters, 'Where is the king?'

'Here I am,' said Arthur, stepping from the shadows. 'Whoever you are, and whatever your business, you're welcome here. Dismount and share our banquet.' And he signed to the servants to lay a place.

'No,' said the green man. 'If I sat down to eat, your board would be bare in a moment. I bring a challenge to the bravest warrior in all this court. Let him take my axe and slice off my head. I'll neither wince nor flinch, and all I ask is that in a year and a day from now he bend his neck just as unflinchingly to my axe-stroke.'

If there had been silence in the hall before, it was nothing compared to the stillness that followed the green man's words. Everyone sat transfixed, waiting to see who would speak first, while the green man looked up and down the line, daring the banqueters one by one to accept the challenge. At last, since no one else had moved, Gawain said, 'This is a foolish challenge. But if all you want is someone to slice off your head, hand me the axe.'

The green man handed him the axe, and he took firm hold of the handle and began shifting it about to test the weight. The green man swept the hair-cape clear of his shoulders, knelt and bent his neck. Gawain crossed himself, lifted the axe with both hands and brought it down in a stroke which sliced through flesh and bone and struck sparks from the flagstones of the floor. The green man's head rolled among the banqueters' feet like a football, and blood fountained from his neck. But he neither flinched nor toppled; calmly, without hurry, he walked forward, picked up his head and swung himself on to the saddle of his horse. He took the reins and fixed his feet in the stirrups – and then he turned the head to face Gawain and the head opened its mouth and said, 'One year and one day from now, Gawain, meet me at the Green Chapel in the Wilderness of Wirral. Remember: keep your word!'

He galloped out of the hall, still holding his head in his hand, and as soon as he was gone the banqueters filled the hall with talk, buzzing like bees in a hive. But Arthur, seeing Guinever's alarm, made light of it. 'This was nothing supernatural,' he said. 'Conjurers perform this kind of illusion all the time. It was an entertainment, like the New Year music and dancing, and it was the wonder I needed to allow me to sit down and enjoy the banquet. Sound the trumpets: the king feasts in Camelot tonight!' But secretly, as the lords and ladies turned with relief to their banqueting, he said to Gawain, 'That was a foolish challenge, and you were foolish to accept it. But now you've given your promise, and you must keep it.'

For most of Arthur's courtiers, the year that followed was no different from any other. There were battles to fight, giants and trolls to slay, pilgrimages to make and contests of archery or horsemanship; there were hunting, dancing, feasting and flirting to charm the hours away. Few of them remembered the green man, and those who did believed Arthur's explanation of his beheading, that it was a Christmas conjuring trick, and thought no more of it. Only Gawain, whose hands had held the axe, knew that it was no trick, and he spent the year like a man condemned, turning more and more to the dark side of his nature, brooding and secretive. 'What's wrong with Gawain?' the young men asked. 'He must have a secret mistress, or a broken heart, to keep him as quiet as this.' The older people watched him withdrawing more and more from the court's gaiety, spending days and nights on his knees, and said, 'Gawain's growing up at last.'

The time for the Christmas and New Year festival arrived, and Arthur invited his lords and their ladies to Camelot as usual. But long before the festivities began, Gawain announced that it was time for him to find the Green Chapel in the Wilderness of Wirral and keep his promise. Sighing (for he never expected to see Gawain again), Arthur ordered the best horse in his stables – its name was Gringolet, and its coat was pearl-white – to be saddled and bridled, with his own hands helped Gawain arm himself, and gave him a shield decorated with the pentangle, the sign of the sealed knot.* When everything was ready, Gawain heard Mass in the royal chapel, embraced Arthur and set off on his journey. There was snow on the fields, and the earth was iron-hard. Birds piped miserably as Gawain galloped north; neither animals nor humans showed themselves. He rode through the forests and hills of Wales, passed the Isle of Anglesey on his left and at last crossed the River Dee (by way of a frozen ford at Holywell) and came to the Wilderness of Wirral. Now, whenever he saw a cottage or a farmhouse, he knocked and asked if anyone knew of the gigantic green man, or had heard of a Green Chapel thereabouts – and people made the sign of the evil eye against him and slammed their doors. For days he wandered, forlorn and lost, and the country grew ever bleaker, a frozen wilderness swamped in snow. It was not till Christmas Eve, when the daylight was fading and his strength was ebbing with it, that he saw signs of civilisation: a castle set in an elm-copse, with honey-yellow firelight streaming from its windows. He knocked with his sword-hilt on the door, and servants flung it open and warmly welcomed him. They helped him change from his ice-stiff riding-clothes to a gown of velvet edged with ermine. They set a chair in the hearth-corner, with a table beside it, and brought him soup in a silver dish, a tureen of fish and a flagon of hot mulled wine. Gradually, as he ate, the chill left Gawain's body; only his heart stayed frozen at the thought of the death he had willed himself.

When Gawain had eaten, the lord and lady of the castle came to welcome him. The lord was a bluff, broad man with a bushy beard and green eyes glinting with glee. The lady was tall and pale; on her breast was a necklace of emeralds, and on her fingers were rings of jade. And there was a third person: a wizened old woman swathed in brown. She said nothing, and Gawain assumed that she had taken a vow of silence; she sat on a chair beside the hearth, listening to the conversation and gazing into the fire. The lord (whose name was Bertilak) and his lady made up for her aloofness, and their cheerful chatter unlocked Gawain's own garrulousness. They were overjoyed, they said, to welcome one of King Arthur's followers, and especially a warrior of such far-flung fame. Gawain tried to turn the talk to the Green Chapel and the huge green man, but Bertilak laughed and said, 'Why think of such things now? It will be midnight soon, and time for Mass.'

So they went to Mass, and afterwards to bed. They spent Christmas Day, and the three days afterwards, in fun and feasting, and there were so many guests, with so much joking and jollity, that only

Arthur's Christmas feast at Camelot could have bettered it. But on the fourth day of Christmas, in the grey dawn, the guests gathered their belongings and slipped away to see in the New Year with their own families. Gawain said to Bertilak, 'I must go too. I must find the Green Chapel, whatever and wherever it is, and keep my promise.'

'Stay a few days more,' answered Bertilak cheerfully. 'The Green Chapel is only half an hour's ride away. On the morning after New Year's day, I'll send a servant to show you the way. In the meantime, enjoy yourself. Tomorrow I'll be hunting deer, and I'll make a bargain with you. At the end of the day I'll give you a token of whatever sport I've had, and you give me a token of your day's sport.'

'Agreed!' said Gawain, though he had no notion what sport might come to a man cooped up in a castle all day long. He soon found out. For next morning, soon after Bertilak and his servants had left for the hunt, with neighing of horses, yelping of deer-hounds and hallooing of horns, the lady of the house, his hostess, came into his bedroom, brazenly boasted that she thought him the most beautiful man she'd ever seen, and begged him to make love with her. Gawain gazed at her ivory cheeks. But he remembered that he was guest in her house, and a man doomed to unheard-of peril in the Green Chapel, and instead of making love he made polite, bright conversation till the time of the mid-day meal, when she kissed him once, went out of the room and was not seen again that day.

That evening Bertilak bustled back from the hunt, and in token of the day's sport served Gawain a feast of venison. 'And your sport, my lord?' he said. 'What token have you for me?'

'Only a friend's kiss,' said Gawain, and kissed him once.

'A fine day's work!' said Bertilak cheerfully. 'Tomorrow I go to hunt boar. Shall we make the same bargain – a token for a token – a second time?'

'Agreed!' said Gawain, though his heart shrank to think what his part in it might be. Next morning, after Bertilak and his followers had view-hallooed their way out of the castle, the lady once more appeared in Gawain's bedroom and offered to make love with him. As on the day before, he made pleasant conversation until noon, and this time she kissed him twice before she left, so that two kisses were the token he had to give Bertilak in exchange for the wild boar's head. On the next day, New Year's Day, Bertilak went fox-hunting, and the lady came a third time to Gawain's room and offered herself. By now, if Gawain had been as he was before he met the green man at Arthur's court, he would gladly have given in and welcomed her to his bed; but now his dread of what was to happen at the Green Chapel next morning, added to his respect for Bertilak, made him spend a third morning in conversation instead of love-making. This time before she left, the lady gave him two remembrances: a belt of green silk embroidered with gold, and a final kiss. When Bertilak came back from the hunt, with a fox's pelt as token of his sport, Gawain gave him the kiss but said nothing about the belt, which he kept to himself and wore next to his skin under his clothes.

They spent that evening feasting. The lady joined them and shared their merriment, and in a chair by the hearth the brown-robed, silent old woman sat gazing at the fire. That night Gawain lay sleepless, listening to the wind howling and the snow blustering outside, and long before dawn he was calling for his clothes. After Mass and breakfast he looked for Bertilak and his lady to say goodbye, and they were nowhere to be seen. But a servant came to him, a round, broad man in a green leather jerkin, and said, 'Hurry, my lord. My orders are to take you to the Green Chapel before the sun is high.'

They rode out of the castle, through the woods and up to the high hills where mist merged with the moorland and mantled the sun. They reached a rock-gully, with stone sides soaring, and the servant said, 'My lord, no further! No one has ever visited the Green Chapel and returned alive. Run, now! Only I will know, and I swear by the saints to say nothing.'

'No,' said Gawain. 'I gave my promise, and I mean to keep it.'

'So be it!' said the servant, and he jerked his green reins, turned the horse's head and galloped into the mist.

Gawain rode down the ravine until it broadened into a snow-wilderness cut by a roaring river. And there in front of him was a mound of rock, rounded like a burial-barrow and covered with grey-green moss. The mound was open at both ends, and a passage led inside to a dark, dank cave. 'If this is the Green Chapel,' thought Gawain, 'then it's sacred to Satan and no church of God.' He bent his head and stepped inside – and at once he saw him, the green man, sharpening an axe till it sparked and glinted in the gloom. He was exactly as he had been in Camelot, except that his head, instead of rolling on the floor, was firmly on his neck. Gawain gave him no warm words, but merely said, 'Sir, I've kept my promise. Strike the blow, and I'll receive it, as we agreed.'

He bent his bare neck, and without a word the green man lifted the axe in both hands and brought it slicing down. And at the last moment, though Gawain's heart was unflinching, his flesh shuddered from the blow, and the green man's axe harmlessly sliced the air.

'You lose, Gawain,' the green man said. 'Admit that I'm the better man.'

'No,' said Gawain. 'That was weakness of the flesh, no more. Strike again!'

Once more he bent his neck, and once more the green axe sheared down. This time the green man, teeth set in a glittering grin, halted it in mid-air, and Gawain felt nothing but a whisper of wind across his neck. 'Don't play games,' he snapped. 'Strike the blow and have done with it!' He bent a third time, and the green man struck again. The rage in Gawain's heart kept him still as a stone, unmoving – but once more the green man held back the stroke at the very point of death, so that instead of slicing Gawain's neck the axe-blade merely nicked him, sending a fleck of blood to the rock below. At once Gawain spread wide his legs, took a grip of his sword and said, 'Enough! The blow was given and taken unflinchingly, as agreed. Your challenge is answered.'

He looked to the green man to defend himself, and found that he had disappeared. In his place, leaning on the axe and laughing, was Bertilak. 'The challenge is answered,' he said, 'and the enchantment is broken. The old woman you saw in my castle was Morgan le Fay, and she placed this spell on me to test you and find the bravest of all King Arthur's followers. There were three axe-blows: one for the kiss you took from my wife on the first day, one for the kisses you took on the second day, and one for the belt you took on the third day and hid from me. Come back with me now, and spend the rest of the New Year festival with us; we'll jest and joke about this test.'

'No, sir,' said Gawain. 'I must go back to Camelot and tell Arthur of Morgan le Fay and her treachery.' And he shook Lord Bertilak's hand, climbed on to Gringolet and galloped away, his friendly farewells masking the fury in his heart to think how he had both passed the test, by following the green man into the Wilderness of Wirral, and failed it, by accepting the kisses and the magic belt. He wore the belt round his waist forever afterwards, and carried a moon-white axe-scar on his neck, in remembrance of the mystery*†.

6

PERCIVAL

Percival and Kay

Percival was the seventh son of King Eburac of York. While he was still a baby his father and all his brothers were killed in battle, and his mother took him to a remote Cambrian farm, to bring him up as far from weapons as possible. He saw no swords, spears or war-harness until he was fifteen; then, one day, he helped some horsemen lost in a forest, and in return they showed him their weapons and told him how to use them. At once his father's and brothers' warlust flared up in him, and despite his mother's tears he set off for Camelot to join King Arthur's court.

Percival was riding a skinny mule for a warhorse and carrying sticks for spears, and when he arrived at Camelot the young lords would have jeered at him for a yokel except that they had other matters on their minds. Half an hour before, a stranger had swaggered into court, upended a wine-cup over Guinever and challenged any warrior in the hall to fight him and punish the insult. Now he was standing outside in the courtyard, waiting – and because the young lords were convinced that a man would need supernatural protection to take such a risk, none of them dared face him. At this point Percival walked into the hall in his darned clothes and carrying his stick-spears, and said cheerfully to Kay, 'Hey, Lanky, which one of these men is Arthur?'

Kay shouted furiously, 'How dare you speak to me like that? Get out of here! Kill the man in the courtyard and put on his armour: then you'll be fit to talk to gentlemen.' The young lords sniggered to hear it. What did it matter now if the stranger was a wizard in disguise? It was only a yokel he would harm. But Percival went outside, and before the stranger could defend himself – for what had he to fear from a boy armed with branches? – threw one of the sticks into his eye and killed him. He stripped the body and put on the man's armour.* Then, instead of going back into the hall, he climbed on to his mule and rode away. Owain spurred after him to ask what the matter was, and Percival said that he would go back to Camelot when the lanky lord apologised for his rudeness, and not before.*

It took eighteen days, as Percival rode through the woods, for his rage to cool. On each of the days he found a robber, a highwayman or a giant, fought them into submission and sent them to Camelot with the same insulting message: 'Tell the lanky lord that his day of reckoning will come.' Arthur's young lords thought the whole thing very funny, but Kay grew angrier and angrier, and in the end Arthur said, 'We'd better find that boy and put a stop to this.' He ordered horses, and he, Kay and Gawain rode after Percival.

In the meantime, Percival was riding in lonely, snow-covered mountains*, and came to a mist-wrapped castle whose walls heaved and breathed as if they were made of living flesh. He asked for a night's shelter, and the gatekeeper said, 'Find somewhere safer, friend. There are ghosts here. The nine hags of Gloucester have eaten up all the countryside; this is the last place left, and tonight they'll gnaw us too.' As soon as Percival heard this he jumped from his mule and insisted on staying. The gatekeeper took him to the Lady of the castle, a girl of Percival's own age, and she ordered her servants to make him up a bed as if there was nothing to fear. Percival slept soundly until the darkest hour of night, when he was wakened by a man's shrill screaming. He ran into the hall and found the gatekeeper writhing on the floor, with a cackling hag hovering over him, tearing him. Percival lifted his sword and sliced off one of the hag's talons; then he turned the swordblade sideways and began beating her skull like a plate till she begged for mercy. 'For pity, sir,' she moaned. 'Put down your sword; tell me what to do.'

'You know perfectly well what to do,' said Percival. 'Take your sisters and leave this place in peace.'

Hissing and snarling, the hag collected her sisters, and they climbed to the battlements and flapped from them like rooks. The mist cleared, the castle walls turned back from flesh to stone, and the gatekeeper's wounds healed as if they had never been.

For the next three weeks the people of the castle saw neither hair nor talon of the hags. Percival spent his days hunting, feasting and riding with the Lady and his nights dreaming of her; he decided that she was the most desirable person he had ever known, and began plucking up

55

his courage to ask her to marry him. One morning he was walking alone in the hills, practising proposals, when he found a duck's carcase in the snow, and a raven tearing it. He stood there lost in thought. Were the raven's feathers as black as his lady's hair? Was the snow as white as her skin? Were the duck's blood-drops as red as the blushes on her cheeks?

He was still standing there, still pondering, when Arthur, Kay and Gawain found him. They stopped out of sight in a copse of trees, their horses' breath steaming in the cold air, to discuss what to do. 'What's to discuss?' said Kay. 'There's only one way to deal with brats.' He spurred his horse to Percival and said sharply, 'Stop staring like a ninny and come with me.' Without answering a word, Percival poked him under the chin with his spear-butt so hard that he fell off his horse, was dragged back across the frozen ground with one foot caught in the stirrup, and ended up at Arthur's feet groaning with a broken collar-bone.

'You're a fool, Kay,' said Gawain. 'You'll get nowhere by snarling.' He, too, rode out of the copse, but instead of galloping at Percival he trotted quietly up, dismounted and waited patiently till Percival raised his eyes, and then said, 'Sir, King Arthur would be glad to speak to you.'

'If he's as polite as that lanky lord,' growled Percival, 'he can save his breath.' None the less he walked back with Gawain, gave Arthur a blunt 'Good morning' and shook his hand. Then he looked at Kay groaning on the ground and said, 'He'll die in a week if someone doesn't set that bone.' He knelt down, straightened Kay's arm and bound up his broken collar-bone. Then Arthur gave him Kay's horse and they rode back to Camelot with Kay in a litter between them, grinding his teeth with pain. It took six weeks for his shoulder to heal, and another six weeks for his temper to mend enough for him to shake Percival's hand and to apologise, before the whole court, for insulting him. From that day on, he and Percival put up with each other, though they were never friends.

The Lady of the Castle

When Percival first went back to Camelot, his quarrel with Kay drove from his mind all thoughts of the raven-haired, snow-skinned, blood-blushing Lady of the Castle*. But the nine hags of Gloucester had no intention of letting him forget her entirely: they planned revenge on him, and she was their bait. One day when Arthur was sitting with Percival, Owain, Gawain and King Hoel of Brittany, listening to complaints and petitions from any of his subjects to cared to visit him, an old woman rode in on a stringy donkey. Her skin was the colour of oozing tar, her teeth were gorse-yellow, her back was bent like a scythe-handle, her legs were bowed and one of her arms ended in a wrinkled stump as if someone had sliced off the hand. She told them of a beautiful girl imprisoned in the Fortress of Marvels in the High Hills, begged Arthur to send men to rescue her, and before they could ask what Fortress of Marvels or which High Hills she meant, she disappeared.

Percival was certain – as the nine hags knew he would be – that the prisoner was his beloved, the Lady of the Castle, and he told Arthur that he would ride to rescue her that very day*. The hags let him quarter Britain for a whole year*, looking for the Fortress of Marvels, and then when he was exhausted and full of despair, they sent him help they hoped would be the death of him. At a river-crossing one day he met a bent old man with a withered arm, who said that if Percival visited the Tall Tower in the Black Mountains, its master would tell him how to find the Fortress of Marvels. But as soon as Percival knocked on the Tower gate, he was stripped, beaten and thrown into a dungeon: this was the trap the hags had set for him. To make sure that he never escaped alive they sent an army of soldiers to tear the tower apart, cut the throats of every living soul inside and burn the remains. There were five hundred defenders in the tower, trapped by the hags' enchantment, and from his dungeon Percival heard their screams as they fought off the siege and struggled for their lives. He bribed the Tower-master's daughter to unlock the dungeon and give him a sword and a horse, and galloped out among the attackers dealing death. He fell on the attackers' commander and killed him, and at once the remaining attackers ran shrieking for safety, and the hags had no choice but to lift their enchantment from the Tower. The Tower-master offered Percival any reward he liked, even his daughter's hand in marriage and half his lands; but Percival asked only to be told how to find the Fortress of Marvels, and rode on his way.

The Fortress of Marvels lay on an island in an enchanted lake, and the first thing Percival saw was a chessboard in the courtyard, with human-sized chess-pieces playing by themselves. He joined the white pieces, taking the place of a knight on horseback, and the black pieces all drew swords and rushed him, whereupon he scattered them like the toys they were and threw the board into the lake. As it sank out of sight, the same withered hag appeared as had visited Arthur's hall, and told him that before he could find the Lady of the Castle he must kill the unicorn which guarded the woods beside the Fortress. Its horn was barbed and poison-tipped, and the hags expected Percival to be spiked on it and die in agony. Instead, as the unicorn charged, Percival side-stepped, brought his sword down and sliced off its head. The head changed in an instant to a black rider on a skeleton horse, a billowing spectre spurring a horse of bones. Instead of wasting energy stabbing the rider's shadow-body, Percival swung his sword at the horse's legs, and the skeleton crumbled to dust. The Rider blew away like smoke on the breeze, and Percival found himself once again in the Fortress hall, surrounded by the nine hags hissing and baring their poison-fangs. He ran at their leader (the tar-skinned crone with the withered hand) and chopped her in half from skull to navel. His sword-blade came out of her body bubbling, and the metal foamed; the hags turned before his eyes to nine grease-puddles on the floor and Percival was left alone in the echoing Fortress. He hurled himself from room to room like a madman, smashing doors, upending furniture, tearing down tapestries and shouting his beloved's name. But the Lady of the Castle, like all the hags' other conjurings, had disappeared from the mortal world as if she had never existed, and in the end all he could do was ride broken-hearted and empty-handed home to Camelot.

7

CULHWCH

Ysbadadan

When Culhwch was fifteen his mother went mad and died, and his stepmother had sons of her own and wanted rid of him. 'It's time you married,' she said. 'Go and pay court to Olwen, the daughter of Ysbadadan, king of the giants.' Until that moment Culhwch had never once thought of girls or marriage, but his stepmother's words wove a spell so powerful that every part of his body, every freckle, every fingernail, began to ache for Olwen. He rode to Camelot to ask Arthur's help, and his stepmother chuckled to see him go, for she knew that soothsayers had long ago told Ysbadadan that on the day his daughter married he would die, and for that reason he killed every suitor who asked for Olwen's hand.

Culhwch reached Camelot in the evening, just as Arthur's courtiers were sitting down to supper, and the gate-keeper said that it was too late to let him in. He offered him mash for his dogs, oats for his horse, a meal of peppered chops and a soft bed, and said that he would be the first person admitted to speak to Arthur in the morning. But Culhwch brushed him aside, rode into the main hall and demanded to be heard. 'My heart's desire is to marry the daughter of Ysbadadan, king of the giants,' he said, 'and I ask you and your courtiers, my lord, to help me find her.' He went through the courtiers one by one, naming every man and woman sitting at supper that night. There were two hundred and twenty of them, giants, mortals, wizards, dwarfs and shape-changers, and not even Arthur or Guinever, who knew every one of them personally, could have recited their names and ranks. Arthur ordered six courtiers to go with Culhwch – they included Kay, Bediver, and the interpreter Gwrhyr (a magician gifted with second hearing, who understood every sound uttered by mortals, supernatural beings, birds, animals and insects)* – and they all rode out of Camelot next morning. After two days' riding they saw a castle in the distance and spurred towards it. But the nearer they went the further away the castle seemed, and for days they splashed across rivers, galloped through forests, cantered past cornfields, and got nowhere. Finally they came to a flat moor that stretched from horizon to horizon. There were no hills, trees, or shrubs: nothing but mossy stones in all directions, and moving among them a flock of enormous sheep, guarded by a tree-sized shepherd and a dog as big as a plough-horse. Kay sent the interpreter Gwrhyr to ask directions, and when he had roared and growled a conversation in giant-language he came back and said, 'He's Ysbadadan's shepherd, and that castle is Ysbadadan's lair. The only way to reach it is to court Ysbadadan's daughter and face certain death. Accept the challenge, and the shepherd promises his help.'

The shepherd took them home, and his giant-wife roasted a sheep for supper. Just before they sat down to eat, she opened a wooden chest by the fireplace, and out jumped a young man with fair curly hair. 'Once I had twenty-four sons like him,' the giant-wife said, 'and Ysbadadan killed all of them but Goreu. He hides in the chest when strangers come, and he's sworn to kill Ysbadadan and avenge his brothers.'

'Let him come with us,' said Culhwch. 'We've sworn to kill Ysbadadan too.'

Next morning Culhwch, Kay and Bediver walked to Ysbadadan's castle, and now that Culhwch had sworn to kill Ysbadadan, the walk was short and the castle near at hand. The castle was so enormous, and they were so small, that although they strode in openly, the guard-dogs took as little notice of them as elephants would of ants. Culhwch stood in the castle hall, cupped his hands to his mouth and shouted, 'Ysbadadan, giant-king, wake up! Prince Culhwch is here to marry your daughter.'

Even though Culhwch's shout sounded no louder than a bat's-squeak in the vastness, Ysbadadan heard it, lifted his shaggy head and growled, 'Servants, where are you? Prop my eyelids on the forks, and let me see this son-in-law.' His servants swarmed up his chest like mountaineers, propped his eyes open with pitchforks, and he stared at Culhwch and the others and said, 'Come back tomorrow and hear my answer.' But as they turned to go he snatched a poison-spear from a rack on the table and hurled it at Culhwch's back. Bediver caught it in

60

mid-air and hurled it back, and it jarred into Ysbadadan's knee, where it looked no bigger than a pin. Ysbadadan roared with pain and said, 'Barbarians! That will give me arthritis till the day I die! Cursed be the blacksmith who made it and the man who threw it!' On the second morning, the same things happened: Culhwch demanded Ysbadadan's daughter's hand, Ysbadadan propped his eyelids open with pitchforks, told them to come back next day, and hurled a second poison spear. This time Kay threw it back, it stuck in Ysbadadan's nipple and he roared, 'Barbarians! That will give me pins and needles till the day I die. Cursed be the man who made it and the man who threw it!' On the third day Culhwch hurled the spear into Ysbadadan's eye, and he shouted, 'Now I'll blink and weep till the day I die!' But on the fourth morning, instead of hurling spears he said, 'These are my conditions. If you fulfil them, and take no more than a year and a day to do it, you can marry my daughter; if you fail, you die. First, bring back the sword of Giant Wrnach, who will not part with it until he is killed by it. Second, bring back twin wolf-cubs fastened with a lead woven from the beard of Dillus the Barbarian, and the hairs must be plucked while he is still alive. Third, there are nine sackfuls of flax-seeds scattered in the wind; bring back every seed and sow it to make a veil for my daughter's wedding-day. Fourth, bring back the tusk of White Turk, king of the boars, to shave my beard for the wedding. Fifth . . .'

The tasks

Ysbadadan went on naming conditions until there were thirty-nine of them*, and it took all Culhwch's concentration to remember them. He hurried back to the shepherd's house, wrote them down on ten white sheepskins, and sent three of his companions to take the skins to Camelot and ask Arthur's help. Then he, Kay, Bediver, Gwrhyr the interpreter and Goreu the shepherd's son rode to the castle of Giant Wrnach, a fortress of black stone blocks the size of carts. Gwrhyr growled in giant-language at the gatekeeper, and then told the others, 'Knife has gone into meat and drink into cup; no one may step inside till morning unless they have a skill to show.'

'I have a skill,' said Kay. 'I polish swords.'

The gatekeeper showed him into the castle hall, and Wrnach ordered a ladder to be hung from the table so that Kay could climb up and show his skill. He gave Kay his sword, with its blade as wide as a ship's rudder and as long as an oar, and Kay polished one side until it glittered. 'That's a useful skill,' said Wrnach. 'A man like you should be travelling with friends.'

'I have friends outside,' answered Kay. 'And they, too, have skills to show.'

Wrnach roared to the gatekeeper to open up, and Culhwch, Bediver, Gwrhyr and Goreu walked into the hall and stood in the shadows with their hands ready on their sword-hilts. Kay polished the other side of Wrnach's sword, and then said, 'Show me the sheath. The wood must be rotten; that's what's tarnishing the blade.' Wrnach handed over the sheath, and Kay replaced the slats in its side. Then he lifted the sword two-handed above his head as if he was going to sheathe it, and at the last moment whirled it round and sliced off Wrnach's head. The head thumped on to the table with the breath hissing out of it, and Culhwch, Bediver and the others drew their swords and prepared to show their warskills. But there was no fighting: as soon as Wrnach's dinner-guests saw that he was dead, they jumped from their places and ransacked the castle, ripping down the tapestries, emptying the chests and carting away the furniture until the humans were left alone in the bare hall with Wrnach's lolling body and gaping head. Kay wiped the gigantic sword and strapped it to a packhorse: Ysbadadan's first task was done.

The companions next went looking for Dillus the Barbarian. He was another giant, an outlaw, and Ysbadadan's orders were to pluck the hairs of his beard while he was still alive, and to weave a lead from them strong enough to hold a pair of wolves. They had no idea where Dillus might be, for he wandered where he liked, walking as lightly from mountain-peak to mountain-peak as mortals tread over stepping-stones. In the end they noticed the smoke of a cooking-fire on the central peak of Plynlimmon, and found Dillus kneeling beside a fire the size of a haystack and roasting oxen with skewers made from poplar-trunks. 'Look at the size of him,' whispered Bediver. 'How can we get near enough to his head to cut it off, never mind pluck out his beard while he's still alive?'

'Let him eat all he wants,' said Culhwch. 'And while he's eating, we'll dig a pit and make some tweezers.'

He, Bediver, Gwrhyr and Goreu dug a pit as wide as a house and as deep as a well, and while they were digging Kay roped two spear-shafts together to make tweezers, and Dillus gorged himself on spitted oxen, mead and beer. When everything was ready, Culhwch and Kay stretched out a trip-rope in the darkness, and Gwrhyr shouted, 'This way, Dillus, and be quick about it! The barbers are waiting.' Dillus lurched to his feet, snarling, groped through the darkness towards them, and was so stuffed with meat and so fuddled with drink that he tangled his legs in the trip-rope, rolled head over heels and ended up standing in the pit with his feet on the bottom and his head sticking out at the top like a vast, red-bearded, roaring cabbage. Kay, Bediver and Gwrhyr shovelled earth into the pit to trap him, and Culhwch and Goreu took a handle of the tweezers each, plucked out the hairs of his beard one by one and laid them on the ground like string. When his chin was utterly bare they hacked off his head with Wrnach's sword, and buried it beside his body. They plaited the hairs into a lead, and Ysbadadan's second task was done.

While all this was happening, Arthur's courtiers had scattered across Britain to carry out the other tasks. Every day Camelot's citizens gaped to see some new wonder arriving: a giant in chains, a shimmering magic cauldron, a cageful of wolves, a tusk of White Turk, king of the boars, gleaming yellow on a scarlet cushion, a bottomless drinking-horn, a talking harp. One by one, Arthur's secretaries crossed off the items on Culhwch's sheepskin lists, and when everything was gathered and Arthur set out to take them to Ysbadadan's castle, the procession of riders, cages, carts and prisoners looked like a circus on the move.

Even so, there was still one task left, and it seemed impossible: gathering the nine sackfuls of flax-seed scattered on the wind, to be sown and grown to make Olwen's wedding-veil. As the year and a day neared their end, and Culhwch and his companions made their way back to Ysbadadan's castle, they were heavy with failure, certain that their death-day loomed. Then Gwrhyr the Interpreter suddenly said, 'Listen! Voices!' They reined in their horses, and from the field by the road they could hear crackling flames and see a mushroom-cloud of smoke, as if a city was burning. But there was no other sound, and the others were amazed when Gwrhyr shouted, 'Hurry! Can't you hear them crying for rescue?', and jumped over the wall into the field. They followed him, and found not a blazing city but an ant-hill, with smoke and flames gushing from its top and a column of ant-refugees streaming out below. Culhwch took Wrnach's enormous word and chopped through the blazing mound like a man shelling an egg, and the ants were so grateful for the rescue that they searched out the flax-seeds wherever the wind had scattered them and carried them to

Ysbadadan's castle, one each, with the last one fetched home by a lone, lame ant on the very last second of the year and a day's last hour.

The end of Ysbadadan

As soon as Ysbadadan saw Arthur's procession of marvels, and Culhwch and his ant-column, he knew that the tasks were complete and he had no choice but to keep his word. He tied a napkin round his neck and beckoned to Culhwch, and Culhwch clambered up with White Turk's razor tusk to shave him. The tusk trimmed beard, skin, ears and flesh to the bone, and Ysbadadan showed no sign of pain, but merely wiped his face and said, 'Son-in-law, take Olwen my daughter, and long life to you!' Then Goreu the shepherd's son drew Wrnach's sword, cut off Ysbadadan's head and spiked it on a pole in the dungheap, and as soon as Ysbadadan was dead all the spells he had ever worked were undone, his dungeon-doors fell from their hinges, and all the people he had killed, including Goreu's twenty-three brothers, were restored to life and ran in cartwheeling with delight. There and then, in the sight of them all, in the sight of Arthur and his courtiers from Camelot, Culhwch and Olwen were married and were crowned king and queen of Ysbadadan's lands.*

8

OWAIN

The Warrior of the Fountain

One Whitsun it was too wet to hunt, and Arthur's lords spent the time telling stories. 'Last year,' said Kynon, 'I discovered a fountain, far from civilisation in the forest, and all I had time to find out was that it was under an enchanter's spell, waiting for some hero to fight him and make him reverse the magic, when I was driven away, coward that I am, by the warrior who guarded it.' Most of the lords took this for Kynon's usual boasting, and thought no more about it. But the story stuck in Owain's mind, and that evening as the others feasted he saddled his horse, slipped away from Camelot and began following Kynon's journey in every detail, riding along a river-valley in the gathering dusk. As he went the rain stopped, the sky lightened, and the moon rose bright as the sun in summer.

After a while, Owain came across two boys in a field. They had stuck their knives in the ground for archery targets, and were shooting at them with ivory bows and arrows flighted with peacock-feathers. A man stood watching them, and when he saw Owain he politely invited him back to his castle to spend the night. There were twenty-four girl servants in the castle, and the lord clapped his hands and ordered them to give Owain a better welcome than any visitor had ever before enjoyed. While they bustled, he told Owain about the enchanted fountain and the warrior who challenged every visitor, and filled him with such eagerness to fight that, for all the softness of the bed the twenty-four girls made up for him, he slept not a wink all night.

Next morning Owain dressed at dawn, ate a quick breakfast and galloped to the fountain to meet the warrior. It was misty, and the dark warrior's clothes and armour blended with the mist as if they were conjured out of it; nonetheless, Owain attacked him with such frenzy that he turned and fled with Owain galloping after him. They came to a castle of square black bricks, and the warrior galloped through the gates with their double portcullises. Owain was close on his heels, and as he passed under the portcullises they snapped down like a shark's jaws closing. The outer one chopped Owain's horse in two, and Owain was trapped between it and the inner portcullis like a prisoner in a cage. If the castle guards had found him there they would have used him for target practice. But just as the alarm was raised, a young girl ran up. She was identical in looks to the boys Owain had seen shooting the day before, and she reached through the bars and closed his fingers round a ring of invisibility, so that when the guards ran up they found nothing in their trap but the front half of the severed horse. Later, when the hue and cry died down, the girl opened the portcullis and helped Owain to a safer hiding-place.

That same evening the fortress was suddenly filled with the sound of chanting monks. Owain started up and snatched his sword. But the child touched his arm and said, 'It's all right. They're giving the last rites to the warrior you wounded.' Towards midnight there was a wail and howl of grief, and when Owain jumped up in alarm the child touched his hair and said, 'They're crying for the warrior you hurt.' At dawn next day every bell in the fortress began to toll, and the child touched Owain's cheek and said, 'They're burying the warrior you killed.' She took him to the window, and Owain saw the streets thronged by a funeral procession, led by the most beautiful woman he had ever seen. She was so like the boys from the meadow and the child from the portcullis that she could have been their elder sister. He called to the girl and asked the beautiful woman's name, and the girl said, 'She's the Lady of the Fountain, wife of the warrior you killed.' Later that day she took Owain to the audience-chamber in the fortress keep, and the Lady of the Fountain asked him to take the dead warrior's place, to become her husband and to protect the fortress and the fountain.

Owain's quest

So Owain became the Warrior of the Fountain, and for three years, while his heart ached for Camelot, he had no choice but to challenge and slaughter every innocent man who passed that way. The enchantment might have lasted forever if Arthur had not finally sent out

Gawain and Kay to look for him. Kynon led them, and they found the
boy archers, the hospitable lord and his twenty-four serving-girls
exactly as Owain had done, and finally came to the fountain. At once
Owain loomed out of the mist, unrecognisable in black armour, and
challenged them. Kay drew his sword and spurred furiously to the
attack, but Owain knocked him senseless with a blow on the temple
from his spearshaft. Then Gawain spurred forward, throwing off his
helmet to give himself clearer vision, and as soon as Owain recognised
him he threw down his weapons and hugged him with tears of joy.
The spell was broken – it would last only as long as Owain fought
passers-by; hugging them had never been expected – and Gawain and
Owain splashed water in Kay's face to revive him; then they all
wheeled their horses and galloped to Camelot.

Owain stayed in Arthur's court for three years after his return, and
then the memory of the Lady of the Fountain tormented him so much
that he set out to try and find her enchanted kingdom once more*. In
the heart of the forest he came to a high, bare boulder, split down the
centre, and in the cleft a lion was sheltering from a hissing, red-hooded
snake. Owain cut the snake in two, and the released lion fawned on
him like a pet cat, licking his hand, arching its back and gambolling.
That evening, while Owain gathered branches and lit a fire, the lion
vanished among the trees, came back with a roebuck in its jaws and
dropped it at Owain's feet. Owain cut slices of the meat to roast, and
was settling down to eat when there was the sound of wailing from the
trees, and he drew his sword while the lion flexed its claws and
growled. 'Where are you?' said Owain. 'And what are you – human
being or ghost?'

'I'm over here,' came the answer. 'My name's Luned; I'm no ghost.'

Owain ran to the edge of the trees and there, in a stone bottle the size
of a water-butt, half buried, was the girl who had given him the ring of
invisibility when he was trapped between the portcullises. She could
not see him through the stoppered bottle, and had no idea who he was;
she told him that she was the sister of the Lady of the Fountain, and
had helped her find a husband from among King Arthur's lords. But
the man had only stayed for three days*, and as soon as he left the
enchanter whose slave the Lady was had sent his sons to imprison her,
Luned, in a stone bottle. Unless Owain, the Lady's husband, came to
rescue her by midnight next day, she was to be burned alive.

'And if Owain knew all this,' said Owain, 'are you sure he'd come to
rescue you?'

'He loves my sister; I'm sure he'd come.'

Owain unstoppered the bottle, but the narrowness of the neck prevented him from rescuing or seeing Luned. Still without telling her his name, he fed her pieces of meat through the gap, and asked her how to find the Lady of the Fountain. But all she would answer was 'Bravery will find the way,' and in the end he gave up, pillowed his head on the lion and slept. Next morning, after sharing a breakfast of cold venison with Luned, he rode off down the forest path with the lion padding beside him. They came to a tower, barricaded against attack, and when Owain knocked the inhabitants opened the door, snatched him and the lion inside and slammed it shut again. A giant had stolen their twin princes the day before, they said, and was coming that morning to demand the princess as ransom. How could they exchange the girl's life for her brothers', or decide which of them should die? The choice was impossible.

'There's a third choice,' said Owain, 'and it's an easy one: fight the giant.'

Soon afterwards the giant came stamping up the path with a small boy under each arm, and roared to the tower-people to surrender or see their princes' heads used as battering-rams. Owain stepped outside and drove his sword into the giant's foot like an enormous thorn. The giant dropped the princes, danced in the air holding his foot and roaring with rage, and as he bent to rip Owain limb from limb, the lion leapt from the battlements and slid down his back with outstretched claws, tearing him till his guts spilled out and he fell dead at Owain's feet.*

The tower-people would have made Owain their king on the spot, and kept him there forever. But he was anxious for Luned, and after a day of celebration hurried back down the path with the lion at his heels. As he came to the clearing he saw a blazing fire, and two boys feeding it with branches. They were the boys he had seen at shooting-practice years before, identical in looks to Luned and the Lady of the Fountain, and as he watched they lifted Luned's stone bottle between them, smashed it and picked her up to throw her on the fire. Owain shouted to them to put her down, and they answered, 'It's midnight, and since Owain isn't here to rescue her, she'll burn.'

'If you think Owain has failed,' said Owain, 'fight me in his place.'

'Keep that lion out of it,' they answered, 'and we'll fight as much as you like.' They conjured up a prison, a box of solid stone, and put Luned and the lion in it. Then they fell on Owain to kill him. His

68

weapons were sword and spear; theirs were logs from the fire, picked up and hurled red-hot. They would soon have crushed him or charred him dead, but the lion suddenly gave a roar which made the forest shudder, smashed the stone prison with one paw-blow and snapped their necks.

Owain swung Luned on to his horse behind him and galloped with her to the castle of the boys' father. The man welcomed him as warmly as if he knew nothing of his sons' deaths, and ordered the twenty-four serving-girls to look after him. But as soon as they were alone with Owain they fell on their knees in tears. They were not serving-girls at all, they said, but princesses. The enchanter had enticed them to the castle, with their husbands, pretending hospitality. But the castle was really a plunder-house, and as soon as they were in the enchanter's clutches he stripped them of all they owned, locked the husbands into a cellar and forced the girls to act as his slaves. Now, furious at the death of his sons, he meant to wait till Owain and the lion were sleepy with food and drink, and then to cut their throats.

Owain said nothing, but as soon as the enchanter came back, chuckling and joking as if nothing was the matter, he sprang from behind the door, wrestled him to the floor and tied his hands behind his back. He beckoned to the lion, and it lifted its paw and bared its claws. 'Spare me,' said the enchanter. 'It was foretold that my power would only last until a man came clever enough to trick me and strong enough to bind me. If you spare my life, I'll turn this plunder-house into an inn, and give passers-by an honest welcome instead of robbing them.'

Owain agreed to this and untied the man's hands. The enchantment was over. The locks of every dungeon fell open, and the enchanter freed the husbands of the twenty-four princesses and a hundred other prisoners, and opened his store-rooms to give their plundered possessions back. That same day, Owain led them all in procession to the castle of the Lady of the Fountain, claimed her as his wife and took her home to Camelot, where he, she and Luned lived the rest of their lives very happily, and the lion lay purring under Arthur's table, as tame as a castle cat.

9

TRISTRAM

Tristram's youth

In the far south-west of Britain, between Cornwall and the waterfall that girds the earth, lay the peaceful kingdom of Lionesse. It was a land of farms and orchards, and its people were bee-keepers, gardeners and cider-makers, too busy and too kind-hearted to take joy in war*. Their kings paid tribute to King Arthur, and for the most part the other people of Britain were happy to leave them in peace: only the savage Hibernians ever troubled them, falling on them from time to time as pirates fall on merchant-ships.

King Meliad of Lionesse was a rose-grower, and for thirty years contented himself with developing new varieties, entering them in competitions and carrying off every prize. But as he grew older and thoughts of death began troubling his mind, it came to him that he should leave his kingdom not just a catalogue of blooms but a son and heir to rule after him. He married a beautiful Cornish princess, Elizabeth – after courting her with a new rose-variety named in her honour, The Thornless – and he was delighted when, some months afterwards, she told him that she was pregnant and the royal astrologers foretold that she would bear a son.

Meliad was in the habit of travelling the length and breadth of his kingdom to visit flower-shows, inspect rose-beds and exchange information with fellow rose-enthusiasts. As the time approached for Elizabeth to bear her child, he tried to cut down on these journeys, to be with her as much as possible. But some errands could not be put off, and one cold morning in November he kissed his wife, climbed on his horse and rode away, saying that he was going only a two hours' ride to collect grafts from a neighbour, and would be back that afternoon. Elizabeth watched from the palace window as he trotted away; by now

70

she was nine months pregnant, and the baby was kicking its eagerness to be born.

As the hours passed, Elizabeth's anxiety turned to icy fear. There was no sign of Meliad, and no news of him. If she had known the truth, she would have sent help at once: for Meliad had been captured by highwaymen and was in a castle dungeon awaiting ransom. As things were, as soon as afternoon turned into evening Elizabeth decided to look for Meliad herself, and rode out into the darkness with just one maid for company.

The night was frosty, and as the horse slid and stumbled on the icy road, Elizabeth felt a sudden stab of pain, and knew that the time of childbirth was upon her. She climbed down from the horse, and her maid made her as comfortable as possible on a bed of leaves. The pains came more and more often, and with each one the cold crept further into Elizabeth's bones, and she guessed that the hour of the baby's birth would be her own hour of death. The child was born just as dawn was breaking, and the maid wrapped him in a cloak and handed him to Elizabeth. She held him tight, kissed him, and had time only to name him Tristram (that is, Soul of Grief) before she died.

Not long afterwards, a search-party from the palace (led by Merlin, who was a friend of Meliad and often visited those parts) found the queen's body on its leaf-bier, and the maid cradling baby Tristram and crying. Two servants hurried the child home to the warmth of the palace, and the others laid Elizabeth's body in state in the cathedral. Merlin, meanwhile, spurred his horse to the castle where Meliad lay imprisoned, blinded the jailers with a magic mist and rescued his old friend, only to break his heart at once with news of his dear wife's death.

Meliad endured his grief for seven years. Then he married the elder daughter of King Hoel of Brittany, and in due course they had three children. At first King Hoel's daughter treated Tristram kindly, and he was brought up respectfully as his father's eldest son and heir. But as the years passed and the queen saw her own sons growing up in Tristram's shadow, blocked from royal inheritance, her heart hardened and she decided to murder him. One summer afternoon she took Tristram and his stepbrothers on a picnic, and while they were playing in the river she set out four cups, three made of pewter and filled with lemonade, the fourth made of silver and filled with poison. She expected that Tristram, the senior prince, would drink from the silver cup. But he was a good-natured boy, and when one of his step-brothers ran ahead saying that he was so thirsty he would die of it, Tristram gladly handed him the silver cup. The poison burst the little boy's heart and killed him. That evening the queen poured another cup of poison for Tristram to drink – and this time, instead of one of her sons it was her husband Meliad who reached for the cup, so that she was forced to knock his hand away and confess what she had done, or see him dead on the floor in front of her.

Meliad shook with fury. 'When a rose-stock turns woody and worthless,' he shouted, 'we burn it – and so we shall with you. Servants, prepare a fire!'

Now, all the twelve years of his life, Tristram (as befitted a prince of Lionesse) had been the gentlest of people, a peacemaker. When he saw his father raging and his stepmother sobbing he threw himself at Meliad's feet. 'Father, in gratitude for my life being spared, please give me a gift,' he said.

'Whatever you ask,' said Meliad.

'All I ask is – spare my stepmother's life.'

Meliad ground his teeth, and signed to the servants to put out the fire. But he swore that from that day on, as long as he lived, he would have nothing more to do with the queen. He banished her from his bed, his board, his gardens and his palaces – and to save Tristram from any more attempts on his life, he shipped him abroad to Brittany, where King Hoel brought him up with his own royal sons.

Tristram stayed six years in Brittany, and learned hunting, hawking, boxing, wrestling and sword-fighting. Even so, and good though he was at such pursuits, he found them repellent and preferred gentler pastimes such as chess, book-reading and playing the harp. And soon, as so often in his life, the very gentleness of his character brought trouble: for Belinda, King Hoel's second daughter, fell in love with him, and when he refused to sleep with her mixed him a cup of poison, exactly as her sister had done in Lionesse. Tristram realised with a sigh that it was time to leave Brittany – and since his father Meliad had died and his stepmother was now queen of Lionesse, he felt it unsafe to return home and went instead to Cornwall, where his uncle King Mark gave him a welcome in the royal castle of Tintagel.

Tristram and Ysoud

Not long afterwards, King Argius of Hibernia decided that it was time to gather tribute from the unwarlike inhabitants of Lionesse. He filled a warship with soldiers, and put his brother-in-law Morant in charge of them. Morant's mother was a giantess, and he was so huge that he could rip up trees and tear cattle apart as ordinary men tear chickens. When the people of Lionesse heard that his warship was approaching they hurried to meet him with casks of cider, barrels of apples, sacks of gold, honeycombs, carpets, and any other tribute they could think of. But even when his ship was loaded to the waterline Morant was still not satisfied, and roared at his men to row along the coast and plunder Cornwall.

News of the Hibernians' approach filled the people of Cornwall with even greater panic than the timid inhabitants of Lionesse. They had long experience in fighting giants – it went back to the days of Corin, their founder and first king, and his wrestling match with Gogmagog – and they knew that resistance was useless unless a single champion could be found, someone so reckless or so furious that he forgot all fear. To their surprise they found just such a champion in Tristram. Word of how the Hibernians had plundered Lionesse so enraged him that he snatched his sword, ran out bareheaded and challenged Morant to single-handed combat then and there. Morant picked him up in his two vast hands, intending to pull his limbs from their sockets as children torment flies – and as soon as he was in range Tristram lifted his sword and smashed it down on Morant's head. The blade sliced through chain-mail, cap, hair, skin and flesh, and the point snapped off and lodged in Morant's skull. Morant dropped Tristram with a scream, fell to the ground clutching his wound, and died. His soldiers lugged his body back to the ship and rowed hastily for Hibernia, while Cornish jeers rained down on them like stones.

After that, Tristram was the hero of Cornwall. The people held feasts and celebrations in his honour, and when he made up a song about the duel, they danced in the streets to the sound of it. But their joy was tinged with sorrow: for when Morant had picked Tristram up to tear him, one of his finger-nails had grazed Tristram's arm. Giants' finger-nails, like everything else about them, are poisonous, and now the wound festered and no Cornish medicines could cure it. Tristram decided that his only hope was to go to King Arthur's court in Camelot and ask Merlin's help. King Mark gave him a ship for the journey, and

73

when Tristram went on board and the sailors bent to the oars, the whole Cornish people lined the shore to cheer him on his way.

As soon as the ship was clear of land, storm-winds snatched it and hurled it into open sea. The sailors cowered; in a blanket on the foredeck Tristram tossed and turned in a fever, heeding neither the gales nor the whimpering of his crew. The storm lasted for four days, and when it stopped they found themselves becalmed by the shore of an unknown country, shaggy with trees. The sailors carried Tristram ashore, lit driftwood fires and made supper, grateful to have firm ground underfoot at last. Next morning they sent scouting-parties inland, and found a large, rich town with a royal castle at its heart, and human beings and giants living happily side by side. They carried Tristram to the castle, and the queen herself made a poultice to heal his wound.

Tristram lay on his sickbed in the queen's apartments for six days. He saw no one but the palace women, and was particularly attracted to one of them, the queen's daughter Ysoud. She shared his love of music, and visited him every afternoon to sing and play with him. The combination of good company and expert nursing soon began to restore Tristram's health – and he was just making up his mind to announce who he was, and to ask for Ysoud's hand in marriage, when he discovered by chance the name of the country he was in, and the news was like a hammer-blow. For this was Hibernia, the country whose champion Morant he had killed, and part of the comforts of the royal apartments consisted of tapestries and furniture looted from Lionesse. He knew that if anyone in the castle discovered who he was they would rip him to pieces; he swore his crew to silence, told everyone he was Tramtris, a nobleman from overseas, and made plans to slip away as soon as he was fit to move.

In the meantime, another visitor came to Hibernia: Prince Palamedes of Syria. The Hibernians held games, feasts and contests of archery and swordsmanship in his honour, and Palamedes won every contest he entered, until no one in Hibernia would stand up to him. At this point he announced that he had come to ask Ysoud to marry him, go back to Syria and be his queen. Tristram's heart was stabbed with jealousy. How could he challenge Palamedes and declare his own love for Ysoud without revealing who he was? In the end, however, matters resolved themselves. Palamedes challenged any gentleman of the court to a duel with swords, and Tristram accepted the challenge, sent for his sword from his ship and so soundly beat Palamedes, despite his wounded arm, that the Syrian prince stormed angrily on board his ship and sailed away. The Hibernians thronged to congratulate Tristram, and the queen noticed that his sword had a broken tip, and that the missing piece was identical to the fragment which had lodged in her brother Morant's head and killed him. King Argius was away from Hibernia at this time on a pirate-trip, and justice rested with the queen. She banished Tristram on pain of death, and Ysoud helped her lover and his men provision their ship, then watched with tear-filled eyes as they rowed away.

After two days Tristram reached Cornwall, and gave his uncle King Mark a full account of his adventures. He was particularly lyrical in his description of Ysoud's beauty, hiding only his own love for her – and he was horrified when Mark said that she would make an ideal queen for Cornwall, and ordered him to go back to Hibernia and fetch her to be his (Mark's) bride. What could Tristram do? He was forbidden to go back to Hibernia on pain of death, and he could not disobey his uncle without revealing that he was a rival for Ysoud's love. He decided to ask Merlin's advice in Camelot – and once again his ship was snatched by storms and cast up on an unknown shore. Here he found an old man facing an ogre, and joined the unequal combat on the old man's side, slicing off the ogre's head with the same chipped sword as he had used on the giant Morant. The old man embraced him with tears of gratitude. 'Ask any reward you like,' he said. 'I am Argius, king of Hibernia, and everything I have is yours.'

So Tristram was able to go back to Hibernia after all, and when the queen saw how Argius favoured him, she dared say nothing about the death of Morant or her own threat against Tristram's life. But she was a witch, with magic powers: she knew the future, and she was content to wait. Meanwhile, Tristram was fighting a battle in his heart between his duty to his uncle King Mark and his own love for Ysoud. Duty conquered, and he went to King Argius and asked, as the favour promised him, to be allowed to take Ysoud back to Cornwall to be the old king's wife. Argius gladly agreed, and ordered a ship to be prepared, fit for a princess. This was the witch-queen's moment. She sent for Ysoud's servant Brangen, who was to go back to Cornwall with her mistress. 'To ensure a happy marriage,' she said, 'take this love-potion, and pour it in Mark's and Ysoud's cups at the wedding feast.'

Those were her orders, but she knew very well that things would turn out otherwise. For the ship carrying Tristram and Ysoud was hardly a day's journey out to sea when flat calm fell. The crew dozed over the oars, Brangen slept, and only Tristram and Ysoud were awake, sitting sadly over a chessboard high on deck. The sun was hot, and Ysoud said that she was thirsty. 'Don't waken Brangen,' said Tristram. 'Look: there's a bottle there beside her.' He poured half the drink for Ysoud and took the rest himself. At once the potion did its work: they fell into each other's arms, and the witch-queen's vengeance for her brother's death began.

The lovers at last reached Cornwall, and Tristram watched despairingly as Mark's and Ysoud's wedding went ahead*. Mark was delighted with his young queen; he loaded Tristram with honours and made him first lord of the royal court, and the more Tristram watched him laughing and talking with Ysoud, spending every moment in her company, the more his good fortune turned to ash. He tried to console himself with music, but complained that the harp was out of tune and smashed it; he tried to read, and tore his book to shreds; he went hunting, and snapped his bow and kicked the dogs till they whined. In the end, he and Ysoud began meeting secretly in Ysoud's apartments. Their loyalty to Mark kept them from making love, but the love-potion filled them with such longing for each other that they spent hours sitting over a chessboard, toying with the pieces and gazing at each other with a passion they dared not satisfy. This was how King Mark found them one afternoon when he came back unexpectedly from hunting – and he locked Ysoud in a tall tower of Tintagel Castle and forbade Tristram ever to see her again. For a time Tristram wrote messages on birch-bark and floated them inside the castle on the millstream; but Mark found out about this, too, and exiled him.

Tristram's death

Exile from Ysoud unhinged Tristram's character. He began to buffet about the world like a rudderless ship; he abandoned music, chess and the other pursuits of the mind, and instead became a fanatical huntsman, pitting his wits (and his hawks and dogs) against anything that ran or hid or flew. His blood-lust extended to human beings, too: whenever he could pick a quarrel, fight a duel or take part in a battle, no one was readier. His reason for living had been snatched away, and he lived like a gambler, staking his own life on every throw*.

One spring evening Tristram was riding through a forest, in a part of Britain he had never visited before. His dogs had alarmed a herd of deer, and he was trying to decide whether to camp for the night and get up at dawn to hunt, or to continue on his way. While he was turning it over in his mind, he came across a small chapel in a clearing, and went inside to pray. Afterwards, the priest-in-charge invited him to supper. He warned him that the forest was dangerous: it was the home of Vivien the Enchantress, and its caves and thickets were full of the skeletons of men she had fallen in love with and enticed to their deaths. She gave her victims a ring, and as soon as it was on their fingers they forgot who they were, where they came from, even the need to eat and drink: love was all they cared about, and it pulsed like venom in their veins. Not long before, the priest went on, Vivien had ensnared King Arthur himself, and now he was wandering with daisy-chains in his hair, while the young men of Camelot quartered the woods to find him.

Tristram recognised in Arthur's state of mind exactly the same ecstasy as the love-potion had produced in his own brain, and decided to find him and help him if he could. There was no sign of Arthur either in thickets or in the open paths; but towards mid-day next day, as Tristram was climbing a bracken-covered hill, a young girl darted out of the undergrowth and begged him to come and help. He ran up the hill after her, and at the top found Arthur stark naked, with his Pendragon-helmet and Excalibur useless on the ground beside him. Three robbers had attacked him and were stripping him of all he owned, and he sat slack-eyed among the bracken and let them do it. They were so busy passing his belongings from hand to hand, chuckling at the weight of the velvet clothes and the glint of the money, that they knew nothing of Tristram until they heard the wind of his sword and felt its blade slice their necks. Tristram kicked the bodies down the hill, and began gathering Arthur's clothes; the girl, meanwhile, went to the babbling king, lifted his hand and took from one of his fingers a small, plain ring, grey as a wisp of smoke. As soon as it was off his finger, it coiled away to nothing in the air, King Arthur's wits returned, and he stood blinking before them, asking who they were and why they had brought him there.

While Arthur was dressing and Tristram was explaining, three armed men shouldered their way through the undergrowth and ran up the hill to help the king. They were lords of Camelot, and would have cut Tristram's and the girl's throats then and there if Arthur had not prevented them. He invited Tristram back to Camelot and offered him a place at the Round Table, and Tristram, who had plans for no other journeys, gladly agreed. As for the girl, she was a servant of Vivien the Enchantress, and was terrified of the revenge her mistress would take on her for saving Arthur's life; but Arthur promised to take her, too, back to Camelot, and to put her under Merlin's protection. They mounted their horses and rode off through the woods, the lords blowing horns and shouting to the others that the king was safe.

Tristram stayed at Arthur's court for over a year, and was one of the most fearless and heroic young men of Camelot: of all the others, only Gawain and Lancelot ever matched his fighting-skill*. Stories of his courage spread throughout Arthur's kingdom and eventually reached Cornwall, where they made King Mark grind his teeth with jealousy. He decided to go to Camelot, creep upon Tristram and stab him; but he was so unused to plotting that instead of travelling stealthily he went openly with a retinue of servants and Queen Ysoud herself riding in a litter. He left Ysoud in a nunnery outside the city, put on a disguise which fooled nobody and crept into the city, unaware that every step he took was watched.

While Mark lurked in Camelot, waiting his chance to plant a dagger in Tristram's back, Ysoud's beauty caught the eye of Bruce the Pitiless, a robber-baron from the nearby hills, whose castle had walls so sheer and was so well-stocked with his brigand-followers that none of Arthur's young men had ever been able to catch him or deal with him. He waited until Ysoud went riding one afternoon, with only Brangen for company; then he leapt out at her and dragged her to the thicket where his horse was waiting to carry them away. Brangen ran screaming for help – and by chance came on Tristram, hunting in the woods, and begged him to come to the rescue. There was a short, sharp duel, Bruce was killed and the two lovers, despite their own or anyone else's plans, were reunited. They rode into Camelot together – and found Mark in chains before the king, accused of hiding under the Round Table with a dagger in his sleeve. The whole matter between him, Ysoud and Tristram was explained, and Arthur agreed to let Mark go free, back to Cornwall, provided that he and Tristram swore an oath of everlasting friendship. Mark muttered and growled, and at last agreed to the oath – but when Arthur turned to ask Tristram to swear, he had disappeared. Once again the conflict between duty and love had flared in his mind, and he had galloped away from Camelot determined never to see Ysoud, Mark, Arthur or any of his Round Table companions again.

To put an even greater distance between them, Tristram sailed to

Brittany, and offered his services in a war King Hoel was fighting against barbarians from the south. He drove the invaders whimpering home, and in gratitude King Hoel offered him the hand in marriage of his youngest daughter, Ysoud. Ysoud! The young girl was amazed at how violently Tristram hugged her to him and snatched at the marriage-offer. He called her Ysoud of the White Hands, but in his sleep he babbled of another Ysoud, Ysoud the Beautiful, far away, until his young wife grew jealous of a rival she had never seen.

Not long afterwards, Tristram was leading the siege of a rebellious southern city, and was climbing a scaling-ladder when a boulder, hurled from the battlements, knocked him unconscious to the ground. The fall opened the wound in his arm where Morant's finger-nail had gashed him long ago, and once again his flesh began to fester. King Hoel's doctors tried every potion and poultice in their spell-books, but the wound grew worse and Tristram gew weaker with every day that passed. In the end he decided that only the Hibernian magic which had cured him before would heal him now – and since the witch-queen, Morant's sister, was long since dead, he knew that the only person who could help him was her daughter Ysoud of Cornwall, however many oaths he had sworn never to see or speak to her again.

Tristram sent messengers to Cornwall, begging Ysoud to come to him. He asked her to hoist white sails if she came herself, and black sails if she refused to help – and every day till the messengers returned he had himself carried to a headland and gazed out to sea, watching for news. When she saw this, the jealousy of Ysoud of the White Hands curdled into fury, and she began plotting Tristram's death. Long before the ship arrived from Cornwall, he was too weak to be carried to the shore, and had to lie in bed at home, sending a servant to the headland each day to watch for sails. Ysoud of the White Hands bribed this servant to lie to him, and accordingly, when Ysoud of Cornwall sailed to Brittany in a white-sailed ship, the servant told Tristram that the sails were black. Despair, added to the poison of his wound, over-whelmed Tristram's heart, and when Ysoud of Cornwall landed and rushed to his bedside, she found him dead and cold. With a cry of grief she took his sword, the one with the chipped blade he had used since youth, and stabbed herself; then she cradled his head in her arms and bent to kiss him, and the unhappy lovers were united at last, in death**†.

10

GERAINT AND YNID

The challenge

Arthur often spent Whitsun at Caerleon, so that when the Masses and thanksgiving-services were over he could invite all his followers to a deer-hunt in the Forest of Dean. One year Guinever slept late, and when she woke up everyone had left for the hunt and the castle was deserted except for a few servants and for Prince Geraint of Cornwall, who had also stayed up late, dancing, the night before. Guinever and Geraint gulped their breakfast, shouted for their horses and hurried off to find the hunt, accompanied by one of Guinever's maids. They had reached open country, the fringes of the Forest, when they met an unknown lord on horseback, accompanied by a lady and a dwarf, and Guinever sent her maid to ask their names. The dwarf answered rudely, 'Why should my lord tell his name to the likes of you?' and flicked the girl's face with his riding-whip so that she came back bloody and tearful; then the dwarf, lord and lady rode serenely on. Furious, Geraint galloped after them: he meant to track the lord to his castle and challenge him to a duel for the dwarf's impertinence.

That evening the lord, lady and dwarf reached a town Geraint had never seen before, and rode through the streets to the castle while the townspeople crowded to their windows to watch. It was a town filled with fighters: armour and weapons hung in every window, and warhorses whinnied in the yards. Geraint thought, 'I'd better wait and see, before I challenge anyone.' He chose the shabbiest house he could find and begged a bed for the night. The owners of the house, a white-haired old man and his beautiful daughter, welcomed him, and while the old man saw to the horse the girl hurried out to buy bread, wine and beef, food fit for such a noble guest. As they ate, the old man said that he was Prince Niwl, and that he had built the town and ruled it until he was dethroned by his own nephew and stripped of all he owned. As for the lord with the dwarf, every year at Whitsun he rode to the town to declare his lady the most beautiful woman in Britain, and to challenge any man who disagreed. 'Sir,' said Geraint, 'if your daughter will let me answer the challenge in her name, and if you'll lend me some armour, I'll fight that lord.'

Next morning the townspeople, and all the visiting warriors and their ladies, gathered on the castle green for the duelling, and the dwarf led his master out in full armour, and challenged all comers to deny that his lady was the most beautiful woman in Britain. Before anyone else could answer Geraint rode forward, in a rusty suit of armour with a cobwebby spear and an old-fashioned sword, and said, 'I deny it, in the name of Ynid, Niwl's daughter.' The duel began, and the proud lord soon had the better of it, hammering Geraint's helmet and shoulders as a blacksmith beats an anvil. But when Geraint stepped aside to wipe the sweat from his eyes, Niwl whispered, 'Remember the dwarf, and the insult you came to punish,' and this stoked his anger as logs stoke fire. He ran at the proud lord with a battery of blows which dented his armour and bruised his ribs, and brought his sword down on the man's head with such force that it split the helmet, cut through cap, hair and skin and ground on bone. The lord staggered and fell, and Geraint dumped him like a dummy across his horse, and told the dwarf to take him to Camelot as he was, bloody and undoctored, and apologise to Guinever for his impertinence.

After this victory, several of the other visiting fighters wanted to challenge Geraint for the honour of their own ladies. But the townspeople would have none of it. They cheered him as hero of the hour, and promised him anything he wanted. He called for Niwl's lands and authority to be given back to him, and for everything to be as it was before. Then he married Ynid and took her home to Cornwall, where his father King Erbin was fighting invaders on every side.

The rescue

Up till now, Geraint had been a modest, sensible young man. But his victory over the proud lord, and the victories which followed it, filled him with an arrogance close to madness, and he began to think himself invincible. He never trained or exercised; he refused to take part in tournaments or to accept challenges; he spent his time with Ynid and left friends and enemies alike to kick their heels. The other young lords began muttering that he was growing soft, that if he spent any longer in women's company he would turn into one himself, and in the end, since no one dared to tackle Geraint openly, his father Erbin asked Ynid's help. Ynid pulled back the covers as Geraint lay sleeping, and stroked his arms and chest with tears running down her cheeks. 'Dear God,' she whispered, 'never let his strength be wasted on my account.'

Geraint half-heard these words in his sleep, and his fevered mind took them as an admission that Ynid was having a love-affair with another man, who would challenge him to fight for her. He leapt out of bed, called the servants to bring his weapons and saddle his horse, and said coldly to Ynid, 'Get up. Order your horse and put on your shabbiest riding dress.'

'Where are we going?'

'On a quest, to see just how much of my fighting strength is wasted. Ride twenty paces in front of me, and don't speak unless you're spoken to.'

Ynid had no idea how she had deserved this treatment, but she meekly dressed and did as she was told. They rode along the wildest road in Cornwall, a haunt of bandits and highwaymen, and as they went, Ynid overheard three cutthroats waiting in ambush, saying, 'This is easy: two horses and two saddles, with no one but a man-woman to fight for them!' Trembling, she waited for Geraint to catch up with her, and said, 'Sir, shall I tell you what I know?'

'I told you not to speak until you were spoken to. Why should I care what you know?' answered Geraint, and signed angrily to her to ride on. Before they had gone three steps the cutthroats leapt out of the bushes and attacked, and Geraint killed them with three easy blows, threw their bodies into the ditch, knotted their horses' reins together and gave them to Ynid, saying, 'Lead these horses fifty paces ahead of me, and don't speak unless you're spoken to.'

They rode on, Ynid leading the horses and Geraint following, and as they passed a copse of trees Ynid heard four bandits plotting an ambush and said to Geraint, 'Sir, shall I tell you what I know?' Once again he snapped at her to keep quiet; once again the bandits attacked and once again he killed them and added their horses to the three Ynid already led. A little later five highwaymen leapt out on them, and Geraint killed them and added their horses to the others. For the rest of that day Ynid led a dozen horses through the woods, not daring to turn round or speak, and Geraint rode a dozen paces behind her, stony-faced. At sunset he rolled himself in his cloak, lay down on his shield and slept, leaving Ynid to guard the horses. They rode all the next morning without incident, and at mid-day came to a town* and paid for their lunch with one of the captured horses. Geraint stayed the rest of that day at the inn, feasting and resting, and Ynid sat in a corner and waited for him to speak to her.

That night when Geraint was asleep, the lord of the town came knocking at Ynid's door. 'How can you travel with a man like that?' he said. 'Leave him, and marry me.'

'Sir,' she answered, 'I'll not desert him; I'll not be called a whore. But bring soldiers in the morning and kill him; then I'll marry you.'

As soon as the lord was gone Ynid shook Geraint awake and told him what had happened. At first he was furious that she had spoken without being spoken to, but at last she persuaded him to get up and dress, and they left the rest of the captured horses with the innkeeper and galloped out of town.*

Geraint's next encounter was with the Little King, a dwarf who ruled a peaceful river-valley and challenged anyone who tried to ride across it. Geraint was ashamed to fight a dwarf, but found the Little King more than a match for him: the duel lasted all day, and it was dusk before Geraint was able to wheel his horse and gallop away, sweaty, exhausted and full of wounds. He would have died of his injuries, if Arthur, Kay and Gawain had not happened to be hunting in those parts, taken him to their hunting-lodge and given him food, rest and doctoring. Even so, he recognised none of them, and as soon as his wounds healed he climbed on his horse and rode away, with Ynid following as before. He was hot for a fight, and fell furiously on three giants he found on the road. They had killed a passer-by and were robbing the body, and Geraint killed all three of them; but the last of them, with his dying strength, hit him a blow which jarred open every wound on his body, and Ynid only had time to jump from her horse and run to him before he lay dead in her arms.

There were other travellers on the road: a black-cloaked lord and six black-hooded attendants. They put Geraint's body on his shield, carried him to the lord's hall beneath the hill, and laid it on a bier. 'Change your clothes, lady,' the lord said to Ynid. 'Sit and eat. He's dead; he'll keep.'

'How can I eat, when my lord is dead?'

'Drink from this cup. Forget him.'

'How can I drink? How can I forget?'

'If you won't drink willingly,' said the black lord, 'you must be forced.' He held the cup to her lips, and when she refused to drink he threw it down and boxed her ears.

Until that moment Ynid had controlled her feelings. But now her love for Geraint, her misery and her rage burst out in a scream that rattled the rafters and sent echoes ringing round the hall. It pierced Geraint's heart, there in the vault of Death under the mountain, and he sat up, lifted his sword and brought it down on the dark lord's head in a blow which chopped him from cap to navel and jarred the sword a blade's depth in the table-top. The dark lord and his servants vanished like the wraiths they were, and Geraint and Ynid were left alone. The veils of madness lifted at last from Geraint's mind and he realised how he had wronged Ynid, how her devotion had rescued him even from the grave. They kissed joyfully, mounted their horses and rode as fast as Geraint's weakness would let them back to the Little King's castle, where doctors treated Geraint's wounds and Ynid and the castle women set about nursing him back to health.

As soon as Geraint recovered, he and Ynid left to finish the quest and go home to Cornwall. They rode side by side, laughing and talking, until the path ahead was blocked by a hedge of mist. It stretched like a curtain from sky to earth, and bristled with wooden spikes, on each of which hung a gaping human skull. Geraint asked Ynid to wait for him, then spurred into the mist – it was like riding through wet silk – and disappeared. He came to an apple-orchard, and on the nearest tree was a hunting-horn. As soon as Geraint's horse set foot on the orchard grass*, a warrior sprang out of the trees on a warhorse, and he and it were armoured from helmet-tip to hoof. Before the man could utter a single word of challenge, Geraint levelled his spear and rode at him so fiercely that he sent him and his horse rolling head-over-heels. Geraint drew his sword, and the man cried, 'Spare me! Take any gift you choose!'

'I want an end to these enchantments,' said Geraint.

'Take the horn and blow it,' said the man.

The horn-blast was like a hurricane which engulfed the orchard in a leaf-storm, uprooted the apple-trees and scoured the sky. When the air cleared warrior, orchard and mist-hedge had all disappeared, and Geraint found Ynid waiting placidly beside the path. They rode back to Cornwall side by side, and ruled there in contentment till the day they died.

84

11

LANCELOT

Lancelot's boyhood

Lancelot's father was Ban, King of Brittany* and Arthur's loyal ally. He kept Arthur's power alive in Gaul, and the Gaulish chiefs hated him for it. Since none of them were strong enough to defeat him single-handed, they banded together and hired a giant, Claudas, to lead them. Under Claudas they sacked and burned the towns of Brittany one by one, until Ban and his pregnant queen Elaine were trapped in their last surviving castle, a single tower ringed by enemies. While stones from Claudas' siege-weapons thudded into the walls and fire-arrows whizzed about their ears, Ban said to his trembling queen, 'I must fetch Arthur, and help, from Britain. Stay here: my generals will guard you till help arrives.' He slipped out of the tower at midnight, and as soon as he was well away his generals opened the gates and let in the enemy. Whooping Gauls ripped down the tapestries, smashed the furniture, looted the treasury and slit the throats of every living soul they found. Their main search was for Elaine, but in the nick of time, as the attack began, she had disguised herself as a servant and fled on a donkey to join her husband. The jolting of the journey was too much for her, and she no sooner found her husband Ban by a lakeside, gazing tearfully at his blazing tower, than she went into labour and died of it. Ban wrapped the newborn baby in a blanket, laid him on the lake-shore, kissed his dear wife for the last time and fell dead beside her from a broken heart.

The lake the dead lovers and their baby lay beside was really not a lake at all, but a magic castle, home of the Lady of the Lake*. Most castles are guarded by moats, turrets and battlements, but the Lady's was protected by its shape. It looked like any other lake, a swirl of water edged by trees and blanketed by mist; but anyone who tried to swim in it found that the water was a mirage, a dream in the mind, and ended up floundering. The Lady lived deep inside it with her fairy-retinue, as ordinary people and their servants lived in stone castles in the mortal world. From time to time they left it to visit the mortal world, and changed shape to do it, disguising themselves as smoke, leaves, dragonflies, jewels, domestic pets or men and women of repellant ugliness. Soon after the deaths of Ban and Elaine, the Lady heard from the lake-depths the sound of a baby crying, swam to the surface and found Lancelot wailing by his parents' bodies on the shore. She picked him up and carried him away, determined to bring him up as her own foster-child. Later, to give the little boy company, she stole his cousins Lionel and Bors, disguising them as greyhounds and slipping them from under their nurses' noses.

In the corridors and schoolrooms of the lake-castle, the three boys mastered every piece of learning known to human beings, and as much of their foster-mother's shape-changing magic as their mortal natures allowed them to understand*. In its paddocks and gardens they practised horse-riding, sword-fighting and other war-skills; they grew up content with each others' company, used to the way their foster-mother and servants changed shape or disappeared even as they spoke to them, and quite unaware that there were other human beings in the world beside themselves. They might have continued in the lake-castle till their deaths – for unlike the Lady and her fairy-servants, who were immortal, they grew older with each passing day. But Merlin, the Lady's lover, pointed out to her that as they reached manhood and the age for marriage they were becoming more her prisoners than her foster-sons, and accordingly, on Lancelot's eighteenth birthday, she carried the three young men to Britain and set them on the road to Camelot, to seek human fame and fortune at Arthur's court.

Lancelot and the four fairy queens

At first, when Lancelot went to Camelot, the young men of the Round Table were amazed at his warskills. Although he was one of Arthur's least experienced followers, his fairy education made him unbeatable at riding, shooting, hunting, wrestling and duelling; whatever challenge was put to him, he met it easily. As time passed, however, they began to mutter against him, and to devise ways of catching him off-guard and defeating him – and their hostility was increased, not lessened, by his charm with pretty girls*, and by the way he won the hearts of every lady at court, from the humblest maidservant to Queen Guinever herself. She favoured him above all Arthur's followers, and delighted in spending hours each day with him, indulging in music, games of bowls and chess, and, after he had been at court for less than a month, in bed.

For his part, Lancelot at first revelled in a way of life so different from his young days in the lake-castle. But restlessness soon gripped his mind. He felt that his victories on the duelling-field or in the bedroom were too easy, and took to riding further and further away from Camelot, looking for adventures which would test his skills and win him acceptance as a true member of Arthur's court instead of a casual, dazzling visitor*. One day, after he and Lionel had spent the whole morning on horseback, he lay down to rest in the shade of an apple-tree, while Lionel stayed on guard. All at once Lionel heard horses' hooves and saw three horsemen galloping for their lives, and a giant pelting after them on a horse the size of a farm-cart. As Lionel watched, the giant caught the horsemen up, clubbed them unconscious and slung them across his saddle like turnip-sacks; when Lionel challenged him, he did the same to him. He carried them to his lair, hung their shields on a tree festooned with the shields of earlier victims, locked them in an underground cave and went to eat his lunch.

Meanwhile, under the apple-tree, Lancelot slept heedlessly on. In the middle of the afternoon Morgan le Fay and her three companion fairy queens rode past, on moon-white horses and with a canopy held by four servants to shade the sun (whose rays no fairy can abide). Everyone thought that Morgan le Fay was mortal, the daughter of King Gorlois and Queen Ygern of Cornwall, and King Arthur's own step-sister. But she was a changeling, a fairy substituted for Gorlois' and Ygern's mortal baby, and she was jealous of her half-brother Arthur and did everything in her power to destroy him*. Like all fairies, she was insatiably passionate, and liked nothing better than love-making with mortal men – and now, as she gazed down at Lancelot asleep under the apple-tree, she thought him the most handsome mortal she had ever seen. She put a spell on him to keep him asleep and ordered her servants to carry him gently to her castle. When Lancelot woke up he found himself in a torchlit hall, its walls glittering with silver and with mosaics of gem-stones and tortoise-shell, and servants brought him the kind of food and wine he had not tasted since his boyhood under the fairy lake. But when he had eaten, Morgan le

Fay appeared and said that he must choose either to live with her forever and forget the mortal world, or die in a dungeon. Lancelot angrily chose the dungeon, and Morgan's fairy-servants dumped him there. But next morning he seduced the servant-girl who brought him breakfast*, and she opened the dungeon's twelve locks, slipped him past the guards and led him to his horse. She told him that the fairy kingdom was guarded by a giant, whose lair was marked by a tree hung with shields; to escape from the fairy spell, Lancelot must rattle the shields until the giant appeared, challenge him to a fair fight without magic and cut off his head. So Lancelot did: he found the tree with its unearthly fruit of shields, and rattled them until the giant (whose name was Turkin) came roaring out of his lair. Then he ran round behind him, cut the tendons of his ankles to topple him and hacked off his head. He took the keys from Turkin's belt, opened the cave and set the prisoners free: not only Lionel and the three horsemen Turkin had captured the day before, but twenty-seven other young men, one for each shield hanging on the tree. They were all King Arthur's followers, imprisoned on the orders of Morgan le Fay; now Lancelot told them to expect him at King Arthur's court in a month's time, on Whit Sunday, and sent them in convoy to Camelot.

Lancelot rode away by himself into the forest, in search of further adventures. And he soon found them: for the four fairy queens, furious at the death of their giant-protector, sent a sorceress, Hellawes, to trap him and destroy him. She disguised herself as a grieving widow, and sent her familiar disguised as a black dog to fetch Lancelot. Lancelot saw the dog sniffing a blood-trail among the trees and whimpering. Thinking that the trail must come from a wounded deer, he followed it, and came not to a deer dying in a thicket but to a black-bearded warrior lying in a coffin in a clearing. Lancelot crossed himself, said a prayer for the dead man's soul and hurried on. Not far off he found a girl crying in the bushes, and a young man writhing in agony beside her. The girl begged Lancelot to help her. Her brother, she said, had fought a brigand from the woods, and had mortally wounded him; but the brigand had gashed him so severely that he lay dying of it, and the only cure was to wipe his wound with a corner of the gravecloth from the enemy who wounded him. Exactly as Hellawes had planned, Lancelot remembered the black-bearded man in the coffin, and galloped back to find him. But instead of the clearing and the coffin he found a chapel, with a graveyard and an outer wall lined with giants, all baring their fangs and daring him to fight. Lancelot drew his sword, but instead of attacking them he held it by the blade and brandished the hilt at them, held high in the sign of the cross. The giants fell back hissing with terror, and Lancelot walked through the graveyard into the chapel. In the centre was the coffin, lit by a candle at each corner, and in the coffin was the brigand's body wrapped in a cloth. Without dropping his sword-cross for a moment, Lancelot drew his dagger with his other hand and cut off a corner of the gravecloth, crusted with the brigand's blood. He hurried out of the chapel – and this time found his way barred not by giants but by Hellawes herself. 'Stop, Lancelot!' she said. 'Put down your sword, kiss me and live in the fairy world forever, immortal and all-powerful.' Lancelot's answer was to brandish the sword-cross at her, and hurry back to the girl and her brother in the wood. He laid the blood-stiff piece of cloth across the hole in the young man's stomach – and at once the wound healed with a sizzle, and the young man, his sister, the castle, the chapel, the dead brigand and Hellawes all disappeared like the phantoms they were. This adventure meant the death of Hellawes: not because of the anger of the four fairy queens, but because she was captivated by love for Lancelot, and no sorceress can lose her heart to a mortal and survive. But Lancelot knew nothing of that, and rode cheerfully on to see what other adventures might come his way*.

The four queens had still not done with him. They saw that his main weakness (apart from unthinking bravery) was kind-heartedness: wherever he saw a wrong to be righted, or felt that he could help some hand-wringing unfortunate, he rushed in without a moment's thought for the consequences. Accordingly, they fixed on Kay, King Arthur's court controller, who was riding to a lonely farm to inspect some cheeses, and egged on three highwaymen to attack him. As Lancelot rode along the forest path, therefore, he was passed first by Kay on a panting horse, and then by three ruffians with daggers in their hands. He spurred his horse, came up behind the highwaymen (who had surrounded Kay and were demanding his saddlebags or his life) and knocked them senseless from their horses. He tied them back-to-back with their own belts, loaded them on one of the horses like bundles of washing, and told Kay to take them back to Camelot and meet him there on Whit Sunday, one month from then*.

As soon as Kay was out of sight and Lancelot was alone once more, the four fairy queens tried their third and last trick to destroy him. He came to a house surrounded by an orchard, and was reaching up to pick an apple when a hawk suddenly flew mewing and squealing overhead. It was no wild bird, but a hunting-hawk with long leather strings fastened to its leg; now these strings tangled themselves in the tree-branches, and the hawk dangled, helpless and furious. A girl ran out of the garden, carrying a falconer's glove and lure, and cried to Lancelot, 'O please, sir, don't let my husband find out I've lost his hawk. Please climb the tree and fetch it down!' Lancelot protested that he was better at fighting than tree-climbing, but in the end his kind-heartedness overcame his reluctance (as the four fairies knew it would), and he unfastened his sword, took off his leather jerkin and struggled up the tree in nothing but his shirt and trousers. He untangled the hawk and passed it gently down to the lady; he was just climbing down himself when the lady's husband appeared, armed with a sword and roaring, 'Lancelot, pray for your soul! Armed, you might have escaped; unarmed, you die!' For answer, Lancelot jumped down on him from the tree and knocked him unconscious. Then he cut off his head with his own sword, dressed and galloped away, leaving the treacherous lady with the hawk in her hand and her husband dead at her feet.

Lancelot and Elaine

Lancelot rode back to Camelot in time for the Whitsun celebrations, and found the thirty rescued warriors, and Kay with his three highwaymen-prisoners, waiting to welcome him. He was the hero of the hour, and for the first time since he went to Camelot every member of the court paid him respect, and he was honoured second only to Arthur and Guinever themselves.

It was in this moment of triumph that the four fairies set their final plot to work against him, this time using not his warmheartedness but two deadly sins that were in him, pride and lust. At the very climax of the Whitsun celebrations, when the minstrels were singing a ballad of Lancelot's adventures in the forest and the young men were hammering on the tables and demanding more of it, there was a clatter of hooves from the courtyard and Gawain came in, dusty and furious. 'Welcome, Gawain,' said Arthur. 'How fares Elaine?'

'Still boiling,' growled Gawain, and frowned so fiercely that no one asked any further questions. When talking began in the hall again, Guinever said secretly to Lancelot, 'Elaine is the daughter of Lord Pelles of Carbonek – and Morgan le Fay has plunged her into a vat of boiling water, like a human lobster, and announced that only the noblest warrior in Camelot can save her life. Since no one knew where to find you, Gawain went to rescue her – and as you see, he failed.'

'If Gawain failed,' said Lancelot, 'how can I succeed?' But the eyes of the court were on him, and he knew that it was a fairy challenge and that he must accept it. He left the feast then and there and galloped to Carbonek*. Servants led him to a room high in the castle keep, and there, in a cistern of boiling water, was a beautiful lady floundering for breath and naked as a needle. Lancelot touched her hands, and at once the enchantment was lifted, the cistern and water disappeared and the lady was left gasping on the floor like a stranded fish. Her servants carried her away to revive her, and her father Pelles took Lancelot for a banquet of celebration*. While they were eating, a dove fluttered in carrying a tiny incense-pot on a golden chain, and the hall was filled with the smell of herbs and spices. A girl appeared, dressed in white silk and carrying a golden cup; as soon as they saw it, Pelles and his courtiers fell on their knees and began to pray.

'What is it?' whispered Lancelot.

'The richest thing anyone on earth can own,' answered Pelles. 'This is the Holy Grail.'

Lancelot bowed his head with the others, and prayed to the Grail. Afterwards they returned to their feasting, and after a while Pelles left them and went to talk with Brisen, the old, wise woman who had been his daughter's nurse. His priests had told him that if Lancelot made love with Elaine and she conceived a child, the baby would grow up more beautiful than his mother and more princely than his father; Pelles hoped that this would make the child a fit future guardian for the Holy Grail, but his only problem was how to persuade Lancelot, who loved no woman in the world but Guinever, to lie in Elaine's bed.

'Leave it to me,' said Brisen.

That same evening, when the banquet ended and the guests went yawning to bed, a servant ran up to Lancelot, breathless and dusty as if he had galloped many miles. 'My lord,' he said, 'Queen Guinever is spending the night at Castle Case, not an hour's ride from here. She sends you this ring, and calls you to come to her.' He held out a ring identical to Guinever's, and Brisen smiled in the shadows to see the sudden passion in Lancelot's face.

Lancelot waited till midnight, then saddled his horse and galloped to Castle Case. The servants there led him in the darkness to a bedroom with shuttered windows and no candles lit; in the bed was a lady he took to be Guinever , and he threw off his clothes and slipped in beside her. They made love all night, and every time Lancelot tried to speak the lady put her finger to his lips and hushed him, so that it was only at dawn, when he unshuttered the windows and began to dress, that he discovered that his bedmate had been not Guinever but Elaine. Furious, he snatched up his sword to kill her. But Morgan le Fay wrapped him in a magic mist and stole him out of time, so that what seemed to him like minutes were in fact days and weeks, and the people of Carbonek gave him up for dead and mourned for him.

In the meantime Elaine's pregnancy ran its course, and she gave birth to a son and called him Galahad. And the priests' prophecy came true, so that by the time Bors came from Camelot to find Lancelot* (with news that Arthur was planning an expedition to Brittany to fight Claudas, the giant who had long ago caused the deaths of Lancelot's father and mother), the baby already seemed more beautiful than his mother and at least as princely as his father.

In due course Arthur came back in triumph from Brittany, and invited all his friends and allies to a celebration at Camelot. Among the guests were Lord Pelles and his daughter Elaine, and they rode to Camelot with a hundred attendants on horses decked in gold. Arthur welcomed Pelles warmly, and paid Elaine the respect due to a lady of noble rank. But Guinever, who knew from Bors about Lancelot's unfaithfulness and the baby son Elaine had conceived by him, greeted her frostily; the women smiled at each other with lips and not with eyes. To make matters worse, this was the moment when Morgan le Fay lifted the magic mist from Lancelot, and he galloped back to Camelot to cheers of welcome from most of Arthur's lords, and chilly looks from everyone who knew of his double unfaithfulness, to Arthur with Guinever and to Guinever with Elaine. As for Lancelot, he was too embarrassed to say anything at all to Pelles or Elaine; all he could think about was sending a message to Guinever and begging her to meet him that same evening and hear his explanation. 'Come to my room tonight,' was her reply. 'Make love to me and prove, once and for all, that you prefer me and not Elaine.'

That night, Elaine said tearfully to Brisen, 'Lancelot's coldness is freezing my heart.'

'My lady,' said Brisen slyly, 'would it warm you if he came to your bed tonight, and held you in his arms?'

'More than any fire on earth,' said Elaine.

Half an hour later, when Lancelot was lying in bed in his nightgown,

Brisen crept into his room and said, 'Are you asleep, my lord? Queen Guinever is waiting.' She took him by the finger and guided him to Elaine's bed, and Lancelot, thinking that the lady beside him was Guinever, began to make passionate love to her; each time he tried to speak Elaine laid her finger on his lips and hushed him, exactly as on the night when Galahad was conceived. And all the time they were kissing and fondling, Guinever lay alone in her own cold bed next door. After a while the lovers fell asleep, and Lancelot, as his habit was, began to dream of Guinever and to sleep-talk about her. So Guinever, lying awake next door, heard her false lover (as she thought him) talking passionately and in detail about her charms, and in the end ran furiously in with a blazing torch, snatched the quilt from Elaine and Lancelot and screamed, 'Traitors! Never show your faces in Camelot again!' Elaine held the bedclothes round her and sobbed, and Lancelot was startled so suddenly out of sleep, and filled with such surprise and shame, that his wits cracked. He snatched a sword and a shirt, jumped out of the window into the rosebed and ran yelling into the darkness – and no amount of guilty tears on Guinever's part, or sending of Lancelot's foster-brothers Bors and Lionel to quarter the countryside and look for him, could bring him back.

For two years Lancelot wandered in the forests, in sharp showers and sharper snows, and people saw his madman's eyes and ran from him. His bed was bracken, his drink was rainwater, his food was berries, nuts and insects. He would have died of it, if one day in a field by a river he had not found a tent beside a tree, and on the tree a shield and two propped spears. He ran forward and began hacking and hammering the shield with his rusty sword. The tent belonged to a man called Bliant, who was travelling in those parts with his wife and a dwarf-servant, and at the sound of the hammering he went with the dwarf to see what the matter was. Lancelot hurled the dwarf aside like a doll, and hit Bliant so hard on the head with the flat of his sword that he fell stunned, blood oozing from his ears. Lancelot ran into the tent, sat in a heap on the ground and humped Bliant's bedclothes over his head – and Bliant's wife ran screaming to tend her husband.

'My lord,' said the dwarf when Bliant sat up at last, 'He's a madman: we'd best kill him before he does us harm.'

'No,' said Bliant, 'we must help him, not harm him. Go to White Castle, and ask my brother for men, clothes and a horse-litter.'

So Bliant's brother came galloping, and six servants took Lancelot to White Castle in a horse-litter, washed him and dressed him in clothes suited to his rank. They fed him and cherished him till his strength returned; but nothing would restore his wits, and one day he escaped, and ran through gorse, bracken and briar till his clothes were as tattered as before. He wandered aimlessly in the woods till he came by chance to the town where Pelles, his nephew Castor and his daughter Elaine all lived. As Lancelot ran through the streets, his hair flying and his feet slopping in the gutters, children followed him shouting names and throwing stones, and only the last rags of lordliness in his mind stopped him turning on them like an animal and tearing them. In the end the watchmen took him to Castor's castle, where he was washed, dressed, fed and given a wickerwork hutch to live in. He became Castor's fool, and visitors to the castle liked to feed him titbits through the grille of his hutch and ask him questions, to see what wild or sorrowful answers he might give. From time to time he put on red velvet robes and went walking in the castle garden, and people crept after him to watch him striding along, muttering, his eyes fixed on empty sky.

One day, several months after Lancelot came to the town, Elaine and her father were walking in the garden of Castor's castle, when they came on the velvet-robed fool sleeping beside a well. As soon as they saw his face they recognised him, and Pelles' servants carried him gently to Castle Carbonek and laid him, still sleeping, in front of the Holy Grail. A priest uncovered the Grail, the dove flew over Lancelot's head, and the scent of incense filled his nostrils and wakened him from madness as gently as people wake from sleep. He saw Pelles and Elaine, and the memory of all that had happened made him sob from shame; but he was too feeble to resist their kindness, and lay a fortnight in Carbonek while Elaine and her servants nursed back his health. At the end of that time he took Elaine's hand and said, 'My lady, you and I are banished forever from Camelot. If your father will give me a castle and some land, I'll gladly spend the rest of my life with you.' Pelles gave him a castle, on an island in the middle of a lake, and Lancelot called it Joyous Isle in memory of his other castle, Joyous Gard near Camelot. For himself he took the name Sinner Lord, and was abrupt and angry with anyone who called him Lancelot. He and Elaine lived many years in Joyous Isle, and their lives were peaceful; but each day at the same time Lancelot broke off whatever he was doing, went alone to the island shore and gazed in the direction of Camelot, and the thought of Arthur and Guinever all but broke his heart.

Then, one morning, Bors and Lionel came to Joyous Isle. For fifteen years, as Guinever had ordered, they had faithfully searched for Lancelot in every corner of the kingdom. Now they found him at last, and gave him the news that Guinever had forgiven him and he was welcome back in Camelot. He could hardly hold back his joy – until he remembered his promise to Elaine, that he would live the rest of his life on Joyous Isle with her. But she generously hid her own heartbreak, freed him from his promise and begged him to go back to Guinever. They took a last sad leave of one another, and Lancelot, Bors and Lionel rode home to Camelot. Arthur said, 'My lord, what can it have been that cracked your wits? Was it love for Elaine, or shame that you made love with her and gave her the child Galahad?' Lancelot said nothing; but everyone at court except Arthur knew the true cause of his madness and the name of the woman he really loved. And from that day on, wherever he went and whatever he did, his passion for Guinever, and Morgan le Fay's plan to use it to topple Camelot, overshadowed Arthur's court like a thundercloud.

12

THE QUEST FOR
THE HOLY GRAIL BEGINS

The Holy Grail

The Holy Grail was a silver bowl used to collect Jesus' blood when he hung on the cross. After the crucifixion Joseph of Arimathea (the man who provided Jesus' tomb) took charge of it, and in due course brought it to Britain. The Grail passed down in Joseph's family for generations, until it came into the guardianship of Pelles of Carbonek. So long as it stayed on earth, people thought, it would ensure peace and harmony among the human race; but if it was ever owned by a sinner it would fade from the world, and war and pestilence would return.*

Pelles' only child was Elaine, and he was anxious, before he died, to see her make a good marriage and have a child who would be a fit Grail-guardian after him. He decided that of all the people of Britain, the noblest were King Arthur's lords, and Morgan le Fay put it into his mind to entice one of them, Lancelot, to Carbonek and trick him into making love with Elaine. In due course Lancelot's and Elaine's son Galahad was born, and he was princely and honourable, a fit Grail-guardian. But his birth was the result of a trick, and it branded Pelles as a sinner. The Grail began to fade from the world, exactly as the prophecy had foretold, and Pelles in desperation asked the Round Table lords to rescue it.

For Arthur's lords, the Grail-quest was even harder than Pelles imagined. They were Christians, every one of them, but they lived in a world of giants, wizards, fairies and black magic. They preferred to leave God's affairs to monks and nuns; they put their trust less in psalms and hymns than in quick-wittedness and fighting-skill. If finding the Grail had been merely a matter of battling ogres and demons, they would have brought it back easily. But the battle was also with themselves, to replace arrogance with humility and self-reliance with obedience to God. The Quest was a battle between good and evil, and the battle-ground was the lords' own souls. They struck real blows and suffered real wounds, but their adventures had the logic of dreams, not reality, and the direction of each lord's quest depended not on outside events but on his own imagination and character.

Galahad

Galahad was brought up by monks, and when he was old enough to begin the Grail-quest his grandfather Pelles sent him to Camelot. For days before he arrived there were omens of his coming. Each Round Table lord had his own fixed place, and no one else ever sat in it. There was one unclaimed place, known as the Seat Perilous. Anyone who sat there soon afterwards suffered injury or death in battle, and for this reason it was always left empty. But one Whit Sunday when Arthur and his courtiers came back from Mass they found, written in gold before the Seat Perilous, the words 'In the four-hundred-and-forty-fourth year of our Lord Jesus Christ, this seat will at last be claimed.' They were still discussing it, buzzing like bees in a hive, when a servant ran in to tell them of another mystery. A block of red marble was floating like cork in the river outside, and stuck in it was a jewel-hilted sword with writing on the blade which said, 'No one but the True Prince will take me from this stone.' Arthur remembered how he, too, had once been proved king by a sword stuck in a stone, and asked Gawain, Percival and others to pull it out. All of them failed.* The lords went back inside, and found new writing before the Seat Perilous: 'This is the place of Galahad, the True Prince.' There was no explaining any of it until the end of the meal, when the servants were clearing the tables and the lords were sitting back to enjoy last cups of wine. Then a priest led a young man, a stranger, into the hall, dressed in red and with an empty scabbard at his side. The priest showed him the writing before the Seat Perilous and said, 'Look, sir. This place is yours.' So everyone knew that the young man was Galahad; there was a hubbub of greeting, and Lancelot embraced the son he had never seen, and kissed him with tears in his eyes. And by the light of candles and torches, Arthur took Galahad outside and showed him the stone floating in the river, and Galahad drew out the sword as easily as if it were stuck in cheese.

97

On the next day Arthur ordered a tournament, and Galahad fought so skilfully, using the sword from the stone, that no Round Table lord could stand against him. That same evening as they feasted, the hall was plunged in supernatural darkness and the Holy Grail appeared. It floated in mid-air above their heads, and the smell of incense filled the air. After a while the Grail faded and disappeared, and Gawain jumped up and said, 'In God's name, I vow to search for the Grail, wherever it is, and not to come back to Camelot till the quest is done.'

One by one other lords stood up and made the same vow, until no less than one hundred and fifty had spoken. Arthur said bitterly, 'If so many of you leave Camelot, how can the Round Table survive? These vows mean death.' But the vows had been taken in God's name and could not be broken. All he could do was stand next day, full of tears, and watch his lords ride away forever, one by one through the echoing streets.

Each lord except Galahad was armed with a sword, a spear and a shield. Galahad carried no weapons but the miraculous sword pulled from the stone. He soon found a shield to match it. On the fifth day of riding he came to a chapel in the forest and found Bagdemagus lying inside, full of wounds, with Owain looking after him. They showed him a miraculous shield hanging beside the altar. It was coloured white, for purity, and beside it similar words were written to those on the sword in Camelot: 'No one but the True Prince will carry me.' Bagdemagus said that he had ignored the writing, taken the shield and ridden on his way. But he had hardly gone a dozen paces when a horseman in white armour had galloped out of the trees and shouted to him to defend himself. Bagdemagus had tried to lift the shield, but it had hung at his side like a block of stone, and the stranger's spear had sliced through his flesh, splintered his bones and sprawled him on the ground. This was the end of his adventuring; he had listened to his own arrogance and not the voice of God, and he would be the first of Arthur's lords to give up the Grail-quest and stumble home. Galahad said nothing, but next morning he took the shield and rode along the same forest path* – and instead of attacking him, the white rider hailed him as the True Prince, the only man on earth fit to bear the shield of purity* and the sword of truth, and immediately vanished into thin air with his horse and was never seen again.

Leaving Bagdemagus to hobble home and Owain to continue the Grail-quest on his own, Galahad rode on along the valley of the River Severn. He saw a castle in the distance and spurred towards it, meaning to ask shelter for the night. On the way he was stopped four times. First an old man warned him that anyone approaching the castle with sword and shield would be ambushed and thrashed; then seven girls on seven white horses called out in chorus that he had passed the point of turning back; then a servant blocked his path and demanded his business; finally seven armed men ringed him with spears and shouted to him to fight or die. Galahad gathered their spearpoints on his shield of purity and snapped them; then he drew his sword and began slicing and stabbing so fiercely that all seven attackers turned and ran. He walked to the castle gate, and the gatekeeper handed him the keys and said, 'Welcome, lord. Your bravery has lifted the spell from this castle and everyone inside it.' He led Galahad inside, along paths and lawns filled with cheering, waving girls. It was not till Galahad had washed, said grace and sat down to supper that he heard the explanation. Ten years before, seven bandit brothers had swaggered into the castle and demanded hospitality. They had eaten and drunk all they pleased, and then begun pawing the castle women and demanding to make love with them. One of the women, the virgin daughter of the castle's owner, had indignantly refused. At this the bandits had tortured her father and brothers to death, one by one, before her eyes, and she had bitterly prayed that just as the castle had fallen to the seven ruffians because of a virgin, so they might lose it because of a virgin, who would fight all seven single-handed and send them scampering. Ever since, whenever any young girl visited the castle, they had jeeringly kept her prisoner to see if she was the virgin in the prayer – and now, thanks to a virgin who was male, not female (for Galahad had never made love with a woman) the prayer had at last been granted. Galahad sent all the captive girls home to their parents, and their fathers and brothers swore never to allow such barbarity again. Two days later a servant brought word that the seven bandits had challenged Gawain, Gareth and Owain on a forest path, and had been slaughtered for their trouble*. Galahad rode on to continue his quest.*

Lancelot

Lancelot left Camelot with Percival, and they rode for several days without seeing or doing anything out of the ordinary. It was at this time that Galahad was fighting the seven bandits and freeing the prisoners in the Castle of the Virgins, and when he left the Castle he was wearing new clothes and carrying the shield of purity, which neither Lancelot nor Percival had ever seen. For this reason, when they saw him in the distance they took him for an enemy* and galloped to attack him – and Galahad saw two unknown men charging him, drew his sword and rode to defend himself. The fight would have been short but deadly if a holy woman who happened to be nearby had not called out Galahad's name in the nick of time. He galloped away down the forest path, and Lancelot wheeled his horse and rode after him, leaving Percival and holy woman where they stood.

Long before he even left Camelot, Lancelot had been tormented by shame to think that his love for Guinever was a sin which would bar him from finding the Holy Grail. Now guilt at nearly killing his own son made his spirits even heavier, and when he could find no trace of Galahad in the woods, he dropped the reins and let his horse wander where it chose. In the darkness of the fourth night, he came to a crossroads, and beside it was a chapel and a tall stone cross. The chapel was derelict and its door was broken, but its altar was covered with silk, and on it stood a six-branched candlestick glowing with light. Lancelot's soul ached to go into the chapel and pray, but whenever he tried to open the rotting door or step over the broken windowsill an iron grille sprang up and barred his path. At last he gave up. He unsaddled his horse, leaned his sword against the chapel wall, lay down beside the cross and tried to sleep.

As Lancelot dozed, torn between waking and sleeping by the misery in his soul, it seemed to him that two white horses trotted up to the chapel, and on a litter slung between them was a wounded man, weeping and calling out in pain. His servants laid the litter on the ground, and the wounded man sat up as best he could and began praying for his suffering to end. Then – or so it seemed to Lancelot – the candlestick floated out of the chapel, and beside it on a silver table was the Holy Grail. The sick man stretched out his hands to the Grail, strength flowed into him and his wounds were healed. He knelt on the grass to give thanks, and the Grail and candlestick disappeared inside the chapel. The man stood up and said to his servant, 'Thanks be to God, who has answered my prayers and cured me. But who is that, lying on the ground beside the cross, and why did he sleep on even when the Grail appeared?'

'Sir,' said the servant, 'only a man utterly stained by sin could so ignore his saviour. Take his horse and his sword: you'll put them to far better use than he will.'

He handed his master Lancelot's sword and helped him on to Lancelot's horse, and the two of them rode away. Then at last Lancelot was able to stir, like a man waking from a dream. He threw himself on his knees, but before he could utter a word of prayer a voice thundered in his ears, 'No, Lancelot! Your presence pollutes this holy place.' He clambered to his feet and set off wearily down the path, brushing bracken aside and crying for deliverance. At last, after walking all night, he came to a hermit's cave and found the holy man muttering Mass inside. Lancelot knelt to pray, and as soon as Mass was over he begged the hermit to hear his confession and tell him how to purge his sin.

The hermit told him that his sin was not just loving Guinever; it was loving her above God himself. He said that the only way for Lancelot to purge his sin was to promise, then and there, to put Guinever out of his heart forever and never see or speak to her again. Lancelot's heart was torn between love for Guinever and love of God; in the end he forced himself to make the promise the hermit demanded, and the hermit made the sign of the cross over him, gave him a horse and a sword and saw him on his way.

Percival

Unlike Arthur's other lords, who were so eager to find the Holy Grail that they galloped in all directions with neither plan nor thought, Percival was a hard-headed, sensible young man. When, therefore, Lancelot rode into the forest after Galahad, he decided not to gallop after him, but to talk to the holy woman and ask her where to find the Grail*. She told him that three men were destined to find the Grail: Galahad the True Prince, Bors and Percival himself. He should follow Galahad to Castle Carbonek, where the Grail and the Maimed King were; above all, since the forces of evil were working against the quest, he should keep himself pure in word and deed, and hold Jesus his saviour always in his thoughts. Percival found this advice impossible to understand, but none the less promised to follow it, and rode on his way. After a while he came to a monastery, and in a side chapel barred by an iron grille he saw an aged, blind, sick man. This was Evalak, a king long ago converted to Christianity by Joseph of Arimathea. He had fought bravely against Christ's enemies, but one day, covered with wounds, he had longed so desperately for the Holy Grail that he had stretched out his hands and taken hold of it, and at once light from the Grail had seared him blind and a voice had said that he would lie naked and bleeding and would be denied death until the True Prince freed him from his suffering. He had lain in the chapel for four hundred years, and his wounds were still fresh and bleeding; he covered his face with a cloth, and lifted it only to listen to Mass each day. The priests begged Percival to stay and tell them news of Galahad, the True Prince. But he made up his mind that they were servants of the evil powers, and that their purpose was to delay him from his quest. He said shortly, 'Time spent talking is time thrown away,' and left the monastery without another word.

Percival came next to the same part of the forest as Galahad, and the evil powers saw their chance to trap Galahad, using Percival as bait. Accordingly, Percival was riding along, whistling, when a gang of goblins suddenly leapt out at him, armed with knives. They stabbed his horse dead, and would have torn him to pieces on top of it if Galahad had not galloped out of the wood with the shield of purity on his arm and the sword of truth in his hand. The trap was sprung. The goblins left Percival standing and turned on Galahad. But the shield of purity dazzled their eyes, and the next thing they felt was the sword of truth, slicing them. They ran for their lives, and Galahad galloped after them, windmilling his sword and filling the forest with fury. Percival stood open-mouthed. Was he doomed, every time he met Galahad, to see him ride off into the woods with no way to follow him? He unfastened the saddle from his horse's carcase and began plodding wearily back to the monastery – and at once, on the path ahead of him, a girl appeared leading a fresh black horse. 'Take him,' she said. 'All I ask in return is that when I come again you pay whatever price I ask.'*

Percival jumped on to the horse's back and spurred after Galahad. But instead of obeying the reins the horse carried him deeper and deeper into the forest. It galloped for four days and nights without stopping, and came at last to a fast-flowing river. Percival felt spray on his face in the darkness, and knew that if the horse threw him into the rapids he would drown. But he could think of no way of stopping it, until he suddenly remembered the holy woman's advice, to trust in God. He made the sign of the cross and prayed – and at once, as if the cross-sign weighed the evil horse down like a millstone, it shook Percival from its back and rushed whinnying and shrieking into the river. Sheaves of flame sprang up, and when the smoke and steam dispersed the horse had disappeared. Percival thanked God for deliverance. Then he lay down on the bank, with the water-roar in his ears, and slept. Next morning when he awoke he found to his terror that what he had taken for a river was in fact the roaring ocean which surrounds the earth. He was on an island in the midst of it, a gaunt rock with water swirling on every side. Even worse, he was not alone. All round him, in every direction, the rock swarmed with deadly creatures: lions, dragons, leopards, vipers and scorpions. He scrambled up the nearest tree, hunched himself in the branches and gazed out at the stony sea, waiting for death.*

After a while Percival saw a sail in the distance, and a boat gradually approached and grounded at the foot of his tree. Percival jumped down and ran towards it, whooping so eagerly that the wild beasts cowered in terror. The boat's sides and decks were entirely covered in white cloth, and an old monk sat on deck. 'Sir,' said Percival, 'whoever you are and wherever you come from, please take me away from here.'

'Not yet,' said the monk. 'You have temptation still to face. Trust in Jesus Christ.'

Even as he spoke, the wind filled the sails and carried the white boat out of reach. There was nothing for Percival to do but climb gloomily back up the tree and wait. What temptation? What could possibly tempt him on a bare rock in empty sea? He sat till noon, and then saw another boat sailing towards him, as black as the first one had been white. This time, instead of a monk, a woman dressed in shimmering black velvet sat on deck. 'Percival,' she said, 'why did you come here? This is the Sea of Death.'

'I came to find the True Prince,' answered Percival.

'If I help you, will you pay whatever price I ask?'

'Gladly.'

The lady's servants put up a sunshade to shelter them, and laid a table with food and drink. The lady poured Percival wine with her own hands, and Percival (who until then had drunk nothing all his life but water, milk or beer) found it so powerful that his head swam and he began babbling about the lady's charms and begging her to make love with him.

'And if I do,' she said, 'will you promise me obedience forever? Will you obey without question every order I give you?'

'I promise,' said Percival eagerly. 'I'll be your willing slave!'

'As you say, so be it,' said the lady, and her eyes glittered like a cat's. She lay down on the sand, and Percival undressed to make love with her. But at the last moment, just as he was laying his sword on top of his piled clothes, he caught sight of his cross-hilt and was reminded at once of his duty to Jesus Christ. He made the sign of the cross, and immediately the sunshade flew into the air and vanished, there was a smell of sulphur and the sea burst into flames. When the fire died down the lady, her servants and the boat had all disappeared, and Percival was standing naked on the shore. He was filled with sudden disgust at his own mortal weakness, and stabbed his sword-point into his thigh till blood fountained. Then he bound the wound with cloth, knelt down as best he could and prayed for rescue. His prayer was hardly done when the white boat appeared miraculously in front of him, and the old monk stepped out and said, 'Percival, did you keep your promise?'

'I kept my promise to Christ,' answered Percival. 'But I made another promise, to a woman dressed in black, and broke it.'

'She was sent by the evil powers to test you,' said the monk, 'just as I have been sent by God to rescue you. Step into the boat, and it will carry you safely where Galahad and Bors are waiting.'

Weeping with joy, Percival gathered his clothes, sword and shield and limped on board the white boat. Wind filled its sails and it carried him safely out to sea.*

13

THE GRAIL-QUEST ENDS

Gawain and Ector

Although Gawain was the noblest of all King Arthur's lords, his part in the Grail-quest was futile from the start – and the reason was that he was more interested in his own entertainment than in actually finding the Holy Grail. For three months he rode through every forest or wasteland he could find, hoping to be challenged by giants, savages, enchanters or devil-worshippers, and found none. He rode for a time with Gareth his brother and Owain, and the only adventure they had was the ambush of the seven brigands from the Castle of the Virgins and the fight which followed it. By the end of July Gawain was bored, with no one to talk to and nothing to hunt but rabbits and magpies. One day he met Ector, riding disconsolately in the opposite direction, and the two of them decided to travel together, to see if two men together could track down the adventures which eluded each one alone. But although they enjoyed each other's company, at the end of a week they had nothing else to show for their travels but short tempers and dusty clothes.

One evening they stopped to pray at a roadside chapel, and afterwards wrapped themselves in their cloaks and lay down on pews to sleep. That night Gawain dreamed that he was standing in a flowery field next to a hayrack. There were one hundred and fifty bulls, feeding at the hayrack, but they suddenly scattered to find other pastures, and the few who came back, months later, were thin and starving. Instead of feeding placidly once more, the returned bulls kicked the hayrack over and fought a bloodly battle, after which the survivors ran out of the field and were never seen again. Ector's dream was just as mysterious. He and Lancelot were riding along a forest path when they were challenged by an armed stranger. He knocked

Lancelot from his horse, stripped him and dressed him in a sack stuck all over with holly; then he sat him on a donkey, drove his horse into the woods and disappeared. Lancelot came to a river, but every time he bent to drink the water sank out of reach, and in the end he climbed back on the donkey and rode miserably home to Camelot. Ector, meanwhile, rode on to a castle, bright with light and filled with the sound of feasting, and the castle owner drove him away shouting, 'No one on a warhorse enters here!'

For all their strangeness, these visions were still only dreams, and Gawain and Ector could have blamed them on nothing more than tired minds*. But next morning Gawain's eagerness for adventure led to an event which allowed no such explanation, and which ended his part in the Grail-quest in an unexpected and bitter way. He and Ector were less than an hour's ride from the chapel when they saw a muffled warrior galloping towards them with his spear outstretched. 'Fine!' muttered Gawain. 'If it's a fight he wants, he'll get one!' And he covered his own face, lowered his spear and charged. They met with a crash that knocked them both from their horses. Gawain had no injuries but a grazed thigh; but when he went to the other man, he found that his spear had passed through the stranger's body and pinned him to the ground. Gawain opened his water-bottle, pulled the cloth from the stranger's face to help him drink – and to his horror found that the man was Owain, one of his dearest friends. He laid him on his horse and walked him gently to the nearest monastery, where he hoped for doctors. But Owain's injuries were fatal, and the monks had time only to give him the last rites before he died.

So Gawain's lust for adventure led him to kill the one man in Camelot, apart from Arthur and Lancelot, he respected most. He asked the abbot of the monastery to hear his confession – and the abbot explained his and Ector's dreams in a way which redoubled Gawain's grief. He said that the bulls signified the lords of Camelot. As the bulls had scattered for new pasture, so the lords had scattered to find the Holy Grail, and the few who returned would squabble and break up the companionship of Camelot forever. Ector and Lancelot, he said, had ridden on horses of pride to look for the Grail, and Lancelot would be stripped of his lordliness, humiliated and forbidden to drink the water of righteousness; in just the same way, Ector's love of war would one day bar him from the happiness of those who feasted with Christ their lord.

What possible answer could Gawain or Ector find for words like these? They left the monks to bury Owain's body and went their ways, Gawain back to Camelot* and Ector vowing to fight the warlust in his heart until he was worthy to see the Holy Grail at last.

Bors

Like Percival, Bors began his Grail-quest by asking a hermit's advice, and was told that if he kept Christ always in his thoughts, renounced sex and ate no meat (which inflames the passions and heats the blood) he would be one of the only three mortals in the world permitted to touch the Grail. As with Percival, the forces of evil heard this promise, and determined to test Bors at every step, to corrupt him and so destroy the whole Grail-quest. They led him first to a tall fortified tower, and as soon as Bors was inside the servants barricaded the gates with tree-trunks, roof-rafters and barrels from the cellar. The tower's owner, a pretty girl, invited him to eat with her, and her servants loaded the table with roast meat, pies, pressed beef and sausages. It was a test of Bors' self-control, and he remembered the hermit's words and ate nothing but three fingers of bread dipped in water. While servants cleared the table, the girl laid her hand over Bors', and its softness made his heart thud in his chest. But instead of murmuring words of love, she told him that a giant, Priadan, was coming to attack the tower next morning, and that unless some champion could be found to fight him, he would tear down the walls and kill everyone inside. She looked at Bors with tear-filled eyes, and squeezed his hand till he promised to fight the giant. Servants showed him to a bedroom, with a bed of carved oak covered with goose-feather quilts and soft silk sheets, and as soon as he was alone the girl slipped into the room and offered to make love with him. Bors was tormented with desire. But he remembered the hermit's advice to renounce all sex, bundled her out of the door, lay down on the stone floor beside the bed and tossed and turned till dawn.

Next morning the servants brought a breakfast of cold meat and beer. Bors was starving. But he refused everything but three sips of water, saying that the time to eat would be when the giant was dead – and the words were no sooner out of his mouth than there was a braying of trumpets from outside, and Priadan strode down the hill with his soldiers yapping at his heels. Bors crossed himself, muttered 'Not by good luck but in your name, O Lord!', and stepped outside to face him. Priadan was as tall as a house, and his fists were the size of boats. He lifted a foot to crush Bors, and Bors held his sword point-upwards above his head, so that Priadan's stamping drove it like a thorn into the sole of his own foot. The giant roared and fell, and Bors ran round and stabbed the artery pulsing in his neck. Boiling water, giant's blood, poured out, there was a whirlwind-roar and Priadan, the tower, the girl and all the servants vanished, leaving Bors alone in an empty field*.

For their next attack, the evil forces waited until Bors was in a thick forest, riding down a path like a corridor between tall, dark trees. He came to a crossroads, and found two men on horseback, leading a third man on a donkey. The man's hands were tied behind his back, and the riders were flogging him with hawthorn branches whose thorns ripped his flesh and spattered the ground with blood. To his horror, Bors recognised the man on the donkey as his own brother Lionel. He was about to gallop to the rescue when he heard a pitiful crying behind him, 'Sir, sir, help me!', and saw a pretty girl (almost the twin of the girl for whose sake he had fought Priadan) struggling with a dwarf who was dragging her into the bushes. What was Bors to do – rescue his brother from a beating, or save an unknown girl from rape? He lifted his eyes to heaven and cried, 'Lord, protect Lionel'; then he spurred forward and hit the dwarf a blow with the flat of his sword that broke his collarbone and sent him screaming to the ground. Bors jumped from his horse to finish him, and at once the girl threw her arms round him and began kissing him and hugging him, and her father and brothers surged out of the trees and began shaking his hand and patting his back in gratitude. By the time Bors broke free, Lionel and the two men beating him had disappeared. Bors galloped after them, and he had gone less than a hundred paces when he found Lionel's body on the path, raw with wounds. He leapt from his horse and gathered up the body – and to his surprise it was not heavy and awkward as most corpses are, but weightless as a bolster. He laid it over his horse's saddle, and walked back to where the men and the girl had been. Instead of trampled grass and mud there was a chapel, and outside it a graveyard with a single table-tomb. Weeping, Bors laid Lionel's body on the tomb and knelt to pray; but before he could utter a word the girl and her relatives ran out of the wood again, swept him on to his horse and rode away with him. They took him to a castle, spread a feast in his honour (at which he refused everything but bread and water, as before), and that night the girl came to his bedroom and offered to make love with him exactly as her twin in the tower had done. Once again Bors spent the night tossing and turning on the bare stone floor, and next morning he dressed and galloped away before anyone else woke up. The first person he saw in the wood was his brother Lionel, scowling and fully armed. 'You left me to die, Bors,' he said. 'You saved a stranger before your own brother. Defend yourself or die.' Bors hesitated – how could he fight his own brother? – and Lionel spurred at him, crushed him to the ground with his horse's hooves and trampled him. He lay bruised and breathless, and Lionel was just bending over him to cut his throat when another lord from Camelot, Colgrevan, ran out of nowhere and pulled him clear of Bors. Lionel smashed his sword-hilt into Colgrevan's face and sent him sprawling. Bors staggered to his feet and reluctantly drew his sword – and at once, as if at a signal, a fireball fell from the sky and charred Lionel and Colgrevan to piles of ash in front of him. They had been wraiths, both of them, sent by the evil forces to trap him. If he had lifted his sword to kill the man he took for his brother, they would have won.

Bors looked round, dismayed and bewildered, and found that in place of the woods and castles were sand-dunes, a beach and a boat, draped in white cloth, rocking at anchor. He groaned: if this was another test, how could he find the strength to survive it? He walked wearily down the beach to the boat – and as soon as he stepped on board he found a man sitting silently on deck, and to his joy recognised him as Percival. They fell into each other's arms weeping tears of joy, and Percival said, 'Now all we lack is Galahad, the True Prince. When he comes, the Grail companions will be complete.'

The companions

Galahad was asleep in a monastery when a young girl hammered on the door, soon after dawn, took him to the shore and showed him the boat with Percival and Bors in it. It was as if Percival's prayers had been answered – and the three companions' joy at finding each other was doubled when they found that the girl was Percival's own sister, sent away to a nunnery many years before. All day and all night they sailed before the wind, and next morning they landed on a marshy shore. Galahad, Percival and Bors were saddling their horses to explore when a swarm of goblins suddenly shrieked out of the trees and attacked them, without warning or explanation. Galahad turned the shield of purity in their direction, and its rays dazzled their eyes and sent them scattering. They fled to a castle on a nearby hill, and Galahad, Bors and Percival galloped after them. The castle hall was full of wraith-warriors, startled from breakfast. They began shouting and scrambling for their weapons, and Galahad, Bors and Percival ran round the hall, slaughtering enemies like stranded fish, until the survivors turned tail and began pelting down the steps and jumping out of the windows, leaving the floor and tables strewn with dead. The three companions stared about them, aghast at the slaughter. Was this murderous fury, even in self-defence, a sin which would end their quest and prevent them ever seeing the Grail? But even as they stood there, the ground gaped open at their feet and swallowed castle, tower and wraiths like the Devil-spawn they were*. Galahad, Bors and Percival ran to the shore and hurled their boat to sea.

At the next landfall, they were hardly ten steps from the shore when a troop of soldiers surrounded them and said, 'Go no further. Either that girl agrees to the custom of the country, or all of you die.'

'What custom?' asked Galahad, loosening his sword.

'Every girl who lands here must give enough blood to fill a silver bowl, to help the leper-princess in the castle.'

'And if she refuses – ?'

'She dies.'

At this Galahad, Percival and Bors drew their swords; but Percival's sister cried, 'No! No fighting! Take me to the princess: she's welcome to my blood.'

The soldiers led them to the castle – and there in a turret room they found the princess stunted by leprosy, and doctors waiting with a knife and a bowl to catch the blood. Percival's sister lay down and bared her arm, the doctors opened a vein, and bright blood spurted into the bowl. After a while Percival's sister said feebly, 'Dear brother, if I die of this, in God's name bury my body in the Holy Land.' The words took her last breath from her and she died; but when the doctors smeared her blood on the princess' leprous stumps, they were at once restored and the princess fell on her knees and thanked God. There was wild celebration – and in the midst of it Galahad, Percival and Bors carried Percival's sister back to their boat and laid her tearfully on the bed.

Lancelot at Carbonek

After Lancelot left the hermit he had many adventures, each sent to test his Christian humility, and his vow never to see or speak to Guinever again carried him safely through them all.* At the end of a year, at midnight, he came to a castle and was astonished to find the gates gaping open. There were no sentries or other human beings in sight – but as soon as he walked towards the gates a pair of lions sprang out of the shadows and menaced him. Before his wanderings began, Lancelot would have used a sword to defend himself. But now he trusted in God and made the sign of the cross instead, and at once the lions crouched at his feet, purring like kittens. He stepped safely round them into the castle. Although every gate was open and every door unbarred, he could still see no one. He crept through the courtyards in the moonlight, his shoes scuffing the cobbles – and at last he heard the sound of a choir, singing psalms from a high tower, and found a chapel streaming with candle-light. He was in Castle Carbonek, in the presence of the Holy Grail.

Lancelot ran up the steps to the Chapel door. At the far end he could see the Grail, on an altar covered by a crimson cloth. And it seemed to him that there was a choir of angels beside it, and a priest saying Mass. The priest lifted his arms as if to hold up the bread that signified Christ's body, and it seemed to Lancelot that instead of bread his hands held up a living man. Lancelot cried out, 'Lord Jesus, help me!', and ran into the chapel – and at once fire flared in his head and he fell helpless on the floor. He felt hands carrying him out of the chapel and laying him gently beside the door. He could neither move nor speak; he was as still as a corpse. The castle servants put him to bed and tended him, and after twenty-four days and nights without moving he opened his eyes like a waking child and said. 'In Jesus' name, what dreams I've had!' Then they knew that the last twenty-four years of his life were no more to him than adventures in a story-book. He was a middle-aged man with the mind of the boy who had long ago gone to seek his fortune in Camelot, and when Pelles, lord of the castle and guardian of the Grail, spoke to him of Galahad his son, and told him sadly that Elaine was dead, it meant no more to him than clouds passing across the sun.

Pelles realised that Lancelot's part in the Grail-quest was over, and that the purpose of his life lay once more in Camelot. He entertained him for four days – tearfully, for he loved him – and on the evening before he left Carbonek spread a banquet in his honour. While they were eating and drinking, the doors and windows of the hall slammed shut of their own accord, and soon afterwards they heard knocking at the door and a man's voice shouting, 'Let me in! In God's name, let me in!'

Pelles answered, 'God allows into Carbonek only those fated to find the Holy Grail,' and when the man outside knocked and shouted even more furiously he said, 'In heaven's name, tell me your name. Who are you?'

'Ector,' answered the man bitterly. 'Lancelot's cousin; King Arthur's loyal companion.' And he turned his horse and galloped away. The dream he had had long ago in the chapel with Gawain had come true: he was barred forever from the feasting of those worthy to find the Grail. Next morning Lancelot, too, left Carbonek and made his way home to Camelot.

Galahad and the Grail

Galahad came to the monastery where Evalak lay, aged and full of wounds, and when he walked into the chapel all the bells rang of their own accord. Evalak lifted himself on his bed behind the grille, turned sightless eyes to Galahad and said, 'Servant of God, take me in your arms; touch me and make me whole.' Galahad went to him, and the iron grille parted like a curtain. He pillowed Evalak's head in his arms, and Evalak said, 'Blessed Lord Jesus, now that I have my heart's desire, the gift I have awaited for four hundred years, take me from the world,' and fell back dead. When the monks laid him out for burial, they found that all his wounds had healed and his body was as unblemished as a baby's.

Galahad stayed two days in the monastery, and then rode on. He met Percival and Bors in the Forest of Dread*, and the three of them travelled together to Castle Carbonek, where they found every door flung wide to welcome them. Pelles spread a feast in their honour, and the Holy Grail appeared, floating into the hall on a silver table. Four angels followed it: two carried candles, the third held the Holy Lance and the fourth a cloth to lay over the Grail. Lastly came a man in priest's robes, and the companions knew that it was Josephus, son of Joseph of Arimathea who had brought the Grail to Britain four hundred years before. He celebrated Mass and the angels served him; when the time came for the consecration he drew bread from the Grail itself, and it seemed to Galahad, Bors and Percival that they were receiving not bread at all, but the body of Jesus Christ their saviour. When the Mass was done Josephus said, 'Now you have seen the mystery of the Grail, the mystery revealed only to the purest men and women on earth. Take the Grail to the Holy Land, for the British people have turned to evil, and the Grail will never be seen here again. Your ship is waiting; go.' So he spoke and disappeared, and for a long time the companions stayed on their knees, praying. Then Galahad took three drops of blood from the tip of the miraculous lance, went to Pelles and anointed him. At once Pelles' sins were washed away. He knelt and blessed Jesus' name, and soon after the companions rode from Carbonek he took priestly vows and went to live the rest of his life in a monastery.

Galahad, Percival and Bors rode to the shore, and found the white boat waiting. Inside was the body of Percival's sister, and the Grail on a table covered with a cloth. As they knelt and prayed, wind filled the sails and carried them to the Holy Land. The boat beached in a quiet creek, and the first thing they did was dig a grave and bury Percival's sister reverently by the city walls. Then Galahad began to carry the Grail into the city, and he felt it grow heavier and heavier till he could scarcely bear the weight. He asked a cripple to help him, a bent, helpless old man. 'How can I?' the man said bitterly. 'For ten years I've neither stood nor walked.' 'Try,' answered Galahad. 'In God's name, try.' As soon as the man touched the Grail he became as lively as a boy, and sprang and danced beside Galahad all the way into Sarras. The people flocked to see the miracle, and Sarras was converted into a Christian city on the spot. Galahad became its king, and the Grail's presence blessed him and his people for months to come.

At the end of a year, on the same Sunday as Galahad was crowned king, he, Percival and Bors went to hear Mass before the Holy Grail. The chapel filled with light, and Josephus appeared amid a choir of angels. He made the sign of the cross and said, 'Galahad, Servant of God, True Prince, come forward and receive the Lord.'* Galahad took communion at the altar. Then he kissed Percival and Bors, and the angels carried him up to heaven, singing hymns to God. As Percival and Bors watched, the Grail and Lance faded from sight; they were never seen on earth again.

In this way the soul of Galahad, the last Grail-guardian, passed from the mortal world, and the people of Sarras sang Masses for his eternal rest. When the ceremonies were over Percival took priestly vows and lived the rest of his life as a monk. Bors left Sarras and travelled home to Camelot, where he told Arthur, Guinever and the surviving Round Table lords everything that had happened since the quest for the Holy Grail began.

14

THE END OF THE ROUND TABLE

Lancelot and Guinever

At first, when Lancelot came home from the Grail-quest to Camelot, the stroke he had suffered in Carbonek seemed utterly to have changed his character. He turned from his former friends, and went out of his way not to see or speak to Guinever. He spent his days on his knees, praying; left to himself he would have become a hermit and devoted the rest of his life to Christ. But Morgan le Fay had no intention of leaving him to himself. He was the lever she meant to use to topple Camelot, and so long as the smallest ember of love for Guinever still glowed in his heart, she knew how to fan it into flame. Instead of sending Guinever to him and letting Arthur find them together – too easy and quick a way to destroy him – she surrounded Lancelot instead with court ladies, fifteen-year-olds who had entered Guinever's service long after Lancelot left Camelot to look for the Holy Grail. First there was one, peeping round the chapel door to ask if he needed a cushion to kneel on. Then there were two, pouring his wine at meals and handing him his napkin. Then there were a dozen, listening wide-eyed to his adventures and giggling at every word. At first Lancelot was short with them. But after a while he began combing his beard, practising dance steps he had not tried since he was a young man, and polishing up new tales every day to stagger them. Guinever was furious. She raged at him for deceit and ingratitude, and banished him from Camelot before he could say a word. Lancelot put on his ragged clothes from the Grail-quest, saddled a donkey and rode to the cave of the hermit Brastias, where he begged to be allowed to live the rest of his life in solitary, repentful prayer. He told no one but Bors where he was to be found, and swore even him to silence.

Morgan le Fay next turned her magic on Guinever. She put it into her mind to give a dinner-party for twenty-four of Arthur's lords, in her castle beside the River Thames in London. The chief guest was Gawain, and among the others were Patrick and Mador, young men newly arrived in Camelot from Hibernia, and Pinel, a Cambrian prince whose cousin Gawain had killed in a duel years before, and who had vowed revenge*. As the lords rode towards London, Morgan le Fay hovered round Pinel like a mist-cloud, and filled his mind with a vengeance-plan. Anyone who had ever eaten with Gawain knew how fond he was of fruit: he finished every meal with an apple, and the custom was to place a dish of apples on the table, and for everyone else to wait until he'd chosen. As soon as Pinel reached Guinever's palace in London, therefore, he slipped into the banqueting-hall and poisoned the ripest apple in the dish.

The lords took their places, Guinever's servants brought bread, meat, wine and all manner of pies and pastries, minstrels sang – and as the feast was reaching its end, the boy Patrick (who was a newcomer to court and knew nothing of Gawain's custom with fresh fruit), bit into the poisoned apple, the veins burst in his neck and he fell dead on the floor. There was uproar. None of the lords (except Pinel) knew anything about it, and Morgan le Fay filled them with the idea that Guinever had invited them to the banquet deliberately to poison them, and that she meant to kill every Round Table lord she could. Because she was the queen, no one made any move to harm her. But Patrick's brother Mador demanded that she stand trial for murder, and the others nodded in agreement. They took her back to Camelot and insisted that Arthur hear the case and pronounce sentence, even though she was his own wife, even though she was the queen.

Arthur was in despair. The punishment for poisoning was death by fire, and unless Guinever found a champion to duel with Mador for her honour and prove her innocent, she was doomed. He called the Round Table lords together, and asked which of them would be her champion. But they all thought her guilty; they looked at the ground and refused to fight. In the end Arthur had no choice but to take Bors aside and order him to accept the challenge as a royal command. Bors reluctantly agreed. But he said, 'My lord, if a better champion comes forward, you must let him fight in my place' – and that same night he galloped to Lancelot's hermit-cave for help.

On the morning of the duel, the Camelot executioners were up at dawn. They set up an iron pillory in the courtyard, and piled it with branches and straw-bales. After breakfast Arthur and his lords began

116

taking their places on benches in the courtyard, and Guinever stood beside them surrounded by priests and nuns. In a side room, young Mador fidgeted, checking his helmet-straps and making sure that his sword slipped freely in and out of its scabbard, and Bors reluctantly armed himself.

At last they were ready, and a trumpet sounded for the duel to begin. But before they could strike a single blow there was a rattle of hooves outside the gate and a stranger galloped in, wearing plain armour without identification and with his helmet pulled down to hide his face. He took Bors' place, and rode at Mador with such force that he knocked him sprawling. They drew their swords and began hacking at each other's shields till the sparks flew. Mador was less experienced than the stranger, but he was young and furious, and the duel lasted for over an hour before he lost his concentration, slipped in the mud and fell. At once the stranger was on him. Mador felt his sword-point at his throat, and took off his helmet as a sign of submission. The stranger helped him up and led him before Arthur. 'My lord,' said Mador, 'the duel was fair, and the verdict is clear. Guinever is innocent.'

Arthur and Guinever hurried to shake the stranger's hand – and the unknown man took off his helmet and they saw that it was Lancelot. Guinever fainted: her maids had to carry her to her room and dab rosewater on her temples to revive her. As for Arthur, he was overjoyed to see his old friend again. Despite Lancelot's attempts to slip back to his hermit-cave, he was bathed, dressed in silk and velvet, and made guest of honour at a banquet in the castle hall*.

Agravain and Mordred

So Lancelot was welcomed back to Camelot, and Arthur and Guinever made more of him than ever. He spent his days with Arthur and his nights with Guinever, and everyone but Arthur knew exactly what was happening. The young Round Table lords shrugged at it. They had lives of their own to live, and the love-tangles of the older generation were none of their affair. But the older lords were furious – and none more so than Agravain, who was devotedly loyal to Arthur and could not bear to see him cuckolded, and Mordred, Arthur's son by incest with his sister Morgaus, who had ambitious reasons of his own for wanting Arthur destroyed. They told Arthur of the love-affair, and offered to prove it. If he stayed away from Camelot for a day and a night, they said, they would arrest Lancelot in Guinever's arms and bring him alive or dead before the king. Reluctantly Arthur agreed. He told the court that he was going boar-hunting, and would stay the night wherever the chase ended: for that reason, as well as grooms and huntsmen, he would take with him the royal butlers and the royal cooks. The party clattered out of Camelot, dogs yapping and horns blowing, and Agravain and Mordred collected a dozen other lords and made their plans.

That night, as usual, Lancelot went to Guinever's bedroom in nothing but his nightshirt. No sooner were they in bed than Agravain, Mordred and the others came hammering at the door, armed to the teeth and shouting to Lancelot to surrender. Lancelot leapt out of bed, bare as a radish, and began frantically searching the room for a sword, a spear, a log, anything to defend himself. In the end he wound the bed-curtain round his arm as padding against sword-blows, slid back the bolt and opened the door just wide enough to let one man pass. Colgrevan squeezed inside, and Lancelot slammed the door behind him, parried his sword-blows with his curtain-wrapped arm, and with his other hand brought a footstool down on Colgrevan's head and felled him like a poleaxed bull. Quickly he and Guinever stripped the body, and strapped Colgrevan's armour round Lancelot as best they could. Then Lancelot picked up Colgrevan's sword and ran out among the waiting lords. Before they realised what was happening, he was swinging the sword and slicing them. Agravain and eleven others fell dead at the first onslaught, and Mordred ran, staggering and bleeding, to find Arthur in the woods and raise the alarm.

By this time Camelot was in uproar. The servants, bleary-eyed and blinking, were pulling on their clothes and running to help the queen. The lords were standing in their bedrooms, shouting angrily for their squires to help them arm. In the confusion Lancelot told his brother Bors to gather as many lords in the courtyard as he could. There, while the lantern-light glinted on their sword-points, Lancelot explained what had happened, and half a dozen of the older lords and a large group of young men agreed to follow him. They galloped out of Camelot in the darkness, leaving Arthur's loyal lords to arrest Guinever and raise the alarm.

While all this was happening, Mordred was pelting through the woods on a foam-flecked horse. He came to Arthur's camp in the boar-marshes and gasped out his tale. Arthur's lords stood round the king, grim-faced. At last the truth was told; at last Arthur knew what everyone else had known for years. Arthur said in a low voice to Gawain, 'Go to Camelot, arrest the queen and burn her.'

'My lord,' said Gawain. 'How can I kill the queen I've honoured all my life? How could I face my good friend Lancelot when he hears of it?'

Arthur turned to Gaheris and Gareth, and said in the same emotionless voice, 'Go to Camelot, arrest the queen and burn her.'

Unlike Gawain, Gaheris and Gareth dared not refuse a royal command. All Gaheris could say was, 'If we go, my lord, we'll go unarmed, as messengers not warriors. We'll shed no one else's blood in this affair.' They took the king's ring as their authority and rode away, while Arthur gave orders for Mordred's wounds to be bandaged and for the whole hunting-party to leave for Camelot at dawn.

It was still dark when Gaheris and Gareth rode into Camelot, showed Arthur's ring and repeated his orders. By the light of pine-torches executioners set up the pillory in the courtyard and surrounded it with branches as before. Guinever's weeping maids dressed her in a flaxen shift, for death, and a group of lords led her outside, where the people of Camelot were gathering to see her die. A priest began to hear her confession, while a hastily-gathered choir sang hymns and the executioners oiled the padlocks on the pillory and checked the straw-bales, ready to start the fire.

Unknown to everyone, Lancelot and his men had followed every one of these preparations from the woods. Lancelot waited until Guinever's confession was finished and the priests began chanting prayers for her soul, while the people closed their eyes and bowed their heads. Then he galloped into the courtyard, cut his way through the crowd, snatched Guinever and rode back to his followers before anyone could lift a hand to stop him. He left a dozen men dead or injured. Most were soldiers or executioners, but among the dead were Gaheris and Gareth: for all their wish that the affair would claim no one else's blood, it had claimed theirs. By the time Arthur, Gawain and the others rode into Camelot, the bodies had been laid in the royal chapel and the court was filled with mourning. 'My lord,' Arthur said bitterly to Gawain, 'see what your "good friend" Lancelot has done. Yesterday you had three brothers living; today, all three are dead.'

Gawain said, 'Wherever Lancelot is, I vow to find him and fight him for these murders, till one of us lies dead.'

Lancelot banished

Arthur sent letters to all his lords, telling them of Lancelot's treachery and summoning them to Camelot; soon there were ant-columns of soldiers on every road. Lancelot, too, made preparations. He stuffed the larders of his castle Joyous Gard, cleaned out its water-springs and repaired its walls. His friends and relatives flocked from Brittany, and he was also supported by Bors, Lionel, Ector and a dozen of Arthur's other lords who had fled with him from Camelot. Each of them brought soldiers, grooms and servants, so that by the time Arthur, Gawain and their men besieged Joyous Gard in the pouring rain, and Lancelot climbed to talk peace-terms with them from the battlements, the place was more like a bustling town than one man's property.

'Put your trust in swords, not walls,' shouted Gawain, his face streaming in the rain. 'Come down and fight.'

'Why should I fight my best friend and my king?' said Lancelot.

'You've no choice,' growled Gawain. 'Come down and fight.'

Reluctantly Lancelot made his preparations. There were three ways out of Joyous Gard, and at each he put a force of foot-soldiers armed with daggers, bowmen, axemen, and horsemen in full armour. Lionel and Bors led the side-groups; Lancelot himself led the centre group, through the high main gate of Joyous Gard. The three groups closed on Arthur's army like squeezing fingers, trying to press them into one cramped space and finish them. For their part, Arthur and Gawain fanned their men out as widely as they could, and sent half a dozen of their wildest followers, moorsmen, to hunt Lancelot down and cut his throat. There were giants on the fringes of the battle, drawn out of hiding by the clatter of weapons. They stayed in the shadows, favouring neither side and content to throttle any human who strayed too close.

It was less like a battle than butchery. The men were too close-packed to do more than hack and stab at random; the rain filled their eyes and darkened their clothes, till it was impossible to tell friend from enemy; wherever they set their feet, they trod on corpses or slithered in blood-soaked mud. Through it all, Arthur, Lancelot and the other lords rode their huge warhorses, trampling everyone in their path and hunting each other down. At one point Arthur's horse stumbled and threw him, and as he scrabbled in the mud, helpless in his armour, Bors jumped from his horse to cut his throat. But Lancelot shouted, 'No! This is no way for a king's life to end! This is no way for Arthur to die, in a hopeless war against his own best friend!' He helped Arthur back on his horse and said, 'In God's name, Arthur, call an end to it! What point is there, whether I kill you or you kill me?' Arthur wheeled his horse without a word, and at that moment Gawain rode up behind Lancelot, and would have cut off his head as he stood there if Bors had not ridden across his path and caught the full force of the blow on his own swordblade. Both swords splintered, and he and Gawain fell to the ground stunned by the collision. If their servants had not carried them like potato-sacks to safety, they would have drowned where they lay in mud and blood.

The fighting went on for weeks. The whole country was up in arms either on Lancelot's or Arthur's side; there was hardly a family without a man caught in the war or worse still, dead. At last word reached the Pope in Rome, and he decided to put an end to it. He sent letters to Arthur and Lancelot ordering them, on pain of excommunication*, to give up their feud. Lancelot was to return Guinever to Arthur; Arthur was to guarantee Lancelot safe-conduct; no blood was to be shed by either of them in Britain again. Truce was declared, and Lancelot set out in a glittering procession to take Guinever to Camelot. The column was led by a hundred horsemen in green velvet, and Guinever followed with twenty-four green-clad girls; behind them rode Lancelot with twelve young pages in white velvet; Lancelot's and Guinever's clothes were sewn with jewels, and the warp of the cloth was silk and the weft was gold. People gaped as the gorgeous procession wound through Camelot to the palace, where Arthur sat in state with Gawain and his other lords. Lancelot and Guinever knelt before Arthur, and Lancelot said, 'My lord, as His Holiness the Pope commands, I return Queen Guinever. And in penance for my sins, I vow to make a pilgrimage, barefoot and in a hairshirt, all the way from Camelot to Joyous Gard; at the end of every ten miles I shall pay for the building of a chapel, and for the chanting of services of repentance, day and night.'

Lancelot's lavishness, as he intended, took everyone's breath away. Arthur would have welcomed Guinever and pardoned Lancelot on the spot, if Gawain had not burst out, 'It's not enough! What use are fine promises to me? How many chapels will bring Gaheris and Gareth back to life? Why should I forgive him?'

'Gawain, Gawain,' said Arthur wretchedly. 'What's to be done?'

'Take back the queen, my lord, and let this criminal leave Camelot unharmed. But let him forget his chapels! Banish him from Britain, and in a year's time chase him to Brittany and crush him. For my part, he owes me his death, and I mean to collect it, face to face.'

Arthur bowed his lead. Lancelot turned furiously, walked out of the court and galloped to Joyous Gard. He filled a fleet of boats with furniture, horses and treasure-chests, and as soon as they were loaded he set sail for Brittany, for exile, and turned his face from the Britain he never expected to see again.

15

THE ONCE AND FUTURE KING

Arthur in Brittany

When Lancelot left Britain in exile, and sailed to Brittany, its people welcomed him with cries of joy. For years they had chafed under Arthur's rule. Once he had been their friend and ally, the router of Romans, the giant-killer. But now he was old; he never set foot outside his British castles and hunting-parks, and they objected to paying taxes to a ruler they never saw. They crowned Lancelot king and tore up every treaty and trading-tie with Britain. In Britain, this added to the discontent the younger lords already felt with Arthur. He was finished, they said. Camelot's glory was a fairy-tale; it was time for him to hand the throne to a better man. For his part, if Arthur had had a suitable son and heir, he would gladly have given up the crown. But his only heir was Mordred, a blusterer who would begin his reign with tyranny and end by handing Britain to the first invader who demanded it. With Lancelot gone, and Bors, Lionel and other senior lords with him, Arthur had no one but Gawain to advise him – and Gawain's advice, on every occasion and whatever the question, had hardened into two implacable words: 'Kill Lancelot!'

Arthur decided that the only way to save his reputation was to win a last foreign victory, the equal of his old campaigns against the Romans or the giants. Wearily he began massing men and ships to make war on Lancelot. The invasion-fleet was enormous: a thousand ships and sixty thousand men. It was the most glittering warfleet ever seen in Britain, and people flocked to watch it leave, pennants fluttering, trumpets blazing, sails billowing and sailors bending the oars in their eagerness, making a race of it. Unfortunately, however, instead of sailing from Totnes or some other south-coast harbour, Arthur had chosen to leave from Cardiff. The outsize fleet not only had to negotiate the Bristol

Channel and the stormy waters off Lionesse, but was hurled south by storms into the Bay of Biscay and very nearly drowned in the roaring waterfall on the rim of the world. More than half the ships broke up and sank, and by the time the others beached in Brittany (not far from Mont St Michel, where Arthur had killed a flesh-eating giant forty years before), the men were terrified and mutinous.

Their confidence was not increased by the kind of war they had to wage. Instead of fighting openly, Lancelot's followers hid in their high-walled towns, and Arthur's men had to build siege-weapons, hurl themselves at one well-guarded town after another, and as soon as one siege was over drag themselves and their weapons to the next town and the next attack. Arthur was always at the head of the attackers, with Excalibur gleaming in his hand, and Gawain strewed enemy corpses like fallen leaves. But this was small comfort to men who had been away for months instead of the weeks promised them, and who shuddered to think what might be happening to their farms and families at home.

In this way, and although they grew weaker and wearier with every day that passed, the British cut a path through Brittany, defender by defender, town by town, until they besieged Lancelot's capital Benwick itself, and bottled him and his lords inside like wasps in a jar. Bors, Lionel and the others urged Lancelot to go out and fight, to order the pitched battle that would end the war once and for all. But he was still unwilling to fight his old friend Arthur face to face, and instead sent out a girl on a pony to ask Arthur's terms for peace. Once again, as on the day Lancelot surrendered Guinever in Camelot, Arthur would gladly have given up the feud – and once again Gawain intervened before he could say a word, throwing his steel-fingered glove at the terrified girl and roaring, 'Tell that coward that Gawain challenges him to single-handed combat, face to face.'

There was nothing for it but a duel. Next morning, as soon as the sun was high, Lancelot rode out of Benwick attended by Bors and Lionel. Gawain was waiting on his warhorse, and in Arthur's army and on the battlements of Benwick the people stood in lines to watch. First Lancelot and Gawain charged, and splintered their spears on each other's shields; then they drew their swords and hacked at each other till sparks flew. They had avoided fighting each other for thirty years, even in fun, for fear of having to admit that either was superior; now the battle was not for reputation but for life. To begin with, Gawain had the best of it, and Lancelot was pressed back as far as the city walls.

But then Lancelot realised that the rising sun was the source of Gawain's strength, and for two hours, till it stood directly overhead, he contented himself with ducking Gawain's sword-blows, parrying and scampering out of range. Noon passed, and Gawain's strength passed with it. But still Lancelot gave him no rest, darting at him, fussing and tormenting him as a terrier tires a bull. At last Gawain fell on one knee, and Lancelot crashed his sword down on his helmet and stunned him. He walked back into Benwick and slammed the gates, leaving Arthur's servants to gather Gawain on a litter and carry him back to camp. The sword-stroke had dented Gawain's helmet and driven a circle of bone into his brain. He lay in a coma for days – and then, in the teeth of his doctors' advice, he challenged Lancelot to a second duel, took a sword-blow on exactly the same place and collapsed again. The doctors warned him that any more pressure on that part of the skull would kill him.

Mordred

At first, when Arthur's huge invading-force left for Brittany, Mordred played the part of a modest, unambitious prince. He said that he was only a caretaker king, and that Arthur would make all decisions and settle all disputes when he came home. But as the weeks passed and there was no sign of the returning army, he began working to make his rule secure. He pretended that news had come from Brittany that Arthur and Lancelot had killed each other and that Arthur had named him heir; he filled the Round Table with grooms and scullions (since there were no lords left) and bribed them to elect him king; he had himself crowned at Canterbury, and pawned the royal silver to pay for a coronation feast. He told Guinever bluntly that she was Britain's queen and that it was her duty to marry him, whereupon she fled to London, barricaded herself in her castle and sent a letter begging Arthur to come home and help.

Even this was not the end of Mordred's wickedness. When the Archbishop of Canterbury told him that he was behaving like a tyrant and that if he persisted he would be cursed with bell, book and candle, he answered, 'Utter one word of a curse, and you'll lose your head,' and drove the Archbishop into hiding in a hermit's cave near Glastonbury. This earned him the hatred of every Christian in the country, and he was popular only with the rabble whose loyalty he bought with cash from the royal treasury and with high-sounding titles like Duke, Milord and Prince. When news came at last that Arthur was sailing to the rescue, Mordred gathered an army of farm-labourer infantry and apprentice-boy generals and ambushed him on Dover beach. There was a day-long battle in the shallows – for Arthur's army, too, was spineless and tatterdemalion, no more than rags of the invasion-force which had set out so proudly for Brittany – and it ended only when Gawain stood up in the bows of the ship where he had been lying sick, crammed his war-helmet on his head and uttered such a roar that both armies, friend and foe alike, scattered for their lives.

This last effort brought Gawain's death. His helmet was still dented from Lancelot's sword-blows, and when he rammed it on his head it reopened the wound in his brain, exactly what the doctors had warned him to avoid. Arthur buried him on the cliff overlooking Dover bay, and ordered a castle to be built to mark the grave. Then, with a heavy heart, he gathered his soldiers and told them to be ready to march on Canterbury next morning, to finish Mordred.

That night, tossing on a camp-bed, Arthur was tormented by prophetic dreams. First he was strapped to a throne, and the throne was nailed to the Round Table, which rolled downhill to a pond full of snakes, dragons and water-worms which tore him limb from limb. Then Gawain's ghost glided into the tent, and told him that if he fought Mordred next day he would be killed, and that he should postpone the battle and send word to Lancelot to bring reinforcements. Arthur woke up in terror, remembering how he had once before dreamed a prophetic dream (when he saw the dragon fight the bear on his youthful voyage against the Romans in Brittany), and how its prophecy had proved exactly true. He sent for his advisers, and they recommended that he offer Mordred peace-terms. If Mordred disbanded his army and acknowledged Arthur as king, he should be offered Cornwall for a kingdom while Arthur lived and all Britain to rule when Arthur died. The promise would never have to be honoured, the advisers said – for while Bediver was taking the peace-terms to Mordred, another lord would be sailing to Brittany to ask Lancelot's urgent help.

Mordred crowed with delight at Arthur's terms. He sent a reply agreeing to everything, but insisted that the two armies should be drawn up facing each other on the marshes near Canterbury, and that he and Arthur should meet in the middle alone and unarmed, to sign the treaty and drink a friendship-toast. And if any soldier on either side produced a weapon during the ceremony, Mordred said, it meant treachery, and war. Arthur wearily agreed to these terms. The two scarecrow armies gathered on the marsh, and he and Mordred walked out unarmed, with servants carrying the treaty, quills and ink and two cups of wine. But just as Arthur was dipping his quill in the ink to sign, an adder slid out of a grass-tussock at his foot, and without thinking one of his servants drew a sword and killed it. At once Mordred began screaming, 'Treachery! A drawn sword! Treachery!', and his soldiers swarmed to attack before Arthur could say a word. Weapons appeared from nowhere, stones and arrows flew, and soon the armies were at each other's throats. In the midst of the struggle, as Arthur watched the remnants of his kingdom collapsing all round him, he saw Mordred whooping to attack him with a sword and his mind flooded with fury. He snatched Bediver's spear, levelled it against Mordred and rammed it through his belly so hard that two arm's-lengths stuck out behind. With his last strength, Mordred slid hand-over-hand along the spear-shaft and hit his father Arthur on the side of the head with a sword-blow that sliced off his ear and buried itself a blade's depth in his brain. Arthur fell swooning and Mordred fell on top of him, stone dead*.

The once and future king

When Mordred's and Arthur's armies saw their leaders fall they dropped their weapons and disappeared like ghosts, leaving the battlefield to corpses. All that day, while crows and seagulls gorged, Arthur lay in a coma, and his last two loyal lords, Lucan and Bediver, lugged Mordred's carcase clear of his body and guarded him. They avoided moving him while it was daylight in case they jarred his wound and killed him. But at twilight, when robbers began creeping out of the shadows to loot the bodies, they struggled to carry him to a safer place. Lucan had been wounded in the stomach, and the effort of carrying Arthur made his bowels gush out and killed him. Bediver was left alone with Arthur. He wondered if he and his king would survive the night. Then, as if in a dream, it seemed to him that he was lying not on a barren battlefield but on the shore of a still, grey lake, and Arthur stirred beside him and said, 'Take Excalibur and throw it into the water, then come back and tell me everything you see.'

Bediver took the sword to the water's edge. But on the way he began admiring the jewelled hilt and the fairy lettering on the blade, and thought, 'How can he mean me to throw such a wondrous thing away? What can come of it but harm and loss?' He hid Excalibur under a tree-root and went back to Arthur.

'What did you see?' asked Arthur.

'Wind and waves,' said Bediver.

'Go back!' said Arthur angrily. 'Do as I tell you! Throw Excalibur into the water, then come back and tell me everything you see.'

Bediver went back to the lake-side. But he thought, 'His wound has made him delirious. Excalibur is the symbol of his power: it would be sin to throw it away.' He covered Excalibur with leaves and went back to Arthur.

'What did you see?' asked Arthur.

'Wind and lapping waves,' said Bediver.

'Traitor!' said Arthur. 'Would you betray your king for the riches of a sword? Throw Excalibur into the water, then come back and tell me everything you see.'

Bediver cleared the leaves from Excalibur, took it to the water-side and threw it hard to the centre of the lake. An arm and hand came out of the water, sleeved in white, caught it and sank back under the surface, and Bediver ran trembling to tell Arthur. 'Quickly!' said Arthur. 'Take me to the lakeside, for my wound is cold.' Bediver dragged him to the water-side, and found a boat bobbing there, and inside it the Lady of the Lake and her fairy attendants. The Lady of the Lake cradled Arthur's head tenderly in her lap, and as the rowers rowed out across the lake Bediver called forlornly after him, 'My lord! Where are they taking you?'

'To Avalon, where all wounds are healed,' said Arthur. 'If you hear no more of me, pray for my soul.'

The boat disappeared into the lake-mists, and Bediver knelt at the water's edge and wept. When he looked up again the lake had entirely vanished: it was as if he had been transported through time and space to an empty, moonlit wood. He ran desperately through the trees, and came on a hermit praying by a freshly-dug grave. 'Where is this place?' asked Bediver. 'Whose grave is that?'

'This is Glastonbury,' answered the hermit. 'All I know of the body is that a lady brought it at midnight, and paid me a hundred gold pieces to bury it.'

Bediver burst into tears and said, 'That was my lord King Arthur. Is this bare wood to be his last resting-place on earth?' He sent the hermit with word to Guinever in London, and she rode at once to see the grave. She made arrangements to sell her castles, land and jewels, and to use the money to build an abbey at Glastonbury, a place of pilgrimage whose heart would be a stone set over Arthur's grave with the words written on it, 'Here lies Arthur, the Once and Future King*.' Then she retreated into a nunnery at Amesbury; soon afterwards she died and was buried by Arthur's side*. When Lancelot and his army came at last from Brittany, they found that there were no more battles to fight and that Lancelot's lover of thirty years and his best friend were dead. Lancelot threw himself sobbing on the grave, crying that he was the cause of Britain's misery, and that his whole life had been nothing but futility and sin. He stayed there for six weeks. He refused to get up, refused to eat or drink, and shrivelled to the size of a child, a mouse, and finally an acorn, when he died. His lords took his remains to Joyous Gard and buried them.*

So the glory of Camelot reached its earthly end, and the lives and deeds of the Round Table lords began to blur from truth into legend. But the memory of Arthur's reign lived on, like a glowing fire, until people began to think that he and his followers were not dead at all but sleeping, and that when Britain once more needed them the horn would blow and they would come galloping to answer it from the cave of dreams.*

HEROES

16

BEOWULF

Grendel

Of all Arthur's former lands, the country emptiest of mortals was Denmark, which had once been ruled by his brother-in-law Lot, king of Orkney. The reason was that Denmark was a lair of giants, trolls and other supernatural beings, and when Camelot collapsed and its soldiers were no longer available to protect the Danish people the supernatural beings fell on them and gorged themselves. Those mortals who could escape fled to Geatland, Brittany or Germany; those who stayed huddled together for safety, and built walled towns and towers to protect themselves.

One such tower was Heorot, built by King Hrothgar. He built it of a double line of pine-trunks, thick as ships' masts, and gold-plated the roof to glitter in the sun. Heorot was big enough to hold every one of Hrothgar's people, and on the day it was finished they crammed inside for a celebration-feast, and their laughter and singing filled the sky. When night came and the feast ended, they bolted Heorot's massive doors, laid mattresses on the floor and slept. They set no guards: who needed them, with the strength of Heorot all round them?

What no one in Heorot knew was that the shrillness of the singing and the thump of the dancing had disturbed Grendel in his water-lair, deep in the swamp. He was a night-wanderer, the monstrous son of a giantess and a water-snake, and his food was flesh. As soon as the moon leapt into the sky, he loped across the fen and began sniffing at Heorot and tearing it with his talons till he found the doors. He ripped them open, reached inside and began munching men like crayfish, sucking the flesh and spitting out the bones. Next morning Hrothgar's people found the fragments of thirty people in the wreckage. They rebuilt Heorot's doors and bronze-plated them, and that night Grendel smashed them just as easily and ate another thirty men. Night after night he fell on the place and gorged himself, till only a handful of Hrothgar's people were left alive. During the day, when the sun was up and all supernatural beings hid themselves, they moved miserably about Heorot, and its rafters rang with their weeping. When night fell and Grendel prowled the moors, they hid in holes like rats and left Heorot empty in the moonlight, gaunt as a rotting ship.

Twelve years passed. The gold peeled from Heorot's roof and woodlice and fungus fed on its wooden walls. Every day Hrothgar's people grew fewer and weaker. The young folk left for safer homes, the old sickened and died, and Grendel sniffed out their graves in the night and munched their bodies. A handful of worthy warriors remained, Hrothgar's hardy helpers, but for all their bravado they could think of no way to punish the predator who preyed on them.

Then, one day as Hrothgar and his people were dining in Heorot, while a minstrel sang sad songs of happier days, a warship swam into harbour, with twenty-five warriors wielding the oars. They were Geats, led by Prince Beowulf, and they moored the ship and swaggered to Heorot with mailshirts clinking and spears held high. 'Hrothgar,' said Beowulf, 'give us permission to sleep in Heorot tonight, when it lies useless under the stars, and we'll rid it of Grendel.'

'You?' scoffed one of Hrothgar's counsellors, a man called Unferth, banging his beermug down. 'Aren't you the same Beowulf who lost that swimming-race against Breca, across the sea from Denmark to Geatland? What good could you do against Grendel?'

'Unferth,' said Beowulf, 'you're letting the beer talk for you. We took that race on years ago, Breca and I, for a dare – why else would anyone go sea-swimming in the depths of winter? For five days we kept pace stroke for stroke, stitching the sea, and we'd have reached Geatland neck-and-neck if the glint of my chainshirt hadn't caught the eye of a water-worm, deep in the weed beside the shore. It took the shirt for a shell, and snatched me in its jaws, hoping to crunch my carapace and suck my flesh; six of its companions left their lairs and nuzzled for scraps at the banquet. But I gave them a different feast from the one they hoped for. I sliced all seven, and laid them dead in a row on the shore of Geatland. That's why Breca won that race.'

Unferth had nothing to say to this. But Hrothgar said, 'Beowulf, you talk of swords and chainshirts – but what use is steel against Grendel? He brushes arrows aside like gnats; his scales split swords and wither spears.'

'I'll wrestle him bare-handed,' said Beowulf. Hrothgar threw up his hands at such self-confidence, and ordered room to be made on the benches for the Geats to sit and eat. That night, after he and his people had left as usual for their burrows, never expecting to see Beowulf or his Geats again, the visitors made up beds on the floor of Heorot and lay down to sleep. Beowulf's warriors kept their chain-mail buckled round them and their swords by their sides, but Beowulf cheerfully piled his weapons by the wall and lay down in his shirt without so much as a dagger to defend himself.

In the dark night, prowling for prey, Grendel sniffed flesh in Heorot, and padded through the fen to find it. He reached his single arm, broad as a barrel, through the shattered doorway, picked up the nearest Geat, tore him to tatters and gulped him down. Then he felt inside for another morsel, and his pincers, scuttling across the floor, fastened on Beowulf's pillow. Before he could disentangle them and fix his grip on flesh instead of pillow-feathers, Beowulf took hold of his arm at the elbow and clung on to it as a bear clings to a tree-branch. Grendel withdrew his arm, and began shaking and twisting it to dislodge Beowulf's grip. But Beowulf clung tight, and he was too near Grendel's elbow for the monster to twist his pincers and tear him, too near Grendel's shoulder for him to bend to the ground and scrape him off. Grendel lifted his arm to bite Beowulf free, and Beowulf fastened his feet in Grendel's armpit, arched his back under Grendel's arm and heaved. Grendel thrashed in the air and roared; he wriggled on the ground and splashed through the shallows of the sea; he picked up a stick in his teeth and tried to prize Beowulf's grip apart. But Beowulf held tight, and gradually straightened his back and shoulders until he burst open a crack in Grendel's arm. The scales slid apart, the flesh tore, the sinews split, and finally the arm-joint snapped from its socket and the arm rolled to the ground with Beowulf still clinging to it. Grendel ran shrieking to his water-lair with his lifeblood fountaining.

The water-witch

Next morning Hrothgar's people swarmed to Heorot like ants. They gaped at Grendel's enormous arm, and their children clambered about on it as if it were a fallen tree. They followed Grendel's trail to the swamp-edge, and found the water seething with water-snakes which

133

had writhed from the depths to feast on his spilled blood. Above all they carried Beowulf and his Geats shoulder-high and held triumph-games in their honour; while the gallants galloped their horses along the shore, Hrothgar's palace women scrubbed Heorot clean of Grendel's blood, hung Grendel's huge arm on chains from the rafters like a trophy, set up tables and benches, and began butchering sheep, cattle and chickens for a banquet. The royal minstrels made songs in Beowulf's honour, comparing him with great warriors of the past*, and the feasting and singing lasted far into the night, so triumphantly that all the night-hunters far across the fens, giants, ogres, trolls and goblins, covered their ears and cowered*.

When the eating and dancing were finished, they moved the tables and benches aside, spread mattresses on the floor and lay down to sleep. On the bench at each man's head were his chain-mail, helmet, spear and sword, ready to snatch at a moment's notice. So they slept, heavy with celebration, and no one heard the padding steps of Grendel's mother as she slid out of the swamp and sniffed her way to Heorot, hungry for revenge. She was a water-witch, a giantess*. Long ago, when the world was still mud and slime, she had mated with a seasnake and made her home in its lair deep under the swamps, where she cherished her foul son Grendel till his death-day dawned. Now she flung open the door of Heorot, murder glittering in her eyes. She was less deadly than her son. She had neither fangs nor pincers, and her chief danger to mortals was her enormous size: she could tear human beings apart like dolls. Her arrival snatched the warriors from sleep and she had time only to pick up one slow old man, Hrothgar's friend and counsellor Aeschere, before fifty armed fighters were firing arrows, hurling spears and stabbing her legs with swords. Roaring with rage, she tucked Aeschere into her armpit and ripped Grendel's bloodstained arm from its ceiling-chains. Then she kicked her way clear of her attackers, hunched out of Heorot and darted into the darkness, shedding spears like porcupine-quills.

Aeschere's kidnapping broke Hrothgar's heart. But his heartbreak was nothing compared to Beowulf's rage at the stealing of Grendel's arm. He gathered a tracking-party as soon as it was light, dogs, hunters, warriors, and marched at their head in full armour*, flashing-eyed and furious. They followed the water-witch's tracks across the fen, to the tree-bordered lake where she made her lair. Will-o'-the-wisps hovered over the surface, and the water-stench hung in their nostrils and made them retch. One of the men suddenly shouted in the mist, the dogs snarled, and they found Aeschere's head ripped from his body and lolling at the water's edge. Blood had trickled into the water, and water-worms were browsing like cattle round a manger. Beowulf set arrow to bow and shot the nearest worm, and its companions tore it to shreds while the water seethed.

Beowulf left the Danes huddled round Aeschere's head, weeping, ran to a tongue of rock and dived into the lake, ferocious and fully-armed. He swam about in the muddy depths, parting weeds like curtains, looking for Grendel's mother's water-lair. She swam at him from behind, snatched him into a high-roofed underwater cave and threw him down on the slimy floor. Beowulf lay half-stunned, foul water streaming from him, and the water-witch crouched in the corner by a glowing fire, where Grendel's body lay bloodstained on the floor. Her hair flowed over Grendel like a shroud, and her weeping filled the cave. Beside her was Aeschere's headless corpse, and stacked by the wall was a heap of armour and weapons from earlier victims, helmets, chainshirts rusty with blood, smashed spears and shattered swords. One of the swords caught Beowulf's eye. It was jewel-hilted and enormous, with a coiling smoke-pattern inset in silver on the blade. He crept forward in the shadows to put his hands on it. The water-witch heard him and whirled with a dagger to disembowel him. But his chainshirt deflected the blow, and he had just time to snatch the giant sword with one hand and her hair with the other before she stood up, snarling, and he was riding on her shoulder like a child at a party. She lifted her hands to tear him, and Beowulf swung the sword and sliced the artery pulsing in her neck. The blade ground on bone, blood scalded his hands, and the water-witch shrieked and fell, so that he was hurled across the floor and lay winded against the wall. He waited until he was sure that the witch was really dead, and then he dragged the huge sword over to Grendel – it was as hefty as a roof-beam – lifted it two-handed and chopped the monster's neck. Grendel's body leapt at the blow as if he were still alive, and his head rolled against his mother's breast. And where his blood stained the swordblade, the metal splintered to the floor in silver icicles, leaving the hilt like a heavy jewelled cross in Beowulf's hands.

All that day Hrothgar's people had been waiting anxiously on the bank. They knew nothing of Beowulf's search, or of his battle in the water-lair; all they saw was air-bubbles breaking the surface and blood welling like mud in a geyser. Then, in the evening chill, Beowulf suddenly broke surface, swam to the bank and heaved Grendel's head

135

ashore by the hair – and at once, as if the deaths of the monster and his mother had lifted all enchantment from the lake, the mist and fires dispersed, the sulphur-stench evaporated, the weeds and water-worms disappeared and the water glinted clean and clear in the moonlight. Hrothgar sent two young Danes diving for Aeschere's body, and his people carried it with honour back to Heorot. Beowulf walked beside them with the jewelled cross, and behind him four Geats spiked Grendel's head on spears and lugged it home.

The treasure-worm

Beowulf and his companions left the Danes mourning Aeschere, and sailed back to Geatland in a ship loaded with treasure. After that the two countries lived in peace and friendship for fifty years, and Beowulf ruled his lands*. He was over seventy when his death-day came, and it was brought on him not by old age or enemies, but thanks to the greed of a servant and the fury of a worm. On a headland near Beowulf's castle was a mound of earth, a funeral-barrow heaped there in ancient times, and the rock-chamber underneath glittered with gem-stones, goblets, rings, swords, helmets, collars and armbands of twisted gold. Three hundred years before, warmed by the heat of the earth's core far below, a dragon's egg had hatched there, and as the years passed the baby dragon had flourished until it was a monster as big as a longship, able to gulp oxen as a chameleon gulps flies. It dozed all day, curled in its treasure-house; at night it flapped out in search of prey, and people saw its fire-glow in the sky and cowered by their hearthsides till the danger passed. In three hundred years no one had ever found the barrow's secret entrance or the treasure. But one day a runaway, a page-boy hiding from a beating, wriggled through a rock-hole, fell head-over-heels in the gaping dark and landed on the jewel-pile. He could hear the dragon's hissing snores, and feel its fire-breath fierce on his face. Its scales glowed in the dark like coals, and by their light he snatched a single goblet, wriggled out of the cave and ran to his master, babbling of wealth and a treasure-worm.

When they saw the goblet Beowulf's followers began clamouring to run to the headland, tear the barrow apart and loot the jewels. 'Not yet,' said Beowulf. 'It's evening, and the dragon will be stirring. Tomorrow as soon as it's dawn and the dragon sleeps, be ready.' They ran to their houses, fetched pickaxes, spades and crowbars, and sat up all night in their eagerness, too full of greed to sleep. And at sunset when the dragon stirred, it knew at once that part of its treasure had been stolen, as a broody hen senses the theft of even a single hatchling from her nest. It roared and spat fire, and the flames licked out of ventholes in the barrow till it seemed as if the headland itself was blazing. The dragon soared out of the cave, its eyes glittering and its talons bared. It swooped on Beowulf's village, charring houses, people and animals, setting trees ablaze, parching vegetable-plots and turning streams and ponds to steam. At dawn the night-flier flapped home to roost in its treasure-house, and Beowulf's people clambered miserably through the sooty wreckage of their farms, counting the cost and burying their dead. That night the dragon circled the settlement again, sniffing out the scent of the boy who had robbed it, reddening the sky. All night it searched, and when dawn once more drove it underground, every house in Beowulf's settlement was rubble and every cart, barn and boat was ash.

Beowulf took the terrified women and children of his settlement to the high hills, and hid them in fissures too narrow to catch the dragon's eye. Then he gathered his warriors and set out for the headland, led by the snivelling boy who had stolen the goblet and roused the dragon's rage. There were twelve of them, and they scurried like fieldmice hunted by a hawk, flattening themselves against the ground, their hearts pounding and their eyes white with fear. They were armed with swords and with bronze-bound shields; Beowulf had a sword, a silver dagger and a man-sized shield forged from solid iron, which had lain in his arms-house since primitive times, scoured each year with oil and sand to keep it from rusting. It was made for a chariot-rider and was too heavy to carry on foot, but it was the only defence he could find against the dragon's scorching breath.

They came to the barrow on the headland, and saw the flame-blackened stones of the entrance, blasted apart by dragon-rage. Beowulf signed to his men to stand back, and they scuttled for safety and peered out at him, timid as toddlers. He stood wide-legged in front of the entrance, planted the iron shield four-square in front of him and shouted in a voice so thick with rage that it was no longer an old man's piping but the proud war-roar of youth that fills a battlefield. 'Wake up, worm!' he shouted. 'Come out and fight!' The shout tore through the treasure-cave and rained roof-rubble on the monster's head. Its eyes opened, alert in an instant. It flicked its tongue to taste the air, then filled its lungs and sent a gust of flame surging from the cave to lick at Beowulf's shield. Then it gathered itself and hurled itself out of the cave with bared talons and snapping fangs. Beowulf struck it with his sword, and the blade bounced from its skin and fell useless on the ground, while the infuriated dragon flapped into the air and hovered above him, snorting fire. He saved his life by rolling on the ground and snatching the iron shield over him like a blanket; even so the dragon's breath heated it red-hot, and Beowulf began to bake like a loaf in an oven.

That would have been the old king's end, if it had not been for the bravery of a warrior called Wiglaf. He was the only man to take action: the others cowered behind their rocks, watching Beowulf writhing and listening to his groans as if they were spellbound. Wiglaf drew his sword, held his shield over his head to ward off the flames and ran forward. The dragon saw him scuttling like a scorpion, and spat a fireball which melted the bronze binding of his shield, burned the leather to ash and charred his hand to the bone. But in the same moment Wiglaf thrust his sword upwards, and by chance the point stabbed an overlap between two of the dragon's scales and sank into its windpipe. Smoke hissed from the hole like steam from a kettle, and the dragon gave a shriek and crashed to the ground. It crouched for a moment, belching fire, then folded its wings and lunged at Wiglaf. It would have bitten him in two, but Beowulf rolled clear of the iron shield, snatched his sword from the ground and hit it a blow between the eyes that dazed it, and it turned its fangs on him instead and tore the flesh from his shoulder as a terrior tears a rat. It was half-stunned or it would have finished him then and there. But its jaws were too weak to close, and even as its fangs ground on bone, Beowulf drew his dagger and slit its underbelly (the only part soft enough to take a knife) from side to side. The dragon's guts flopped like blood-soaked ropes. Its eyes glazed and the life sprayed out of it in blood and steam. Wiglaf levered its jaws free of Beowulf's shoulder, working as well as he could one-handed, and dragged Beowulf clear. He propped him against the barrow-wall, and started tearing his tunic to staunch the wound. But Beowulf could feel dragon-poison sliding through his body, and knew that when it reached his heart he would die of it. 'The treasure,' he whispered. 'Show me the riches from the treasure-house.'

Wiglaf ran in at the shattered door, gemstones skidding underfoot like pebbles, and in the shaft of daylight from the entrance he could see the dusty goblets, helmets, collars and armbands of a bygone age, their golden ornament peeling with passing time. He filled his shirt with jewels and ran back to Beowulf carrying a sooty golden banner, the pride of the treasure-house, which had not been unfurled in daylight for three centuries. Beowulf gazed on the treasure with glazing eyes, while the eleven warriors and the page-boy crept from their hiding places, too timid to pelt past their dying king and loot the gems. Before they could make a move the dragon-poison choked Beowulf's heart and he rolled dead at Wiglaf's feet.

So Beowulf gave his life to save his people, and the women and children ran to the headland with cries of grief. They gazed at Wiglaf's charred hand, at the gash of dragon-fangs on Beowulf's neck, and most of all at the worm itself, lying huddled on the heath. The men would have skinned it and built a trophy-hall round it, but its hide was too tough to cut; as it was they stretched it out, one hundred human paces from snout to tail, and rolled it over the cliff-edge into the sea. Then they built Beowulf a funeral-pyre, heaping it with gems and gold, and sang dirges and danced funeral-dances in his honour. When everything was burnt they built a new barrow to bury the ashes, a mound on the headland which could be seen a day's sailing out to sea. And with the hero, on Wiglaf's orders, they buried the jewels, gold and other riches from the treasure-house and hid the entrance, and there the treasure has remained ever afterwards, as useless to mortals as it ever was.

17

STORIES OF CUCHULAIN

Cuchulain's boyhood

Setanta, nephew of King Conchubar of Ulster, lived with his father
Sualtim and mother Dechtire in a remote country castle. His nurses
were always prattling about the glories of his uncle Conchubar's court,
about the marble floors polished like the sun, the gold-inlaid furniture,
the jewelled cups and the king's scarlet velvet robes. 'At that court,
even the footmen are lords,' they said. 'There are one hundred and
fifty princes there, every one a king's son, and they spend their days
riding, shooting and playing games on the palace lawn.' These stories
set Setanta's mind on fire, and when he was seven he said to his
mother, 'Please take me to Conchubar's court to play with them.'

'You're far too young,' she answered, 'and it's far too far.'

The boy said nothing, but that afternoon he took his hurling-stick
and silver ball, and set out to find his uncle's palace for himself. He
made the journey shorter by hitting his ball ahead of him, then
throwing his hurling-stick after it and running to catch them both
before they fell. He went on in this way until he came to his uncle's
palace, and on the lawn in front of it the hundred and fifty princes
were practising wrestling-falls. No one paid him any heed: they went
on armlocking, feinting and falling as if he wasn't there. But he soon
forced them to notice him. Though most of them were twice his size
and age, he began using wrestling-throws of his own on them and
tossing them about like dolls. Servants ran to fetch King Conchubar,
and he watched while Setanta beat every one of the hundred and fifty
princes, then welcomed him to court and gave him the honours due to
a royal prince. From that time on, however much the other princes
muttered, Setanta was their leader by the king's decree, and by the
time he was twelve he had mastered hunting, riding, duelling and

every other royal skill.

There was a rich blacksmith in those parts called Culain. One spring day he set a feast in his house and invited Conchubar and all his nobles. 'Hurry, Setanta,' said Conchubar. 'Ride beside me in my chariot.'

'Not yet, uncle,' said Setanta. 'The boys need me to finish their game. Ride on ahead, and I'll follow your chariot tracks and catch you up.'

Conchubar and his nobles galloped to Culain's house, unyoked their horses and went in to feast, and as soon as everyone was seated Culain unchained his mastiff and set it to guard the house. The dog was as tall as a pony, black and fierce; its eyes were rubies and its teeth were knives. It loped in seven paces round Culain's whole estate, and then settled on guard by the gate, ready to rip out the throat of any stranger who went out or in.

Evening came, and the princes finished their game on Conchubar's palace lawn and went home to bed. Setanta set out for Culain's house, following his uncle's chariot-tracks and shortening the road by hitting his ball ahead of him and throwing his hurling-stick after it as he always did. It was dark when he reached the house, and the mastiff snarled out of the shadows to rip his throat. Setanta had no weapons but his stick and ball. He struck the ball so hard that it flew down the dog's throat, tore through its entrails and splintered its bones; then he whirled it by the hind legs and dashed out its brains against a stone. When the lords ran out from the feast, instead of Setanta dead they found the dog broken and bleeding on the ground. Culain glowered and said, 'With my watchdog dead, who'll protect my house and guard my herds? Bad luck to you, Setanta: you've ruined me.'

'I'll make up for it,' said Setanta cheerfully. 'I'll find the finest puppy in Ireland and train him for you, and in the meantime I'll guard your property myself.' So, for the next few months while he was training the puppy, he looked after Culain's house and herds, and was known ever afterwards not as Setanta but by the nickname Cuchulain, 'Culain's dog'.

By the time Cuchulain was sixteen no other prince could match him for strength, good looks or fighting-skills. He was the only young man in the kingdom fit to wear his uncle's armour and able to control the royal horses and chariot*, and he would have been proclaimed champion of all Ulster if he had not had two rivals, Laoghaire Winner of Battles and Conal Cearnach, his own cousin, the eldest of the hundred and fifty princes who had learned warskills with him on Conchubar's palace lawn. Each young man had his supporters, and the rivalry between them swelled from insults to arguments, from arguments to quarrels, from quarrels to fights, until the end of it would have been civil war if Conchubar had not ordered Cuchulain, Laoghaire and Conal to go to Ailell King of Connaught and ask him to choose between them. Ailell put them in a banqueting-room separate from all his other guests, and as soon as they were settled at table let three wild-cats into the room and locked the door. Next morning he found Laoghaire and Conal clinging to the rafters like bats for safety, and Cuchulain holding off the cats with his drawn sword. 'Was that a fair test?' Ailell asked Laoghaire and Conal. 'Do you bow to Cuchulain as champion?'

'We do not,' they answered. 'We were trained to fight men, not cats.'

This answer threw Ailell into panic. He could neither judge fairly between the young men, nor refuse to judge for fear of war with Conchubar. In the end he decided to tell Conchubar his decision not openly but by a trick. He took Laoghaire aside, said, 'Hail, champion!' and gave him a bronze cup studded with rubies; he took Conal aside, said, 'Hail, champion!' and gave him a silver cup studded with emeralds; he took Cuchulain aside, said, 'Hail, champion!' and gave him a gold cup studded with diamonds; then he sent all three of them home to Conchubar. So there was no agreed decision, and the arguments began again, twice as vicious are before, and Conchubar could think of no way of stopping them*. Then, one night as the court was feasting, a giant galloped into the hall, a four-metre monster with yellow eyes and an axe slung over one shoulder. He stood wide-legged in front of them and said, 'The champion of all Ulster will be the man who chops off my head tonight, and tomorrow bends his neck to my axe as willingly as I to him.' Laoghaire swaggered forward, took the axe and chopped off the giant's head, and the giant picked it up, set it back on his neck and galloped out of the hall without a word. Next day, when he came looking for Laoghaire the would-be champion was nowhere to be seen, and the contest was between Conal and Cuchulain. The same thing happened: Conal willingly hacked off the giant's head, but next day when the giant returned he was nowhere to be found, and the contest was between Cuchulain and Cuchulain's own fear. Cuchulain sliced off the giant's head, and then laid his own neck on the block while the palace women sobbed and the princes clutched their sword-hilts with trembling hands. The giant lifted his axe till it reached the roof, and brought it whistling down. But at the last moment, seeing Cuchulain neither flinch or wince, he turned the blade so that it missed Cuchlain's neck and rang harmlessly on the floor. 'Stand up, Cuchulain,' he said. 'The championship of Ulster is yours, and may disaster come on all who challenge you.' With these words he disappeared, everyone in the hall cheered Cuchulain, and Laoghaire and Conal were forced to crawl out of their hiding-places and bow to him as champion.

The Brown Bull of Cuailgne

One morning King Ailell of Connaught said to Queen Maeve as they were lying in bed, 'You're an even finer woman now than on the day I married you.'

'What d'you mean?' said Maeve. 'When I married you, I was the finest woman in all Ireland. You were lucky to get me.'

'Nonsense,' said Ailell. 'I was richer, and far more nobly born.'

The argument seesawed backwards and forwards all morning, and that afternoon, to settle it, Maeve and Ailell had all their treasure laid in two heaps on the palace lawn, their flocks and herds driven in from pasture, and their shoals of carp, gaggles of geese and flocks of ducks rounded up for counting. They found that in every single thing, from brooches to bedspreads, from footmen to falcons, from rabbits to rolled gold, they were exactly equal – except one. A bull had been calved in Maeve's cattle-byres, and when he grew up he'd decided he was too proud to belong to a female and had crossed over into Ailell's herd; he was the best bull in all Connaught. He gored or trampled every cowherd Maeve sent to drive him back, and she was as furious as if she'd had no cattle of her own at all. 'What's to be done?' she asked MacRoth her herald. 'I won't be outclassed because of a single bull.'

'Lady,' said MacRoth, 'let me go to Cuailgne in Ulster and ask the loan for a year of the Brown Bull of Cuailgne. He'll sire so many calves for your herds that you'll never be outclassed again.'

So it was agreed, and MacRoth went to Cuailgne to beg for the bull. At first King Daire was flattered to be asked, but then he overhead MacRoth's servants saying that it was a good thing he'd agreed, or Maeve's army would have taken the bull by force. At once he sent MacRoth home empty-handed except for a message that if Maeve wanted the bull she could fetch it herself, and Maeve invited every prince and lord in southern Ireland to join the fight. The armies gathered in Connaught, and there were so many of them that their evening cooking-fires lit up the plain as bright as day. While they were sorting out orders of precedence among themselves*, Maeve went to consult a wise woman about the war. 'Tell me how you see my soldiers,' she said.

'I see them crimson and I see them red.'

'How can that be? Is it the kings of Ulster reddening them?'

'No. All the kings of Ulster, Conchubar, Eoghan, Celtchair and the others, are lying at home in their weakness, with their warriors spider-webbed by a fairy spell*. There's a boy, smooth-chinned, gentle as a deer and fierce as a dragon, and by his own force of arms he is reddening your men.'

'A boy? What boy?'

'Cuchulain, Hound of Ulster.'

When she heard this Maeve laughed aloud and went back to her army. 'The Brown Bull of Cuailgne, and all the wealth of Ulster, have no one but a boy to guard them,' she said. 'All we have to do is choose a leader and attack.' That night, while the men joked about the loot that would be theirs next morning, the chiefs met to elect a war-leader, and the man they chose was Fergus MacRogh, because he had once been King of Ulster* and knew every field and fold of the countryside. Fergus was reluctant to lead armies against his former people, and sent secret messages to the chiefs of Ulster to warn them of the danger. One by one, the kings lolled in their weakness and laughed in the messengers' faces; only Cuchulain went out to fight. He cut an oak-sapling, twisted it into a circle, wrote a warning on it and forced it over a pillar-stone on the border, and next morning the stone was bare, the warning was gone and the tracks of an army led clearly through the snow into Ulster and disappeared into the forests. All day Cuchulain followed them, and found roads hacked through woods and passes cut in mountain-sides to let them through.

The army marched through Ulster as it pleased, and no one lifted arrow to bow to stop it. In the end the soldiers sacked Cuchulain's own home, slaughtering the people and burning the buildings, and he appeared on a hillside with the fire of his fury blazing about him, and vowed to take revenge on every man in the army. Fergus and his warriors shook with terror. But Maeve said, 'Is that all there is to Cuchulain? Can't you see he's just a half-grown boy? Call him to a meeting; bribe him with a place at the head of our troops, and offer him a palace of his own as soon as Conchubar is killed.'

MacRoth the messenger rode to Cuchulain, ashen-faced with fear, and called him to a meeting in the morning. But that night Cuchulain stuck scythes in his chariot-axles, dressed his horse in a coat sewn with spikes and knives, and galloped through the army like a whirlwind, carving a crimson path. One hundred men were killed, and the same thing happened on the next night and the next, until the troops were too terrified to eat, sleep or rest. 'Go again,' said Maeve to MacRoth. 'This time accept whatever terms he makes.'

'These are his terms,' MacRoth reported when he returned. 'He challenges the men of Ireland to meet him in single combat, one each day. While the duel lasts, the rest of the army can march unmolested. But as soon as Cuchulain kills his man, the army must make camp and stay where it is till the next day dawns.'

'Ridiculous!' said Fergus.

'No,' said Maeve. 'It's better to lose one man each morning than a hundred every night. Go yourself, and tell him we accept.'

Fergus rode to Cuchulain, taking no one with him but a young man called Etarcomal. They found Cuchulain practising spear-throws in a clearing, and Etarcomal was amazed to see Fergus, a general in all his power, kneel to Cuchulain, shake his hand and talk to him as gravely as if to a king in council. When Fergus rode off Etarcomal lingered. Cuchulain asked what he was staring at, and he answered sneeringly, 'I'm staring at you. They say you're the best fighter of your age in Ireland, and no one can deny your skill in a scythe-wheeled chariot against sleeping men. But how long would you last, fighting single-handed against a fully-grown, fully-trained fighting-man?'

'Come tomorrow and see for yourself,' snapped Cuchulain. But as he thought about it that day and night, he decided that Etarcomal's rudeness was no reason for killing him, and that he owed him his life out of affection for his old friend and teacher Fergus, whose squire Etarcomal was. Next morning, therefore, when Etarcomal swaggered into the clearing with his sword drawn and fury in his face, Cuchulain said, 'Turn round and go back, and no harm will come to you.'

'Never,' said Etarcomal.

Cuchulain drew his sword, chopped the ground from under the soles of Etarcomal's feet and sent him sprawling on his back. 'That was the first warning,' he said. 'Go back, and no harm will come to you.'

'Never,' said Etarcomal.

Cuchulain made a second sword-stroke, and this time sliced the hair

145

from Etarcomal's head without drawing a drop of blood.

'That was the second warning,' he said. 'Go back, and no harm will come to you.'

'Never,' said Etarcomal.

Cuchulain struck a third time with his sword, and the blow was so fast and the sword was so sharp that Etarcomal felt nothing, and never knew he was dead until the halves of his body fell sideways like the pieces of an apple. Cuchulain tied him behind a chariot, and the horses dragged him back through the mud to Fergus' camp.

Next morning Natchrantal went to fight Cuchulain, and found him leaning against a pillar-stone. Cuchulain threw on his war-cloak so quickly that he pulled up the pillar-stone inside it, and Natchrantal's blow rattled on it and splintered his sword, whereupon Cuchulain whirled his own sword and cut off his head. In the next few days Cuchulain killed Rae, Cur, Ferbaeth and every other fighter sent against him except Larine, the young brother of his friend Lughaidh, and him he took in his hands and shook as a terrier shakes a rat, so that the young man's head lolled and his hands trembled to the end of his life.

While all this happening, the Morrigu, the war-goddess, took the form of a crow and perched on a pillar-stone beside the Brown Bull of Cuailgne. 'Beware!' she cawed. 'Cuchulain is alone, and the men of Ireland are thousands. Hide yourself, or you'll be Maeve's property before this war ends.' The startled bull kicked his heels and stampeded with his harem of cows to a secluded river-valley far away – and that was exactly what the Morrigu wanted, for the valley was no more than a morning's march from Maeve's army, and she wanted its nearness to stir the men to battle so that she could gloat over the fighting and glut herself on death. She turned her fifty witch-attendants into heifers, and led them against Cuchulain in a storm of trampling hooves and tossing horns, so that Cuchulain only saved himself by running waist deep into the river and leaving the witches (who could not cross running water) bucking and shrieking on the bank. He hurled his spear at the Morrigu and took out the eye in her face, and she and her furies vanished, spitting hate*. While Cuchulain was still weak from this attack, Maeve sent not one warrior against him but six enchanters, and though he had no weapons to use on them but slingstones, he killed every one of them. After that, seeing that she had broken her agreement with him, he fell on the army so furiously by day, and galloped his scythe-chariot so murderously by night, with bocanachs and bananachs howling on his weapon-points, that neither man,

146

horse nor dog dared stand against him.

'What's to be done?' said Fergus. 'There must be one hero in Ireland fit to fight him.'

'There is,' said Maeve. 'Ferdiad MacDaire, his best friend, who trained with him, learned with him, and knows every war-trick as well as he does.'

'You'll never persaude Ferdiad to fight his own best friend.'

'Leave it to me,' said Maeve. 'And while I'm persuading him, you go and fight Cuchulain yourself.'

'He'll kill me.'

'Why should he kill his old friend and teacher? You'll have the best of it.'

Fergus was sure that his death was calling him. But when Cuchulain saw him coming, he held his sword point-down and said, 'Go back, Fergus, and no harm will come to you. How can I kill my friend, my teacher?'

'Cuchulain,' said Fergus. 'For the sake of our friendship, for the sake of all I taught you, do one thing for me. Pretend to give way to me, in the sight of the whole army; refuse to fight.'

'I give way to no one,' said Cuchulain.

'Do this for me, and when the last battle comes and you appear before me in weakness and in wounds I'll give way to you. The whole Irish army will follow me, and the war will end without more blood.'

This promise persuaded Cuchulain. The watching soldiers saw him sheathe his sword and run from Fergus. 'After him!' they shouted. 'Cut him down!' But Fergus walked back to his camp without a word, and they would have thrown jeers at him like stones if they hadn't been so afraid of him: the only man in Ireland to make Cuchulain turn tail.

While this was happening, Maeve went to persuade Ferdiad Mac-Daire to fight. Her servants gave him honey-wine to drink, and she offered him wealth, lands and a royal wife if he fought Cuchulain and won.

'And if I refuse?' said Ferdiad.

'My poets will make satires against you, and my Druids will raise blisters of shame on your body. In nine days you'll die of it.'

Ferdiad's head swam with the honey-wine, and he thought it better to die on Cuchulain's spear-point than by blisters and satires. He agreed to fight Cuchulain next morning. He and his people spent a heavy-hearted night, and in the grey dawn he rode out and found

Cuchulain waiting by a river-ford with the sun rising behind him.

'Is it you, Ferdiad?' Cuchulain said as Ferdiad rode up on the other side of the ford. 'Are you and I, best friends, to fight?'

'In all Ireland,' answered Ferdiad, 'only you could bring me honour, not shame, by killing me, just as I alone could honour you. Defend yourself!'

All that day from dawn to twilight they fought with round-handled spears, quill-spears and ivory-shafted spears, and the weapons flew between them like bees in summer till their shields were dented and their spear-points blunt and useless. At dusk Ferdiad said, 'Let's leave these weapons, Cuchulain, for it's not by them that the fight will end.' He and Cuchulain kissed three times, and that night they shared the same camp-fire as true friends should. Next day they fought from dawn to dusk with long-handled pikes, and at evening kissed and shared camp as before, sleeping on herb-pillows to soothe their wounds. On the third day they used axes and maces, and reddened each other from dawn to dusk. If it had been the custom for birds to fly through warriors' bodies, they could have passed clear through their wounds that day and scavenged mouthfuls of flesh for their nestlings; when twilight came Cuchulain and Ferdiad barely had the strength to kiss each other before collapsing on their beds for their servants to tend their wounds.

On the fourth day they fought with swords and shields in the ford itself, and the river ran red with blood. They hacked the leather shields and struck sparks from the metal rims; they chopped, ducked and parried; their feet flung up curtains of water to hide them from the bank. They were equally matched, and though either could have killed the other they pulled back their blows for friendship's sake, hoping that the gods would intervene and end the fight, or that one or other would yield without a death. But the only god watching was the Morrigu. She was hungry for revenge on Cuchulain for wounding her, and when she judged the moment right she flew in Ferdiad's face like a shrieking crow, distracted him from turning aside the sword-blow he was making, and buried his blade in the flesh of Cuchulain's thigh. Red fire blazed in Cuchulain's brain, and he drove his sword hard into Ferdiad's chest above the shield-rim. The blade stuck out an arm's length from Ferdiad's spine, and he toppled into the stream while Morrigu's bocanachs and bananachs screeched their glee. Cuchulain groaned, threw down his weapons and knelt to take Ferdiad in his arms; but his friend was dead, and no amount of sobbing over his body in the silent stream would buy back a moment's life.

Cuchulain's servants gently disentangled him from Ferdiad's body and carried him to a secret cave, out of reach of Maeve's vengeance. They bathed his wounds in a pool, and threw in herbs and healing plants till the water-surface was strewn with green. Then they laid him on a sheepskin bed, and his flesh was so raw that he could bear no blankets and they had to cover him with grass. In the dead of night one of his servants galloped to the ruins of Cuchulain's home, where Cuchulain's father Sualtim lay in an enchanted sleep. He shouted the news of his son's injuries in Sualtim's ears, and the words shook the spell from Sualtim as cold water snatches a man from drunkenness. 'Is it the sky bursting I hear?' he said. 'Is it the sea going backward, the earth breaking, or the groaning of my son in his weakness?' He looked around him at the corpses of his people and the smoking ruins of the castle, sacked by Maeve's army. Then he harnesssed his horse Grey of Macha and galloped to warn King Conchubar. 'Men are being killed, women raped, cattle stolen!' he shouted outside Conchubar's castle gate, and no one stirred or answered. He galloped into the castle hall, among the heaps of sleeping warriors, and shouted, 'Men are being killed, women raped, cattle stolen!', while the iron shoes of Grey of Macha struck sparks from the marble floor. The sparks and the shouting disturbed Conchubar's warriors in their sleep, and they sat up, yawning, and gazed at Sualtim with slack, incurious eyes. Sualtim wheeled Grey of Macha to face the king, and the horse reared so suddenly that the sharp edge of Sualtim's shield caught him under the chin and sliced off his head. His body slumped, and the shield clattered to the ground with its straps till tangled in the horse's bridle, so that when Grey of Macha galloped through the hall he dragged the shield rattling beside him, with Sualtim's head lying inside it and shouting, 'Men are being killed, women raped, cattle stolen!'

Sualtim's death lifted the sleep-spell from the warriors of Ulster, and the Morrigu and her bocanachs and bananachs kicked them awake, shrieking at them to ride out and kill. Not long afterwards, in their camp on the plain, Maeve's army heard a rumble like the coming of a thunderstorm or the breaking of surf on shore, and the plain was filled with wild beasts stampeding from the woods.

'What is it?' said Maeve. 'MacRoth, climb the hill and see.'

MacRoth climbed the hill, and after a while came back and said, 'In the far distance a grey mist; in the mist a blizzard; in the blizzard spear-points like stars on a frosty night. The men of Ulster are marching against us.'

These words caused panic, and Maeve and Fergus had to calm it by mounting their horses and galloping round slapping order into their men with the flat of their swords. They organised the soldiers into a defensive ring with their spears pointing outwards, and the men trembled on guard all night in the darkness, waiting for dawn, while the Morrigu taunted them in the shape of a lean, grey-haired hag, hopping from spear-point to spear-point with her bocanachs and bananachs howling at her heels. It was Maeve's plan to wait till the warriors of Ulster attacked, then to open the jaws of the ring and close it behind them, trapping them. But when dawn came and Conchubar attacked, his onslaught was so fast and Maeve's troops were so terrified by the Morrigu that the ring-trap broke before it could be sprung, and in the light of the rising sun frightened men were butchering each other in a confusion of blood across the plain.

In the midst of the battle, when Maeve saw that neither side was getting the victory, she called out to Fergus, 'Take your chance, now! It's Conchubar breaking your men, Conchubar who stole your throne. Kill him, and end the war!' Red rage blazed in Fergus' brain, and he began stalking Conchubar over the battlefield, close as a cat, silent as his shadow in the welter of warriors. He waited till he and Conchubar were alone in an open space, then sprang round in front of him and lunged with his spear. Conchubar lifted his shield to parry the blow, and at the shriek of metal against metal every shield in the army screamed in sympathy, filling the sky with shrieks like starlings flocking before a hawk.

'What's that?' said Cuchulain, lifting himself on his sickbed in the cave. 'Who is attacking Conchubar, and why am I not there to defend him?'

'Lord,' said the servants, 'there's no part of your body unwounded, not a hair, not a fingernail; your flesh is so raw that you can bear no blankets; even the grass we warm you with is propped on sticks. Lie still.'

They tied him with ropes to stop him leaping from the bed and opening his wounds. But he put forth all his strength, burst the ropes and scattered them and the grass into the high air. Then he roved about the cave looking for weapons, and found the yoke-pole of his chariot. He picked it up, biting his lips from the sorrow of his wounds, and ran naked into the battle scattering enemies like stones. In the midst of the fighting he found Fergus and Conchubar hammering each other's shields like anvils.

'Fergus!' shouted Cuchulain. 'I demand that you give way before me, as you promised if I appeared in weakness and in wounds. Give way!'

'Never,' said Fergus.

'Give way, or I'll grind you as a mill grinds malt.'

'Never,' said Fergus.

'Give way, for the third time of asking, in the name of the gods.'

At the thought of the gods' anger Fergus hesitated and drew back three steps – and the men of Ireland took it for yielding, dropped their weapons and ran, sweeping Fergus, Ailell and the other kings from the battlefield as a flood sweeps twigs. Conchubar and the warriors of Ulster ran after them, stabbing and slicing, and choked the ford with corpses while the Morrigu and her bocanachs and bananachs howled with glee. Not a thousand men from the whole invading horde were left alive, and they scattered like sheep in the woods and were not seen again. When the fighting was done Cuchulain threw away the last splinters of the chariot-pole, snatched up a sword and cut the tops from three mountains like a man slicing eggs: they are the three bare hills of Meath, a memorial to this day to the men lost in the war over the Brown Bull of Cuailgne.

As for the bull himself, when Maeve saw the battle lost and her army scattered she went secretly to the valley where the bull and his heifers were pasturing, and drove them across the border to Connaught and her own royal cattle-herd. 'We came to get the bull,' she said grimly to himself, 'and get him we shall, however many lives it costs.' But as soon as the bull saw that he was once again owned by a woman, he stampeded his cows into the herd of Maeve's husband Ailell, and there locked horns with the White Bull of Connaught, leader of Ailell's herd. All day they tried to gore and crush each other. Their eyes were fireballs; their hooves sent sods flying; they reddened the ground with each other's blood. Darkness fell, and all through the night Maeve's men could hear them bellowing and battling. Next morning, in the sunrise, they saw the Brown Bull of Cuailgne with the White Bull dead on his horns, and he carried his enemy back across the border into Ulster and home to his own pasture of Cuailgne. And as he stood there, legs apart, bellowing for victory, the heart burst in his body, blood gushed from his nostrils and he died, so that every moment of the war, and every warrior's death in it, was utterly in vain.

Cuchulain's death

The war over the Brown Bull of Cuailgne changed Cuchulain's character. The violent deaths he dealt in the war, and especially the killing of his blood-brother Ferdiad, scarred his mind with an arrogance more like a tyrant's than a champion's, and he began to do exactly as he pleased, without pity or explanation, to enemies and friends alike. Once, sulking because his uncle Conchubar went off to a banquet without him, he would have cut the throats of everyone in Conchubar's palace if the minstrels had not distracted him with music until Conchubar hurried home and apologised. When Blanad, wife of Curoi the Enchanter (who devised the tests which proved Cuchulain champion of Ulster) told Cuchulain that he was the only man in the world she loved, he showed no hesitation in kidnapping her or in killing Curoi when he came to demand her back*. After this Curoi's son Lughaidh forgot his old friendship for Cuchulain, vowed revenge and began gathering an army to attack him. Maeve (who was by now a grey-haired, wild-eyed old woman) saw her chance to revenge herself on Cuchulain at last. She went to the three witch-daughters of Calatin the enchanter, reminded them how Cuchulain had murdered their father and brothers in the war for the Brown Bull of Cuailgne*, and stirred them to sap his brain with their magic and lure him out to fight.

The witches put on cloaks of invisibility and flew on the wind's wings to Conchubar's court, where Cuchulain was listening to music on the sunny lawns. They began tearing up the grass, making stalks, oak-leaves and fuzz-balls appear like fighting-men and filling Cuchulain's ears with a babble of warcries that only he could hear. He leapt to his feet, eyes starting and lips trembling, and it was all the other lords could do to stop him snatching his sword and hacking at empty air.

'He's possessed,' said Conchubar. 'Take him to Deaf Valley, and on no account let him leave it, whatever he sees or hears, until these enchantments are over or Conal Cearnach comes.'

The lords took babbling Cuchulain to Deaf Valley, a place so hidden and so tranquil that no war-noise ever penetrated it, and entertained him there with feasting, music, conversation and games of draughts and chess. But in the darkness of night Calatin's witch-daughters swooped on the place, and once more filled Cuchulain's eyes with the sight of a phantom army and his ears with the sounds of war. He jumped out of bed and buckled on his weapons, the eldest witch took mortal form and led him by the hand to his chariot, and he galloped out of Deaf Valley with his warspears red in his hand, his war-whoop on his lips and the hero-light blazing round his head*.

Lughaidh's army, gathered in their camp, heard the thunder of Cuchulain's horse's hooves, and cowered. But Lughaidh shouted, 'There's nothing to fear. We'll trap him by trickery, not strength.' He organised the men into a long line across Cuchulain's path, and ordered them to make a fence of their iron shields linked together. He picked the six best warriors in the army, divided them into three pairs and placed each pair outside the shield-fence facing Cuchulain, with a Druid beside each of them. 'When Cuchulain comes,' he said, 'let the warriors pretend to fight each other, and let the Druids ask Cuchulain to throw his spears and end it. No one can refuse a Druid's request, and Cuchulain will be forced to let his spears out of his hands. Each of them is fated to kill a prince – and so they shall, for we'll turn them on Cuchulain himself.'

The men took their places and Lughaidh sat on horseback inside the fence of shields, ready to gallop up and snatch the spears. So they waited, and presently Cuchulain galloped down the path with the sunrise behind him, crimsoning his hair. At once the six warriors began duelling, and as Cuchulain rode up to the first pair the Druid ran out beside his chariot and shouted. 'End it, Cuchulain! Throw your spear and end the fight!' Cuchulain threw the spear, and there was such force in his cast that the iron head passed through the Druid's body, passed through the bodies of the warriors, flew over the shield-fence and fell at Lughaidh's feet. He snatched it up and hurled it back, shouting, 'Die, prince!'; but by this time Cuchulain had wheeled his chariot, so that the spear missed him and instead fulfilled the prophecy that it would kill a prince by killing Cuchulain's driver Laeg, Prince of Charioteers.

Cuchulain galloped to the second pair of duelling men, and their Druid ran out and asked for his second spear. As before, he threw it so that it killed the Druid and the fighters and fell at Lughaidh's feet – and this time when Lughaidh hurled it back it struck Cuchulain's chariot-horse, Grey of Macha, Prince of Steeds, in the belly, so that the horse overturned the chariot, threw Cuchulain on the ground and galloped off, dragging its bowels after it across the plain. Cuchulain picked himself up and ran to the third pair of fighting-men. The Druid asked for his third and last warspear, and he killed him and the warriors exactly as before. But this time when Lughaidh hurled back the spear, it passed through Cuchulain's own body, and he felt his bowels slide out round his sword-belt and knew that his death-day had come.

'Lughaidh,' he gasped, 'let me go to the lake and drink before the last battle, and if I don't come back you can kill me there.' He staggered to the lakeside and bent to drink. Then he went to the pillar-stone beside the lake, out of sight of the army, lashed himself upright to it with his sword-belt, and shouted with his last strength to his enemies to come and finish him. Lughaidh and his men surged forward. But Cuchulain's shout had also summoned Grey of Macha the chariot-horse, and it galloped frenziedly up and down the line of warriors, snapping at their necks with its razor-teeth, till every one of them but Lughaidh was dead, and the agony of the horse's wounds drove it clattering into the lakeside mists and out of sight.

Lughaidh stood for a long time on the blood-sodden ground, gazing at Cuchulain standing by the pillar-stone, and not daring to attack for the dazzle of hero-light round his head. But then the Morrigu, in the shape of a carrion crow, fluttered down and perched on Cuchulain's shoulder, and Lughaidh realised that he was dead. He ran forward and sliced off his head – and as it fell to the ground the warrior-dazzle dimmed round it, leaving the flesh pale as snow on a winter night. Lughaidh unhitched Cuchulain's body and laid it beside the head on the crimson ground.

So died Cuchulain, Hound of Ulster, Prince of Champions, not gloriously in battle but by enchantment and trickery. When Conal Cearnach galloped to the lakeside and found his body, he killed Lughaidh, gave Cuchulain to his people for burial, and went in furious search of Fergus, Laoghaire, Erc, Cunlaid and the other warlords of Ireland. He cut off their heads, and the heads of Calatin's three witch-daughters, and made a cairn of skulls beside Cuchulain's grave. The warriors of Ulster wrapped Cuchulain's head and body in silk, buried them with bitter lamentation, and set up a stone to mark the grave. And from that day on, though Cuchulain's mortal self was lost to humankind, the glory of his deeds was long remembered in songs and stories. People often heard him in the ears of their dreams, galloping his war-chariot through Ulster's forests and across its windy plains.

FOLK STORIES

18

WELSH STORIES*

Pwyll, Rhiannon and Pryderi

PWYLL, PRINCE OF DYFED

Pwyll was a shape-changer, the fairy prince of Dyfed. One day he went deer-hunting, and he and his dogs became separated from the rest of the party. All at once, in a water-meadow in a valley, he saw another pack of dogs cornering a stag. They were the most magnificent animals he had ever seen, with moon-white skin and glowing coals for eyes. He drove them from the wounded stag and let his own dogs finish it – and no sooner was it dead than a huntsman rode up, stony-faced with rage. 'What kind of barbarian are you,' he said, 'to drive off someone else's dogs and steal his stag?'

'Sir,' said Pwyll politely, 'I apologise. What can I do to make up for it?'

'Help me kill the Prince of the Underland, my enemy Havgan.'

'How can I do that?'

'Change shapes with me. Live in my castle for a year, and at the end of it Havgan will fight you for the ownership of all the lands from the mountains to the sea. Strike one blow only – and however much he begs you to finish him, hold your hand. Every blow but the first redoubles his strength instead of weakening him.'

So Pwyll changed shapes with the stranger. The stranger, whose name was Arawn, went back to Pwyll's castle and spent the year disguised as Pwyll, and Pwyll went to Arawn's castle, where the servants, the lords and even Arawn's wife treated him exactly as if he were Arawn. At the end of a year Havgan, prince of the Underland, challenged him to fight for all the lands from the mountains to the sea, and Pwyll hit him a blow that splintered his shield and sent him

157

sprawling, mortally wounded. 'For God's sake finish me off,' begged Havgan. But Pwyll shook his head, and Havgan said, 'Then I know that you're a shape-changer, not Arawn, and that my death-day has come. Tell Arawn that all the lands between the mountains and the sea are his,' and died.

Pwyll changed back into his own shape and went home to Dyfed, and on the way he met Arawn and told him everything that had happened. When he reached his own castle, and his servants bustled to pull off his boots and fetch him wine, he asked curiously, 'What have I been like, this last twelve months?'

'Kinder and more generous than before,' they answered.

After that Pwyll and Arawn often hunted and feasted together, and sent each other presents: hawks, hounds, jewels, leather-bound books embossed in gold. But although Pwyll enjoyed Awawn's company, he pined for a wife and child of his own. Every day he saw the same woman on his hunting trips, riding a pale grey horse along a distant ridge, and in the end he fell in love with her and sent servants to invite her to the castle. They reported that although she never spurred her horse or let it do more than canter, she outran them however hard they galloped. At last Pwyll went out himself. But instead of galloping after the woman, he reined in as soon as she came near and said, 'For God's sake, and for the sake of the man you love most in all the world, stop and talk to me!'

The woman reined in her horse and lifted her riding-veil. She told Pwyll that her name was Rhiannon and that the reason she rode alone was that she cared nothing for the young man she was engaged to marry, Gwawl prince of the Sun, and that she loved another prince. And to Pwyll's amazement, when he asked her beloved's name, she lowered her eyes and said, 'His name is Pwyll, Prince of Dyfed. It's you I love.'

'But how can we marry, if you're engaged to Gwawl?'

'There's only one way,' said Rhiannon, and told him what to do. Her wedding with Gwawl was fixed for a year from that day, in her father's castle, and on the evening before it Pwyll rode to the castle gate, wearing beggar's clothes and with a tattered knapsack on his back.

'Alms!' he said. 'Fill my knapsack with table-scraps, for the love of God.'

Gwawl the Sun-prince, eager for good luck on his wedding-eve, invited Pwyll inside and began filling his knapsack not with scraps but with choice cuts of meat, loaves of bread, cheese-cakes and honeycomb. But the more he put into the knapsack the emptier it seemed. 'How will we ever fill it?' he asked at last.

'There's only one way,' said Pwyll. 'A royal prince must stand inside it, and tread down the food like a farmer treading grapes.'

'Whatever you say,' said Gwawl. But as soon as his feet were in the knapsack it changed its shape to a fishing-net, and Pwyll tangled Gwawl inside it upside-down and hung it from the rafters. Then he began banging it with a stick, and refused to stop until Gwawl, bruised and furious, promised to go back to the Sun-kingdom and give up all claim to Rhiannon. There was a wedding next day after all, but the bridegroom's name was Pwyll, and instead of bright sunshine the weather was overcast, as if the sky was sulking.

PRYDERI

Pwyll and Rhiannon lived happily in Dyfed for a year, and at the end of it Rhiannon was pregnant and went to Arberth to bear her child. She had six midwives to help her, but her labour lasted three days and nights, and on the third night they all fell asleep and when they awoke found the baby born and Rhiannon unconscious beside it.

'We'll be blamed for neglecting her,' said the oldest of the midwives. 'We'd better do something, fast.'

The midwives hid the baby in a cupboard, killed a puppy, smeared Rhiannon's mouth with its blood, threw its bones at her feet and ran out of the room screaming that she'd eaten her own child in a fit of madness. Rhiannon was judged guilty – how could she not be, when it was her word against six, and the baby was nowhere to be found? – and she was condemned to live in a barrel at the town gate, and whenever strangers arrived, to tell them the story of her crime and carry them into town like a beast of burden. As for the baby, the midwives spirited him away from Arberth till they could think what to do with him.

The lord of a nearby manor, Gwent-under-the-woods, was called Tiernon. He had a fine brood mare, and expected a string of thoroughbred foals from her. But she always foaled at night, and the foal disappeared each time before anyone could catch a glimpse of it. On the next occasion, therefore, Tiernon decided to stay up all night and watch. He sat in the stable by the pregnant mare with a drawn sword in his hand. Nothing happened until midnight, when the mare foaled – and at once the stable began to shake, the ground heaved and an enormous hand, taloned like an eagle's claw, reached up from the Underland to snatch the foal. Tiernon hacked it with his sword, and it vanished with a hiss and flare which seared his eyes. When the fumes cleared he found the mare and foal unharmed, and beside them on the ground was a baby boy.

Tiernon took the baby into his own home and fostered him. But as the years passed and the child grew it became obvious that he was no ordinary toddler but a shape-changer, able to take on the appearance of any creature or thing he chose. It was a great annoyance to the child's nurses, and an even greater mystery to Tiernon, until one day he went visiting to the town of Arberth and found a woman in a barrel at the gate, telling a wild-eyed tale of murder and child-eating and begging him to ride her into town like a pack-mule. At once Tiernon guessed who his foster-son really was. He sent servants to fetch the boy to Arberth and restored him to his mother Rhiannon and his father Pwyll. Pwyll, overjoyed, offered Tiernon the pick of all the treasure in Dyfed. But Tiernon refused and went home with nothing but cries of thanks ringing in his ears.

So Pryderi came to Dyfed. He lived the rest of his childhood in Arberth, and grew up as a fairy prince. And when Pwyll tired of living in the mortal world – for though shape-changers are immortal and never grow old, they do grow bored – he succeeded to his father's throne.

Branwen and Bran

Branwen and Bran were giants, children of the sea-king Llyr and a mortal woman. They had a giant brother, Manawydan, and two mortal half-brothers, Nissyen and Evnissyen. Nissyen was a peacemaker whose soft words could turn aside any quarrel; Evnissyen was a trouble-maker, and delighted in causing fights.

One day the giants were sitting on a headland, gazing out over the broad face of their father the sea, when they saw thirteen ships, each rowed by a hundred men and containing a hundred warriors and their horses, scudding over the water from Hibernia. A man stood in the leading ship, dressed in royal robes and holding a shield upside-down as a token of peace. The ships beached and the visitors swarmed up the headland and bowed to the giants. 'I am Mallolwych, king of Hibernia,' said their leader, 'and I want to make an alliance between our countries, and to mark it by marrying Branwen, if she agrees.'

Branwen gladly agreed, and arrangements were made for the Hibernians to row back next morning, after spending the night in a sumptuous wedding-feast. The feast was held outdoors (for no house had ever been built big enough to hold Bran, Branwen or the other giants), and Nissyen and Evnissyen, Branwen's mortal half-brothers, heard the laughter and singing and came out of their houses to find a noisy wedding-dance taking place on the headland under the stars.

'No one asked our opinion,' grumbled Evnissyen. 'Why were we allowed no part in this?'

'It doesn't matter, brother,' said Nissyen soothingly. 'If Branwen's happy, why should we interfere?'

But Evnissyen would not be satisfied. He crept in the darkness to where the Hibernian warhorses were stabled, and cropped their lips to the teeth, their ears to the skull and their tails to the flank.

Next morning Mallolwych's grooms found the mutilated horses, and ran to tell their master that the giants had insulted him and that he should break off the wedding and declare war instead. But Bran said soothingly, 'My lord, this was nothing but a prank. I'll replace every injured horse, and give you the giants' cauldron of rebirth in recompense. Any dead person boiled in the cauldron leaps out as whole as ever, except that they lose the power of speech.'* This generous offer persuaded Mallolwych, and the wedding-feast went ahead. Next morning the Hibernians bolted three of their ships together to carry Branwen, and the fleet rowed out with oars flying and trumpets sounding to take her home.

Branwen lived happily for a year as queen of Hibernia. No visitors to her palace went away ungladdened: she gave them brooches and jewelled rings, and her musicians made up songs in their honour. She bore a son, Gwern, and gave him to the palace women to bring up. But the happier she was, the more her happiness irritated the mortal lords and ladies of Hibernia. 'Why must we have a giantess for queen?' they muttered. 'Why couldn't Mallolwych take a wife from among his own kind?' In the end they told Mallolwych that unless he punished Branwen for the insult done him in Cambria (when the horses were mutilated) they would dethrone him and find some other king. Mallolwych sighed, but there was no help for it. He gave Branwen a kneading-trough the size of a horse-pond, told her to spend her life in the palace kitchen, kneading bread-dough day and night, and sent the royal butcher to box her ears with his blood-stained hands every evening when he finished work.

Branwen endured her humiliation for three long years, but then she could stand no more of it. She caught a sparrow, trained it to chirp giant-speech, and sent it fluttering to Cambria to beg her brother Bran to rescue her. Bran gathered an army of giants and mortals, packed them into ships, sat harpers and viol-players on his shoulders to play war-music, and led his armada to Hibernia, wading through the shallow sea ahead of it. Mallolwych retreated across the river Liffey, and threw magic rocks into it to smash any wooden, stone or metal bridge the giants built over it. But Bran discovered the trick, spread-eagled himself across the river with his feet on one bank and his hands on the other, and counteracted the magic by making a bridge of living flesh.

Mallolwych was cornered, and Bran sent his peace-making step-brother Nissyen to discuss treaty-terms. 'What shall I do?' moaned Mallolwych. 'Will it be enough if I give up my throne, and hand the kingdom to Branwen's son Gwern, toddler though he be?'

'It may be enough,' said Nissyen. 'You can persuade Bran easily. Build a house big enough to hold him. It will be the first giant-palace ever made in the world, and the effort and expense will flatter him. Hold the peace-conference and the crowning-ceremony inside.'

Mallolwych did exactly as Nissyen advised. The house was built, large enough to cover a wheat-field, and when it was finished all the Hibernians and giants crowded inside.* Bran bent his head to pass through the doorway and gazed round in astonishment, as one who had never seen the inside of a building before. Peace-terms were agreed, wine was drunk and nurses brought the child Gwern to be crowned king of the two united countries. At once the trouble-maker Evnissyen, furious at being allowed no part in the ceremony, jumped up, snatched the little boy and threw him on the fire, where he burned to death.

There was pandemonium. Everyone drew their weapons, and soon the ground swam with blood. Bran stood up, lifted the roof of the house from the walls and tossed it away like matchwood, and roared till the ground shook. He began trampling the Hibernians, and they died like flies. Mallolwych ran to the room where the cauldron of rebirth stood, and he and his men began cramming dead bodies into it and stoking the fire, working desperately to bring their soldiers back to life. When Evnissyen saw what they were doing, he foolishly decided to try to damp the flames with his own body. He lay down in a pile of corpses, and Mallolwych's men tossed him into the cauldron with the others. As soon as Evnissyen felt the first touch of the scalding water, he flung out his arms and legs with such force that he split the cauldron into pieces. The water and the corpses spilled on the ground; the Hibernians' hopes of rebirth were gone.

So, thanks to Evnissyen's unexpected help, the giants won the fight in the end. But there were only eight survivors, Bran, Branwen and seven mortals – and when Branwen saw the slaughter her marriage had caused, and thought about her poor charred baby Gwern, her heart broke for misery and she died. Bran said to his followers, 'We must take care that nothing like this ever happens again. Cut off my head, take it back to Cambria and plant it on White Rock Cliff. So long as it looks out across the water, no fleet will ever invade our land again.' Sadly the men did as he asked. They transported the enormous head from Hibernia, planted it as Bran had ordered, and it kept watch for invaders for generations.**

Manawydan

When neither Branwen nor Bran came back alive from Hibernia, their giant brother Manawydan was broken-hearted. He asked his friend Pryderi, prince of Dyfed, what to do, and Pryderi said that what he needed was a wife and kingdom of his own. He said that if Pryderi's mother, Rhiannon, was willing to marry Manawydan, he, Pryderi, would share his kingdom of Dyfed with them as a wedding-present. So it was arranged, and the four rulers, Manawydan, Rhiannon, Pryderi and Pryderi's wife Kigva, feasted, hunted and enjoyed themselves for a whole happy year. Then, one evening when they were watching the sunset from a hilltop beside Arberth, instead of the sun settling slowly in a bed of rosy clouds, darkness snapped down like a slamming lid. By dawn the next day the entire countryside was empty. There were no birds or insects, no animals, no people in the villages, no soldiers or servants in Arberth Castle. The buildings stood untouched, but Manawydan, Rhiannon, Pryderi and Kigva were the only four beings visible north, south, east or west.

'What's the point of staying?' said Manawydan. 'With no beasts in the fields, no game in the woods, no fish in the rivers, we'll starve to death.'

'We'll go to Albion,' said Pryderi. 'We'll set up a business there, and live on that.'

They went to Hereford in Albion, and set up a business making saddles. Manawydan taught Pryderi the skill of colouring the leather with azure chalk in a way no other leather-worker in Hereford could match, and soon no one bought saddles from anyone else in Hereford, and the other saddle-makers began gathering round Manawydan's and Pryderi's shop, throwing stones and shouting threats.

'Let me go out and kill them,' growled Manawydan.

'No,' said Pryderi. 'We're kings, not criminals. We'll start a new business somewhere else.'

They went to Worcester, and set up in business making leather shields. But the same thing happened: as soon as people saw the azure finish on the leather, they wanted no one else's shields, and the other shield-makers started throwing stones at Manawydan and Pryderi and shouting threats. They went to Gloucester and started making shoes with worked-leather uppers, azure straps and gold buckles, and although they gave work to the goldsmiths who made the buckles, they put every other shoemaker out of business and were faced with stones and threats exactly as before.

'I keep asking you to let me kill them,' said Manawydan.

'No,' said Pryderi. We'll go home to Dyfed, and see how things are there.'

They went back to Dyfed, and found that although there were still no people, the woods were stocked with game and the rivers with fish, as they had been before the mysterious darkness. They set about hunting, trapping and angling, and Pryderi's shape-changing skills and Manawydan's giant's stealth made them experts at it. Then one day, after a year of this, Pryderi had taken the shape of a wolf-hound and was stalking a wild boar when the boar ran into a deserted castle and disappeared. When Pryderi followed, he found a fountain with a carved marble rim in the courtyard, and hanging above it was a golden bowl, flashing and glowing as if it held the rays of the sun itself. Pryderi changed back to human shape, stood on the marble rim and stretched up to touch the bowl – and at once he stuck there, stretched tight like a man on the rack, and his voice locked in his throat before he could say a word.

That evening, when Pryderi failed to come home, Manawydan was all for crashing through the woods to look for him. But Rhiannon said, 'Let me go. A shape-changer will travel twice as fast and see twice as far.' She changed into a barn-owl and flew over the countryside till she saw the castle and Pryderi suspended in the courtyard. And when she changed back to human shape, stood on the marble rim and tried to tug him free, she too stuck fast, and her voice locked in her throat before she could say a word.

'Now what shall we do?' said Manawydan to Kigva. 'Without Rhiannon my wife and Pryderi my friend, I've no heart left for living here.'

'Harvest the cornfields,' said Kigva. 'When that's done, we'll try our luck in Albion again.'

'I'll start with West Field,' said Manawydan. But he found nothing in West Field but naked stalks: every corn-ear had been broken off and stolen. He moved on to North Field and South Field and found the same thing there. 'There's nothing for it,' he thought. 'I'd better sit in East Field all night, and guard that crop.'

He sat on guard all night by the nodding grain-heads of East Field, and at dawn next morning, as if the rising of the sun was a signal, a horde of mice appeared from nowhere and swarmed over the corn. Each mouse swung on a corn-head, nibbled the ear away, then scampered off leaving nothing but the stalk. Manawydan jumped about trying to trap the mice. But they were too quick for him, and the only one he caught was a pregnant female, heavier and slower than the others. He put her inside his purse, pulled the string tight and took her home.

'What have you there?' asked Kigva.

'A corn-thief: one that must pay the price.'

'Hanging! You're a king, Manawydan. What king goes about hanging mice?'

'Robbery was the crime and hanging's the punishment,' said Manawydan. But to spare Kigva's feelings, he took the mouse to the hilltop beside Arberth, and built a gallows by propping a wooden spoon on two kitchen forks. He was testing the balance when a priest came by, the first human being seen in Dyfed since the mysterious darkness years before.

'In God's name, spare that mouse,' said the priest. 'What sin can a mouse commit against a king?'

'Never mind,' said Manawydan. 'I know the sin, and I know the punishment.'

The priest went on his way, and Manawydan was lifting the mouse out of his purse to string it up, when a bishop came by in full regalia.

'My son, I beg you, spare that sinner's life,' he said.

'I'm sorry: no,' said Manawydan.

The bishop went on his way, and Manawydan carried on with his work, and was knotting a string round the mouse's neck when an archbishop rode by on a donkey, with a dozen choirboys trotting at his side.

'Manawydan, spare that mouse and I'll give you a horse for it.'

'No.'

'A thousand horses.'

'No.'

'All the horses in all the lands between this hilltop and the sea.'

Manawydan realised that he was dealing not with priests, bishops or archbishops but with a wizard. He looked the stranger squarely in the eye and said, 'I'll set the mouse free in exchange for Pryderi, Rhiannon, and all the people of Dyfed you enchanted.'

'Anything. Only please release that mouse.'

'First, promise that everything will be as it was, and that there will be no more spells.'

'I promise,' said the wizard, and Manawydan unfastened the string from the mouse's neck and let it go. As soon as its feet touched the ground it changed into a beautiful, pregnant woman, and the archbishop changed into Llywd the Grey, king of shadows. He had stolen Pryderi and Rhiannon and bewitched their people to pay back the trick Pryderi's father Pwyll had long ago played on Gwawl the Sun-prince, when he hung him up in a fishing-net and beat him till he gave up his marriage to Rhiannon.

So Rhiannon and Pryderi were freed from enchantment, and found themselves at home in Arberth, quite unharmed. And all the mice which had gnawed the cornstalks scampered after them and turned back into human beings, the villagers and farmers snatched from Dyfed long ago. Tht night Manawydan, Rhiannon, Pryderi and Kigva gave a party, and the noise of celebration was so loud that it spread as far as Hereford, Worcester and Shrewsbury, and all the saddlemakers, shield-makers and shoemakers there turned over in their beds and muttered, 'Will those creatures never give us peace?'

Math, Gwydyon and Lleu

HUMAN FOOTSTOOLS

Most people are safer at home than on the battlefield. But it was exactly the opposite for Math, prince of Gwynedd. When he went to war he was perfectly safe, but when he sat peacefully at home he had to keep one foot forever touching a girl who had never slept with a man: if he lost contact even for a second, the slightest accident (a fly landing on his hand, a speck of dust in his eye) could kill him. His human footstool was a girl called Goewin. She came to him when she was eight years old, and kept him safe for seven years until she was fifteen. Because living with one foot on a girl made travelling difficult, Math stayed at home all this time, and his nephews Gilvaethwy and Gwydyon ran his kingdom.

One day when Gilvaethwy and Gwydyon were drinking beer in the castle hall, Gwydyon noticed his brother gazing at Goewin and sighing like a bellows, and guessed that he was in love with her. 'If you want her that badly,' he said, 'why don't you make love with her?'

'How can I make love with her, when Math keeps one foot on her day and night?' said Gilvaethwy.

'Leave it to me,' said Gwydyon. But instead of tricking Math directly, he called for his horse and went to visit Pryderi, prince of Dyfed. Pryderi had just been given a present, the first herd of pigs ever seen in Cambria, and Gwydyon said coaxingly, 'My lord, what will you take to part with them?'

'What have you got?' said Pryderi.

Gwydyon took Pryderi to a clearing, where the night before he had laid out twelve branches, twelve rope's ends, twelve toadstools and twelve candle-stumps tied with yellow wool, and the branches had turned into racehorses, the ropes' ends into bridles, the toadstools into warships, the candle-stumps into greyhounds and the wool into leashes of yellow gold. 'Are these a fair exchange?' asked Gwydyon, and when Pryderi eagerly agreed he rounded up the pigs and galloped them to Gwynedd like stampeding cattle. When his men asked what the hurry was, he said, 'I don't want to be anywhere near Dyfed tomorrow morning, when those presents of mine turn back to branches, candles and toadstools,' and next morning he put his ear to the ground, jumped up cheerfully and said, 'They're after us!'

So war began between Dyfed and Gwynedd over a herd of pigs, and

Math was forced to lift his foot from Goewin, put on his armour and go to fight. On the first night he was away Gilvaethwy and Gwydyon broke into his bedroom and raped Goewin, and as soon as they were gone she fled in shame from Math's castle and never went back.

Gilvaethwy, Gwydyon and Math fought the men of Dyfed up hill and down dale for seven weeks, and the fighting only ended when Gwydyon challenged Pryderi to a single-handed magic contest, enchanter against shape-changer, and the soldiers on both sides dropped their weapons and went to watch. Gwydyon stirred up a whirlwind against Pryderi, and Pryderi changed into a sapling and bent before it; Gwydyon split the earth to uproot him, and Pryderi changed into a hawk and soared overhead; Gwydyon hurled a fireball to scorch him, and Pryderi turned into a dragon, gulped the fire and swooped to earth; Gwydyon opened up a lake of standing water, and dragon-Pryderi plummeted into it in a cloud of hissing steam, and only saved his life by changing into a salmon and darting upstream before Gwydyon could drain the lake and leave him high and dry. That was the end of the contest: Pryderi had vanished, and his generals gloomily disbanded their army and called off the war.

As soon as the fighting was over, Math had to hurry home and put his feet on a girl immediately, or die. His servants told him how Gilvaethwy and Gwydyon had raped Goewin, and Math, resting his feet on his chimney-sweep's five-year-old daughter, waved aside their excuses and announced their punishment. He turned them into a stag and a hind, and made them roam the woods till they produced a fawn, then into a boar and sow till they produced a piglet, and finally into a wolf and a she-wolf till they produced a cub. The shame of having to mate with his own brother and produce animal offspring was too much for Gilvaethwy: he hurried into exile as soon as his human shape returned. But Gwydyon stayed at court, and in time became Math's loyal friend and adviser once again.

LLEU

After a while, Math began looking for a new human footstool to replace the chimney-sweep's sooty daughter, and Aranrhod, Gwydyon's sister, presented herself. She claimed that she had never in her life made love with a man. But Math held out his magic wand and told her to jump over it, and when she lifted her skirt a baby fell out on the floor, with a drop of blood which Gwydyon gathered in a silk handkerchief and put in his pocket. Aranrhod left the court in a fury, Math kept his feet on the chimney-sweep's daughter, and Gwydyon shut the handkerchief in a box in his room, went to bed and thought no more about it. In the middle of the night the box-lid opened and a tiny child crawled out, still wrapped in the handkerchief which Aranrhod's blood had stained. Gwydyon was so delighted with him that he decided to bring him up as his own son.*

The boy grew twice as quickly as any human child. By the time he was four he could out-ride, out-run, out-swim and out-shoot any eight-year-old in the castle. On his fifth birthday Gwydyon took him to Aranrhod's castle, told her the story of his birth and asked her to choose a name for him. Aranrhod was furious. 'What has he to do with me?' she raged. 'How can he have been born from a drop of my blood? He's a bastard of your own – and he'll get no name from me!'

Gwydyon said nothing, but left the castle and took the boy for a walk along the beach. They came to a heap of seaweed, out of sight of the castle, and Gwydyon sat down crosslegged beside it and told the boy to do the same. He changed the pair of them into shoemakers, changed the seaweed into leather and showed the boy how to cut it and stitch it into shoes. When the shoes were finished Gwydyon made a driftwood boat, and he and his son sailed round the headland into town. People flocked to buy the miraculous shoes, and Aranrhod herself came down from the castle to buy a pair. While Gwydyon fussed about, measuring her shoesize, the boy made a sling of waste leather and fired a pebble so skilfully that it sent a wren spinning from its perch on the boat's side.

'What a clever child,' said Aranrhod admiringly. 'How pleased you must be to have a son so bright.'

As soon as the word Lleu ('bright') left her lips, Gwydyon changed the shoes back to seaweed, the boat back to driftwood, and himself and the boy back to their proper shapes. 'You've named your son,' he said to Aranrhod. 'Lleu you called him, and Lleu he'll be.'

'He'll also be cursed,' she answered. 'He'll never be armed unless his own mother arms him, and he'll have to fight his enemies bare-handed.'

Gwydyon looked after Lleu until he was nine years old, and as full-grown and strong as a young man twice his age. Then he said, 'Time to visit your mother again,' and the two of them walked to Aranrhod's castle, this time disguised as musicians, men of peace. They played and sang for Aranrhod, and she paid them with gold and begged them

169

to stay the night. As soon as it was dark, Gwydyon used his magic to fill the air round the castle with the shouts and trumpet-calls of a gathering army, and at dawn, when Aranrhod's guards looked out, he turned the sea to a forest of invading ships. 'Every man in the castle must help to defend it,' said Gwydyon. 'Arm us, lady, and we'll lay aside our music and fight for you.' But as soon as Aranrhod finished arming Lleu with her own hands from head to toe, Gwydyon snapped his fingers and turned the army to wind-blown leaves, the forest of ships to sea-shells, and himself and Lleu back to their proper shapes. 'You've armed your son,' he said to Aranrhod. 'Now he'll fight fully-armed forever.'

'Maybe so,' said Aranrhod. 'But he'll be cursed forever, too. No woman will ever marry him, from any race of beings on earth, and this curse will last as long as he lives.'

THE MAGIC BRIDE

Gwydyon took Lleu home, and looked after him until he was fifteen years old, when he looked like a man of thirty, well past marrying age. Then he went to ask Math's advice. 'It's simple,' said Math. 'If no woman will marry him, from any race of beings on earth, we'll make him a wife by magic.' He called for oak-leaves, broom and meadow-sweet, fashioned them into a girl and called her Blodeuedd (Flowers). Then he gave Lleu a castle and lands to rule, and the young couple settled down to married life.

For as long as fresh-picked flowers keep their perfume, Blodeuedd kept her love for Lleu. But just as perfume fades and dies, so her love fell away, and she found a mortal lover called Goronwy, and plotted with him to kill Lleu and steal his lands. Lleu was a magic being, grandson of the sea, and he could never be killed so long as he kept one foot on land or in water; so Blodeuedd waited until he was stepping into his bath, and then, when he had one foot on a stool and the other in the air, she let Goronwy in, Goronwy fired a poison-arrow and the head snapped off in Lleu's thigh. With a shriek of pain Lleu changed into an eagle and soared away, to roost on cliffs and treetops till the poison took effect and his death-day came.

After a while, word reached Gwydyon that there was a new, mortal prince in Lleu's castle, and he disguised himself as a beggar and went to see for himself. He lodged with Lleu's old swineherd, and next morning, when the man drove his pigs to pasture, he was astonished to see one of the sows run out of the sty, swift as a greyhound, and disappear into the woods.

'She does the same thing every day,' the swineheard said. 'She must have a secret food-hoard, hidden in the hills.'

As soon as Gwydyon heard the word 'hills', he changed into a hawk and soared to find the sow. She was feeding, high in the hills, on scraps of maggoty meat at the foot of a tree beside a stream, and on the topmost branch was an eagle, sick and swaying, with flesh-flakes peeling from it like onion-skins. Gwydyon changed back to his own shape, sang a spell to charm the eagle from the tree, and as it landed in his arms changed it back to Lleu. He carried the sick man home to Math's castle, and in seven weeks Math's doctors found an antidote for the poison and nursed Lleu back to health.

As soon as Lleu recovered, he, Math and Gwydyon went to punish Blodeuedd and Goronwy. They changed Blodeuedd from a flower-woman to a bird with a round, flower-petal face, and banished her from daylight, letting her feed only at night out of sight of other birds. She was the first owl ever seen in the world, and Blodeuedd has been a Welsh name for 'owl' ever since. As for Goronwy, Lleu challenged him to a duel to the death, and they positioned themselves on each side of a fast-flowing stream and aimed their spears. Goronwy planned to stab Lleu with his spear as he was jumping across the stream, and so had no protective foothold in water or on land. But Lleu stabbed first, and his spear-thrust spreadeagled Goronwy's body against a rock and pinned him there. Lleu buried the corpse, left the spear-stuck rock by the stream as a memorial, and went peaceably home to rule his lands. But in the years that followed his mother's curse prevented him from marrying, and in the end he grew bored with the mortal world and went to live with his grandfather the Sea. He became the brightness of wave-tips, and we still see him today as white horses, scudding over the ocean's surface and galloping to land.

19

ENGLISH STORIES

Golden apples

THE MAGIC CASTLE

An old, sick lord told his three sons that his only hope of survival was to hold the golden apples of immortality, and asked them to ride to the three corners of the world to find them. The two older brothers jumped on their horses and rode away. But they knew that as soon as their father died all his money would be theirs, and instead of searching for the golden apples they went to a town where no one knew them and set about enjoying themselves. As for Jack, the youngest son, he rode alone over hill, dales, valleys and mountains, through woolly woods and shaggy sheepwalks, till he came to a cottage on the edge of the forest, with an old man rocking on the porch. The old man's hair was so long that it covered his shoulders like a shawl; his skin was so wrinkled that it hung from his face like pouches; his voice was a whisper of dry, dead leaves.

'Come in, young man, and welcome. Rest here tonight, and tomorrow I'll give you a fresh horse and see you on your way. But whatever you do, lie straight in your bed tonight. There will come blindworms and vipers, trying to lie in your lips and snuggle in your ears, and if you move so much as a hair you'll turn into one yourself.'

Jack went to bed, and lay straight all night despite the horror of the creatures sliding over his lips and ears. Next morning after breakfast the old man gave him a black horse and a ball of black yarn and told him to fling the yarn over the horse's ears and follow it. Jack did as he was told, and the horse galloped so that the wind behind could not catch the wind before, until it came to a second cottage by a second wood, with a second old man rocking on the porch. The old man's hair covered him from head to toe like a blanket; his skin hung from his face like knapsacks; his voice was the rattle of corn inside the husk.

'Come in, young man, and welcome. Rest here tonight, and tomorrow I'll give you a fresh horse and see you on your way. But whatever you do, lie straight in your bed tonight. There will come spiders and scorpions, trying to force up your fingernails and sting your eyes, and if you move so much as a hair you'll turn into one yourself.'

Jack went to bed, and lay straight all night despite the terror of the creatures scrabbling at his nails and eyes. Next morning after breakfast the old man gave him a silver-grey horse and a ball of silver yarn to fling over its ears, and it galloped so that the wind behind could not catch the wind before, until it came to a third cottage by a deep, still lake, with a third old man rocking on the porch. The old man's eyelids hung down like shutters; his fingernails curled like ram's-horns to his elbows and his toenails to his knees; his voice was a rustle of mouse-paws on mossy paths.

'Be quick, young man! The Castle of the Golden Apples sleeps for one hour only, in the middle of the day. Go to the lakeside, ride the swans to the island, run through the castle and pick the apples without delay. Whatever you see, hurry past: if you stop more than once you'll fall into an enchanted sleep yourself.'

He took a goosequill pipe from his sleeve, and at its sound three swans swam to the lake-shore and carried Jack to the island where the Castle of the Golden Apples lay. Four giants guarded the shore, with boar's-tusk fangs and spears like trees; but they lay in a heap in an enchanted sleep, and Jack picked his way between them to the castle gate. The gate was guarded by dragons, basilisks and fireworms, whose breath charred the ground as they snored; Jack picked his way among them and ran through the echoing courts to the kitchen. On the floor, tumbled in sleep, were cooks, scullions and kitchen-maids, and knives, bowls, whisks and rolling-pins lay unattended on the tables. Jack hurried into the orchard, picked three golden apples and ran quickly back. But this time he found a spiral stone staircase beside the kitchen door, and ran up to it to explore the rest of the castle. He found footmen asleep in the hallways, minstrels snoozing in their galleries, lady's-maids dozing over their sewing, and in a bedroom, fast asleep on a golden bed, a beautiful girl in a blue velvet dress. 'One stop!' thought Jack. 'If I stop more than once, I fall into an enchanted sleep myself.' He bent to kiss the girl, and in the same movement slipped a ring from his finger on to hers; then, before she could stir or wake he ran down the stairs, past the fire-breathers at the gates, past the snoring giants and back to the lakeside where the swans were waiting. He set his feet on two of the swans' backs and took hold of the third swan's upstretched wings for balance. As he did so one of the golden apples rolled out of his pocket to the ground – and the sound of it woke all the dragons, basilisks and fireworms and sent them roaring after him. If he had not had his feet over water instead of land, they would have caught him where he stood and finished him.

THE BROTHERS

Jack took his two golden apples to show the old man with the ram's-horn fingernails and toenails, and the old man said. 'You've done well. Before you go, please pay me my reward. Cut off my head and throw it in the well.'

'What sort of reward is that?'

'Do it: you'll see what sort it is.'

Reluctantly Jack drew his sword and cut off the old man's head. As soon as he threw it into the well the cottage changed into a bustling inn, the garden changed into rolling water-meadows and the old man changed into an acrobat cartwheeling across the grass. Jack left him entertaining the guests at the inn, galloped back to the second old man's cottage and showed him the golden apples. The old man asked for the same reward, and when Jack cut off his head he turned into a sword-swallower, gulping knives and munching fire. Jack rode to the first old man and gave him the same reward, and the old man turned into a conjurer, pulling coloured flags from his mouth and pigeons from his sleeves. Jack left him where he was, saddled his own horse in the stable and rode to the town where his two wicked brothers were carousing. And that night while he slept his brothers stole into the bedroom, put two mouldy apples in his pocket and galloped off with the golden apples to cure their father.

Next morning when Jack rode up to his father's castle he was surprised to hear bells pealing and people cheering, and amazed when his father met him at the gates, as hearty as if he'd never had a moment's illness in his life. The old lord hurried Jack into the hall to hear his adventures. But when Jack took the wrinkled, mouldy apples out of his pocket, his brothers ran from the shadows with soldiers, accused him of plotting to poison their father and arrested him. The old lord's eyes filled with tears, for he loved Jack best of all his sons. But the accusation was made and Jack's guilt seemed clear. He summoned his executioner and told him to take Jack to the woods outside the castle and cut off his head.

For all the executioner's terrible trade, he was a kindly man with children of his own. While he was bundling Jack into the execution-cart, loading his axe and driving out of the castle gates he put on a show of frowning ferocity, but as soon as they were out of sight of the castle he lifted the blindfold from Jack's eyes, cut his ropes and said, 'Jump out and clear off. I'll think up some story to explain it.' Jack jumped gratefully out of the cart, and as soon as his feet touched the ground a bear ran out of the woods, gathered him in its arms and gave the executioner exactly the story he was looking for. He whipped his horse and galloped pell-mell back to the castle, and the bear nuzzled Jack's neck and said, 'Lie straight, young man, and fear nothing. You're safe with me.' Jack lay straight and quiet, and the bear carried him to a clearing in the woods where the sword-swallower and the conjurer were waiting. The bear put Jack down, pulled off its own head and revealed itself as the third magic old man, cartwheeling round the clearing in a bearskin and carolling, 'You're safe with us! You're safe with us!'*

Jack stayed for weeks with the three magic brothers in the woods, learning the skills of tumbling, sword-swallowing and conjuring, and all the while his heart ached for the girl he'd kissed in the Castle of the Golden Apples, and he rubbed the place on his finger where the ring had been, and sighed. Then, one day, the girl herself rode to Jack's father's castle at the head of a prancing procession, told the old lord that she meant to marry the boy who'd kissed her, and asked to see the old lord's sons. Jack's eldest brother swaggered forward.

'Was it you who kissed me?' asked the girl.

'Of course it was.'

She took the ring from her finger and asked him to try it on – and as soon as it touched the skin of his ring-finger it grew to the size of a barrel-hoop and slipped over his arm, his head and his whole body while the castle servants put their hands to their faces to hide their glee. The second brother stepped forward, and the ring shrank on his finger-end till it would hardly have circled a sparrow's leg, while the servants stuffed their mouths with their sleeves to hide their glee.

'Have you no other sons?' the girl asked the old lord. 'I had a son called Jack,' he began sadly – and before the words were out of his mouth Jack and the three magic brothers ran into the hall, cartwheeling, stilt-walking and sword-swallowing while Jack's father gaped and his wicked brothers hid in the shadows and glowered with rage.

'Was it you who kissed me?' asked the girl.

'Of course it was,' said Jack – and when he tried on the ring it fitted perfectly. The girl linked her arm in his and led him where her pageboys were prancing in procession.* They rode to the Castle of the Golden Apples, with the three magic brothers stilt-walking, swordswallowing and cartwheeling beside them, and were never seen in those parts again.

The Black Bull

THE THREE DAUGHTERS

A poor washerwoman had three daughters, and nothing to give them but her skill in washing clothes. One day the eldest daughter said, 'Mother, bake me buns and boil me beef, for I'm going to seek my fortune.' She took the food in a basket, walked all night and walked all day, and at evening came to the house of a witch and her daughter beside the wood.

'If it's your fortune you're seeking,' said the witch, 'stay here by the window and watch. You'll know it when it comes.'

The girl gazed out of the window all the first day and all the second day, and saw nothing. On the third day a carriage drew up at the gate, with a coachman, four prancing horses and two liveried footmen. 'My fortune's here. Goodbye!' shouted the girl, and drove off in the carriage while the witch's daughter watched from the shadows with envy in her eyes.

The washerwoman's first daughter was never seen in those parts again. Some time after she disappeared, the second daughter said, 'Mother, cut me cake and slice me sausage, for I'm going to seek my fortune.' She walked all night and walked all day, and at evening came to the same witch's house beside the wood. For three days, as the witch instructed her, she gazed out of the window and saw nothing, but on the fourth day a carriage drew up at the gate, with a coachman, six prancing horses and four liveried footmen, and she drove away while the witch's daughter watched from the shadows with envy in her eyes.

The washerwoman's second daughter was never seen in those parts again. Soon after she disappeared the youngest daughter, Meg, said, 'Mother, please butter me bread and choose me cheese, for I'm going to seek my fortune.' She went to the witch's house beside the wood, and for a week of days looked out, as the witch instructed her, and saw nothing. Then, on the first day of the second week, the Black Bull of Norroway lumbered down the road, and the witch said 'There you are. You came to seek your fortune, and there it is.' She bundled terrified Meg on the bull's broad back, and she and her daughter watched them leave with malice in their eyes.

The bull carried Meg all day, all night, until they came in sight of a grey-green castle in a river-valley. 'This is my first brother's house,' he said, 'and it's here we must stay tonight.' The people of the castle helped Meg from the bull's back, turned the bull loose into a clover-field, and gave her a magnificent banquet and a goosefeather bed to pass the night. Next morning, as she was climbing on the bull's back ready to ride, they gave her a grey-green apple, sweet-scented and unblemished, and said, 'Don't cut it till you're in the first great need of your life.'

The bull carried Meg all day, all night, all day, to a yellow castle beside a stream. 'This is my second brother's house,' he said, 'and it's here we must stay tonight.' The people of the castle entertained Meg exactly as before, and in the morning gave her a sweet-scented, unblemished pear and told her not to cut it till she was in the second great need of her life. The third castle was purple-velvet, and this time Meg's gift was a sweet-scented, unblemished plum and her advice was to save it until she was in the third great need of her life.

Soon after they left the third castle, Meg and the bull passed into a dark valley overhung with cliffs, and there was no daylight. The bull set Meg down by a rock and said, 'Wait here. Unless I fight and kill the Guardian of Glass Valley, we'll never get out of here alive. Sit on this rock, and if everything turns blue and sunny, you'll know I've won; if everything turns blood-red, you'll know I've lost. Above all, don't move. If you alter your position even by a hair, I'll never be able to find you here again.'

Meg sat on the rock and waited. After a while the sun began to shine in a blue sky, the cliffs round her and the ground underfoot turned blue, and she knew that the bull had won his fight. She was so overjoyed that she lifted one foot and crossed it over the other, and the result was that when the bull lumbered back up the valley, his black coat spotted with blood from the battle, though she could see him

177

perfectly, he neither noticed her sitting there nor heard her cries, and never saw or spoke to her again.

THE THREE GREAT NEEDS

Heartbroken, Meg got up to walk on her way. At once her feet began slipping and sliding, and she found that the rock underfoot and the rock-walls behind her had turned to mirror-smooth, ice-slippery glass. The Guardian of Glass Valley might be dead, but the Valley still remained, and she was trapped like a spider in a bowl: the more she scrambled up the sides, the more she slithered back, bleeding and exhausted. At last there was nothing for it but to crawl on hands and knees round the edge of Glass Valley, looking for a way out. For days she found nothing and saw no one, and she wondered if this was the first great need of her life, and if it was time to cut open the apple the bull's first brother had given her. But before she had need of that, she came to a blacksmith's forge on the valley floor, with the glass walls rearing like a glacier behind it, and sobbed out her story. 'Is that all?' said the smith. 'Work for me, seven years without complaining, pumping the bellows and holding the tongs, and I'll make a pair of iron shoes to help you out.'

For seven years Meg pumped the bellows and held the tongs, and though her brain swam and her cheeks baked in the heat of the furnace, she never once complained. At the end of seven years the smith made her a pair of iron shoes set with spikes, and since he knew no other way of fastening them, nailed them to her feet. She clambered and groped her way up the smooth sides of Glass Valley, and every step meant agony; at last she climbed over the rim, staggered out and crawled back to the cottage of the witch and her daughter and begged for shelter.

'It's a good thing you're here,' said the witch. 'Last night the prince of Norroway left a suit of clothes for cleaning, black leather spotted and stained with blood, and whoever can clean them is to be his wife. I've tried and my daughter's tried, and the stains sink in ever deeper. You're a washerwoman's daughter: you can earn your keep by cleaning them.'

Meg dragged herself to the cleaning-stones on her rags of feet, laid the leather clothes flat and began rubbing them with a wash-leather, as her mother had taught her long ago, to clean off the blood. As soon as the wash-leather touched them the blood-stains vanished, the leather shone, and Meg's feet healed as if they'd never known a moment's injury. She ran back to the cottage with the clothes over her arm, and the witch snatched them and cackled, 'Thank you, my dear. You've made my daughter's fortune,' and locked her in the attic in case she saw the Prince of Norroway or spoke to him. That night the prince came to fetch his clothes, the witch's daughter smiled a gap-toothed smile and told him she'd scrubbed and struggled to get them clean, and he had no choice but to agree to marry her in three days' time.

That night, alone in the attic, Meg remembered the apple she'd been given in the first brother's castle of the Black Bull of Norroway. This was certainly the first great need of her life. She cut the apple in two, and instead of pips it was filled with pearls. She called to the witch's daughter and said, 'Let me sing outside the prince's door tonight, and these pearls are yours.'

'Done!' said the daughter. But she ran straight to her mother, and her mother gave the prince a sleeping-potion in a wine-cup. That night, Meg sat outside his door and sang,

> 'Seven years I served for thee;
> Glass Hill I climbed for thee;
> Thy clothes I washed for thee;
> Wake up and turn to me.'

But the sleeping-potion clogged his ears so that he heard not a single word, and by the time he called for his breakfast next morning Meg was locked in her attic again and nowhere to be seen. It was the second great need of her life, and she sliced open the pear she'd been given in the second brother's castle of the Black Bull of Norroway. Its core was of twisted gold. She called to the witch's daughter and said, 'Let me sing another night outside the prince's door, and this gold is yours.'

'Done!' said the daughter. But once again she ran straight to her mother, and once again the witch gave the prince a sleeping-potion in a wine-cup. All night long Meg sat outside his door and sang,

> 'Seven years I served for thee;
> Glass Hill I climbed for thee;
> Thy clothes I washed for thee;
> Wake up and turn to me.'

But the sleeping potion clogged his ears as before, and by the time he

179

called for his breakfast next morning, Meg was locked in her attic and nowhere to be seen. It was the third great need of her life, and when she cut open the plum she found instead of a stone a diamond quarried from Glass Valley, as big as a pigeon's egg. 'Let me sing one last night outside the prince's door,' she said to the witch's daughter, 'and take this stone for your wedding-crown.'

'Done!' said the witch's daughter, and her mother prepared a sleeping-potion as before. But just as the prince was lifting it to his lips, he heard a faint lowing of cattle from the meadow outside his window, as if the bull's three brothers were calling him, got up to look, knocked the wine-cup over and spilled the wine. He went to bed, thinking nothing of it, and had hardly slept five minutes when he heard Meg singing outside his door,

> 'Seven years I served for thee;
> Glass Hill I climbed for thee;
> Thy clothes I washed for thee;
> Wake up and turn to me.'

The prince ran and opened the door, and Meg fell into her true-love's arms. They were married next morning, and every bell in Norroway pealed in celebration. As for the witch and her daughter, they sat down to comfort themselves by counting out the pearls, gold and diamond they had cheated out of Meg, and found nothing in their hands but apple-pips, a pear-core and a plum-stone. Shrieking with rage, they galloped like maddened cattle to the edge of the meadow, tumbled over the rim of Glass Valley and never troubled the mortal world again.

The bogles and the moon

The moon was forever hearing tales of what went on in swamp-country when her back was turned. In the end she decided to go down and see for herself. At the end of the month, leaving a single sliver of light in the sky, she wrapped herself in a black cloud-cloak, pulled the hood over her gleaming silver hair and slipped down to earth.

The place she choose was muddy and slippery. The path was bordered by clumps of reeds and grass, and on each side wide pools, dark and fathomless, rippled in the breeze. It was pitch dark. The only light was a shimmer from the moon's own silver shoes, a glow as faint as candle-flame in the howling dark. As the moon picked her way along, dim night-creatures, owls, bats and furry moths, fluttered past, and she could hear the bogles' eerie wailing and see their will-o'-the-wisps dancing in the misty fields. Every so often, when the moon's foot went too near the edge of the narrow path, bony fingers reached quickly up from the water's depths: the bogles were alert for prey.

At first, nothing could catch the moon. Her tread was as light as gossamer: she stepped nimbly, easily, from tussock to tussock; the bogles snatched in vain.

Then the moon's silver shoe slipped on a stone. She took hold of a handful of reeds to steady herself, and at once they coiled round her wrist and held her fast. More and more reeds snaked out of the darkness, till the moon was a prisoner, trapped and shivering.

All at once in the distance she heard the thin sound of a human voice, calling for help. A man was lost in the swamps, splashing past the pools and puddles, writhing clear of the bogles' clutching hands, sobbing desperately for help. The moon knew that unless the man had light to find his path, he would soon be bogles' meat. She shook the hood clear of her head, and let her silver hair stream down her back. In its sudden light the man saw firm land ahead of him, jumped thankfully on to the path and ran safely home. But the same silver light attracted bogles from all the surrounding swamps. Shielding their eyes against the light, they clustered round the moon and tied her even tighter, covering her with reeds and stones till every glimmer of her light was gone. Now there was no hope for creatures lost in the swamps at night. Without light, everything that passed was doomed. Cackling and whooping, the bogles slithered back to their oozy dens to wait.

At first, the people who lived in the swamp-village thought nothing was wrong. At the beginning of each new month, it was always dark; the moon always took days to show herself. But as the weeks passed, each night as dark as the last, the swamp-bogles grew hungrier and bolder. They took to prowling outside the windows of the houses, so that people had to bolt their doors, stay awake all night, and build roaring fires to keep the evil things at bay.

For two months this was how things were. The villagers were in despair. Then, one night, sitting with his cronies round the fire in the village inn, a farmer suddenly slapped his thigh and said, 'Of course! That must have been the moon who saved me, that night when I was

181

lost in the swamp. I saw a shining and I found my path; but I never thought till now that it was the moon. She's the bogles' prisoner – and I know where she is.'

Everyone ran for lanterns, pitchforks and scythes. A crowd surged down the village street, waving lights and jeering at the bogles to show how brave they were. Then, at the edge of the village, they stopped so suddenly that those at the back fell cursing into those in front. The village wise woman, a toothless crone everyone took for a witch, was standing there, a guttering candle in one hand and a bony finger held up to her withered lips. 'Shh!' she hissed. 'You'll not scare bogles with yells and scythes. Cover your lanterns and feel your way through the swamp with sticks. Put a pebble under your tongue, each one of you, to stop you whispering and letting the bogles know where you are.'

They did as she said. A straggly line of men poked and picked its way along the paths between the swamp-pools. Many of them were sure they were walking into bogles' larders: they cast fearful eyes into the dark on either side, and muttered prayers for safety in their hearts.

At last they came to a pile of stinking, rotting weeds, and a heap of stones like the cairns men build to mark a grave. At once they did as the wise woman had advised. They threw open their cloaks and showed their lanterns all at once, and the sudden light sent the bogles shrieking for cover. The men began prising up the stones and dragging away the reeds. Soon, from the ground below, there was the glitter of silver, and they saw the face of a woman more beautiful than any seen on earth before or since. The swamp-pools for metres round were lit as bright as day; the moon's reed-manacles slipped free of her wrists and she soared into the sky, like a dazzling beacon to light her rescuers home.

From that day to this the moon has kept a special watch on travellers in swamp-land. But she takes care never to put herself in the bogles' way again, and never ventures down to earth. She soars high out of reach in the sky, and her face is all earth-dwellers ever see.

20

SCOTTISH STORIES

Assipattle

Assipattle was the seventh son of a seventh son. All day long his father and brothers herded cattle, and in the evening they sat at the kitchen table and whittled cowhorn spoons. And all day long Assipattle lay on the ashpile by the fire with his hands behind his head, dreaming of the day when he would marry a princess and inherit a castle and lands to rule.

Assipattle's father's farm lay in the very north of the country, close to the roaring river that girds the world. And in that river, swimming like a monstrous eel against the current, lived the Stoorworm. Its eyes were lakes, its teeth were precipices, and its tail was long enough to wrap twice around the earth. When it felt hungry it heaved its head to land, flicked its tongue and began swallowing human beings like a lizard gulping flies.

The Stoorworm's favourite food was children, and every year, as soon as its head loomed over the headland, the king's soldiers of Assipattle's country trussed seven boys and seven girls like parcels, the Stoorworm flicked them into its gullet and they were never seen again. This went on until the only child left in the land was the king's own daughter, a princess just turned fourteen. The royal soothsayers advised him to truss her and leave her like all the others, but the king sat tight in his castle and set his face.

'Send messengers all round the kingdom,' he said. 'If a champion can be found to kill the Stoorworm, his reward will be my daughter's hand in marriage, and a castle and lands to rule.'

'But what if we find no champion, highness?'

'I'll fight the beast myself.'

The messengers rode out, and champions gathered from every

corner of the kingdom. At first there were three hundred and thirty-three of them, feasting and drinking at the king's expense. But as the weeks passed and the day of the contest came nearer, they grew ashen-faced with panic and slunk away; a week before the fight only thirty-three were left; three days after that there were three; two days later there were none, and the king ordered his royal boat to be moored by the shore, ready to ferry him to fight the Stoorworm, and his royal armour to be fetched from the attic and polished. 'Either it'll protect me against the worm,' he muttered, 'or it'll give me a glittering funeral.'

On the evening before the fight, Assipattle was snoozing on the ashpile when he heard his mother and father talking. 'Look out my best clothes,' his father said, 'and make sure Teetgong's saddled and bridled, as soon as it's dawn. I'm going to watch that fight.'

'How can I bridle Teetgong? You know he won't stand still for anyone but you.'

'It's easy. If you want him to stand still, you pat his right shoulder. If you want him to prance, you stroke his left ear. If you want him to gallop, you blow on that goosequill whistle in my pocket.'

As soon as everyone else was snoring, Assipattle filled a porridge-pot with embers from the fire, took the goosequill whistle from his father's pocket and crept to the stable. At first Teetgong shied and reared, but he patted its right shoulder and at once it stood quiet while he saddled and bridled it. He climbed into the saddle and stroked Teetgong's left ear, and the horse pranced out in the moonlight. The clatter of its hooves woke Assipattle's father and brothers, and they ran out cursing to catch the thief. But before they could even mount their horses, Assipattle blew the goosequill whistle and Teetgong galloped away so fast that the wind snatched Assipattle's breath and set the embers glowing in his porridge-pot.

They came to the coast, and Assipattle patted Teetgong's neck, jumped down and let him loose to pasture on the headland. Not far out to sea was a dark, green island, breathing gently: the Stoorworm's head. And bobbing in the bay beside the shore was the king's royal boat, with the royal ferryman dozing at the oars. Assipattle put the pot of embers down and began gathering driftwood and dry seaweed. The ferryman heard wood and weed, woke up and said, 'What's that you're doing?'

'Lighting a fire,' said Assipattle. 'Why not step ashore and warm yourself?'

'Don't be daft,' said the ferryman. 'Suppose someone sneaked up while I was away, and stole this boat?'

'Please yourself,' said Assipattle. He cleared the fireplace, and then suddenly began scrabbling at the earth and shouting, 'Stay away! Stay away!'

'What's the matter now?'

'Nothing! Stay away! I never even mentioned gold –'

As soon as the ferryman heard the word 'gold' he splashed out of the boat to shore and began scrabbling in the dirt of Assipattle's fireplace. And as soon as the way was clear, Assipattle snatched up his pot of embers, jumped into the boat and set sail for the Stoorworm, leaving the boatman waving his fists in the air and cursing.

All this while the sun had been rising, until its rays shone full into the Stoorworm's face and wakened it. The Stoorworm opened its jaws and yawned, and the yawn sucked a cataract of seawater into its mouth and down its throat. Assipattle set his course straight for the yawning gap, and the cataract swept him under the Stoorworm's portcullis-teeth, into its cavern-mouth and on down its gullet with a flotsam of seaweed, dead fish and ship's planking rushing along beside him. At last the boat grounded on a shelf of flesh and Assipattle threw out his anchor, hauled down his sail and splashed out to explore, carrying the pot of coals to light his path. He threaded his way along the Stoorworm's passages and tunnels like a man in a labyrinth, and at last came to the liver, hanging overhead like an enormous purple cliff. He clambered up it till he found a fold, emptied the potful of embers inside and blew on them to make them glow. The liver-oils sputtered into flame, and as soon as the Stoorworm's whole liver was sizzling like a sausage Assipattle ran back to his boat and hauled up the anchor.

He was just in time. The Stoorworm felt the fire-agony deep inside, and the pain made it writhe, retch and gulp water to quench the flames. Assipattle's boat spun like a twig in a torrent, and he clung to the mast while the whirlpool bucketed all round him. At last, with a convulsive heave, the Stoorworm opened its mouth and spewed out a flood of water that carried Assipattle, his boat, and all the children the Stoorworm had ever swallowed back to land, up the beach and on to the headland where Teetgong was feeding placidly and the ferryman was cowering in a heap with his fingers over his eyes, moaning that he was too young to die.

The Stoorworm continued to lash and writhe, snorting steam and belching fire. But the flames reached the very heart of its liver, and at

185

last, overcome by agony, it flung itself out of the sea and reached up with its tongue to snatch the moon from the sky and crush the fire. But the tongue missed its target, snapped off one of the moon's horns and sent it crashing to earth, and the Stoorworm fell with it and broke in pieces as it fell. Its tongue made a trench between the countries of Denmark and Sweden, and sea-water rushed in to fill it. The teeth from its jaws made the Shetland Isles, and its tail-splinters made the Faroes. With its dying strength the monster coiled its body into a ball, hugging its own agony, and sank like a stone to the bed of the northern sea. Even then it was so huge that its humped flesh stuck up above the surface in the shape of the country mortals call Iceland, and its liver-fires blaze underground there to this very day.

As soon as the Stoorworm's death-agony ended and the smoke cleared, Assipattle mounted Teetgong, stroked its left ear, pranced in procession with the rescued children to the king's palace and asked for the princess's hand in marriage. So his dreams for himself came true, and he ended up with a wife, a castle and lands to rule. As for his father and brothers, they set up a quarry in the place where the moon's horn fell to earth, and their moon-horn spoons were famous in those parts ever afterwards.

Loyalty

When the king of the Western Isles died, he left all his lands to his eldest son, all his wealth to his second son, and nothing to his youngest son Iain except a lame grey mare. 'If that's how it is,' thought Iain, 'then that's how it must be.' And he mounted the mare and rode off to seek his fortune. He rode an hour and walked an hour, and at evening stopped to eat his supper while the mare browsed on the grass beside the road. As they were eating a man rode up on a high black horse, and its hoof-beats whistled in the trees like wind.

Iain looked at the black horse, and thought it the finest animal he'd ever seen. He was astonished to find the stranger gazing with the same admiration at his old grey mare. 'You've a fine animal there, king's son,' the stranger said. 'I don't suppose you'd like to trade?'

'If that's how it is,' thought Iain, 'then that's how it must be.' He and the stranger traded horses, and the stranger mounted the old grey mare and rode away. Iain put his foot in the black horse's stirrup, and at once the horse turned its head and said, 'Mount, king's son, mount.

Think of any place you'd like to be in the three parts of the wheel of the world, and you'll be there as fast as thought.'

'Underwaves,' thought Iain as soon as he was firmly in the saddle. At once he found himself riding as easily along the seabed as if he were on dry land. Prince Underwaves sent messengers to fetch him, and as soon as he arrived said, 'King's son, bring back the daughter of the king of Greece before sunrise tomorrow to marry me, or your head will roll.'

Iain rode out with a heavy heart, but the black horse turned its head and said, 'Ride, king's son, ride. No horse has ever been seen before in the lands of the king of Greece. Use this knowledge how you will.' Before Iain could answer a word he was out of Underwaves and riding in bright sunshine to the castle of the King of Greece. The people whispered to one another, 'Two heads, six legs, a man's shoulders and a tail. What kind of monster is it?' But when the king's daughter looked out of her castle window she saw no monster, but a handsome man on a handsome animal, and ran to Iain and asked him to let her ride.

'Of course,' said Iain. He helped the princess up on the saddle in front of him, and at once the land of Greece vanished and they were riding along the seabed together to Prince Underwaves.

'Well done, king's son,' said Prince Underwaves. 'You've brought the princess, and the wedding can take place tomorrow.'

'Not so fast,' said the princess. 'There'll be no wedding until I have in my hand the golden cup my mother held at her wedding-feast, and *her* mother held at hers.'

'Fetch it, king's son,' said Prince Underwaves. 'Fetch it by sunset, or your head will roll.'

Iain rode out with a heavy heart, but the horse turned its head and said, 'Change your shape, king's son. No cat causes comment in the lands of the king of Greece. Use this knowledge how you will.' Before Iain could answer he found himself growing whiskers and a tail, and he crouched in the saddle with the wind in his fur till the black horse rode into Greece, when he jumped down and padded into the king's castle so quietly that no one paid him the slightest heed. He jumped on to the table, snatched the golden cup in his jaws, and the black horse carried him to Underwaves almost before he changed back from cat to man.

'Well done, king's son,' said Prince Underwaves. 'You've brought the cup, and the wedding can take place tomorrow.'

'Not so fast,' said the princess. 'There'll be no wedding until I have on my finger the silver ring my mother wore at her wedding-feast, and *her* mother wore at hers.'

'Fetch it, king's son,' said Prince Underwaves. 'Fetch it by sunrise tomorrow, or your head will roll.'

Iain rode out with a heavy heart, and this time, instead of carrying him at once to the lands of the king of Greece, the black horse turned its head and said, 'Fetching that ring is the hardest task of all. Whatever I ask you to do, do it without question. And first, put spurs on your feet and a whip in your hand, and drive me beyond all stopping.'

'If that's how it is,' thought Iain, 'then that's how it must be.' He fitted spurs and took a whip, and at the first flick of the lash the horse sprang from Underwaves to Overland and set its hooves on the summit of Snow Mountain. Quickly, before its hooves sank in the yielding snow, Iain spurred it and whipped it, and it sprang through the clouds and set its feet on the summit of Ice Mountain. The hooves started skidding on the ice, and Iain once more set set spurs to the horse and whipped it. It sprang through the clouds and set its hooves on the summit of Fire Mountain, and when they were safely clear of the smoke and flames it turned its head and said, 'Now, king's son, run to the smithy on the plain, and fetch an iron peg for every bone in my body. Hurry back and peg them into me.' Iain did as he was told, though his heart thudded every time he hammered a peg into the horse's flesh and the horse rolled its eyes and groaned. At last every peg was in place and the horse said, 'Ride to Fire Loch and wait on the bank, whatever you see or hear, till I return.'

They came to Fire Loch, and Iain watched forlornly on the bank as the horse splashed out into the water. He groaned to see blood welling from the peg-holes; he sobbed to see flames springing up where the blood stained the water; he drummed his hands on the ground for grief when fire and smoke engulfed the horse. All day he lay heart-broken, and just as the sun was setting behind the Loch, the smoke disappeared, the flames sank back into the water, and the horse staggered wearily to land. Every peg but one had vanished from its body, leaving raw wounds, and on the one remaining peg was hung a silver ring. 'Quickly, king's son,' gasped the horse. 'Pull out the peg and take the ring.' Iain pulled out the peg and put the ring on his little finger, and the horse collapsed at his feet and lay with blood seeping from every wound. Iain flung himself on its neck, and at the hug of his arms and the wet of his tears on its skin, the horse lifted its head and said, 'King's son, we've a long way to go. Get on my back and whip me and spur me beyond all stopping.'

Iain was sure that the slightest movement would be the horse's death, but he did as he was told, and as soon as the horse felt spurs and whip it shed its weariness, sprang over Fire Mountain, Ice Mountain and Snow Mountain, and set Iain safely down beside Prince Underwaves, with the ring glinting on his finger.

'Well done, king's son,' said Prince Underwaves. 'You've brought the ring, and the wedding can take place tomorrow.'

'Not so fast,' said the princess. 'There'll be no wedding till I have a castle to live in, with a well of fresh water deeper than the well in the castle my mother had for her wedding and the castle *her* mother had for hers.'

'Build it, king's son,' said Prince Underwaves. 'Build it at once, or your head will roll.'

Iain looked at the black horse, and the black horse laid back its head and whinnied. The sound of the whinny attracted every sea-creature in the shallows and the deeps, coal-fish, crabs, sardines, seals, halibut, herring, hake, and they set to work to build a castle, using coral for building-blocks, amber for window-panes, kelp for banners and bladderwort for ropes. They studded the walls with pearls, garnets and carnelians as befitted a princess' palace, and when everything was ready the horse led the princess, Iain and Prince Underwaves into the courtyard and stamped its foot on the ground, and at once a well opened in the sea-floor, as deep as darkness and as wide as day, with fresh water bubbling to fill it from far underground.

The princess looked at the coral castle and clapped her hands. Then she looked at the well and frowned. 'It won't do,' she said. 'It isn't finished.'

'How d'you mean, my dear?' asked Prince Underwaves.

'Look inside, and see,' she answered. But when he bent over to peer into the well she put her hands on his back, pushed him in and said, 'Stay there and drown. There'll be a wedding by sunset, and the groom will be the young man you sent on errand after errand, threatening him each time with death.'

She and Iain mounted the black horse, and it sprang in one bound from Underwaves to the plains of Greece, and galloped to the gate of the princess' father's castle. Then it turned its head to Iain and said, 'One last favour, prince's son. Before you go inside to your wedding, draw your sword, shut your eyes and cut off my head.'

'How can I do that?' said Iain, and tears filled his eyes at the thought of killing such a loyal friend.

'Do it,' said the horse. 'I helped you fetch princess, goblet and ring; I built and dug for you; for your sake I crossed the Mountains of Snow, Ice and Fire; I filled my flesh with iron pegs out of loyalty to you. Now it's your turn: do this one thing for me.'

'If that's how it is,' thought Iain dismally, 'then that's how it must be.' He and the princess dismounted, and he drew his sword with a heavy heart and shut his eyes. He felt the blade slice through flesh and crunch through bone, and he heard the thud as the horse's head hit the grass. But when he opened his eyes the horse had disappeared, and in its place the princess was hugging a black-haired, velvet-suited prince, her twin brother turned into a horse by an enchanter long years before.

Iain, the princess and the prince walked together into the castle of the king of Greece, and the bells pealed and the people cheered to see them. And before the day was out the princess married Iain, and they, the prince and everyone in the lands of the King of Greece lived happily all the long years of their lives.

Dougal and the Wizard-king

Most supernatural beings hated mortals the way a country's true people hate invaders who overrun their lands. Some, especially giants and trolls, used to lie in ambush for mortals and eat them. Others, such as elves, goblins and other shape-changers, preferred to take on mortal disguise and make mischief in the mortal world, or to steal mortal children, teach them supernatural skills and keep them for their own.

A fisherman on the Isle of Arran once caught a wooden box in his nets, and inside was a baby boy. The fisherman called the baby Dougal, and brought him up as his own son. When the boy was fourteen years old a ship came to Arran, and on deck was a man juggling with three spiked balls. 'Lend me your son for a year and a day,' he said, 'and I'll teach him to juggle too.' The fisherman agreed, and after a year and a day Dougal came back juggling seven balls. 'Lend him to me for another year and a day,' the stranger said, 'and I'll teach him many other skills.'

The year and a day passed, and when there was neither sight nor word of Dougal, the fisherman sailed to the mainland to look for him. He asked help from the Old Man of the Forest, a being so old that his fingers were as gnarled as oak-twigs and his beard was as silver as birch-bark and wound in seven coils round his waist*. 'Your son is the prisoner of the Wizard-king,' he said. 'Go to the castle and ask for him – and whatever choice they give you, be sure and choose the worst.'

The fisherman went to the Wizard-king's castle and asked for Dougal, and the king threw fourteen pigeons up in the air and asked him to choose between them. Thirteen were plump and proud; the last was ragged-winged and pitiful. The fisherman picked it up and said, 'I'll choose this one.'

'Take him, and bad luck to you both,' roared the furious Wizard-king.

The fisherman laid the ragged bird on the grass, and at once it changed into Dougal. 'Hurry,' said Dougal. 'He'll come after us to get me back, and the only escape is to use his own tricks to baffle him. First I'll change into a greyhound, and you take me to market and sell me to no one but the Wizard-king. And whatever you do, don't sell my collar and lead but keep them by you.'

The fisherman did as he was told. Dougal changed into a greyhound, with a studded collar and a plaited-leather lead, and his father took him to market and offered him for sale. People crowded round, eager to buy, but the fisherman refused all offers until he sold the dog to the Wizard-king himself for a hundred gold pieces. The Wizard-king led the dog away by a string round its neck, and the fisherman kept the collar and lead for himself. At once they turned back into Dougal: while the Wizard-king was bargaining, he'd changed himself from dog to lead.

'We're a hundred gold pieces better off,' he said to his father. 'But he'll come after us again. This time I'll change into a racehorse. Offer me for sale, and don't let anyone but the Wizard-king buy me – but make sure he never gets his hands on the bit or bridle.'

So it was. Dougal changed into a racehorse and his father offered him for sale in the market. People crowded to buy, and he refused them all until the Wizard-king came up.

'How much?' asked the Wizard-king.

'A thousand gold pieces.'

'He looks worth it,' said the Wizard-king. 'But let me try him out. Let me ride him once round the market-place and see for myself.'

'No,' said the fisherman. 'I don't trust you.'

'My dear friend,' said the Wizard-king. 'Of course you can trust me. Here's the money in advance.' And he handed him a bag of gold. The

191

foolish fisherman fell on the coins to count them, and the Wizard-king snatched the bridle, leapt on to the racehorse and galloped away. The gold coins changed to horse-droppings in the fisherman's hands.

As soon as the Wizard-king reached his castle he took the racehorse to the stable. 'Rub him down and feed him,' he said, 'but whatever you do, don't take off his bit or bridle.'

The stable-lads rubbed the horse down and fetched oats.* They were astonished when the horse lifted its head and said in a human voice, 'Please take off the bit and bridle and let me eat.'

'We can't,' they answered.

'Then take me to the river and loosen it a little, to let me drink.'

'No harm in that.'

As soon as the bridle was loosened Dougal slipped the bit out of his mouth, turned into a silver-grey salmon and swam away downstream, leaving the stable-lads gaping. There was a flash of lightning, all the castle-bells jangled an alarm, and the Wizard-king ran to the river, changed into an otter and swam to catch the salmon.

For hours the salmon and the otter darted and plunged between pools, rocks and weeds. The salmon began to tire, and just as the otter lunged to capture it, it used its last strength to change into a swallow, and darted away in the evening air. The Wizard-king changed into a falcon and flew in pursuit.

Swallow-Dougal, exhausted, fluttered down beside a lady sitting in her garden, and turned himself into a ring on her finger. 'In a moment,' said the ring, 'a pedlar will come to the gate and ask to buy me. Don't answer: just throw me on the fire.'

As the ring finished speaking, the Wizard-king appeared at the gate disguised as a pedlar. 'Sell me your ring,' he said. The lady threw ring-Dougal into the fire, and the Wizard-king changed himself into a blacksmith and reached into the flames with tongs to fetch him out. Dougal rolled out of the fire and changed himself to a grain of corn on the corn-pile. The Wizard-king changed into a cockerel and began pecking up grains of corn – and Dougal changed into a fox and with a single snap of his jaws bit off the Wizard-king's head and ended his enchantments forever. Then he changed back into human form, married the lady, found his father, and they all went back to Arran and lived happily ever afterwards.*

The loch-wife

TAM AND THE FARMER'S DAUGHTER

The loch-wife lived in the depths of a cold sea-loch, with only the Laidly Beast* for company. Her heart ached for a husband, and one day she stuck her head out of the water beside a lonely fisherman and said, 'Give me your first-born son on his twentieth birthday, and you'll never want for fish from now till then.'

'Done!' said the fisherman, who knew very well that he was past fifty and childless. At once fish started flinging themselves into his boat, and it was soon so laden that the oars bent like bows when he rowed it home. He thought no more about the bargain, even when at the end of a year and a day his wife bore a baby son and called him Tam; for nineteen years, while Tam grew and thrived, the fisherman brought his boat home laden every evening, and they became the wealthiest fisher-family in all those parts.

Then, on Tam's nineteenth birthday, his father suddenly remembered his part in the loch-wife's bargain, clapped his hand to his head and groaned.

'What's the matter, Dad?' asked Tam.

'In exactly a year from today, you're promised to the loch-wife as a husband, and there's no way out of it.'

'We'll see about that,' said Tam. 'Go to the blacksmith's and fetch a sword.' The fisherman fetched a sword as long as a chair, but when Tam shook it in the air it flew into a hundred splinters and Tam said, 'Fetch me another.' The fisherman fetched a sword as long as the kitchen-table, but when Tam shook it in the air it flew into a thousand splinters and Tam said, 'Fetch another.' The fisherman fetched a sword as long as a shelf and twice as heavy, and Tam shook it in the air and said, 'This will do fine.' He sheathed the sword, mounted his horse and rode on his way, and before long he came on a dog, an otter and a hawk quarrelling over a sheep's carcase beside the road. 'No need to tear out each other's throats,' he said. 'Why not share, like friends?'

He chopped the sheep-meat into six parts, and gave three to the dog, two to the otter and one to the hawk. 'For this,' said the dog, 'if you ever need speed of running or flick of paw, remember me.'

'For this,' said the otter, 'if you ever need speed of swimming or twist of jaw, remember me.'

193

'For this,' said the hawk, 'if you ever need speed of flying or crook of claw, remember me.'*

Tam rode along the loch-side till he came to a rich farmer's house and offered his services as a cattle-boy. 'Fair enough,' said the farmer. 'But don't expect wages. You'll get food and drink according to the amount of milk the cattle give, and as for cash, you can keep whatever you find in the fields each day.'

Next morning Tam took the cattle to pasture, and an amazing sight it was to see, a man on horseback with a sword at his side the length of a shelf and twice as heavy, leading a herd of cows. But the grazing was thin, and when Tam drove the cattle home that evening they gave so little milk that the only food he'd earned was a crust of bread and the only drink was a sip of loch-water. 'This won't do,' he thought. 'Tomorrow we'll go further on, and see what we'll see.'

Next morning Tam drove the cattle to the far side of the loch, where green pastures stretched as far as the woods and hills, and they grazed and fattened all day while Tam lazed in the sun. But at evening, just as it was time to drive the cattle home, the sky darkened and a bristling giant loomed over Tam and roared, 'Hi! Ho! Hogarach! These are my pastures, those are my cattle, and you're a dead man.'

He picked Tam up to squeeze the life from him. Tam drew his sword, fast as thought, and sliced off his head with the roar still rumbling in his throat. The crash of the giant's body on the ground split open his treasure-cavern: jewels, ivory, gold, all glinting in the sunset-glow. But Tam left everything where it was except for a single gold ring and drove his cattle home for milking. That night, and for many nights afterwards, they gave such quantities of milk that Tam was head of the herdsmen's table in his master's house, and every day while the cattle browsed he ransacked the giant-treasure and put it in a safe hiding-place until he needed it.

Before too long Tam's cattle had nibbled all the grass in the pasture to bare stubble, and he climbed a pine-tree by the loch to look for new grazing. 'Through the wood and over the hill,' he said to himself. 'There's grassy parkland as far as the eye can see.' He drove his cattle through the wood and over the hill, and they grazed and fattened all day long while Tam lazed in the sun. And at evening, just as it was time to drive the cattle home, the sky darkened and a bristling, two-headed giant loomed over Tam and roared, 'Hee! Haw! Hogaraich! This is my parkland, those are my cattle, and it's your blood that will quench my thirst tonight.' He picked Tam up to squeeze the blood

194

from him, and Tam drew his sword, quick as thought, and sliced off both his heads with the screech still whistling in his throats. The crash of the giant's body opened up a second treasure-cavern even more magnificent than the first*, and Tam left everything where it was except for a coat of velvet sewn with gold thread, and drove the cattle home. For months afterwards he spent his nights as head of the chief servants' table in his master's house, and his days, while the cattle browsed, ransacking the treasure and hiding it away until he needed it.

THE LAIDLY BEAST

That was how things were until two days before Tam's twentieth birthday. Then, when he drew his cattle back for the evening milking, he found the milkmaids sobbing on their stools till the tears made puddles in the milking-pails. They told him that the Laidly Beast, the loch-wife's foul underwater pet, had reared its head out of the water and demanded human flesh, and unless some hero could be found to fight it it was coming back next morning to eat the farmer's daughter. The farmer had offered his daughter's hand in marriage to any warrior who killed the Beast, but the only man to offer was Balin the Boaster: the girl was doomed.

'We'll see about that,' said Tam. Next morning, instead of driving his cattle round the loch, through the woods and over the hill, he left them pasturing on the thin fields of his master's farm, strapped on his sword and hid in a copse of trees beside the loch. At sunrise servants led the farmer's daughter out in a weeping procession to the loch-side. Balin the Boaster swaggered beside them, swinging his sword and uttering roars of rage, but as soon as the servants went back inside and there was no one to see, he left the girl to her fate and cowered behind a rock. The loch began to seethe and swirl as the Laidly Beast heaved itself from its water-lair, and soon its head broke surface. It fixed its eyes on the trembling girl, flicked its tongue and surged through the shallows towards her, tall as a house. It was baring its fangs to snatch her, when Tam ran out of the trees and sliced its neck as he had sliced the pasture-giants. The Laidly Beast lolled in the water, its blood hissing like a geyser, and Tam strung the head on a bowstring and dropped it at the girl's feet. 'Take this to your father,' he said, 'and if you agree to marry me, tell him to prepare a wedding.'

Tam rode off to lead his cattle to pasture, and as soon as he was out of sight Balin the Boaster jumped out from behind his rock, flourished his sword in the girl's face and said, 'Tell them Balin killed the Beast, or die.' He slung the head over his shoulder and swaggered back to the farm with the girl beside him, and all the while they were clapping his shoulders, shaking his hands and bustling about preparations for the wedding, she said nothing at all, merely looked at the ground and wept. Her father could think of no reason for it until that evening, when, just as the priests began lifting their hands and muttering wedding prayers, Tam drove his lowing cattle into the yard, ran into the farmhouse in his muddy herdsman's clothes and demanded his bride.

'You?' said the farmer. 'You killed the Laidly Beast?'

'I did.'

'And you want to marry my daughter? A cowherd?'

'I do,' said Tam. He ran out, put on the gold-sewn velvet robe from the second giant's hoard, fetched the gold ring from the first giant's hoard, put it on the girl's finger and married her before there was any more argument.

Next morning Balin the Boaster was sent to herd the cattle, and Tam rowed across the loch to fetch his father and mother and introduce them to his bride. The boat was hardly halfway back when the loch-wife stuck her head out of the water, hissed, 'It's his twentieth birthday, and it's my husband he'll be, not hers,' and bundled him overboard to her water-lair. The father and mother rowed miserably to shore and told their story, and they, the farmer, the daughter and the servants gathered on the shore and gazed across the loch with streaming eyes.

'We'll never get him back,' Tam's mother sobbed.

'Such a fine young man,' his father sobbed.

'Husband for a day, and forever gone,' the farmer's daughter sobbed.

Everyone took up the sobbing, and the sound of their voices rolled across the lake like singing from a choir. The noise tickled the loch-wife's ears in her water-lair, and she stuck her head out of the water and said, 'I like your music. Sing again!'

'Not a note,' said the farmer's daughter, 'unless you show me Tam's face above the waves.'

The loch-wife brandished Tam out of the water like a puppet, and at the sight of him the people on the bank howled and groaned. 'I like your music,' the loch-wife said. 'Sing again!'

'Not a note,' said the farmer's daughter, 'unless you show me Tam's body above the waves.'

The loch-wife moved closer to the shore, Tam waved his arms and wriggled his body above the waves, and at the sight of him the people on the bank howled and groaned. 'More!' hissed the loch-wife. 'Sing more of it!'

'Show me his legs,' said the farmer's daughter.

The loch-wife moved still closer to shore, and as soon as Tam's legs were clear of the water he wriggled free and scampered safely to land. The people on the bank gave a cheer of joy, and it turned at once to a groan as the furious loch-wife snatched the farmer's daughter in Tam's place and carried her away to her island lair.

'Now what shall we do?' groaned her father. 'The loch-wife sinks any boat that rows out across the loch. On that island roams a swift-running deer; inside the deer is a swift-flying raven; inside the raven is a swift-swimming trout; inside the trout is an egg, and inside the egg is the loch-wife's life. There's nothing we can do.'

'We'll see about that,' said Tam. He put his fingers to his lips and whistled, then shouted, in a voice that echoed across the loch and round the hills, 'Speed of running and flick of paw!' At once the dog he had fed on three shares of the sheep's carcase long ago leapt out of the woods, ran across the loch to the island without so much as a splash, chased the swift-running deer and brought it crashing down with a single flick of paw. As the deer fell a raven soared out of its mouth. Tam shouted, 'Speed of flying and crook of claw!', and the hawk he had fed long ago on one share of the sheep's carcase hovered in the air, swooped on the swift-flying raven and sent it splashing into the loch with a single crook of claw. As soon as the raven hit the water a trout leapt out of its mouth. Tam shouted, 'Speed of swimming and twist of jaw!' and the otter he had fed long ago on two shares of the sheep's carcase dived into the loch, caught the swift-swimming trout and tossed it to land with a single twist of jaw. The trout fell at Tam's feet on the loch-side, and as it fell a glass egg rolled out of its mouth and smashed on the pebbles, and the loch-wife's life coiled into the air like a smoke-wisp and disappeared.

Now it was safe to row to the island*, and Tam brought his bride home with great rejoicing. And what with their own joy in each other, the gladness of their families, and the giants' hoards waiting in their hiding-places to bring them prosperity for the rest of their lives, it would be hard to say if any couple in Scotland was ever happier.

21

IRISH STORIES

The hunger-beast

A hunger-beast, looking for a home, leapt down the throat of Cathal, king of Munster, one of the five kings of Ireland. It snuggled down in his stomach and began gurgling and growling for food. It became quite usual for Cathal to eat ten loaves, a side of bacon and six dozen eggs for breakfast, and as for his evening meal, whole herds of sheep, goats, cattle, a warren of rabbits and a poultry-yard of geese, ducks, chickens, swans and peacocks were fattened just to keep him satisfied. It was bad enough when he stayed at home in his own castle. But when he went visiting, what with the hunger-beast growling inside him, the hundred hunters he took to catch his dinner and the hundred cooks he took to prepare it, he ate every one of his unhappy hosts out of house and home.

There was a poor student at the university of Armagh, called Conor, and he began adding up the number of creatures King Cathal ate at a sitting and the number of beasts still left alive in Munster, and dividing one figure by the other. 'There'll be nothing left,' he thought. 'In half a year he'll have eaten everything that moves. I'd better put a stop to it – and if I can make my own fortune on the way, good luck to me!'

He packed a grindstone in a haversack, put on his cloak, picked up his stick and walked to the castle of Pichan, the richest sheep-farmer and fruit-grower in all Munster. Pichan was sitting in his orchard with his elbows on his knees and his head in his hands, sobbing his heart out. 'What's wrong with you, Pichan?' asked Conor. 'It's a lovely day. The trees are so fruit-laden that their branches kiss the ground. What have you to sob about?'

'Cathal's coming this way tomorrow,' sobbed Pichan. 'He wants ten barrels of apples, ten cauldrons of porridge and ten bathtubs full of cream – and that's just the snack before he starts his breakfast.'

'Leave it to me,' said Conor. 'If I rid you of his eating forever, what will you give me?'

'One sheep from every fold between the mountains and the sea,' said Pichan. 'But you'll never do it.'

'Oh yes I will,' said Conor. 'Just have the apples, the porridge and the cream ready, and tell your servants to do exactly as I order them, and to deafen their ears to everyone else.'

'I'll try anything once,' said Pichan. And so, when King Cathal arrived next morning at Pichan's castle, with his hundred hunters and his hundred cooks, rubbing his hands and asking what was for breakfast, he found the ten barrels of apples, the ten cauldrons of porridge and the ten bathtubs of cream waiting on the table, and Conor sitting with his haversack on his back and his hands folded in front of him.

'Good morning to you,' said Cathal, cramming his mouth with apples from his left hand and porridge from his right.

'Good morning, sire,' said Conor. And that was all he said. But as the king went on gulping porridge, munching apples and swilling cream, he took the haversack from his shoulder, the grindstone from the haversack and began slowly, carefully, to sharpen his teeth.

'Good heavens, man,' said Cathal at last. 'Doesn't that hurt? What the devil are you doing it for?'

'Simple, sire,' said Conor. 'I see from the way you're nibbling that snack that you're a man with appetite, just like myself, and I'm sharpening my teeth to get down to serious eating with you later on.'

'Serious eating?' scoffed Cathal. 'I could eat you, and everything you eat, ten times over and still go hungry.' Conor said nothing, but went on sharpening his teeth, and Cathal said angrily, 'I challenge you to an eating competition: dish for dish, bite for bite, through one whole day. Pichan will provide the food.'

'Done!' said Conor. 'On one condition: we must both eat nothing at all from now until this time tomorrow, to whet our appetites.'

'Done and done!' said Cathal, and the two shook hands on it. All that day Pichan's servants kept watch over Cathal to see that no morsel of food or drink crossed his lips, the hundred hunters and the hundred cooks leapt and cheered for the first holiday they'd had in months, and Conor and Pichan walked from one sheepfold to the next between the mountains and the sea so that Conor could choose the sheep he would have when he kept his promise.

By evening the hunger-beast was groaning and muttering inside Cathal's stomach, and as the night wore on and no food came its way it began stamping, howling and pummelling its fists. But Cathal was a king, he'd given his royal word, and he was being watched: not a morsel of meat or a drop of drink touched his lips all night. Next morning he hurried downstairs for breakfast, and found Conor waiting for him, with a fire in the hearth, a spit as sharp as a sword, a stack of bowls and dishes, and baskets of bacon, beef, butter, bread and honeycomb.

'Good morning to you, Conor,' said Cathal. 'Will breakfast be long delayed?'

'No, sire,' said Conor. 'Sit down in that high-backed chair, and I'll see to it myself.' But as soon as Cathal sat down he shouted, 'Hooks! Nails! Ropes!', and Pichan's servants ran out of the shadows and trussed the king to the chair so that he could move neither hand nor foot. Cathal shouted to them to untie him, but they might as well have been stone deaf; he shouted for his hunters and cooks to cut him free, but the minute Conor said he'd see to the meal himself, they'd run outside to continue enjoying their holiday. There was nothing Cathal could do but sit and drool as Conor sliced bacon and fried it, buttered bread, spooned honey and made cheerful conversation all the while. 'Have you seen fat sizzle like it? What about this honeycomb? Wouldn't you swear it was liquid gold? Just smell the freshness of this bread . . .' Cathal ground his teeth and groaned, and the hunger-beast inside him began caterwauling, cursing and clambering up and down the tubes of his body like a ferret in a rabbit-run. Conor took no notice. He went on frying, buttering and breakfasting, and above all he went on talking, till Cathal's eyes were as good as propped on stalks and the hunger-beast was ranting inside him like a pirate in a prison-cell.

'This is a fine breakfast,' said Conor. 'But it's ashes and wormwood to the food in the dream I had last night. I dreamed that I'd entirely lost my appetite. I wanted nothing; food withered and drink dried on my lips; I was wasting like a leaf in autumn. There was only one cure: to visit the Old Man of the Larder and ask his help. The Old Man lived in Bacon Castle on Milk Lake, and the way to get to it was to row in a boat whose planks were beef-ribs, whose thwarts were sides of ham and whose oars were venison. The lake was peaceful and placid at first, but as I rowed a storm blew up and churned it to butter, so that if I hadn't jumped out on to Cheese Island I'd have drowned in it. The island was wide and long, and at its heart lay Bacon Castle. Every stone of the castle was made from fourteen hundred rashers of salt bacon; the windows were rind and the battlements were lumps of lard. The gatekeeper's name was Butterkin, and his clogs were bread-rolls, his clothes were pancakes and his stick was a cinnamon-twist. He took me to his master, the Old Man of the Larder, who was fishing in a wine-pond with a marrow-bone rod and a line of sausages, and each cast brought up roast chickens, chops or breaded veal. The Old Man let me sleep that night in a bed of cream cheese, and I'd have sunk and drowned if the servants hadn't given me a mattress of toast to float on. Next morning the Old Man told me the cure for my lost appetite. I was to build a fire of oak-branches, in front of a tethered king, and breakfast on bacon, beef, bread, butter and honey till the juice ran down my chin*. "Go now," he finished, "in the name of cheese, and may honey-baked-ham protect you, curds-and-whey guard you and bubbling stew safeguard you for evermore."'

So Conor told his dream, and with every word he wafted a spitful of meat or a bite of bread in King Cathal's direction, before cramming it into his own mouth and relishing it. The hunger-beast inside Cathal heard the dream and smelled the food. Sometimes it lay still and listened; sometimes it danced up and down and roared; in the end it climbed up Cathal's gullet into his mouth and opened his teeth like a trapdoor to peer out and sniff the air. As soon as Conor saw the glitter of eyes inside Cathal's mouth, he held out a particularly juicy, particularly savoury steak and said, 'I'd welcome your opinion, sire. Is this well enough done to eat?' The beast lunged out of Cathal's mouth to snatch the steak, and before it could dart back in again Conor slammed the king's jaws shut with one hand, picked up the spit with the other and spiked the beast into the fire's red heart. There was a hiss, a roar and a bang, and the hunger-beast sprang to the gable like a spitting cat, jumped howling into the sun-glare and never set hoof or talon in Ireland again.

That was how Conor freed King Cathal from the hunger-beast, and Munster and all Ireland with him. And what with the sheep from Pichan's folds, and the herds of cattle and flocks of goats lavished on him by the grateful king, he became the richest man in Christendom, and his animals stood shoulder to shoulder on every blade of pasture from the mountains to the sea.

Finn, Oona and Cucullin

The giants of Ireland were building a causeway across the sea to Scotland. It was hard work, what with the weight of the stones, the coldness of the water, and the seals which kept swimming up and splashing water into their faces. But what made it worse was that every time they turned their backs Finn MacCool started scattering the stones as fast as they'd laid them down. 'What's the matter with you?' they muttered. 'Don't you want this causeway built?'

'No, I don't,' said Finn. 'And I'll tell you why in just one word: Cucullin.'

At the name Cucullin all the giants dropped their clubs and howled. He was a Scottish barbarian, so huge that even to giants he seemed a giant. His tread made earthquakes and his footprints were lochs and glens; he snatched meteorites out of the sky and punched them into pancakes; he'd thrashed every giant in Scotland, and boasted that as soon as the causeway was finished he'd do the same to the Irish giants, beginning with Finn MacCool.

'You can finish the causeway yourselves,' said Finn. 'I'm going home to Oona.' He pulled up a firtree for a walking-stick and tramped through the woods to his house on Knockmany Hilltop. People had often asked why he and Oona lived on a hilltop, where the wind blew their candle out before it was lit and every drop of fresh water ran the other way, and though he always answered, 'We like fresh air, and we can always dig a well,' the real reason was that he could see all the way over the sea to Scotland, and there was plenty of time to hide if Cucullin loomed that way.

'Finn!' shouted Oona when he stuck his head through the doorway, and gave her a kiss that rattled the rafters. 'What brings you home so soon?'

'Cucullin,' said Finn. 'I can't work for fear of Cucullin. If he punches meteorites to pancakes, what hope have I?'

'This skulking is ridiculous,' said Oona. 'There's only one thing to be done – and your talk of meteorite-pancakes gives me an idea how to do it.' She lit a bonfire on the hilltop, put her fingers to her lips and blew a whistle loud enough to stun seagulls in the sky.

'What did you do that for?' said Finn.

'To fetch Cucullin.'

'What? D'you want me pummelled to a pancake? What have I done to deserve such a wife?'

'Stop blathering, and do exactly as I tell you. Go round the neighbours and borrow twenty griddle-pans without handles. Then dress yourself in baby-clothes and lie down in the cradle. Hide a lump of cheese under the pillow, and whatever else you do, don't forget that all Cucullin's strength is in his right-hand middle finger.'

'But what – ?'

'Hurry up. He's coming.'

Sure enough, the earth was shaking and the sea was shivering as Cucullin splashed across from Scotland, kicking the causeway down and scattering giants like hay-stalks. Finn scuttled round his neighbours gathering griddle-pans without handles, and while he changed into baby-clothes and hid in the cradle Oona baked the griddles in the middle of twenty round loaves, made a twenty-first for luck, then piled them on the table with a barrel of milk, a boulder and a hundred cabbages beside them. No sooner had she finished when Cucullin stuck his head through the doorway, and Finn covered his head with baby-blankets and cowered.

'Is this the house of Finn MacCool?' roared Cucullin.

'It is – and it's lucky for you he's not at home.'

'What d'you mean?'

'Some boaster called Cucullin is supposed to be coming to fight him, and he's stamped out in a fury to look for him.'

'Is that so?' said Cucullin. 'And what would you say if I told you *I* was Cucullin?'

'I'd say you're lucky he's not here to hear it,' said Oona. 'Have you never *seen* Finn MacCool?'

'No, but I'll gladly wait here for him,' aid Cucullin.

'That's fine for you. But before you come in, the wind's changed, and the draught's howling through the door. Would you mind rotating the house from west to east? That's what Finn always does.'

This made Cucullin open one eye wide in astonishment – and it astonished Finn even more, cowering under the bedclothes in the cradle. But neither of them said a word, and Cucullin pulled his right-hand middle finger three times till it cracked, put his arms round the house, lifted it clean off its foundations and rotated it from west to east.

'That was neighbourly,' said Oona, when Cucullin came panting inside again. 'Now, there's one other little job. Before he stamped off to look for you, Finn was lifting his fist to punch open the hill for a water-spring. If you did that for him, he might excuse you a beating when he comes back home.'

This made Cucullin open both eyes in astonishment, and Finn hunched under the bedclothes till his chin tangled with his toes. Cucullin went outside with Oona, measured the rock carefully, then pulled his right-hand middle finger nine times till it cracked and punched a rock-channel so wide and so deep that human beings were ever afterwards able to sail boats in it.

'Thank you very much,' said Oona. 'Now, why don't you come inside and eat some breakfast, to build up your strength for Finn?' She sat Cucullin at the table, next to the boulder, the milk-barrel and the cabbages, and handed him one of the griddle-loaves. 'Test your teeth on that,' she said. 'Finn won't miss one loaf.'

Cucullin bit into the griddle-loaf, and at once began clutching his jaw and dancing till the ground rocked under him. 'That's two of my best teeth gone!' he roared. 'What kind of bread is this?'

'Finn-bread,' said Oona. 'But perhaps it's too hard for ordinary teeth. Try another.'

She handed Cucullin a second griddle-loaf, and he bit into it and yelled exactly as before. 'What are you doing to me, woman? Any more of this, and I won't have a tooth left in my head!'

There's no need to shout,' said Oona. 'You'll wake the baby.' As she spoke, she gave the cradle a kick, and Finn did his best to caterwaul like a hungry child. 'There, you see?' said Oona. 'The only thing that'll keep him quiet is a loaf of his father's bread.' She gave Finn the twenty-first fresh-baked loaf, the only one without a griddle-pan inside it, and Finn gobbled it down in two bites and howled for more.

'That's a fine boy you have there,' said Cucullin. 'What must Finn's jaws be like, if his son's baby teeth manage bread like that?'

'He's a fine boy sure enough,' said Oona. 'Baby, darling, show the nice giant how you squeeze juice from stones.'

Finn sat up, with the baby-bonnet pulled round to hide his whiskers, fetched the cheese from under his pillow and wrung it like a dishcloth till pale liquid trickled over the floor. 'Can you do that?' he asked Cucullin, in as babyish a voice as he could manage.

'Of course I can!' said Cucullin. He picked up the boulder from the table and began wringing it. But however much he cracked his knuckles, dug in his thumbs and twisted his wrists, not a drop of liquid fell from the stone. In the end it crumbled to splinters in his fingers, and he brushed his hands and said, 'If the son can do that, what sort of hands can the father have? I'll be going before Finn gets back, if it's all the same to you.'

'That's a wise decision,' said Oona. 'But before you go, wouldn't you like to see the baby's fists and feel his teeth?'

'I would indeed,' said Cucullin. 'I'd dearly like to see fists that squeeze juice from stones and feel teeth that much bread like iron.'

He leaned over Finn in the cradle, and Finn grabbed his right hand with both fists, rammed it into his mouth and bit off the middle finger with a snap like a badger-trap. Cucullin howled with pain, and his howl shrank to a kitten's whimper as the strength oozed out of him. He collapsed on the floor in a heap of dust, and it took Finn and Oona all the rest of the morning to brush him out of doors and scatter him to the winds. From that day on the Irish giants were able to finish their causeway in peace, and no other giants, from Scotland or anywhere else, ever troubled them again.

Kathleen

THE GREYHOUND-HUSBAND

One day the eldest of the three daughters of King Coluath O'Hara put on her father's magic cloak and wished for a husband, the finest young man in Ireland; at once a coach-and-six galloped up and the finest young man in Ireland carried her away to his castle and married her. The second daughter put on the magic cloak, wished for the second finest young man in Ireland as husband, as a coach-and-four galloped up and the second finest young man carried her to his castle and married her. The youngest daughter, whose name was Kathleen, put on the magic cloak and wished for a greyhound, and when she opened the door there he was: handsome, fast, with a coat as sleek as silk.

In the evening of the first day of the first daughter's marriage her husband asked, 'Would you have me as I am by day or by night?', and when she answered 'By day' he changed before her eyes into a stag, and spent each day as a prince and each night as a stag from that moment on. The second daughter's husband asked the same question, and when she gave him the same answer he spent each day as a prince and each night as a seal. As for the greyhound, every night in Kathleen's room he laid his greyhound-skin beside the fire, changed in an instant into a handsome husband, and stayed by her side until it was dawn and time to become a dog again.

A year passed, and one night Kathleen gave birth to a baby boy. She laid him in the bed between herself and her husband – and a tawny owl flew in at the window, picked the baby up by the shawl and carried him away. 'Hush! Hush!' Kathleen's husband quickly said. 'Whatever you do, don't shed a tear for him.' Another year passed, and the same thing happened: Kathleen gave birth to a baby boy, a raven flew in and carried him away, and her husband begged her not to shed a tear. The third year she gave birth to a little girl, and this time when a white swan carried the child away she was so heartbroken that she let fall a single tear, and caught it in a handkerchief. Her husband was angry, but by then it was done and there was no way to mend it.

At the end of seven years King Coluath O'Hara and his queen gave a feast in honour of her daughters. The two elder girls rode up with their husbands in their carriages, and Kathleen sat with them at the banquet with her greyhound-husband at her feet, sharing every bite of food. That night, when the guests had gone to their rooms, the queen took a lantern in her hand and went to say goodnight to her daughters, and was amazed to find her eldest daughter sharing her bed with a stag, her middle daughter with a seal and her youngest daughter Kathleen with a handsome man. Then, on her way out of Kathleen's room, she tripped on a greyhound-skin lying on the floor, and she picked it up crossly and threw it into the fire. At once, with a flash and a bang, it disappeared, and Kathleen's husband leapt out of bed and raced away like a greyhound after a hare, with Kathleen panting behind him as fast as she could run.

They ran all night and they ran all day. The greyhound-husband did his best to leave Kathleen behind, but for all the stitch in her side and the panting in her chest she kept up with him, pace for pace. At last they came to a clump of bullrushes and flung themselves down exhausted. 'Go home!' panted the greyhound-husband. 'Go home! I'm a prisoner of the queen of the Underland*. She cast a greyhound-spell on me, and said that if anyone ever broke it I'd be hers in the Underland till the day she died. Leave me here! Go home! We can never be happy in the Overland again.'

So saying he pulled up a bullrush, stepped into the opening where the stalk had been, and vanished. Without a moment's hesitation Kathleen pulled up another bullrush, stepped into the opening, and found herself in the Underland beside her husband. He was very angry and very sorry, and said, 'You're here now, and you can never go back. You must stay in the Underland forever. But we can never be together. I'm the queen's prisoner, and I must go to her.'

THE UNDERLAND

For a night and a day Kathleen and her husband walked through the Underland. The greyhound-husband kept begging Kathleen to leave him and find happiness with someone else; but she took no notice, and kept pace with him, step by step.

At evening they came to a cottage and stopped for the night. The greyhound-husband soon went to his room to sleep, but Kathleen sat by the fire, talking to the woman of the house. As she sat there, a little boy ran to her, hugged her and cried, 'Mummy!' His hair was as fair as the feathers of an owl. The woman of the house put him gently to bed, and then said to Kathleen, 'You've come at last! When he was a tiny baby, an owl carried him here from the Overland, and asked me to care for him till his true mother came.' She gave Kathleen a pair of golden scissors and said, 'Use these to help any poor people you see. If you snip a corner from their rags, everything they wear will turn to cloth of gold, and you'll know you're on the right path. Use them well, and when it's time, come back here and fetch your son.'

Next day Kathleen and her greyhound-husband walked on through the Underland. Once more the greyhound-husband kept begging her to leave him and find happiness with someone else, and again she took no notice and kept pace with him, step by step. That evening they came to another cottage and stopped for the night. The greyhound-husband soon went up to bed, and Kathleen sat talking to the woman of the house. A second boy ran to her, hugged her and cried, 'Mummy!' His hair was as dark as a raven's wing. The woman of the house put him to bed, and explained that a raven had brought him when he was a tiny baby, and left her to care for him till his true mother came. She gave Kathleen a silver comb and said, 'Use this to help any sick people you see. If you run it through their hair, all the disease will vanish from their bodies, and you'll know your path is right. When it's time, come back here and fetch your son.'

Next day Kathleen and the greyhound-husband walked on as before. The greyhound-husband begged Kathleen to leave him, but she took no notice and kept pace, step by step. They stopped for the night in a third cottage, and this time after the greyhound-husband had gone to bed a little girl ran out, hugged Kathleen and cried, 'Mother!' It was the daughter the swan had taken when she was a tiny baby. Her skin was as soft as swansdown, and she was as graceful as a swan, but when Kathleen stroked her face she saw with a pang of sorrow that one of the little girl's eye-sockets was blank and empty. Then she remembered the single tear she'd shed when the child was taken. All this time she'd kept the handkerchief, and now she took it out and tenderly wiped her daughter's face. As soon as the tear in the handkerchief touched the child's eye-socket it turned miraculously back into the missing eye. The woman of the house put the little girl to bed, and gave Kathleen a goosequill pipe. 'Take this,' she said, 'and keep it till your moment of greatest need. Then blow it, and it will help you find happiness.'

Next morning when Kathleen woke up, her greyhound-husband had disappeared. Though it broke his heart, he'd left her so that she might find happiness with someone else; he'd gone on alone to serve the queen of the Underland. Kathleen had no idea how to find him, or where in the Underland the queen's palace might be. All day she wandered, searching and calling, and at evening she sat down in despair beside a hedge. There was a shape beside her, which at first in the dark she took for a bundle of rags. But then it stirred and she realised that it was a beggar-child. Filled with pity, she took out her golden scissors and snipped a corner from the rags. At once the beggar-child's clothes changed to cloth of gold, and Kathleen's heart leapt to think that she was on the right path after all. Next day she continued on the same road, and this time when she lay down to rest she found next to her a sick old woman covered with spots and sores. Kathleen took out her silver comb and drew it through the woman's straggly hair, and at once the spots and sores vanished, the shrunken old woman changed into a healthy girl, and Kathleen knew that her path was right.

Unfortunately for her, the ragged child and the sick old woman were, like the greyhound-husband, in the power of the queen of the Underland, and ran straight to show their mistress what miracles the golden scissors and silver comb had worked. The queen's soldiers arrested Kathleen, dumped her in a dungeon and threw away the key*.

As Kathleen sat in the dungeon wondering what was to become of her, her greyhound-husband crept down to visit her. By the light of a flickering lantern, he and Kathleen talked sadly through the barred window in the dungeon door. 'What can we do?' he said. 'Tomorrow I must marry the queen, and drink a potion to forget all my former life. Oh Kathleen, this is surely our moment of greatest need.'

As soon as she heard these words, Kathleen remembered the

goosequill pipe. She put it to her lips and blew, and a dove fluttered down from the sky, perched by the dungeon door and said, 'In the courtyard is a hollow tree; in the tree is an egg; in the egg is a life, and the way to happiness.' With a whoop of joy the greyhound-husband ran from the dungeon, took an axe and split open the hollow tree. Inside was a glass egg, with the wicked queen's life coiled like a wisp of smoke. He smashed the egg, the smoke vanished into air, and the queen and her soldiers disappeared with it forever*. All the dungeon doors swung open, the queen's bewitched prisoners threw off their spells as easily as people wake up from sleep, and in Overland Kathleen's elder sisters found that instead of a stag and a seal, they could have their beloved husbands as human beings by night as well as day.

As soon as every enchantment was lifted, Kathleen's husband fetched her from the dungeon. 'There's a wedding planned for tomorrow,' he said, 'and it would be a shame to waste it. Will you marry me again, Kathleen, live in this castle and rule the Underland with me?'

That's exactly what they did. Wedding-bells pealed all through the Underland, and after the celebrations Queen Kathleen and her husband fetched their owl-son, raven-son and swan-daughter, and rewarded the women who'd looked after them. Then they all lived happily ever afterwards.

ADDITIONAL STORIES, ALTERNATIVE VERSIONS AND NOTES

THE BATTLE BETWEEN GIANTS AND GODS
page 2

The traditional site for the giants' stone-pile was in the Greek countryside near Phlegra. The giants were earth-children and could never be killed so long as they kept some part of their bodies in contact with Mother Earth. This is why the gods found them impossible to defeat: every time they were toppled from the stone-pile to earth they gathered new strength from the ground and sprang up again, healed from all wounds. Hercules solved the problem by weakening them with arrows, then, while they were lying dazed on the ground, lifting them clear of Mother Earth and clubbing them dead in mid-air. The plain of Meteora in Greece is, to this day, littered with enormous boulders, which country people say are giants' bones and fragments of their stone-pile.

THE GOLDEN APPLES *page 2*

The golden apples of immortality were Mother Earth's wedding-present to the king and queen of the gods. They grew in a secret orchard in the mountains of Africa, tended by tree-nymphs and guarded by a serpent with a hundred coils. The only being in the world, apart from the gods, who knew their hiding-place was Hercules, who was sent to steal them as one of the twelve labours imposed on him by the wicked mortal king Eurystheus. The gods forced Eurystheus to send the stolen apples back – and when they were stolen again, this time by the giants, they sent Hercules to find them and return them to the garden. Meanwhile, they tried to renew their immortality by eating ambrosia and drinking nectar. But although the magic in these substances was powerful, it prolonged life rather than making it eternal, and the gods knew that without the golden apples they were doomed.

In another version of the story, the golden apples belonged to the gods not of Olympus but of Asgard, in the skies over the northernmost countries of the world. They were guarded by Freia, goddess of beauty and of death, and it was when the giants kidnapped her (and the golden apples with her) that the gods' feud with them began.

For more about the golden apples, see pages 172 and 213.

AVALON *page 2*

The giants kept the golden apples on an island in the far west of the world, as remote from the gods as possible. Its name was Avalon, and it was perpetually hidden from view by a curtain of spray from the waterfall which girds the world. Despite such chilly surroundings, the golden apples guaranteed warmth and sunshine to the island itself, and gave it a mild climate and fertile fields throughout the year. It was a place of rest and healing, and many of the world's heroes went to live there at the end of their mortal lives. (In some versions of the story of King Arthur, he was one of them: see page 128).

Some accounts make the rulers of Avalon not giants but nine Fairy Queens, led by Morgan le Fay (see page 235) or by the Lady of the Lake (see page 233). Others say that Avalon was the same place as fairyland, and that mortals might stumble into it by accident (as Elidor did: see this page). The monks of Glastonbury Abbey in Gloucestershire claimed that Avalon was a real place, the countryside round Glastonbury Tor, and that the burial-chamber known as 'Arthur's grave' (see page 243) lay at its heart – a claim which has drawn pilgrims to Glastonbury from that day to this.

GERYON *page 2*

When the giants scattered across the world after their war against the gods (see page 2), Geryon was the only one who travelled west instead of north. He settled on a mist-shrouded island in the Atlantic Ocean, alone apart from a dwarf-servant, Eurytion, and a two-headed guard-dog, Orthrys. The only god who knew his hiding-place was the Sun, and he put Geryon in charge of a vast herd of sun-cattle, and told him to guard them with his life. For years Geryon was safe in his remote hiding-place; but then Hercules found out where he was and set out west to deal with him. (It was on this journey that Geryon's relative Albion tried to ambush Hercules: see page 2.) Like most giants, Geryon had several heads, and he

also had three bodies; unless all three were fatally wounded in the same instant, there was no hope of killing him. Hercules sailed to the island, clubbed Eurytion and Orthrys dead, and then, instead of trying to shoot Geryon's three bodies simultaneously with three arrows, he hid among the cattle-herds. Geryon parted the cattle, peering about him this way and that – and when his side was turned towards Hercules, Hercules fired with such force that one single arrow passed through all three of Geryon's bodies and sprawled him dead.

THE GIANTS OF BRITAIN *page 3*

The British giants' shyness of the world, and their uncanny power to hide themselves from it (see page 2), meant that very few mortals have ever met a giant or seen one face-to-face. But although giants themselves were seldom seen, there are signs of their presence all over Britain. Some are large and spectacular, like the Giants' Causeway in Ireland (thousands of stone pillars in the sea, which legend says were supports for a bridge which carried the giants dry-footed between Ireland and Scotland), or Fingal's Cave in the Hebrides (a cave as large as a cathedral, with enormous stalagmite-columns to support the roof). Other remains are the circles of standing stones in many parts of Britain (which legend says were giants' cattle-folds), and the banana-shaped *logan*-stones they set up on hilltops and headlands, to rock themselves on as they sat and enjoyed the view. (For another explanation of one group of standing stones, the stone-circle at Avebury, see page 218.)

ELIDOR *page 3*

Centuries after the time of the giants, a Christian monk called Elidor, from St David's Abbey in Wales, told of a strange

211

and supernatural adventure he had had as a boy. He said that one day, bored with lessons, he ran away from school and hid in a wood. As he lay on the bank of a stream he saw a passageway, like a narrow cave-mouth tangled with tree-roots. He wriggled through it, and found himself in a country of tiny people, exactly like human beings but small enough to ride hens for horses and hunt mice for stags. He made friends with their king's son, and played a game with him using half a dozen balls the size of pigeon's eggs, leathery to the touch but made of gold. When he wriggled back through the tunnel to the outside world, he tried to take one of the golden balls with him, but at the last moment he tripped and fell, and the ball rolled back into the land of the tiny people and was lost forever. He was never able to find the cave-mouth or stream again, and never discovered if the place he had found was Avalon (see page 210), and if what the tiny people thought of as golden balls were really the long-lost apples of immortality.

THE WOODEN HORSE *page 3*

Odysseus, a wily Greek commander, devised the trick of the Wooden Horse when his people could find no other way of getting into Troy. The Horse was huge, hollow and filled with armed men. The Greeks left it on the plain in front of Troy, pretending it was an offering to the gods, and sailed away. The Trojans thought that if they captured the Horse the gods would be angry and sink the Greek fleet, so they dragged it into Troy and left it standing in the centre of the city. That night, thinking the siege over and the Greeks gone for good, they held a wild celebration – and when all the city guards were drunk and snoring, the Greeks in the Horse opened it up, murdered the watchmen and flung open the city gates, while their companions turned their ships and sailed back to sack the city.

AENEAS *page 3*

Aeneas' mother, the goddess Venus, helped him escape from Troy's blazing ruins. He took with him his aged father Anchises, his son Ascanius, a band of followers and the statues of the gods of Troy, and sailed south to found a new kingdom, a second Troy. Storms battered his ships and drove them off-course; his followers were attacked by sea-monsters and harassed by the gods' anger; Aeneas himself visited the Underworld and saw a vision of the future greatness of Rome, the nation he was one day to found. He sailed to north Africa, where Queen Dido fell in love with him; but the gods forced him to abandon her and sail to Italy. Here he made an alliance with one tribe, the Latins (and married their princess Lavinia), and fought fierce battles with others (led by Turnus, prince of the Rutulians). It was not till he had made peace with all his enemies that he was able to found the settlement of Alba Longa, near a bend of the river Tiber where one day the city of Rome would stand.

BRUTUS *page 4*

The Latin word *Brutus* means 'brutal' or 'beast-like', and fits Brutus' wild nature as a boy and also the story that he killed his parents. Some people also connect it with the Greek word *brithos* ('weight'), and spell it Brithos or Britus: hence, perhaps, the origin of the future name of the British Isles, and of the Britons who live in them (see page 8).

THE PILLARS OF HERCULES *page 6*

In the days before people knew that the world is a sphere, they imagined it as saucer-shaped, edged by a wall of solid rock. Beyond the rock-wall was a swift-running river, which in due course fell over the rim of the universe in a gigantic waterfall tumbling into the abyss beyond. When the giants scattered after losing their war with the gods (see page 2), Geryon clambered over the rock-wall, swam to an island in the river beyond, just before the currents gathered towards the waterfall, and thought himself safe. But when Hercules went looking for him (see page 2), he used his club to batter a gap in the rock-wall, sailed through and so reached the distant river and Geryon's island. The river is the sea we now call the Atlantic Ocean; the sides of the rock-passage used to be known as the Pillars of Hercules; the narrow gap between them is nowadays called the Straits of Gibraltar.

THE FIRST SETTLEMENT *page 7*

Ever since the legend of this Trojan settlement was first told, people have wondered where it was. One favoured spot is the innermost corner of the Bay of Biscay, somewhere between Santander in Spain and Bayonne in France. The area is still the home of the Basques, one of the most ancient of all European peoples, and their language is unlike modern Spanish or French, and is remarkably close in sound and vocabulary to the ancient language of Cornwall.

GOGMAGOG'S LEAP *page 8*

As with the story of the first Trojan settlement in Europe (see this page), people have often wondered where exactly the landing of the Trojans in Britain, and the fight between Corin and Gogmagog, took place. A likely spot for the Trojan landing seems to have been the place now called Totnes in Devon, and the place where Corin fought Gogmagog lay some-where near the mouth of the River Dart. (The river-mouth is full of jagged rocks and boulders, like lumps of fossilised giant's flesh; the underwater rocks are dull orange in colour, as if stained with blood.) There are other, less likely, sites: near Cambridge, for example (dozens of kilometres inland), are two low hills known as Gog and Magog, as if they were two halves of a giant turned to stone. But even if Corin killed Gogmagog with a sword, chopping him in half as he did his enemies in Gaul (see page 7), how did the pieces get so many kilometres inland, out of reach of the sea?

THE SPRINGS OF SUL *page 10*

The springs of Sul lay on the banks of the river Avon, about sixteen kilometres upstream. A constant flow of boiling water bubbled up from underground, and the air was filled with sulphur. People made channels and cisterns to cool the water, and thought that anyone who drank it or bathed in it would be cured of disease. The healing springs were famous all over Southern Britain, and thousands of people visited them each year. When the Romans conquered Britain (see page 13), they renamed the goddess of the springs Sulis-Minerva, and built a huge temple in her honour, complete with swimming-pools and treatment-rooms. A town grew up round it: in Roman times it was called Aquae Sulis ('The Waters of Sul'); now it is the modern town of Bath in Somerset, and its water still bubbles unfailingly.

KING LEAR *page 11*

Shakespeare used the story of Leir and his daughters as the basis for his play *King Lear*. (He intermingled it with a second story involving the aged Duke of Gloucester and his two sons, Edmund whom he wrongly trusted and Edgar whom he wrongly despised.) In Shakespeare's version, Leir's story ends tragically. Instead of Cordelia defeating her sisters in battle, they defeat her. She is thrown into prison and murdered. Meanwhile, Goneril and Regan are quarrelling for power. Goneril poisons Regan, and kills herself when Regan's husband the Duke of Albany finds out. Lear, a miserable, broken old man, carries centre-stage the body of Cordelia, the only one of his children who truly loved him. He tries to revive her, and when he fails his heart breaks and he, too, dies.

THE FOUNDING OF ROME *page 12*

The wicked King Amulius of Alba Longa in Italy (the town founded long before by Aeneas: see page 212) had seized his throne by ousting his brother Numitor. He made Numitor's daughter Rhea Silvia a priestess, unable to marry or have children who might grow up to snatch back the throne. But the war-god himself made Rhea Silvia pregnant, and when her twin sons Romulus and Remus were born, Amulius executed her and tried to kill the babies by floating them down the river Tiber in a basket. They were washed ashore, where a she-wolf suckled them and a shepherd found them and brought them up as his own children. When they were grown-up they avenged their mother's murder by killing Amulius, and restored their grandfather Numitor to his rightful throne. Then they set about founding a new city of their own. Romulus was ploughing a furrow to mark the line of the city walls when Remus jumped over it, saying scornfully: 'What enemies will this keep out?' Romulus lost his temper and killed him. So Romulus was the sole founder of Rome, and the city was named after him. After his death the gods took him into heaven, and the Romans built him a temple in the city, from which

he protected and helped his people ever afterwards.

BELIN AND BRENN *page 12*

Like Ferrec and Porrec (see page 12), Belin and Brenn were brothers who quarrelled from the moment they left their mother's womb. They were the sons of King Dunvallo, and both coveted his throne. As children they slapped, pinched and bit; as young men they wrestled, threw stones and fought with sticks; as adults they gathered armies and turned quarrelling to war. Belin declared himself king, whereupon Brenn sailed to Norway, married the Norwegian king's daughter and invaded Britain with a navy of Norwegian ships. But the ships were sunk in a storm, and Belin captured Brenn's wife and held her hostage. Brenn fled to Gaul, made a second marriage, with the daughter of the chief of the Allobrogians, and assembled a second invasion-fleet. He landed his soldiers near Dover, and Belin drew his British army up on the beach, ready to defend his throne to the death. Before a blow was struck, however, Belin's and Brenn's aged mother Tonwenna walked through the lines of soldiers, fell on her knees and begged her sons to make peace and turn their anger on joint enemies instead of on one another. Her tears were so affecting that the young men shook hands, united their armies and set sail for Gaul and Germany, where they conquered every hostile tribe. It was because the Romans sent an army to help the Germans that Belin and Brenn marched on Rome. They captured it (so Roman historians glumly report) in 390 BC, slaughtered its people, burnt its buildings and looted it. After that Brenn stayed in Italy, harrying the Roman survivors with merciless cruelty until he was himself killed in battle; Belin went back to Britain, loaded with booty, and brought his country more peace and prosperity than his people had ever known.

CUNOBELIN *page 13*

Cunobelin's education in Italy gave him a love of Roman clothes, customs, manners and the Latin language. When he returned to Britain as king, he built a new capital city (Camelodunum, modern Colchester), and lived there in a palace like an Italian villa, surrounded by consuls and senators in Roman style. In Colchester each year he gathered the silver which was to be sent as tax to Rome, melted it down and stamped it into coins. (They were the first coins ever minted in Britain; a handful still survive.)

After Cunobelin's death the Romans expected the same loyalty from his son Caratacus. But Caratacus rebelled, and tried to return to the old British ways. This led to another Roman invasion, and Caratacus was captured and led through the streets of Rome in chains.

One of Shakespeare's plays, *Cymbeline*, is named after Cunobelin, and its chief character is a British king friendly to the Romans. But Shakespeare's story has little to do with the legendary Cunobelin: it mainly concerns the king's beautiful daughter Imogen, her vow of faithfulness to her Roman husband Postumus, and the efforts of two villains, Iachimo and Cloten, to destroy her.

BOUDICA *page 13*

Although relationships were generally good between Britain and Rome, there were occasional flare-ups. One of the fiercest happened in the time of the crazy Roman emperor Nero. The British king Prasutagus, chief of the Iceni tribe, had always been on good terms with the Romans, and they in turn had helped and

traded with his people, and built an impressive Roman town next to his royal castle at Camelodunum. (It was this town that King Coel later renamed Colchester: see page 216.) Prasutagus wanted friendship with Rome to continue after his death, so in his will he made the emperor Nero joint heir with his own queen Boudica.

Instead of sharing the kingdom, however, Nero decided to take all of it. He sent soldiers to snatch as many British warehouses, farms and villas as they could. Queen Boudica raised an army of resistance-fighters to drive them out. She was famous for galloping across battlefields in a war-chariot whose axles ended in scythes, reaping enemies like cornstalks; her red hair streamed in the wind and she wore glittering, gold-plated armour and swung a double-handed warsword till the Romans cringed and ran. The Roman governor of Britain, Paulinus, happened to be far away at the time, leading his legions against barbarians in Cambria; to give her followers no hiding-place, no excuse not to go to war, Boudica burnt Camelodunum to the ground, then moved westwards and did the same to the Roman settlements at Verulamium (modern St Albans) and London. At last news of the uprising reached Cambria, and Paulinus swung his legions and hurried to attack. The well-trained Roman army massacred the Britons at the battle of Mancetter (a village not far from modern Nuneaton); when Boudica saw that resistance was useless, and that she would end up in chains as a Roman slave, or be crucified as a criminal, she drank poison.

Since few Britons in Boudica's time could read or write, no account of her adventures appeared until she was mentioned by the Roman historian Tacitus (whose uncle was an officer in the legion which defeated her). Tacitus spelt her name Boudicca; a century later a short-sighted scribe mis-copied it as Boadicea, and she has been famous by that name ever since.

OLD KING COEL *page 13*

Coel ruled Britain from Camelodunum, the city built long before by Cunobelin (see page 215); he renamed it Colchester after himself. He took power by killing King Asclepiodotus, who had hated the Romans and sliced off the heads of any he found; for this reason, the Romans were delighted when Coel came to the throne, and sent one of their noblest generals, Constantius, to help him rule. Constantius married Coel's daughter Helen, and became king after Coel's death. (He and Helen had a son, Constantine, who later went to Rome to become emperor, and on the journey was converted to Christianity.)

Very little else is known about King Coel except for the nursery-rhyme:

Old King Cole was a merry old soul,
  And a merry old soul was he;
He sent for his pipe, and he sent for his
  bowl,
  And he sent for his fiddlers three.

(If Coel had done any of this he would have been a remarkable man indeed, for he lived 800 years before the fiddle was invented and 1200 years before Sir Walter Raleigh brought pipe-tobacco from the New World to Britain.)

MAXEN'S DREAM *page 14*

The Welsh legend-collection *Mabinogion* (see page 249) gives a different account of how Maximian came to rule, and then desert, Britain. In it he was renamed Maxen, and was Roman emperor, the most powerful man on earth. One day he dreamed that he travelled to a distant country across the sea, and found there a castle with doors and roofs of gold and jewel-studded walls; inside were two princes playing chess, an old man moulding chess-pieces from a bar of gold, and a beautiful princess who threw her arms round him and welcomed him as king of the island. When Maxen woke up, he set out to repeat his dream-journey, and every detail fitted: voyage, castle, boys, old man, princess. He ruled Britain for seven years, and the Roman people grew so irritated by his absence that they appointed a new emperor and sent Maxen a riddling, insulting message of warning, 'If you come, if ever you come to Rome . . .' Maxen replied, 'If I come, if I come to Rome . . .', and set out with an army, sharing its leadership with the two young chess-playing princes, now grown-up. (Their names were Kynan, or Conan, and Avaon.) They conquered Armorica, Germany and northern Italy, and eventually besieged and captured Rome itself. After this journey of conquest Maxen stayed in Rome, Kynan went to rule Armorica (renaming it Brittany), and Avaon took the rest of the army back to Britain. But the returning soldiers spread word of richer, far more prosperous countries to the south, and this was why so many Britons later decided to leave Britain forever and settle in Brittany.

SHAPE-CHANGERS; MERLIN *page 21*

Just as human beings were a mixture of the two basic elements earth and water, so shape-changers were a mixture of air and fire. They were the wind's relatives, and like it had the power to take on any shape they chose, large or small, powerful or gentle, visible or invisible. They generally kept out of the way of human beings (whom they regarded as slow-witted and lumbering, prisoners of passing time); when mortals caught glimpses of them, they called them phantoms, genies, will-o'-the-wisps and loreleis.

One thing above all others which made shape-changers take on human form was when they fell in love with mortal men or women. They appeared to them as human beings, made love with them and disappeared again. This love-making always resulted in pregnancy, and the children (whether born of mortal fathers and immortal mothers or vice versa) lived in the mortal world but seemed to ordinary people to possess miraculous, superhuman powers. They were favourite prey for Satan, and unless they were given Christian baptism the instant they were born, they were sucked into Hell and became the Devil's unholy servants.

Merlin (born to a mortal mother and a phantom father, and plunged in holy water as soon as he was born) was one of the most famous of all shape-changers, known to the mortals he helped as the Prince of Enchanters. In pictures and storybooks he is often shown as an old man with a long white beard; in fact, since shape-changers live untouched by time, he preferred the appearance of a handsome young man, never aging as the mortals round him aged. One of the reasons for this preference was his addiction to mortal women: he fell in love, instantly and utterly, with every pretty girl he met. This caused him problems with a fellow shape-changer, the Lady of the Lake (see page 233), who changed herself into a mortal girl, seduced Merlin and kept him prisoner in an underground cave until he agreed to love her alone. Merlin refused, and the love of the Lady of the Lake gradually turned to hate. She tangled him in a magic thornbush (which seemed to him like a prison of coiling cloud) and forgot him entirely – and since no one else could undo the spell she cast, he has been trapped in his thornbush cell ever since. He no longer appears in the mortal world, and is nothing more than a disembodied voice calling out for help to every passer-by.

DRAGONS *page 22*

Dragons were an evolutionary dead-end, an attempt to make living creatures out of earth and fire. They were related to lizards, toads and crocodiles, and their remote ancestors were dinosaurs. They came in many sizes: the ones we most often hear about, because they preyed on cattle and even, sometimes, on humans, were the size of houses, but others were much smaller, the size of chickens, mice or gnats. Like all amphibians, dragons were cold-blooded, and depended for life on finding an external heat-source to warm them up. They liked to lie underground, basking in caves as near as possible to the molten core of the earth; failing that they flew as high as they could, seeking the sun's heat unfiltered by clouds. When they were at their most active, they could breathe fire; but this quickly drained the heat from them, and they preferred to rely on knocking their prey senseless with wing-blows, or ripping it to pieces with their talons and razor-fangs.

THE TWO DRAGONS *page 22*

The Welsh legend-collection *Mabinogion* (see page 249) says that in the time of Lud (the king whose capital was Lud-town or London), three supernatural plagues attacked Britain: a race of robbers who could never be defeated because they controlled the winds and so heard every whisper of a plan made against them, a giant who stuffed all the king's food into a magic bag and stole it, and a pair of dragons which screamed so loudly each Mayday Eve that every man in Britain grew pale, every woman miscarried, every child fainted, and every animal, plant and flower withered and died. Lud dealt with the robbers by uttering warplans not directly into the wind but through a bronze tube which took the message straight from his lips to his companions' ears (the first time trumpets were ever used in battle). He dealt with the giant by toppling him to the ground and threatening to water all Britain with his blood unless he changed his ways. To deal with the dragons he dug a hole in the ground, filled it with mead (a powerful drink) and covered it with a cloth. The dragons were attracted by the smell, sank on the cloth into the hole to lap up the mead, and when they were helplessly drunk Lud bundled them up, transported them to Mount Erith and buried them.

In some versions of the myth, when Vortigern's men released the dragons, they not only billowed out of the ground but fought, and the white dragon killed the red one. This makes an exciting story – each time a drop of dragon-blood spills on the ground, it sizzles a hole in it as acid sizzles iron – but it hardly fits the explanation Merlin later gave of the omen (see page 22): if the dragons stood for Aurelius and his ally and brother Uther, why should they fight?

THE GIANTS' RING *page 23*

One of King Aurelius' most pious acts was to give Christian burial to the 400 British lords slaughtered by the Saxons at the Avebury 'peace'-conference (see page 20). The Saxons had dumped the bodies in a pit, without prayer or ceremony; now Aurelius' men reverently reburied the bones in a Christian grave, and priests sang Masses for the victims' souls. The grave was like a flat field, covered with green turf; but Aurelius wanted a more impressive memorial. Merlin suggested that he should send workmen to Hibernia, dismantle the Giants' Ring (a circle of stones on Mount Killaurus) and rebuild it on the field at Avebury. It was easy

enough to sail to Hibernia and to beat off the natives (who strongly resisted the idea of having their Giants' Ring stolen), but moving the stones was much more difficult. There were dozens of them, and they varied from the size of a small dog to jagged boulders as big as carts. For days, while the furious natives prowled the woods all round, Aurelius' masons, carters and surveyors tugged, heaved, levered and pushed the stones, trying to dislodge them from the ground: in vain. Then Merlin offered to do the job himself, single-handed, and while they scoffed he turned himself into a whirlpool of wind, a tornado, and sucked the stones from their sockets as easily as men pull teeth. Aurelius' men shipped them to Britain and carried them to Avebury, where they set them up in the circle still known to this day as the Avebury Ring.

There are other explanations of how the Avebury Ring came to be there – for example that it was part of a Sun-temple built by Stone Age people thousands of years before King Aurelius' time. (Others claim that the British nobles' burial-ground was not at Avebury at all, but at Amesbury nearby, or even at Stonehenge.) But the story of Merlin and the stones neatly explains why the Hibernian people were so hostile to King Aurelius, and why, when Vortigern's son landed in Hibernia (see below), they flocked to join his army and help him invade Britain.

AURELIUS' DEATH *page 24*

In another version of the myth, Aurelius's death had nothing at all to do with Renwein: in fact she disappeared from the story long before Vortigern was burnt in his tower (see page 23), and what happened to her is never told. In this account, Vortigern's son Paschent escaped to Hibernia after Aurelius became king, and made an alliance with Gilloman, the Hibernian clanchief outraged by Aurelius' and Merlin's theft of the Giant's Ring (see page 218). Gilloman provided Paschent with an army and they sailed for Cambria, where Uther led the British defence against them. While this was happening, Aurelius was struck down at Winchester by a mysterious illness, and one of Paschent's Saxons, Eopa (not Ambron, as in the other version of the myth) volunteered to disguise himself as a Christian doctor and poison him. Eopa shaved off his Saxon beard, trimmed his hair in a monk's tonsure (the ring of bare scalp in the centre of the head), put on sackcloth robes and wheedled his way into Aurelius' palace in Winchester. He poisoned the king and disappeared. Meanwhile, in Cambria, Uther defeated the Hibernian invaders, killed Paschent and Gilloman, and was setting off back in triumph for Winchester when news came that his brother was dead and he was king.

THE FIREBALL-DRAGON *page 27*

Some people explain the fireball-dragon as a comet, something whose existence no one would even have suspected in Uther's time. A comet is an ice-ball hurtling through space, so fast that the ice on the outside forms gas and bursts into flame, giving the comet the appearance of a fireball with a glowing tail. Most comets have vast orbits, and are only seen once in ten thousand or a million years, but one comet in particular, Halley's Comet, appears regularly (and can be seen in southern Britain) every 76 years. It appeared in 1066, shortly before William the Conqueror invaded Britain, and in the time of Uther, 500 years before, it would have passed over Britain in the years 458 and 534.

TINTAGEL AND DAMELIOCK *page 28*

In the legend, Tintagel was a lighthouse-like tower built of huge stone blocks on a promontory of needle-cliffs. It was surrounded on three sides by sea, and the fourth side was connected to land by a neck of rock so narrow that people could cross only in single file, and one careless step to left or right would mean plunging to death on the cliffs or in the sea below. (This spectacular position made Tintagel easy to guard: three or four soldiers could hold a whole army at bay.) Castle Dameliock, about ten kilometres away, was an enormous fortified camp, ringed by three high walls and three ditches. Its remains, and remains said to be those of Tintagel, can still be seen.

Some versions of the legend make Tintagel not the place where Arthur was conceived but the place where he made his court. (See Camelot, page 221.) But it was too small and too remote to be the capital of a whole kingdom: it is far more likely to have been just one of his royal castles, a useful bolt-hole in troubled times.

SIEGE-WEAPONS *page 28*

Uther's siege-weapons were either ones left behind by the Romans or copies of Roman originals. The **battering-ram** was a tree trunk with a bronze-covered spike at one end and dozens of carrying-handles. Men ran with it at full tilt and smashed it into the doors or gates of the place they were besieging; with luck the doors would be torn from their hinges and the besiegers could pour inside. The **ballista** was a giant catapult (worked by twisted rope and mounted on a wooden frame): it fired boulders the size of cattle, and was used to pound walls to rubble or to demolish buildings inside the place being besieged. The **fire-bow** worked in a similar way, but shot enormous arrows tipped with bundles of blazing straw. The **siege-tower** was a wooden scaffolding on wheels. It had several storeys, and was armour-plated against attack. The besiegers rolled it hard up against the defenders' walls, and while archers on the top storey kept the enemy at bay, people on the lower storeys attacked the walls with pickaxes, spikes and battering-rams.

ARTHUR'S BIRTH *page 28*

In another version of the legend of Arthur's birth, he was not a mortal being at all, the son of Uther and Ygern, but one of the most ancient gods of Britain, Artos the Bear. When Christianity came to Britain, Artos withdrew with the other ancient gods to the sky (where he became the star Arcturus). But from time to time he felt the urge to return to earth and take on human shape, and on these occasions he entered the body of a mortal woman at the moment she conceived a baby, and was born in due course as her mortal son.

MORGAUS *page 29*

The legends give several different accounts of Arthur's sister Morgaus. In some accounts she is called Anne or Belisent; in others she is confused with Morgan le Fay: see page 235. Some legends make her not Arthur's full sister at all (daughter of Ygern and Uther) but his half-sister, one of the three daughters of Ygern and Gorlois, king of Cornwall. (The others are Elaine, who has no future part to play in the story – she is not the same Elaine who marries Lancelot: see page 90 – and Morgan le Fay.) Nonetheless, and whatever Morgaus' true relationship to Arthur, all legends agree about what happened to her after she grew up: that story is told on page 32.

ARTHUR'S EDUCATION *page 29*

In some versions of the legend, as well as his princely education from Ector, Arthur was given a second education by Merlin. Because Arthur's parents were human, he was made of the wrong elements to become a fully-fledged shape-changer: earth and water instead of air and fire. But Merlin taught him all the magic skills he could (chiefly herb-lore and sleight-of-hand, which is nowadays called conjuring), and also changed him from time to time into such creatures as frog, fly, hound, eagle, stag or trout, so that he could sample for himself the lives they led.

UTHER'S DEATH *page 29*

In some accounts of Uther's last days, he and his soldiers were the people besieged in St Albans, and the Saxons were the besiegers. Uther was mortally sick, and was convinced that he was being secretly poisoned. He refused to eat any food unless it was first tasted before his eyes by the cook who made it, and drank nothing but water from one closely-guarded well in the heart of the castle. The Saxons got round these precautions by disguising one of their men as a well-guard and giving him a phial of poison to put down the well. The polluted water killed Uther and everyone else who drank it. At first everyone took the epidemic for a plague from God, a punishment for Uther's treatment of Gorlois (see page 28); then they discovered the poison, filled the well with earth and sealed it, and the epidemic stopped.

ARTHUR'S SWORD *page 32*

Arthur's sword was made on the magic island of Avalon, a place in the far west of the world where noble heroes' souls went after death and where there was a cutting from the tree of the golden apples of immortality (see page 210). It was lent, from time to time, to mortal kings and heroes of particular bravery, and after their deaths returned to Avalon. (For how this happened at the end of Arthur's time on earth, see page 127.)

In some versions of the legend, Excalibur did not appear in a stone at all. Instead, Arthur owned a perfectly ordinary sword, and shattered the blade in a duel with someone who challenged his right to ride through a mountain-pass. Merlin rescued him from death (by throwing a sleep-spell on his adversary), and took him to a mist-enshrouded lake nearby (home of the enchantress Nimue, who later became Lancelot's foster-mother: see page 86, and later still fell in love with Merlin himself: see page 217). As Arthur and Merlin stood on the lake-shore, they saw Nimue gliding across it, and a white-robed arm rising from the water brandishing Excalibur. (For what happened next, see page 233.)

THE BATTLE OF BADON *page 34*

In another version of the legend, there was no plot by the eleven kings against Arthur, and no magic by Merlin to topple their tents. Instead, their loyalty to Arthur was won gradually, over a series of twelve battles against the Saxons (who were led by Hengist's son Orca, now a very old man, and his heathen hordes from north of the River Humber). At each of the battles – which took place all over Britain, from the Lincolnshire–Humber border in the north-east to the Severn estuary in the west, Arthur saved the lives of one of the hostile kings, until by the twelfth battle, at Mount Badon near Bath, they were all fanatically loyal to him.

CAMELOT *page 34*

All the legends of King Arthur agree that although he had castles and palaces in several parts of Britain, and often visited each of them, his main court was at Camelot. There is, however, absolutely no agreement about where Camelot was. There are four main possibilities: Winchester (where Arthur's father Uther had his court: see page 27), Caerleon (where Arthur and Guinever were married: see page 35), Cadbury Castle in Somerset (a hill-fort dating back to prehistoric times) and Camelford in Cornwall (not far from Tintagel).

THE ROUND TABLE *page 34*

There are several other accounts of how the Round Table came into existence. In one, it was not made for Arthur at all but for his father Uther, and was given to Arthur as a wedding-present when he married Guinever (see page 35): this table had places for 150 nobles, and Arthur found it hard to find so many men in Britain deserving the honour. (The legend further says that as each man was appointed to the table, Merlin caused his name to appear on it in letters of gold, which stayed bright and glowing until the day of his disgrace or death.) In another legend, Arthur went to kill a water-monster in Carr Marshes, and found a broad, flat stone floating on the water. The stone was the altar of St Carantacus, lost long ago in the Severn, and in gratitude for Arthur's finding it the saint fastened a cloth round the monster's neck and led it out of the marshes as docile as a kitten, then gave Arthur the altar to make into the Round Table. In the most extravagant Round-Table legend of all, Arthur built the table to stop his nobles squabbling over seniority at a Christmas feast – and since there were no less than sixteen hundred of them, each requiring a place, the Table was the size of a small field.

Most Round-Table stories date from the eleventh century, about six hundred years after Arthur's own time. It was an age of chivalry, when noble followers of the king were known as Knights, and it is in this form, as Knights of the Round Table – Sir Lancelot, Sir Gawain, Sir Bedivere and the others – that many people still think of Arthur's followers today, even though it is utterly unlike the pattern of names or ranks in Arthur's time.

In Winchester Great Hall a real Round Table exists, hung on the wall like an enormous dart-board. It is made of English oak, is divided into sections like the slices of a cake, and each slice has the name of the owner (Sir Galahad, Sir Kay, Sir Mordred) painted on it in ornate lettering. King Arthur is shown in one of the panels, sitting on his royal throne and holding Excalibur; in the centre of the table is painted the royal rose of England; there are places round the table for twenty-four knights.

For a religious explanation of the origin and shape of the Round Table, see page 239.

GUINEVER *page 34*

In some versions of the legend there is only one Guinever, and her love-affair with Lancelot and betrayal of Arthur (see page 117) are straightforward failings in a character which is never too honourable from the start. In other versions there are two Guinevers, 'good Guinever' and 'bad Guinever'. One is an honourable lady, the daughter of Leodegran; the other is a wicked fairy, her exact double, who from time to time smuggles her away in a charmed sleep, takes her place and does evil for which everyone later blames 'good Guinever'. This alternative legend inspired the story of Lanfal (see page 223),

and so delighted later myth-tellers that they invented still more Guinevers, saying that Arthur had three or more wives one after the other, all called Guinever, all identical in appearance, and each with a different character, bad or good.

Some people say that Guinever is a form of the Welsh name Gwen-hwyfar, and that she was a Welsh princess; others say that her name was Guanamara, that she was a Roman orphan brought up by King Cador of Cornwall, and that she ended her days not at Amesbury or as Arthur's queen in Avalon (see page 243) but as a nun in the church of Julius the Martyr in Caerleon, City of the Legions beside the River Usk.

THE LOOTING OF LONDON *page 35*

There is a legend that while Arthur, Merlin and their 38 followers were in North Britain wooing Guinever (see page 34), a mob of Saxons and giants took advantage of their absence to attack and loot London. They piled their booty on wagons and began carting it away. But in the nick of time word reached Gawain, and he galloped to London with 700 men, fell on the looters and cut them to pieces. Gawain himself sliced the giants' chief Choas in two, from the crown of his head to the base of his spine (much as Arthur sliced Lucius Hiberius in the ambush of the Roman legions: see page 39), and beheaded another giant called Sanagran. When the Londoners saw what was happening they flocked out to join the fight and drive the enemy away for good.

This story is so close to the account of Arthur's wooing of Guinever that it is probably a simple mis-remembering (changing names and places but keeping many of the details); it also fits badly into the time-scale of Arthur's early reign, which would have made Gawain no more than two or three years old.

222

ARTHUR'S CONQUESTS *page 36*

Some accounts say that Arthur's and Guinever's celebration was not held immediately after their wedding, but came much later, after years of struggle and conquest. The soberer myth-makers limit these struggles to Britain and Brittany, and describe Arthur breaking the power of Saxons, Picts and other heathens in those parts. But more fanciful chroniclers extend his conquests for anything from nine to twenty-five years, and envisage him ruling not only Britain and its offshore islands (eg the Orkneys and Shetlands) but also places as remote as Norway, Iceland, Germany and Poland.

LANFAL *page 36*

In the legend of 'true' Guinever and 'false' Guinever (see page 222), only one person noticed that 'false' Guinever was taking 'true' Guinever's place in the wedding-feast with Arthur. The man's name was Lanfal, and when Arthur refused to listen to his warnings he left Caerleon in disgust and stayed away for a whole year.

One day Lanfal was seduced by an enchantress called Triamor. She heaped him with fairy riches, but warned him that they would turn to ashes and pebbles if he ever spoke her name aloud. Lanfal rode to Camelot in pomp so glittering that no one but 'false' Guinever recognized him as the man who had insulted her at the wedding-feast. Arthur gave a banquet in his honour, and while the king's attention was distracted by some musicians, 'false' Guinever leaned over and asked Lanfal to be her lover. He refused angrily, saying that he was in love with the most beautiful woman in the world, Triamor – and as soon as he spoke the name the rings turned to pebbles on his fingers and his clothes turned to ashes,

leaving him naked before the court. Arthur threw him into prison for sorcery, but 'false' Guinever suggested an even severer punishment: he should be executed, she said, unless his beloved Triamor turned up within a year and a day, and was indeed, as he claimed, the most beautiful woman in the world. Word of this reached Triamor, and she galloped to Camelot. As soon as she showed her face at court, 'false' Guinever was suddenly struck blind, and realized that she had lost the contest of beauty. She fled from Camelot until her sight returned, leaving 'true' Guinever on the throne, and that same night Triamor carried Lanfal to her magic kingdom and they were never seen again.

THE GIANT OF MONT ST-MICHEL *page 38*

In some versions of the legend, as well as Arthur's dream about the dragon and the bear (see page 38), another event gave him courage for his forthcoming battle against the Romans. He and his army landed on the coast of Brittany, and camped there for several months till the European kings and their soldiers joined them. The area was ruled by Arthur's ally King Hoel, and one day he came to Arthur with tears in his eyes and said that his only daughter, Helen, had been snatched by a flesh-eating giant and carried to his lair on Mont St-Michel. Mont St-Michel was a gaunt rock, jutting out to sea and almost entirely cut off from land: it could be reached dry-shod only at low tide, and the giant discouraged visitors by lobbing rocks at them. Arthur decided to attack by boat, at a time of day when the giant was least expecting it, and late that evening he, Kay and Bediver rowed out to the rock and beached their boat. Arthur left Kay and Bediver on guard and began climbing to the giant's cave on the pinnacle of the rock, outside which the giant was roasting meat on a bonfire for supper. Halfway up the hill Arthur found an old woman weeping over a freshly-dug grave. She said that the grave was Helen's, that the giant had tried to rape her, and that when she resisted he had choked the life from her. When he heard this Arthur gave a roar of rage, and the giant at once threw down the human leg he was gnawing and came to investigate. He punched Arthur so hard on his leather helmet that blood oozed from his nose and ears, and while he was reeling, the giant bear-hugged him, intending to squeeze him to pulp and eat him. Fortunately Arthur, dazed as he was, still kept his grip on Excalibur, and the harder the giant squeezed the deeper he forced Excalibur's point into his own heart. The two of them, Arthur and the giant, rolled down the hill pinned by Excalibur in an embrace of death, and crashed on to the beach beside Arthur's boat. Kay and Bediver hurried to hack the giant's grip apart, and Arthur fell on the sand panting for breath and with every rib in his body cracked and bruised. Kay and Bediver used Excalibur to saw the giant's head off; then they heaved the body into the sea and rowed with heavy hearts back to the mainland to break the news to Hoel of his daughter's death. Hoel ordered a church to be built on the cliff-top in his daughter's memory, and Mont St-Michel has been a place of pilgrimage ever since. As for Arthur, by the time the European kings and their soldiers arrived to join his army his wounds had healed, and his victory over the giant gave him confidence to face the fifty giants who led the Roman battle-line (see page 39).

In some versions of this legend, when Arthur tells the story of his fight with the giant of Mont St-Michel, he compares it with another battle, fought years before against a giant called Retho who infested the peak of Mount Erith (the Welsh mountain-top where Vortigern built his magic tower: see page 20). Many kings and warriors had challenged Retho to single combat, and Retho had killed every one of them and sewed their beards on his cloak for trophies; now he promised Arthur that as he was the most famous of all the kings to challenge him, he would sew *his* beard at the place of honour highest up the cloak. While he was still boasting and jeering, Arthur tripped him, cut off his head with Excalibur, and trimmed off Retho's own beard as a war-trophy. (He buried the beard-sewn cloak in a Christian cemetery, as it was all that was left of the honourable Christian warriors who had fought the giant. As for Retho's beard, Arthur had it woven into cloth and made into a cloak, and he wore it over his armour when he went to war.)

ARTHUR EMPEROR OF ROME *page 40*

Most versions of the legend end as this one does, with Arthur returning triumphantly to Britain, to rule his own kingdom free from enemy attack. But a few accounts – those which paint Arthur as a world-conqueror on the scale of Alexander the Great or Charlemagne – say that in the year after his defeat of Lucius Hiberius he marched on Rome itself, that the Roman emperor Leo abdicated in his favour and that the Pope crowned him emperor of Christendom, the one man to whom every other mortal king bent the knee.

'HANDY' *page 41*

In some accounts, the nickname Handy (*Beaumains*) was given not to Gareth but to one of his brothers (usually Agravain), and the reason for it is unexplained. Some say that outstandingly large or skilful hands are typical possessions of sun-spirits, and that the name is a survival from the oldest British legends of all, in which Gawain and his brothers were not mortals but demigods. Others, from a much later time, after the Norman conquest, say that *Beaumains* (or, in some versions, *Maindur* or 'Hardhand') was not a nickname but a surname (like Beecham, i.e. *Beauchamp* or 'Fine fields'), and referred to the whole family.

GAWAIN AND GALERON *page 43*

Some versions of the story of Galeron and Gawain made no link between the million Masses and the return of Galeron's lands. The ghost appeared, and Gawain agreed to pay for the Masses out of his own pocket; later, on another occasion entirely, Galeron challenged him to fight for the lands, and the two men battled each other to exhaustion, and were so badly wounded that the fight would have ended in both of their deaths if Guinever had not ordered a stop to it. Gawain and Galeron lay sick of their wounds for weeks, and when they recovered Gawain gladly handed back the lands, and in return Galeron swore loyalty to King Arthur and became a member of the Round Table.

GYNGALYN *page 44*

In some legends of Gawain, he had a son, perhaps by this unknown lady in the field. The boy's name was Gyngalyn, and his mother never told him who his father was. When Gyngalyn was fifteen he went to Camelot, and Gawain (not knowing who he was) taught him the skills of riding, shooting and sword-fighting. Because he had no known father, Arthur and his courtiers nicknamed him Libeaus Desconus, or 'The Handsome Mystery'.

One day a terrified maidservant went to Camelot and begged Arthur's help against enchanters who had ensnared her mistress, the Lady of Sinadun. Gyngalyn rode with the girl, and on the way to Sinadun fought and beat every mortal, giant or wizard who tried to bar the way. One of his victories was against a giant called Mawgin who was attacking a castle – and after the duel the castle's fairy owner trapped him by magic into staying for a whole year, and it was only thanks to the maid's reminders that he remembered his mission and rode on to Sinadun.

Gyngalyn found no one in Sinadun Castle but musicians: the place was full of pipers, singers, harpers and viol-players, and the air throbbed with melody. He sat down to listen, and at once the castle shook as if in an earthquake, the musicians melted into air and the two enchanters Mabon and Yvan appeared and challenged him. He killed Mabon, and would have sliced Yvan too if he had not vanished just as the blow fell. Gyngalyn was gathering his breath when a snake with a woman's face slithered across the floor, coiled round him and begged him to kiss her. Gyngalyn had inherited all his father Gawain's good manners (see page 46), and agreed to kiss her although his lips were stiff with fear. The kiss turned the snake into a beautiful woman, and lifted all enchantment from the castle. Gyngalyn took the lady back to Camelot and married her; then they settled in Sinadun with the loyal maidservant and lived happily ever afterwards.

THE WIFE OF BATH'S TALE *page 47*

Chaucer used the story of Ragnell as the basis of *The Wife of Bath's Tale* in *The Canterbury Tales*. He changed several of the details – Gawain was not named, for example, and the young man who married Ragnell had to find the answer to the riddle himself or die, as punishment for raping a girl – and he gave the story a different final twist. In his version, the new wife asked her husband if he would prefer her ugly for 24 hours a day (and chaste, safe from pursuit by other men), or beautiful (and chased); when he answered, 'My will is yours. In this marriage, you are sovereign,' she became forever beautiful and forever faithful as well, so making neither partner in the marriage sovereign, but both equal (as, the Wife of Bath insists, all true marriage-partners ought to be).

THE PENTANGLE *page 50*

The Pentangle, or sealed knot, is a single ribbon or line twisted to form a five-pointed star without breaking. It is a powerful sign in magic, and also in the ancient Jewish religion and in Christianity, where it was believed to ward off devils. (If Gawain had been carrying his pentangle-shield when he met the withered old woman in Lord Bertilak's hall, she would have been revealed for the enchantress she really was: see pages 50, 53.)

The writer of the poem *Sir Gawain and the Green Knight*, anxious to present Gawain as the flower of Christian chivalry, says that the Pentangle is the ideal sign for him because he is faultless in every five ways possible. His five senses are the keenest of any man's on earth; his five fingers never fail him; he is protected by the five wounds Christ received on the cross and by the five joys Mary (Christ's mother) had in her son (Annunciation, Birth, Resurrection, Ascension and Assumption into heaven); he practises the five virtues of generosity, kindness, piety, politeness and self-restraint.

GAWAIN AND THE TURK; GAWAIN AND CARL OF CARLISLE *page 53*

Several other Gawain stories used similar ingredients to those in *Gawain and the Green Knight*. In one, he was challenged by a 'Turk' (that is, a dwarf) to a series of unlikely deeds, culminating with slicing off the Turk's head – which broke the enchantment and restored the Turk to normal human size. In another, he, Kay and Bishop Baldwin were hunting near Carlisle when they lost their way. They went for shelter to the castle of Carl of Carlisle, a giant who kept four monstrous pets (bear, boar, bull, lion) from whose claws no mortal guest ever escaped alive. Carl welcomed them, but asked them, in return for his hospitality, to perform a series of bizarre tests, including hurling a spear at him and lying in bed beside his wife without doing more than kiss her. Kay and Baldwin indignantly refused the tests, but Gawain accepted them out of politeness, and went on (at Carl's request) to sleep with his daughter and then to cut off Carl's own head – whereupon the enchantment was broken, Carl changed into an ordinary human being and his savage pets became ordinary household creatures.

PERCIVAL AND THE ARMOUR *page 55*

In some accounts, Percival was so unused to armour that he had no idea how to unfasten it, and when Owain went to call him inside he found him struggling with the fallen warrior's breastplate and muttering, 'Why won't this iron shirt come off?' Owain helped him strip the corpse and dress in the armour, and although Percival refused to go back into Camelot with him, the two of them were friends from that time on.

PERCIVAL'S UNCLES *page 55*

When Percival left Camelot he was still armed only with sharpened sticks. He learned how to use a real sword from his uncles, who had castles in the forest, and proved his skill by slicing through a wooden pillar in his second uncle's hall. In some accounts, his first uncle was King Pelles of Carbonek who guarded the Holy Grail (see page 96); in others, his second uncle showed him a miraculous, blood-dripping sword and a man's head on a platter, and Percival was so ignorant of the world, and so incurious, that he failed to ask what those strange sights meant.

THE LADY OF THE TOWER *page 55*

In some accounts, it took Percival far longer than eighteen days to reach the hills, and his way led through tangled forest. One night he asked for shelter in an ivy-clad, lonely tower, and was hospitably entertained by the eighteen young men who lived there and by their foster-sister, the Lady of the Tower. That night the Lady went to his room and offered to sleep with him if he would only stay next morning and defend the tower against a robber-baron and his gang who had vowed to sack it and kill everyone in it. Percival agreed to help, but insisted on sleeping alone. Next morning the robbers fell on the tower like crows on a carcase, and he rode out, threw a stone from a sling and knocked their leader from his horse. The rest of the robbers at once deserted to the Lady's side, and the robber chief had no choice but to swear to let her live in peace. Percival stayed for three weeks to make sure that the oath was kept, and at the end of that time the Lady asked him to marry her; but he said that he had a lanky lord to teach good manners to, and rode on his way.

PERCIVAL AND THE GIANTS *page 56*

In some accounts, Percival forgot the Lady of the Castle as soon as he was back in Camelot, and fell in love instead with a girl called Angharad. He had no experience of women, and no better idea of courting her than to say bluntly, 'You're pretty. I love you. Sleep with me.'

'Of course I won't,' she answered.

'I won't speak to a Christian soul till you change your mind,' he said sulkily, and rode out of Camelot. At dusk he came to a circular valley, a bowl of fields surrounded by hills, full of gigantic houses made of square stone blocks. He saw nobody, and no one spoke to him; he made for the castle at the valley's heart and asked for a night's shelter. A young girl welcomed him, and sat him down to a banquet with her giant father and two giantling brothers. As they ate, she kept looking at Percival with tears in her eyes, and whispered, 'What a pity that such a fine young man must die first thing in the morning, when my father's giants attack.'

'Why should I die?' asked Percival.

'No Christian who stays the night in this castle lives to tell of it,' she answered.

'We'll see about that,' said Percival. 'Let me sleep in the stable, beside my horse and weapons, and tomorrow can look after itself.'

Next morning a horde of giants swarmed to the castle from their stone houses, and the chief and his sons ran to Percival's bedroom to kill him. As they hammered on the door and roared at him to come out and have his limbs ripped from his body, he crept up behind them, stabbed the giantlings dead and held his sword-point to the artery in their father's knee until he surrendered. Percival herded the giants to Camelot and baptised every one of them as Christians. They promised never to attack Christian travellers again, and Arthur sent them in peace to their valley homes. As Percival stood on the battlements watching them leave, Angharad went to him and said, 'If only you'd kept your promise, and not spoken to a Christian soul, I'd have slept with you.'

'You lose,' said Percival. 'I've spoken to no one but heathen giants. Have you heard me utter a word since I came back to Camelot, till now?' After that Angharad would have given in and slept with him, but the thought of the giant-chief's beautiful daughter had wiped all love for Angharad from his heart, and he refused to have anything to do with her.

PERCIVAL AND THE FAIRIES *page 57*

In some accounts, Percival had other adventures during the time of Kay's recovery and before he set out to find the Lady of the Castle. He was out hunting one day when he passed, without realizing it, out of the mortal world into fairyland. Everyone he saw there looked normal and human, but they were beings who lived beyond mortal time and without human feelings and emotions. Percival killed the Black Oppressor, a tyrant who murdered every guest in his castle; he visited the King of Sorrow, whose servants bathed the bodies of dead warriors back to life; he took as his servant Edlym Redsword, a man scarlet from head to toe, who wore scarlet armour and rode a scarlet horse, and with his help killed the Serpent of the Mournful Mound, in whose coils lay a stone which gave its possessor all the gold he or she might ever want; he killed giants, freed maidens and righted wrongs on every side. Finally he fought in a tournament against the enemies of the Empress of Constantinople, married the Empress and reigned with her for fourteen years. When he left her court at last and found his way back to Camelot he discovered that all his adventures and his fourteen years' reign in fairyland had taken no longer than a couple of mortal days.

GAWAIN AND PERCIVAL *page 57*

In some accounts Gawain rode to help Percival find the Lady of the Castle, but was sidetracked into an adventure of his own. He stayed the night in a castle, and was challenged to a duel by a lord whose father he had killed years before; Gawain refused to fight, and persuaded the lord to let Arthur judge the case, and by the time they finished discussing it Percival had vanished in the woods. It was a year before Gawain and Percival found each other again (when Percival went by chance to the angry lord's castle); they rode together to the Fortress of Marvels, and sent to Camelot for reinforcements to help them fight the hags.

CULHWCH'S COMPANIONS *page 60*

Arthur chose each of Culhwch's companions because of some special skill. Kay (Arthur's foster-brother: see page 29) could go without sleep for nine days and nights on end, and the wounds of his sword were always fatal. Bediver was faster than any other three warriors together: he could make three fatal spear-thrusts in the time it took other men to make one. Gwrhyr the interpreter was a silver-tongued persuader, able to pacify even the most furious of adversaries. Culhwch's other three companions were Arthur's nephew Gwalchmei (whom some identify with Gawain, but whose skill, unlike Gawain's, was that he never failed to do whatever he undertook), the wizard Menw, who could make himself and his fellow-travellers invisible, and the guide Kynddilig, who could find his way in strange countries more easily than most people could in their own castle yards.

Each of the tasks Ysbadadan set Culhwch was concerned with the wedding, and involved dealing with a magic (and often deadly) adversary. Culhwch had to force the giant Amathaon to plough the flax-field, using a plough-share wrested from Amathaon's giant brother Govannon and four giants turned into oxen as a punishment for bloodthirstiness. He had to fetch honey for the feast from a bee-less swarm, wine from a never-failing drinking-horn poured into a bottomless cup, milk from flasks which kept it fresh by racing the sun across the sky, and food from an unfillable basket, boiled in a sun-cauldron stolen from Hibernian giants. Entertainment was to be provided by a harp which needed no player and a flock of birds with human voices. Before Ysbadadan's beard could be shaved for the wedding it had to be softened in the blood of the Black Hag, stored in the magic flask of Gwydolwyn the Dwarf; the shaving was to be done with the razor-tusk of White Turk, king of boars, who could only be hunted by a team of demons and ogres, each hard to find, harder to persuade and even harder to supply with magic horses and magic dogs. There were thirty-nine tasks altogether, and (apart from remembering them) it was impossible for any one man to do them all in a year and a day. Culhwch solved this problem by undertaking only the main tasks himself, with his companions Kay, Bediver and Gwrhyr, and asking Arthur to share out the others among the wizards, shape-changers and giant killers of Camelot. The stories of how each task was done do not survive, but by the end of a year and a day every one of Ysbadadan's commands had been carried out.

In some versions of the story, Ysbadadan refused to give up his throne and life so easily. Arthur and Culhwch led a siege of the magic castle, and it was only when Ysbadadan's followers surrendered that he agreed to let Culhwch marry Olwen. Caw of Caledonia, who had gathered the tusk of White Turk, king of the boars, used it to shave Ysbadadan, Goreu beheaded Ysbadadan, and Arthur forced Ysbadadan's surviving followers to accept Culhwch as their king before he led his own courtiers home to Camelot.

In some versions of the story, Owain's memory of the Lady of the Fountain was jogged by the girl Luned (her younger sister: see page 66), who visited him at Camelot and slipped a ring of memory on his finger. She disappeared immediately afterwards, leaving him no way of finding his way back to the enchanted castle. He began a desperate search, and his wanderings took him to every corner of Britain, and lasted until the clothes rotted from his body, his skin grew a shaggy fleece and he was forced to eat grass and berries like an animal. He would have died, but one day he strayed into a fairy garden, and the princess' servants smeared him with an ointment which drew the fleece from his skin in tufts, cured his wits and restored his strength. He repaid the kindness by killing an ogre who was threatening the kingdom; then, ignoring all the princess' pleas that he would marry her and stay in fairyland forever, he began his wanderings again, and soon afterwards came to the cave where the serpent was threatening the lion (see page 67).

THREE DAYS *page 67*

It was a sure sign of supernatural beings that they had no idea of mortal time. They were undying and unaging, and only knew about days, months and years by hearsay. For this reason, what seemed to a mortal like years (for example the three years Owain spent with the Lady of the Fountain) might seem to an enchanted being no more than days, minutes or the blinking of an eye.

THE PRINCESS OF THE TOWER *page 68*

In some versions, the princes were the sons of the lord of the tower, and their sister was a beautiful heiress, looking for a husband. When Owain's lion killed the giant, the lord of the tower wanted him to marry the girl and accept her dowry of lands and riches, but he said that he already had a wife (the Lady of the Fountain) and rode on his way to rescue Luned and find her.

LIONESSE *page 70*

Lionesse (also called Leonois and Lyonesse) was a fabulous kingdom, stretching from the coast of Cornwall to the Scilly Isles. Like the continent of Atlantis in the myths of another people and another time, it was a place of perpetual happiness, seldom touched by argument, civil war or fighting of any kind. In the end, its prosperity so annoyed the water-spirits of the Atlantic Ocean that they drowned it in a tidal wave. (The Scilly Isles are its memorial: once its mountain-tops, they now survive as warm, lush islands in the middle of stormy seas.) Ever after it disappeared, Lionesse has lived on in people's memories, the vision of a magical western land of peace and plenty, far beyond the tensions of everyday mortality. (Some accounts connect it with Avalon, the beautiful island where deserving heroes go after death: see page 210).

TRISTRAM AND PALAMEDES *page 76*

In some versions of the story, one of the guests at King Mark's and Ysoud's wedding was an unknown prince from overseas. He made up and sang a wedding-song, and it so pleased King Mark that he offered the stranger anything he wanted. At once the stranger announced that he was Palamedes, prince of Syria (the man Tristram beat in the duel over Ysoud in Hibernia: see page 74), and that the prize he wanted was Ysoud herself. King Mark was beside himself with grief, but he was afraid to break his promise, and tearfully handed over his new young bride. Palamedes took Ysoud to his ship, which was rigged and waiting by the shore, and set sail for Syria. But before the ship was out of range, Tristram spurred after them and sang a song so heartbroken that Palamedes turned round and came back to land out of sheer curiosity. As soon as he set foot on shore, Tristram challenged him to a duel, and the affair would have ended in death if Ysoud had not intervened. 'What will you do to prove that you love me?' she asked Palamedes.

'Whatever you ask,' he answered.

'Then go away and never speak to me again.'

So Palamedes' love for Ysoud was dashed for the second time, and he went broken-hearted back to Syria. Ysoud begged Tristram to elope with her, as far from Cornwall and King Mark as possible: but Tristram's simple, honourable nature overcame his feelings (as it so often did), and he took her to Tintagel instead and handed her back to Mark.

In later versions of the story, set in chivalric times and hence written after the Crusades (when Christians and Saracens fought for the Holy Land), Palamedes was a Saracen knight, a heathen, and religious enmity was added to his love-rivalry with Tristram. In one of these accounts, they met for a third time (during Tristram's stay at King Arthur's court: see page 78), and once more fought a duel over Ysoud. It ended when Palamedes surrendered, swore eternal friendship for Tristram, was baptised a Christian (with Tristram and Sir Galleron acting as his godfathers) and became one of King Arthur's most loyal followers, until the war between Arthur and Lancelot began, when he fought on Lancelot's side (see page 120).

TRISTRAM'S ADVENTURES *page 76*

Accounts of Tristram's adventures vary with each new telling of the legend. Some writers are concerned with the unwarlike reputation of warriors from Lionesse and Cornwall (see page 70), and their stories show Tristram being jeered at as a cissy, then revealing his fighting-skills and beating two, four, ten or a dozen thunderstruck opponents. Others, imitating the adventures of Hercules or Odysseus in ancient myth, tell of him fighting giants and monsters, overcoming superhuman evil by nothing more than bravery. Others again (from chivalric times) picture him as a knight like any other, duelling with dragons, righting wrongs, rescuing damsels in distress and forever taking part in jousts and tournaments.

The main group of stories concerns Tristram's relationship with King Mark of Cornwall. In each of them Mark is a coward, constantly harassed by enemies, and has to swallow his pride and ask for Tristram's help, only to banish him fretfully again as soon as the enemies are defeated and he finds him in Ysoud's arms.

TRISTRAM AND LANCELOT *page 78*

When Tristram first went to Camelot (see page 78), Arthur gave a feast in his honour, and the young men competed in wrestling, racing, archery and swordfighting. Tristram won every event he entered, until a stranger with shabby clothes and a rusty sword, and with his face hidden by a cloth, challenged him to a sword-fight. Tristram (who was exhausted after his day's exertions) wanted to finish the fight quickly, and swung the flat of his sword so hard against the stranger's head that he knocked him unconscious – and was horrified when the cloth slipped from the man's face and he saw that it was Arthur himself, disguised. When Arthur recovered, however, he laughed at his defeat and asked Lancelot, the best swordsman in the court, to see if he could do any better. Wearily Tristram lifted his sword to defend himself; but tired though he was, he was still a match for Lancelot, and the duel lasted until both men wounded each other at the same moment, threw down their swords and shook each other's bloodstained hands as a sign of friendship.

Tristram only ever fought Lancelot on one other occasion, when he saw him in full armour with his helmet pulled down over his face, and mistook him for his Syrian rival Palamedes (see page 76). Lancelot was surprised that his old friend should challenge him, but took it for a trial of strength and said nothing. The duel lasted for four hours, and it was only when both of them dropped their swords and fell on the ground exhausted that Lancelot lifted his helmet and Tristram realized, to his shame, who his adversary had really been.

In some accounts of the visit of King Mark and Queen Ysoud to Camelot (see page 78), after Tristram rescued Ysoud from Bruce the Pitiless, he took her not to court but to Lancelot's castle Joyous Gard, where they were entertained royally through all the days of King Mark's treason-trial. All the time they were there they shared the same apartments and the same bed; but Tristram put his drawn sword between them as they slept, and so was able to prove to King Mark (when the trial was done and the friendship-oaths were due) that his and Ysoud's love was noble, untainted with desire.

TRISTRAM AND YSOUD UNITED *page 79*

After Tristram's and Ysoud's deaths, King Mark discovered from Brangen about the magic potions, and realized that what he had taken for lovers' treachery was in fact no fault of theirs at all. Full of remorse, he ordered that they be buried in two graves side by side in Tintagel churchyard. After some time, so the story goes, a vine grew up from Tristram's grave and another from Ysoud's, and they twined and united on the churchyard wall. Three times the cemetery-keeper chopped them down, and three times they grew again, more luxuriantly than before.

TRISTAN AND ISOLDE *page 79*

Wagner used the legend of Tristram and Ysoud as the basis of his opera *Tristan and Isolde*. He was chiefly interested in their yearning, ecstatic love, and in expressing it in music: he reshaped the story to fit this view. In his opera the magic potion begins as a poison-draught, prepared by Isolde to punish Tristan for carrying her away to marry King Mark against her will. At the last moment Brangäne (the maid-servant) substitutes a love-potion, and when the lovers drink it they lose track of everything in the world but their passion for each other. In Cornwall, they continue to meet secretly after Isolde's marriage to King Mark, and when Mark finds them and banishes Tristan, Isolde promises to follow her lover into exile. King Mark's servant Melot wounds Tristan in a duel, and Tristan's servants take him into exile on a litter, leaving Isolde heartbroken. In the last act of the opera we see Tristan, near to death, waiting for Isolde to come to him. Her ship is sighted in the distance, and she lands just as Mark, Melot and the soldiers arrive in a pursuing ship. Tristan dies in Isolde's arms, and while Mark and the others watch in pity and horror, she sings a rapturous farewell to her beloved before dying herself of a broken heart.

THE INNKEEPER'S SON *page 83*

In some accounts, Geraint and Ynid met a boy on the road, with bread, meat and wine for some reapers in a field. He took Geraint and Ynid to his father's inn, waited till they were settled and then treacherously ran to tell the lord of the town of their arrival and of Ynid's beauty.

GERAINT AND THE LORD *page 83*

In some versions of the story, when the lord heard that Geraint and Ynid had fled, he spurred after them with eighty soldiers. Ynid timidly warned Geraint of the approaching dust-cloud, and he snubbed her yet again for speaking before she was spoken to. Geraint killed all eighty soldiers, but spared the lord's life, merely tumbling him from his horse and leaving him sprawled on the ground like an upturned beetle.

THE LAST CHALLENGE *page 84*

In versions of the story from chivalric

times, Geraint found a silk tent in the orchard, and inside were two golden thrones. A girl sat in one of them, and when Geraint went to the other she warned him that its owner killed anyone who sat in it. Geraint recognized this as the final challenge of his quest, sat on the throne, and duly fought a day-long duel with the warrior on the warhorse before he was able to blow the horn and end the enchantment.

BAN *page 85*

Some myth-writers, irritated at the idea that Lancelot should have come from over the Channel, say that his father was not from Brittany at all, but was King of Benwick (a place they located either in Hibernia, Pictland or the countryside near Camelot). But the word Benwick means no more than 'Ban's home-town', and there is no reason to disbelieve the main legend, that Lancelot was French. Malory, in *The Morte d'Arthur*, gets the best of both worlds by identifying Benwick as 'Beaune, where the wine comes from.'

THE LADY OF THE LAKE *page 85*

The Lady of the Lake (also called Nimue the Enchantress and Vivien) was a shape-changer, and fell disastrously in love with Merlin (see page 217). In some accounts, she was an evil character (perhaps even Morgan le Fay in disguise), and her aim was to destroy the human race. She gave Arthur the magic sword Excalibur (see page 221), and only agreed to let him keep it if he repaid her with any gift she cared to ask; then she sent another magic sword to Camelot, offering it to any of Arthur's followers who could draw it from its scabbard, and when Balin succeeded she demanded his head as Arthur's promised gift. (Balin forestalled his execution

by using the sword to chop off the Lady's own enchanted head.) In most accounts, however, she was a benefactress, not a harmer, of the human race, and in particular protected Arthur and the other lords of Camelot. She thwarted several of Morgan le Fay's evil plots against Arthur (see page 234), and when it seemed that the Holy Grail was doomed to leave the mortal world forever, she took human shape, married Pelles its guardian, and arranged for her foster-son Lancelot to sleep with Elaine and father Galahad (see page 91). When Morgan le Fay finally triumphed against Camelot (using Lancelot's love of Guinever to break up the Round Table companionship), the Lady of the Lake rescued Arthur from death and took him to the magic island of Avalon, where his wounds would be healed and he would be reunited with Guinever forever (see page 243).

LANCELOT'S EDUCATION *page 86*

Lancelot's education, half human and half fairy, was very like the education Merlin gave to the boy Arthur (see page 220). But whereas Merlin, from the start, meant Arthur to return to the world of mortals, and therefore taught him magic skills performable by humans, Nimue never expected that her foster-sons would leave her, and taught them a jumble of mortal and fairy skills whether they could cope with them or not. When Lancelot, Lionel and Bors returned to the human world, their fairy knowledge was at first a help to them; but gradually, as they spent more and more time with humans, it faded in their minds till it was no more than dreams. Lancelot's chief fairy legacy from Nimue was lustfulness: like all shape-changers and their pupils (except Arthur, whom Merlin trained otherwise), he had no morality, and no sooner saw a pretty woman than he wanted to sleep with her. His life in the mortal world was affected by the battle in his soul between lust and Christian goodness, and in the end the battle destroyed him, Guinever, Arthur and the fellowship of Camelot: see Chapter 14.

THE LADY OF ASCALOT *page 87*

One of the saddest stories of girls who fell in love with Lancelot is the tale of the Lady of Ascalot, from chivalric, knightly times. The Lady lived with her father and brothers in Ascalot Castle near Winchester (or, some say, in Astolat near Guildford), and her brothers were just old enough to have become apprentice knights. Arthur and his lords went to that part of the country for a tournament, and Lancelot, who wanted to test the others' mettle, decided to go, and to fight, in disguise. He stayed for a while at Ascalot Castle, preparing himself, and during this time the Lady of Ascalot, his host's daughter, fell in love with him. By chance one of her brothers fell ill, and Lancelot borrowed his armour for the tournament, and so went disguised as a novice. To everyone's delight but no one's surprise (for his disguise fooled nobody), he beat everyone who challenged him, but in the fighting he was wounded and went back to Ascalot Castle to recover. As the weeks passed, the more he regained his strength and the more the Lady lost hers; by the time he was fit enough to return to Camelot, she was a walking wraith. Soon after his return, he and Arthur were walking by the river when they saw a boat drifting slowly downstream, ornately painted and covered with an awning of cloth-of-gold. It held the body of a beautiful woman (the Lady of Ascalot), and in her hand was a letter saying that Lancelot was the noblest and the cruellest man alive, and that his rigorous devotion to another lady – everyone but Arthur knew that this was Guinever, though the letter named no names – had caused the Lady's death.

Tennyson's poem *The Lady of Shalott* is based on this story.

Some other versions place the story much later in Lancelot's life, four or five years after the quest for the Holy Grail (see Chapter 115), and link it to the discovery of his love-affair with Guinever and the breakup of the Round Table (see Chapter 14). In them, Gawain discovered that Lancelot was recovering from his wounds at Ascalot Castle and that the Lady was in love with him, and told Guinever. When Lancelot went back to Camelot, Guinever jealously banished him from court (as she did after his affair with Elaine: see page 93), and he obeyed, bewildered. But soon afterwards Patrick died from eating the poisoned apple at Guinever's table (see page 116), and Lancelot came out of exile to fight a duel and save Guinever's life. At the very moment of his triumph, the boat with the Lady of Ascalot's body drifted downriver, and her letter made it clear that although the Lady had loved Lancelot, he had always been loyal to the queen. Guinever and Lancelot were reconciled, and Arthur rewarded Lancelot for saving Guinever's life by giving him the castle and lands called *Joyous Gard*, or 'Fortunate Estate'. It was because of his favouring of Lancelot above Gawain that Agravain and Mordred decided to tell Arthur of his love-affair with Guinever, the event which led to the fall of Camelot (see page 117).

LANCELOT AND THE CART *page 87*

One May morning Queen Guinever was riding in the forest with ten young lords of Camelot when she was kidnapped by Maleagans, son of King Bagdemagus. He said that he had loved her in secret for years, and that she would remain his prisoner until she slept with him. Guinever and her followers were kindly treated, but were kept prisoners in Maleagans' castle; the only one to escape was Guinever's page-boy, and he took a message to Lancelot, who galloped to the rescue. On the way, however, Maleagans' archers ambushed him and shot his horse dead under him; he was forced to hitch a lift in a passing cart (some say a wood-cutter's cart, others a dung-cart), a peasant vehicle unsuited to a lord of his rank and dignity. After many adventures and delays (including being thrown into a dungeon by the four fairy queens, and escaping only thanks to a magic ring given to him by Nimue his foster-mother), he crossed a rope-bridge over a torrent, killed the lion and bear which guarded the other side, and finally reached Maleagans' castle. He fought Maleagans for Guinever and won, and the Queen and her courtiers duly returned to Camelot. But the story got out of how Lancelot, that proud and haughty warrior, had been forced to go riding in a peasant's cart, and whenever people wanted to humiliate or infuriate him, they made a joke of it.

MORGAN LE FAY *page 87*

There are several other accounts of who Morgan le Fay really was. Some say that she was the same person as Arthur's mortal sister Morgaus, and that she learned evil and magic at the nunnery where Uther sent her for safe-keeping (see page 29). Others says that she was the witch Morgana, daughter of Darkness and one of the three Fates. Others even identify her with her deadly enemy, the Lady of the Lake (see page 233), and say that she was a shape-changer who lived in an underwater palace. But most accounts make her the changeling child of King Gorlois and Queen Ygern of Corn-

wall, King Arthur's half-sister and deadly enemy. In these stories, she was forever plotting to destroy Arthur and to topple his kingdom Camelot; but her plans were blocked each time by the good fairy Nimue, Lady of the Lake. When Morgan le Fay smuggled her mortal lover Accolon into Camelot, with orders to steal the magic sword Excalibur and kill Arthur, the Lady of the Lake turned the sword against Accolon himself and so foiled the plot; when Morgan le Fay sent Arthur a magnificent gold-and-silver cloak, the Lady of the Lake warned him, just as he was about to put it on, that it was smeared with poison. To punish this interference, Morgan le Fay first tried to steal Lancelot, the Lady's foster-son (see page 86), and when this failed, she formed the cruel plan of making Lancelot fall in love with Arthur's queen Guinever, so breaking the fellowship of Camelot and revenging herself on the Lady of the Lake in a single scheme.

Morgan le Fay was accompanied everywhere she went by three other fairy queens, her daughters: Morganetta (Morgan the Less), Nivetta (the Snow Queen, or Queen of Northgales) and Carvilia (or Queen of the Waste Lands). After Camelot's fall, when there was no more wickedness for her to do in Britain, she and her daughters settled in the narrow Straits of Messina between Sicily and Italy, where they appeared to sailors as will-o'-the-wisps, luring them to shipwreck on hidden rocks.

LANCELOT AND BAGDEMAGUS' DAUGHTER *page 88*

In some accounts, the girl who brought Lancelot his prison breakfast was the daughter of King Bagdemagus, and instead of seducing her Lancelot agreed, if she set him free, to help her father fight in a tournament against his rival the king of

North Wales. The king of North Wales brought eighty men, and Bagdemagus and Lancelot had forty; in the end only Lancelot and Bagdemagus, of their side, were left standing, but they fought with such ferocity that the others began to draw back, and when Lancelot knocked the king of North Wales from his horse and broke his thigh, the tournament was at an end and Bagdemagus' side had won. After that Bagdemagus vowed to go to Camelot and serve King Arthur, and in later years he was one of Lancelot's most loyal friends. It was when Lancelot was riding back to Camelot from the tournament that he heard of the shield-tree giant, and went to rescue the thirty prisoners (see page 88).

SIR GILBERT AND SIR MELIOT *page 89*

In accounts of this story from times of chivalry, all the people (except for Hellawes, who remains a sorceress) are knights or their ladies: the black-bearded brigand is Sir Gilbert the Bastard, the thirty giants are thirty gigantic knights (and Lancelot subdues them by a show of bravery, not by brandishing a cross), and the young wounded man is Sir Meliot de Logris, a knight distantly connected with Arthur's court, to which he goes when he is cured, to meet Lancelot on Whit Sunday with Kay's prisoners (see page 89) and the thirty knights rescued from the giant's cave (see page 88).

LANCELOT AND KAY *page 89*

Like the story of Lancelot, Gilbert and Meliot (see above), this one was slightly altered in chivalric versions of the Middle Ages. In them, Kay's three attackers were not highwaymen but knights, enemies of the Round Table, and Lancelot defeated them in fair fight and made them promise, on their honour, to meet him at Camelot on Whit Sunday and swear loyalty to Arthur. That night, while he and Kay were sleeping in a friendly castle, he changed armour and horses with Kay and slipped away: thus, Kay was mistaken for Lancelot and got home to Camelot unmolested, and Lancelot was mistaken for Kay, was challenged to duels and tests of knightly skill wherever he went, and defeated his opponents (who included Gawain and Sagramore) so dazzlingly that Kay ever afterwards had a reputation for unbeatable warskill.

PELLES AND CARBONEK *page 91*

Each version of this legend set Pelles and his home in a different place. In some, guardianship of the Holy Grail (see page 96) gave him supernatural powers, and he was ruler of a magic kingdom whose location was not precisely fixed: you found it by searching for the Grail, and discovering it was a metaphor for self-discovery. (The kingdom's geographical location depended on who was telling the story, and ranged from the banks of the river Rhine to the Holy Land.) Less mystical versions of the story placed Pelles' kingdom in France, and called his castle Corbin; English story-writers converted Corbin to Corby, and said that Pelles was lord of an estate and castle there, about five days' riding from Camelot.

LANCELOT AND THE DRAGON *page 91*

In some versions of the story, not content with having Lancelot rescue Elaine from the cistern of boiling water, Pelles also asked him to kill a fire-breathing dragon coiled round a holy tomb. When the dragon's body was dragged clear of the tomb, golden writing appeared on the stone wall: A ROYAL LEOPARD WILL SLAY THIS DRAGON, AND WILL SIRE A LION TO SUR-

PASS ALL OTHERS. Pelles took this to be a prophecy of the birth of Galahad, and because of it he arranged for Lancelot to sleep with Elaine (see page 91).

BORS *page 92*

After Lancelot's disappearance (see page 92), Elaine was courted by Lord Bromel, who wanted to marry her and was prepared to bring up the child Galahad as his own son. But Elaine refused him, saying that she would stay loyal to Lancelot even though she never expected to see him again. Bromel at once vowed to find Lancelot and kill him, and Bors' first tasks, when he rode out from Camelot, were to challenge Bromel to a duel on Lancelot's behalf, beat him in fair fight, and make him give up both his hatred of Lancelot and his courtship of Elaine.

At the banquet to celebrate this victory, the dove with the golden incense-pot and the girl with the Holy Grail appeared to Bors, exactly as they had to Lancelot (see page 91), and Bors begged Pelles to let him stay the night in a castle blessed by such wonders. Pelles answered that he was unworthy. Only the most perfect human beings were welcomed, and even Gawain had failed the test. Bors none the less insisted, and was shown to bed with the warning that he might have magical and unwelcome adventures. Sure enough, in the middle of the night a red-hot spear flew through the air and wounded his shoulder; it was followed by a shower of fire-arrows, and by a leopard, a lion and dragon. Wounded as he was, Bors killed the leopard and lion, and just as the dragon opened its jaws to swallow him, a hundred tiny dragons scampered out of its mouth and tore it to pieces. Next an old man appeared, with adders draped round his neck like scarves. He told Bors the story of the Holy Grail (see page 96) and ordered him to leave the castle at once and go back to Camelot, where he would find Lancelot safely returned from his enchantment. The old man was suddenly surrounded by a group of children, nuns and priests, with the dove and the girl carrying the Holy Grail, and the light from the Grail dazzled Bors' eyes and blinded him. When he could see again, all supernatural sights had disappeared and his adventure (or his dream) was done. Next morning he hurried back to Camelot and told his story – and that was how Guinever came to hear that Lancelot had slept with another woman and given her a child.

THE HOLY GRAIL *page 96*

In another version of the story, the Grail was not a bowl but a silver goblet, the cup Jesus drank from at the Last Supper. It was usually seen with the Holy Lance, the spear which pierced Jesus' side on the cross, and which ever afterwards had the power to heal people as well as harm them. The Holy Grail and Holy Lance became two of the most sacred relics of the Christian church. The name Holy Grail came, people thought, from the medieval French *San Gréal*, a version of *Sang Réal* or 'royal blood'.

Other accounts of the Grail, by contrast, say that it was an invention of Christian myth-writers, and had nothing at all to do with Christ. In Celtic sun-magic, a bowl of water was placed in such a position that the priests could predict the exact moment when it would be struck by a shaft of sunlight as the sun moved across the sky, and sick people were persuaded that if they washed in the water at the moment when the priests predicted, the sun-god's healing shaft would cure their sickness. When Christian writers heard this story, they added details from Christ's crucifixion and made the bowl of water into the Holy Grail and the shaft of light into the Holy Lance. The most famous healing-story connected with the Lance is Galahad's use of it to cure Pelles, the king made lame by sin.

THE SWORD IN THE STONE *page 97*

Most surviving versions of the Grail-story were written in medieval times, and used it to teach lessons about Christian goodness, piety and nobility of soul. In these versions, the sword in the stone was a test of Christian purity. Only the most perfect human being in Christendom could pull it out, and any others who tried would first have their imperfection revealed (by failing) and would then suffer injury or death in battle (like people who unjustifiably sat in the Seat Perilous: see page 97). This was why Gawain and Percival hesitated to try the sword, only did so on Arthur's explicit orders (see page 97), and suffered for it (see pages 101, 106); Lancelot refused even to try, knowing in his heart that he was not, and never would be, sinless.

MELIAD *page 98*

In some versions of the story, Galahad's guide on the path was Bagdemagus' servant, a young man called Meliad. As soon as the white rider disappeared, Meliad begged Galahad to take him as his companion on the Grail-quest. Galahad refused, but he let Meliad ride with him until the road forked, when he went right and Meliad went left. Meliad had ridden for less than half an hour along the left-hand path when he saw a table laid for a feast, and beside it, on a wooden throne, a crown studded with jewels. He picked up the crown to admire it – and a black-bearded warrior galloped out of the trees, roared at him for a thief, and stabbed him so viciously that the spear stuck upright in the ground, with Meliad hanging from

it like a gaffed fish. The black-bearded man galloped away with the crown, and Meliad would have bled to death if Galahad had not ridden up and carried him back to the monastery, where there were doctors to tend his wounds. This was the only adventure Meliad ever had: he had one chance to prove himself pure-hearted enough to seek the Holy Grail, and he failed.

GALAHAD'S SHIELD *page 98*

The shield was coloured white, for purity, and it was made for Evalak, king of Sarras in the Holy Land, the first person converted by Joseph of Arimathea after he received Christ's body from the cross. Evalak kept the shield hidden by a cloth until he was in danger in battle, when he uncovered it and the shape of a cross appeared on it and routed his enemies; as soon as its work was done it faded, leaving the shield pure white exactly as before.

Some years after Evalak's conversion, he and Joseph sailed to Britain with Joseph's son Josephus, and together they converted the British to Christianity. They built a castle called Carbonek which, like the Holy Grail itself, had the power to vanish from the sight of anyone sinful or unworthy. When Josephus lay dying, he took the white shield and drew on it with his own blood a red cross (in the shape later known as the Cross of St George); then Evalak gave it to a holy man to hang behind the altar in a monastery until, centuries later, Galahad the True Prince came to claim it.

In some accounts, Evalak changed his name to Mordrain after his conversion, and was known as Mordrain throughout his Christian life. For the rest of his story, see pages 101 and 112.

GAWAIN, GARETH AND OWAIN *page 99*

Soon after Meliad's adventure with the jewelled crown and its black-bearded protector (see page 238), Gawain rode by chance to the monastery where Meliad lay recovering. He asked for Galahad, and when he heard that he was riding in the direction of the River Severn, decided to spend the night in the monastery and follow him next morning. That evening Gareth and Owain also arrived at the monastery, and the three of them rode on together. By sunset they had just reached the edge of the hill overlooking the Severn Valley and the Castle of the Virgins, when the seven ruffians, still smarting from their fight with Galahad (see page 99), saw them coming and ambushed them. Gawain, Gareth and Owain each speared one brother, then jumped from their horses and fought the other four till they, too, lay dead. By the end of the fighting, however, they were so dazed and dizzy that they mistook their direction, and instead of riding on to the Castle of the Virgins and meeting up with Galahad they turned their horses and headed back the way they had come.

GALAHAD AND THE DEVIL *page 99*

Christian versions of the Grail story gave Galahad several other allegorical adventures, each intended to point a religious moral. In one, soon after his meeting with the white rider (see page 98), the monks of a monastery asked Galahad to rid them of a supernatural voice cackling from inside a grave. Galahad stood in front of the grave, and his purity and honesty shone so brightly that the Devil himself, who had been infesting the grave in the likeness of a dead man, flew back to Hell in a flurry of cinders.

GALAHAD, LANCELOT AND PERCIVAL *page 100*

In some versions of the Grail story, it was the shield of purity which made Galahad unrecognizable to Lancelot and Percival. It marked him as being devoted to God and set him apart from sinners – and because of their sinful natures neither Lancelot nor Percival could make out his appearance, and only the holy woman (whose life was also pure, dedicated to God) could see him for who he was.

PERCIVAL AND THE HOLY WOMAN *page 101*

In some accounts the holy woman was no chance passer-by, but was sent by God to set Percival's feet on the path to the Holy Grail. She was his aunt, formerly a queen in Cambria, and she had retired to religious life after the death of her husband. Among other things, she told Percival that his mother had died of a broken heart on the day he left her to go to Camelot (see page 54); this news added to Percival's heavy-heartedness as he began his quest. She also gave him a religious explanation of the making of the Round Table (see page 34): she said that Merlin made it in memory and in the likeness of the table Christ and his disciples used at the Last Super, that it symbolized a sacred fellowship, and that so long as it lasted the people of Britain would live in Christian harmony and peace.

TWO HORSES *page 102*

In one version of this story Percival was offered not one miraculous horse, but two. As he stood in the wood gazing after Galahad (see page 102), a boy on a pony came up leading a warhorse. Percival asked to buy it, but the boy refused. Shortly afterwards, the boy reappeared in tears, saying that a stranger had waylaid him and stolen his horse. Without a moment's hesitation, Percival borrowed the boy's pony and rode after the stranger to challenge him, but the man killed the pony under him and jeeringly rode away. Percival was bewailing his own foolishness when the second horse (the black devil-horse) was led to him by the innocent-seeming girl.

PERCIVAL, THE LION AND THE DRAGON
page 103

In some accounts, Percival cringed from the savage creatures until he saw a dragon carrying away a lion-cub in its jaws. Incensed with fury, he killed the dragon and returned the lion-cub to its mother, who thereafter trotted beside him and protected him from danger. Later, the dragon's owner (an enchantress) bitterly blamed Percival for killing her pet, and he retorted that the lions were sacred to Christ, and were therefore superior beasts to dragons (which were creatures of magic and sorcery); not surprisingly after this blunt answer, the lady swore to follow him to the ends of the earth, and to punish him as soon as she caught him off his guard.

PARSIFAL *page 104*

In another version of the Grail story, which renamed Percival Parsifal and made him the hero instead of Galahad, he was not so much an honest simpleton as a 'holy fool' whose innocence protected him from sin. Instead of facing sexual temptation from one naked lady on a seashore, he was surrounded in a magic garden by the servants of an enchantress, and his simplicity of soul made him utterly unaware that they were trying to seduce him: his mind was so fixed on God that there was no room left in it for human frailty.

In this version, the Holy Grail and Lance were in the power of the evil wizard Klingsor, and Parsifal strayed by accident into Klingsor's kingdom and was arrested. His simplicity and honesty made it clear that he was the man destined to break Klingsor's power and rescue the Grail, and Klingsor tried to kill him by hurling the sacred lance at him. It hovered harmlessly in the air in front of him, and when Parsifal took hold of it and made the sign of the cross with it, Klingsor's power was broken and the Grail was saved.

This version of the story was popular in medieval Germany, and in the nineteenth century Wagner used it as the basis of his music-drama *Parsifal*.

THE VISION IN THE CHAPEL *page 106*

In some accounts. Gawain's and Ector's dreams were not the only magic signs they saw in the chapel. When they woke up next morning, and were shaking out their cloaks and grumbling about the lack of breakfast, a supernatural darkness fell, blacker than the night just past, and an arm draped in red cloth floated towards them from the doorway. It held a burning candle, and a horse's bridle hung from it; it glided up the chapel to the altar and disappeared, and daylight returned. Later, in the monastery, the abbot said that the hand symbolized God's love, the candle-flame the light of faith and the bridle self-control; these were qualities essential for anyone who hoped to find the Holy Grail, and Gawain and Ector had forgotten them all for the sake of pride-in-war.

GAWAIN AND GALAHAD *page 107*

Some versions of the story did not send Gawain back to Camelot out of remorse, as here, but gave him still one more humiliation. He and Ector were riding along the shore one day when they heard sounds of fighting, and found a group of men attacking a castle, while others defended it. Gawain, still hot for adventure, rode to join the fight. But in the turmoil he suddenly realized that he was facing Galahad himself, and was so severely injured by a blow from Galahad's sword that he was a month in bed recovering from it. He realized that this blow was the one Lancelot had spoken of when Gawain failed to pull the sword from the red marble block at Camelot (see page 97), and as soon as he was fit enough to ride he left Ector (who had loyally broken off the Grail-quest to stay with him) and made his way home to Camelot.

BORS AND THE GIRL *page 108*

In some versions of this story the girl was not an enchantress but a true Christian, victim of a scheming older sister, and Priadan was an ordinary warrior and not a giant. On the night before the fight, Bors was tempted not by the girl but by mysterious, prophetic dreams, though he kept them at bay by the same two strategies: praying and sleeping on the floor instead of the luxurious bed. Next morning, after killing Priadan, he made all the people of the area swear loyalty to the girl instead of to her sister (much as Galahad did with the fathers and brothers of the girls in the Castle of the Virgins: see page 99), and then rode on.

THE DEVIL-CASTLE *page 110*

Christian accounts of this story made the people in the castle not wraiths conjured by the Devil but wicked men who had committed incest with their sisters, thrown their own fathers into prison, pillaged monasteries and murdered every priest or nun they could find. Death was the only possible punishment for such a list of crimes, and because Galahad, Percival and Bors were no more than the means by which Christ exacted punishment, they avoided blood-guilt and could carry on the Grail-quest without stain of sin.

LANCELOT'S ADVENTURES *page 111*

Most of Lancelot's adventures between leaving the hermit (see page 101) and arriving at Castle Carbonek (see page 111) were invented to point Christian morals, and their main interest was religious. He was insulted by a boy of lowly rank and put up with it because what the boy said was true; the Devil appeared to him in a vision and showed him what happened to those who turned from Christ; he saw a vision of angels; he was beaten in a tournament and realized that it was because he trusted in warskills instead of Christ; he was trapped in a river-gorge between cliffs, forest and rushing water, and was attacked but not harmed by a mysterious, black-armoured warrior; finally, when he had learned to put all his faith in Christ, he was guided to the miraculous ship where the body of Percival's sister lay (see page 110), and shortly afterwards Galahad joined him and they sailed for a year and a day, enjoying each other's company, until they landed not far from Castle Carbonek and Galahad left Lancelot to continue the Grail-quest on his own.

GALAHAD'S ADVENTURES *page 112*

In the Forest of Dread Galahad came to a sulphur-spring, with geysers of boiling water hissing into the air and poisoning the ground. He plunged his hand unhesitatingly into the heart of the spring, and his purity so cooled it that it became clear, unpolluted drinking-water, and was known ever afterwards as Galahad's Fountain. Later, in a monastery crypt, Galahad saw the tomb of Simeon the Martyr. Simeon had ill-treated Joseph of Arimathea, and for this was condemned to lie not in a quiet grave but in a coffin of blazing stone, a taste of hellfire, until the True Prince rescued him. Galahad walked unflinchingly into the flames, and at his coming they shrank and died until Simeon was able to rest in peace.

One version of the story says that after Galahad met Percival, the two of them wandered for five years all over Britain, fighting giants, casting out devils and righting wrongs, until they met up with Bors and continued their real quest, for the Holy Grail. Thanks to these miraculous five years, the story claims, evil and supernatural beings are scarce in Britain to this day.

GALAHAD'S DEATH *page 113*

In one version of the story, Galahad asked Jesus in Carbonek to grant him the power to choose the moment of his own death. When he saw the Grail unveiled for the second time, in Sarras, he knew that the hour had come, prayed to be free of mortal life, and was carried by the angels into heaven.

GUINEVER'S DINNER-GUESTS *page 116*

Apart fron Gawain, Patrick, Mador and Pinel, the lords at Guinever's dinner-party – princes drawn to Camelot from all parts of Britain, Brittany, Europe, North Africa and the Holy Land – were Agravain, Aliduk, Astamor, Blamor, Bleoberis, Bors, Brandiles, Ector, Gaheris, Galihodin, Galihud, Gareth, Ironside, Kay, La Cote Male Taile, Lionel, Mordred, Palomides, Persant and Safer.

PATRICK'S TOMBSTONE *page 117*

In the rejoicing over Lancelot's return to Camelot, and the plotting which followed it (see page 117), no one bothered about who had really poisoned the apple which killed Patrick. Mador accepted the verdict of the trial-by-combat, and on his brother's tombstone put the words 'Patrick, prince of Hibernia, whose veins burst after he ate an apple poisoned by an unknown hand'. But soon afterwards, Pinel the poisoner fled from Camelot and went home to Cambria, and Arthur's soothsayers announced that he was the guilty man. At once, Mador changed the writing on the tombstone to 'Patrick, prince of Hibernia, poisoned in place of another by Pinel the treacherous', and from that day on there was enmity between the royal families of Hibernia and Cambria.

EXCOMMUNICATION *page 121*

If the Pope, a Cardinal or an Archbishop ordered anyone to be excommunicated, that person was barred from all worship in the Christian church. Furthermore, anyone else who befriended, helped or sheltered them risked excommunication too, so that they became outcasts in their own countries, and were doomed either to live as outlaws or to flee to some part of the world where Christianity and its laws were unknown.

THE BATTLE BETWEEN ARTHUR AND MORDRED *page 127*

In some accounts, the battle between Arthur and Mordred was a much more glorious affair. It took place on the flat downland of Salisbury Plain, and over 100,000 men were killed, including the princes of eastern Britain (Kent, Essex, Surrey, Sussex, Suffolk and Norfolk) who fought for Mordred, and the Western princes (of Lionesse, Cornwall, Devon, Wessex, Somerset and Shropshire) who favoured Arthur. In these versions, the magic lake into which Bediver threw Excalibur (see page 128) was located not between Dover and Canterbury, but on Salisbury Plain not far from Glastonbury, where Arthur's body was later buried (see page 129).

ARTHUR'S GRAVE *page 129*

The chief proof that the grave at Glastonbury was Arthur's came in the twelfth century, when the tomb was opened and the bodies were exhumed. The burial-chamber lay five metres below ground-level, and consisted of a stone slab supported by stone pyramids, with a coffin hollowed out of a single oak-trunk. On the stone was written 'Here lies the famous King Arthur, with Guinever his wife', and among the bones in the coffin lay a lock of blonde woman's hair which looked fresh and whole until one of the monks picked it up and it crumbled to dust. The male bones were enormous. As the Welsh historian Giraldus, who watched the exhumation, wrote, 'The abbot measured the shin-bone against the leg of the tallest man there, and it reached seven centimetres above his knee. The space between the eye-sockets and eyebrow-bones was as wide as the palm of a human hand. The skull was pitted with a dozen sword-strokes, the deepest and widest of which was probably the wound which killed Arthur.'

GUINEVER'S DEATH *page 129*

In some accounts there was a gap of several years between Guinever's paying for the building of Glastonbury Abbey and her own death and burial there. She spent the time as a hermit at Amesbury, doing good works and with only five court ladies for company. In other accounts she neither died nor was buried, but went with the Lady of the Lake to Avalon and lived there forever as Arthur's queen.

LANCELOT'S LORDS *page 129*

In some accounts, Lancelot's death was due simply to despair that he had betrayed Christ for Guinever throughout his life. Before he died, he made Bors, Lionel and the other lords vow to spend their lives doing penance for his sins by fighting the heathen in the Holy Land, and as soon as he was buried at Joyous Gard they set sail from Britain for the last time and were never heard of again.

THE ONCE AND FUTURE KING *page 129*

No one knows for sure where Arthur and his followers lie sleeping. Britain is honeycombed with underground caves and potholes, and there are folk-legends about sleeping knights in many parts of the country, from Alderley Edge in Cheshire to Wookey Hole in Somerset, from Merlin's Cave at the foot of Tintagel Rock in Cornwall to Gaping Ghyll in Derbyshire. The folk-tales usually tell of local people who strayed into the caves by accident, failed to waken the sleepers and could never find them again however hard they tried. In a typical story, a drunken eighteenth-century horse-dealer called Dickon of Selkirk was taken by a strange old man in a magician's cloak – Merlin? – to a cave deep under the Eildon Hills in the border-country between England and Scotland. He found a row of stables lit by flickering torches, in each of which was a stone horse with a stone knight sleeping beside it. On a table in the centre lay a hunting-horn and a sheathed sword, and the stranger said to Dickon, 'Whoever dares to draw the sword and blow the horn will rescue Britain from all her enemies.' Dickon stretched out his hand, but instead of drawing the sword first he blew the horn, reversing the spell. The old man, the horses, the knights and the cave all vanished, and Dickon was found outside next morning with a broken neck, as if he had fallen over the cliff in a drunken stupor. Nothing has been seen or heard of the old man or the sleepers under the Eildon Hills, from that day to this.

In another story, from the Welsh legend-collection *Mabinogion* (see page 249), Rhonabwy, a soldier sent to track down a bandit called Iorweth, spent one night in a magician's house, and slept on a yellow oxhide which gave prophetic dreams. In his dream he and his companions were riding through a forest when they met a giant, green from head to foot and translucent as a firtree with the sun behind it, and the giant said that he was Iddawg, that he, not Bediver, took Arthur's peace-terms to Mordred (see page 126), and it was because he deliberately garbled them that Mordred and Arthur fought each other. He took Rhonabwy and the others to a wide, mist-shrouded plain, and showed them the tents and cooking-fires of an enormous encamped army, thousands of men and animals, all many times human size and as insubstantial as smoke. Sitting on thrones were two gigantic kings, Arthur king of Britain and Owain king of Cambria, and they were playing chess with gold pieces on a silver board. Arthur asked Iddawg, 'Where did you find these little men?', and laughed bitterly at the idea that Britain should now be ruled by pigmies instead of the heroes of his own time. He and Owain continued their chess-game, and refused to interrupt it even when a savage fight began between Arthur's bored young warriors and Owain's flesh-eating ravens. When the game ended, messengers brought Arthur gifts from every country in the world, and Kay stood up and said to the assembled lords, 'All of you who follow Arthur, come to Camelot; everyone else, join us there as soon as the truce ends.' At this the whole ghostly army began to move, and there was such a commotion of shouts, hoof-beats and weapons that Rhonabwy woke up from his dream, and never found out where the magic meeting-place had been, what the truce was and why it should end, or what great need would bring Arthur and his followers galloping from Camelot to the mortal world.

BATTLE-SONGS *page 134*

One of the minstrels' songs compared Beowulf to Sigemund the Dragon-slayer, whose chief exploit was killing a treasure-worm in its lair under a high, grey rock. The worm guarded a hoard of gem-stones, diamonds, rubies, emeralds and amethysts; it was as high as a firtree, and spat fireballs at any bird, beast or human being that went too close. Sigemund faced it armed with nothing but a sword, and the worm hissed in scorn, knowing that its fireballs would shrivel him long before he was near enough to stab or slice. But instead of stabbing, Sigemund whirled the sword round his head and hurled it like a javelin. The sword pinned the worm to the rockface and blocked its windpipe, and with no outlet, the worm's own internal fires generated such heat inside its body that it burnt to ash, whereupon Sigemund's servants swept the soot from the gem-pile and carried away enough jewels to fill their whole ship's hold.

Another song told of battle-weariness, peace-making and treachery between the followers of two proud clan-chiefs, Hnaef and Finn. Finn married Hnaef's sister Hildeburh, and wanted to unite the clans into one, but Hnaef's followers resisted and many warriors were killed on both sides, including Hnaef himself. Hnaef's surviving followers, led by Hengest, took shelter in a hall as well-built and as strongly-fortified as Heorot, and when Finn could find no way of dislodging them he abandoned slaughter and turned instead to generosity and peace. He promised Hnaef's followers a chest of rings and golden armbands as compensation for their dead; his men built Hnaef a funeral-pyre on the seashore, heaped with blood-stained armour, treasure and the bodies of the dead, and let greedy fire burn all; Finn hoped that enmity would fly away with the fire-smoke, and leave everlasting friendship between the clans. Hengest and his men stayed on in Finn's hall as honoured guests, but all the time Hengest was nursing vengeance in his heart, and as soon as his chance came he buried his sword in Finn's back, led his men to sack Finn's hall and murder his people, and took Hildeburh home in triumph to her own kingdom.

GIFTS *page 134*

As the Danish custom was, Hrothgar rewarded Beowulf at the banquet by loading him with gifts: a gold-sewn banner, a jewelled sword, a helmet, chainshirt, collars and rings of gold, and eight horses, matching as apples, with gold-embossed bridles, one of which also carried a jewel-sewn war-saddle made especially for the king. Beowulf took these gifts home to Geatland, used them to buy as much land as could be covered by seven thousand oxhides, and so became a king with territory of his own to rule.

CAIN'S CHILDREN *page 134*

The family of giants to which Grendel and his mother belonged traced its ancestry to

Cain, son of Adam and Eve and the third human being in the world. He murdered his brother Abel in a fit of rage (so becoming the world's first murderer), and God punished him by making him an outcast, doomed to wander the world until he died. In the course of his wanderings Cain coupled with supernatural beings, spirits, even animals and plants, and peopled the earth with monsters. Some of them, in turn, interbred with giants, and so Grendel's ancestors were born.

BEOWULF'S ARMOUR *page 134*

Beowulf's armour was the most princely ever seen in those parts: though it had little effect on supernatural beings, it over-awed mortal enemies before a blow was struck. His helmet was steel, bound with silver and inset with plaques showing wild boars (the emblem of Beowulf's people) and a mesh of metal fit to shatter any sword. His chainshirt was sewn with gemstones, glittering in the sun like light in a flashing stream, and he carried a magic warsword lent him by Unferth (the man who mocked him in Heorot for losing the swimming-race: see page 132). Like King Arthur's sword Excalibur (see page 220), this one had a name, Hrunting, and its edge had been tempered in blood, not water, and smeared with dragon-poison so that no man injured by it ever recovered from his wounds. Beowulf took it politely, realizing that this was Unferth's way of apologizing for his drunken rudeness; but no mortal sword, however powerful, would have helped him against Grendel's mother, and when he swam up from the water-lair at the end of the battle he gave it back to Unferth, unused.

BEOWULF AND THE THRONE OF GEATLAND *page 136*

The king of the Geats was Beowulf's

uncle Hygelac, and he extended his lands by raiding-expeditions east to Sweden and south to the kingdom of the Franks. On one of these raids Hygelac was killed, and Beowulf only escaped, after butchering thirty enemy soldiers, by plunging into the sea with their mail-shirts over his arm and swimming the hundred kilometres home to Geatland. When he told Hygelac's queen that Hygelac was dead, she invited him to take over the throne of Geatland, since her son was a baby, too young to rule. Beowulf refused, preferring to guide and help the boy as he grew up. In due course the young man was old enough to rule without advice, and it was not until after he, too, was killed in war (against marauders in Sweden) that Beowulf accepted the throne at last, and ruled all Geatland until the day of his battle with the treasure-worm (page 136).

CUCHULAIN AND THE THREE WIZARDS
page 141

Cuchulain was no more than a child when he first used his uncle's chariot and horses. He rode out to look for adventure, and came to the castle of the three wizard-sons of Nechtar the Warrior. Their habit was to murder anyone who visited them unannounced, and they saw no reason to spare Cuchulain just because he was a beardless boy. He unyoked his horses in the heat of the afternoon and lay down on the brothers' lawn, in the shade of the chariot, to take a nap. One after another, the brothers ran out of their castle and attacked. The eldest brother, Foill, was protected by a spell which prevented any sharp edge or point from piercing his skin, but instead of using weapons Cuchulain threw his hurling-ball at Foill's forehead, so hard that it passed clean out of the back of his skull and air whistled through the hole. Tuachal, the second brother, could only be killed by the first spear-thrust or sword-stroke; after that, each blow redoubled his strength. Cuchulain dealt with him by snatching his own poison-spear and stabbing him with it before he could catch his breath. The third brother, Fainnle, had the power to change into a swallow and swoop out of danger, but Cuchulain wrestled him into the castle lake and cut off his head while his feathers were too wet to let him fly. His victory over the three brothers so impressed his uncle King Conchubar that he let Cuchulain keep the armour, chariot and wind-horses for his own.

THE TESTS *page 142*

When the test of the wild-cats failed, Laoghaire, Conal and Cuchulain were sent to Ercol. He first made them fight a pack of witches which ripped their clothes from their backs and shredded their skin. Laoghaire and Conal retreated in dismay, but Cuchulain cut the witches to ribbons with his sword and brought back their cloaks as trophies. Then Ercol himself attacked the three young men, sent Laoghaire and Conal scampering, and would have beaten Cuchulain too if Cuchulain had not killed his horse under him, chained him to his chariot and dragged him home.

Laoghaire and Conal refused to accept these tests as fair, and Conchubar sent the three young men to the wizard Curoi for a decision. Curoi challenged them to fight him, one at a time, at midnight. He appeared to Laoghaire and Conal as a giant throwing ripped-up trees for spears, and hurled them into the dung-heap; he sent witches and a seaworm against Cuchulain, and Cuchulain chopped the witches to pieces and dealt with the sea-worm by thrusting his hand down its gullet and wrenching out its heart. Then giant-Curoi appeared, and before he could pick Cuchulain up and hurl him into the dung-heap with the others, Cuchulain leapt with one bound on to his shoulders and sliced off his head.

Laoghaire and Conal still refused to accept Cuchulain as champion, and it was because of this that Curoi (who had more lives than could be ended by one slicing of his head) made himself into the axe-giant and galloped to Conchubar's feast to issue the beheading-challenge (see page 142).

THE GAILIANA *page 144*

So many warriors, from so many Irish kingdoms, went to join Maeve's and Ailell's army that there was no way of avoiding quarrels between them, arguments about who should cross first or last over fords and rivers, strike the fatal blow in boar-hunts, lead the centre attack or guard the wings in battle. Maeve and Ailell decided that the simplest solution was to keep the men separate in national troops, each with its own commander, and for the commanders to meet together as a war-committee under a single leader. (Fergus MacRogh was later chosen for this job: see page 144.). Seventeen troops of men accepted the arrangement; but the eighteenth, the Gailiana or Men of Leinster, refused to admit equality with anyone else. They were the best equipped, best disciplined and bravest warriors in Ireland, they said; their servants were so efficient that they could catch, cook and serve a meal and ready their masters for sleep before other men's servants had so much as unfastened one buckle on their masters' armour. 'What are we to do?' said Maeve. 'If the Gailiana stay as a troop, the army will be torn by jealousy forever. We'd better trap them and kill them.'

'No,' said Ailell. 'We should fight the men of Ulster, not each other. Divide the Gailiana among all the other troops, so that there are no more than five of them, with their servants, at any one camp fire. Split them up, and they'll have nothing to boast about.' So he and Maeve divided the Gailiana, five to each camp-fire through the other seventeen troops. But even apart from each other, and scattered throughout the army, the Gailiana still kept their superiority, and their boasting made them almost as unpopular as the enemy.

THE FAIRY CURSE *page 144*

The reason why no warrior in Ulster but Cuchulain was able to go and fight was a curse put on them by the fairy-wife of a farmer called Crunden. She married him on condition that he never mentioned her name to anyone else, but he was so proud of her that one day, drunk at a fair, he boasted that she could outrun even the wind-horses of the king. At once the king threw Crunden into jail and told his wife that he would be killed unless she at once proved his boast true. She was nine months pregnant at the time, and begged to be allowed to wait until her child was born. But the king and his nobles insisted, and she ran the race, beat the horses, and gave birth to her child in full view of everyone at the finishing-flag. She was physically unharmed by her experience, but furious: she put a curse on the king and his nobles, saying that whenever they had need of strength in battle, they would be as weak as a nine-months-pregnant woman forced to run foot-races. Only Cuchulain, who was not at the fair, escaped the curse.

FERGUS MACROGH *page 144*

Fergus was one of the least sensible princes in Ireland. When he was King of Ulster he married a woman called Ness, and she persuaded him to let her son

247

Conchubar, a child, rule for a year so that when Conchubar grew up his children could have the honorific title 'king's son' or 'king's daughter'. All through the year of Conchubar's reign Ness gave bribes to every lord and lady in Ulster, and at the end of it, when Fergus asked for his kingdom back, they said, 'You thought so little of us that you gave us a child to rule us. We'll keep Conchubar as king.'

Fergus swallowed the insult, and lived in Conchubar's shadow for a dozen years. Then he began plotting revenge. First, he trained Conchubar's nephew Cuchulain in warskills, hoping that one day he would unseat Conchubar and give him (Fergus) back his throne. Then, when Maeve and Ailell attacked Ulster, he hotheadedly joined their expedition, and was made its leader because he knew the countryside. Then he slept with Maeve, and while they were in each other's arms Ailell crept up on them and stole Fergus' sword, replacing it with a wooden toy which made him the laughing-stock of the army. Finally, Fergus went as one of the champions who had to fight Cuchulain single-handed, and unsuccessfully tried to talk him into surrendering.

HEALING THE MORRIGU *page 146*

Cuchulain's magic was so powerful that only he could heal the wounds he made, even if his victim was a goddess. The Morrigu therefore kept appearing before him in human shape, hoping for help; but he always recognized her and refused. Then one hot day, plagued with thirst, he begged for a drink from a one-eyed old woman milking a cow, and rashly added the words, 'May the giving give the giver good.' The disguised Morrigu gave him a drink at once, and her eye was healed.

BLANAD'S DEATH *page 152*

Feirceirtne, Curoi's jester, rode disguised to Ulster to avenge his master's death. He came on Blanad standing alone on a clifftop overlooking the sea, ran at her in a fury and toppled both her and himself to death on the rocks below.

CALATIN AND HIS SONS *page 152*

After Maeve agreed to let only one man at a time fight Cuchulain (see page 145), and he killed everyone who challenged him, she began to fear that she would lose every man in her army, one by one. Calatin the enchanter suggested a solution. 'I have twenty-seven sons and one nephew,' he said. 'All are identical to me in looks: we could use magic to make Cuchulain take us for just one man, and finish him with our poison-spears.' Maeve eagerly agreed, and next morning Cuchulain found himself ringed by what seemed like twenty-nine mirror-reflections of the same warrior. Calatin, his sons and his nephew threw their poison-spears at the same moment, and Cuchulain gathered them on his shield like a porcupine's quills and began hacking off the shafts. While he was distracted by this, the others wrestled him to the ground and twisted his face in the mud to smother him. He would have had no chance if Fiacha, one of Maeve's men who thought it shameful for twenty-nine men to masquerade as one, had not rushed up and sliced off their right hands with a single sword-sweep. Cuchulain jumped up, caught his breath, and while Calatin and the others were still hopping about clutching their bleeding stumps, chopped them to morsels and fed them to the Morrigu's starving bocanachs and bananachs.

If Cuchulain had not been under an enchantment, a series of grim omens would quickly have persuaded him not to go to war. His chariot-horse Grey of Macha at first refused the yoke, and wept tears of blood when Cuchulain coaxed it to obey him. He asked his mother for a farewell drink, and each time she gave him the cup it was filled with blood. He passed a girl washing clothes on stones by the river, and the tears she wept and the clothes she washed were as red as blood. He found three hags roasting a hound on rowan-spits; they gave him a haunch of it to eat, and as soon as his teeth touched the meat strength ebbed from his own leg and thigh, for the hags were Calatin's daughters and the hound was himself, the Hound of Ulster. These omens convinced him that his death-day had come and that the coming battle would be his last. But his pride, added to the witches' enchantment, gave him no choice but to ride and fight whatever the consequences.

These stories come from a collection called *Mabinogion* ('Tales of Youth'). The four stories in this chapter, people thought, were like main branches on a tree of tales, and other ideas were added like twigs or leaves. Other *Mabinogion* tales are the story of Maxen's Dream (page 216), the story of Lud and the Two Dragons (page 217), the stories of Percival (Chapter Six), Culhwch (Chapter Seven), Owain (Chapter Eight) and Geraint and Ynid (Chapter Ten), and the story of Rhonabwy's Dream (page 244).

The cauldron of rebirth was originally the Sun's property – the boat in which she rode round the earth each day, dying at dusk and being reborn at dawn – but it was stolen by a giant called Llassar Llaes Gyngwyd and hidden in his underwater lair in Lough Neagh in Hibernia. The gods harassed Llassar Llaes Gyngwyd with storms and earthquakes until he left the Lough, carrying his cauldron, and went into hiding as a servant of the king of Hibernia, with his wife, a straw-haired hag twice as big as he was. They lived with the king for fourteen years, and Llassar Llaes Gyngwyd delighted everyone with the beautiful leather shoes, shields and saddles he made. But he and his wife bred a family of brawling, ever-hungry giantlings, and the king could think of no way to quieten their howling or stop them eating him out of house and home. In the end he left a dozen barrels of beer lying about, and when the giants had drained them and were roaring drunk, he threw them into the cauldron of rebirth, piled wood round it and set fire to it. The giants noticed nothing until the cauldron was red-hot, and then Llassar Llaes Gyngwyd jumped out with a roar, picked up the cauldron as if it were an acorn, and hurled it into the Irish Sea to cool it, with his wife and brats inside. He never set foot in Hibernia again, and gave the cauldron to Bran's father Llyr, god of the sea (which is how it came into Bran's possession, for him to give to Mallolwych). As for Llassar Llaes Gyngwyd, his wife and their giantlings, they went to live in Caledonia, where they were the ancestors of all the brigand-giants who infested that part of Britain.

In some versions of the story, the Hibernians planned a trap for Bran and his followers. The roof of the enormous house was supported on one hundred stone pillars, and on every pillar they hung a bag containing an armed man. But one of Bran's followers (some say it was Evnissyen, others one of Bran's fellow-giants) went to inspect the house before the conference.

'What's in these bags?' he growled.

'Nothing but flour,' they said. He reached inside, bag after bag, took the warrior's skull in his fist and crushed it.

'What are you doing?' they asked him.

'Grinding the flour,' he said.

BRAN'S HEAD *page 163*

Some versions of the story set these events in the time of Caratacus the British prince who opposed the Romans (see page 215). He would have planted Bran's head on the southern shore of Albion, to warn against Roman attack, but his wicked uncle Casbellaun, who favoured Rome, put on a cloak of invisibility and began slaughtering Caratacus' men, who could see no one to fight against but only a swordblade slicing through the air. Casbellaun spared Caratacus' life (because he was soft-hearted about his relatives), but Bran's head was never planted, and the Romans invaded and took Caratacus back to Rome as a prisoner of war.

In another version of the story, also set in earlier times, the head was planted on the White Rock in London (later the site of Guinever's castle, and then of the famous Tower); it protected Britain for many generations, until Arthur came to the throne, announced that he would guard Britain himself and needed no magic heads to help him, and dug it up.

THE FIVE PRINCES *page 163*

In some versions of the story, five Hibernian princes and their mothers survived the massacre as well as Bran and the Cambrians. They hid in the hills of their empty country, and in due course the five princes grew up, married each other's mothers and had children of their own. They divided Hibernia between them, and were the first five kings of Ireland; they and their descendants repopulated the island.

ARANRHOD'S CHILDREN *page 169*

Aranrhod was right to claim that she had never slept with a man: her babies' father was an immortal, Wave son of Sea. The first child (the baby born when she lifted her skirt to jump over Math's magic wand) was called Dylan. He was more at home in water than on lands, and soon escaped from the mortal world to live in his father's element. The second baby (the one born miraculously from the blood-drop) could never be harmed so long as he kept one foot on land or in water: this was the secret his wife had to discover before he could be killed (see page 170). In some accounts, the second baby was not Aranrhod's at all but Goewin's, conceived when Gilvaethwy and Gwydyon raped her (see page 168): it was because she was pregnant that Math sent her away from court. In these versions, the arguments that followed, about naming and arming the child, were between Gwydyon and Goewin, and Aranrhod took no part in them.

JUBAL THE BEAR *page 175*

In some versions, the bear was not one of the three magic brothers but a young man called Jubal, and he carried Jack to a camp in the woods filled with men and girls who spent their time not in conjuring or tumbling but in hunting, racing and playing games, until the girl from the Castle of the Golden Apples came to fetch a husband and they all went to watch with 'bear' Jubal gambolling at their head. After Jack was proved to be the girl's rightful husband, they all rode back to the Castle of the Golden Apples, and the three magic brothers conjured, cart-wheeled and stilt-walked to entertain at the wedding-feast.

THE TEST *page 176*

In some versions, the test of husbands was done not with a ring but with a handkerchief spread on the floor. Jack's brothers were asked to step on it, and it turned to a pool of water under the oldest brother's feet and a pool of mud under the second brother's feet. Only for Jack did it remain a handkerchief, and he danced, cartwheeled and somersaulted on top of it while the servants laughed for glee.

THE OLD MEN OF THE FOREST *page 191*

In some versions, there were two Old Men of the Forest. The first Old Man knew nothing except how to find his elder brother (a man so old that his fingers were as gnarled as hawthorn-twigs and his cobweb-silver beard wound round his waist in seven times seven coils); it was the elder brother who told Dougal's father how to find the Wizard-king and how to choose between the pigeons.

FEEDING THE HORSE *page 192*

In some versions, the horse tricked the stable-lads into letting it drink by refusing all normal horse-food (such as oats or hay) and eating nothing but salt beef until its tongue was black and swollen from thirst. Afraid that it would die, the stable-lads took it to the river to drink – and so the trick was worked.

THREE SHAPE-CHANGERS *page 192*

In some versions, there were three shape-changers, not one: the Wizard-king and his two sons. The sons accompanied their father everywhere (as Morgan le Fay's shape-changing daughters accompanied her: see page 235), but they took no part in the transformations until Dougal became a salmon, when they and their father changed into three otters diving, three hawks swooping on the swallow, three labourers building the lady's garden wall (and asking for ring-Dougal in pay-ment), three blacksmiths poking in the fire and three cockerels pecking up the corn.

THE LAIDLY BEAST *page 193*

Another story of the Laidly Beast con-nects it with St Columba. He was travell-ing through Scotland, converting the natives to Christianity, and stopped be-side the loch to preach to a large gathering of heathen. While he was preaching, one of his servants called Mocumin decided to go for a cooling swim, and the Beast sensed his movements in the water and reared up its head to devour him. Just in time, the St Columba made the sign of the cross in the air and shouted to the Beast to leave him, in the name of Christ. The Beast cowered back to its lair, Mocumin was rescued, gasping with terror, and the heathen were so impressed by the miracle that they were converted to Christianity on the spot.

THE DOG COMPANION *page 194*

In some versions, although the otter and the hawk vanished after the share-out of the meat, the dog trotted at Tam's heels as his companion throughout his adven-tures. It saved his life twice, by distract-ing the attention of one of the second giant's two heads (see page 195) while Tam sliced off the other, and by barking and snarling at the Laidly Beast during the battle (see page 195). (In these versions the Laidly Beast had three heads, and it took Tam three days, and three battles, to kill it.)

THE GIANT'S TREASURE *page 195*

In some versions, the second giant kept his treasure not in a cavern but in a castle, guarded by a witch with a magic club which ground anything it touched to dust. Tam cut off the witch's head, but she picked it up and stuck it back on her neck without turning a hair, and it was not till he wrestled the club from her and ground her to dust that he was able to enter the castle and see the treasure.

THE BLACK HORSE *page 197*

Some accounts made Tam not a fisherman's son but a prince, and gave him no ordinary horse but the Black Horse of the Winds. The horse was able to outride the swiftest storm, and when Tam needed to reach the loch-wife's island he spurred it from loch-side to island in a single leap.

TWENTY-SEVEN MOUTHFULS *page 201*

In some accounts, the Old Man told Conor a more complicated, less easy cure for his loss of appetite. In the red embers of an oak-wood fire he was to roast three times nine mouthfuls the size of pheasant's eggs, and each mouthful was to contain eight different kinds of grains (wheat, barley, rye and so on), eight seasonings and eight sauces. He was to wash the meal down with as much milk as twenty men might drink, 'thick milk, yellow bubbling milk, milk that gurgles down the throat'. It was this last detail, the gurgling milk, which finally tempted the hunger-beast to leap from Cathal's mouth.

UNDERLAND *page 206*

Underland is another name for Tir na n'Og, the Land of Youth, a fairy kingdom whose inhabitants never aged or died. It lay under our mortal world, and was an exact mirror-image of it, with lakes, fields, trees, farms and animals exactly like ours. Except for its location, it was an equivalent of the island of Avalon (see page 210): a place where deserving human beings might find eternal happiness at the end of their mortal lives.

THE HEN-WIFE'S CHILDREN *page 208*

In some versions, instead of the beggar-child and the sick old woman Kathleen cured the two daughters of the wicked queen's hen-wife, and the hen-wife ran to tell her mistress about the magic scissors and comb. The queen demanded the scissors and the comb, and when Kathleen agreed to hand them over if she could spend a night with her husband for each of them, she gave the husband a sleeping-potion, so that all Kathleen could do was gaze all night at his beloved face and weep.

THREE CREATURES *page 209*

In some accounts, as well as the dove, a hawk and a fox also answered Kathleen's piping. The glass egg with the wicked queen's life was in a duck, the duck was in a ram and the ram was inside the hollow tree. When Kathleen's husband split the tree, the fox killed the ram, the duck flew into the air and the hawk swooped on it, making it drop and smash the egg.

FAMILY TREES

BRUTUS, CORIN AND THEIR DESCENDANTS

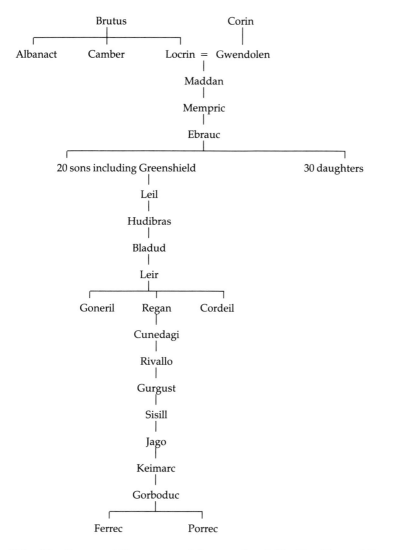

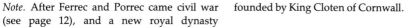

Note. After Ferrec and Porrec came civil war (see page 12), and a new royal dynasty founded by King Cloten of Cornwall.

ARTHUR'S FAMILY TREE

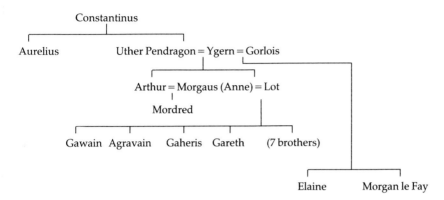

N.B. In some accounts, Margaus is the daughter of Ygern and Gorlois, and therefore not Arthur's full sister: this makes Mordred not his brother-son but (something far less harmful or sinful) his nephew. The seven brothers of Gawain, Agravain, Gaheris and Gareth, long after the fall of Camelot, became kings of distant lands in the far west of the world, so fulfilling Merlin's prophecy (page 27).

GAWAIN'S FAMILY TREE

TRISTRAM'S FAMILY TREE

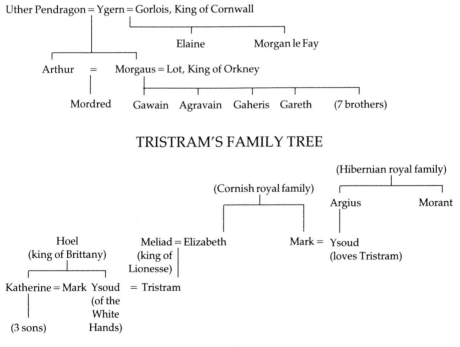

LANCELOT'S FAMILY TREE

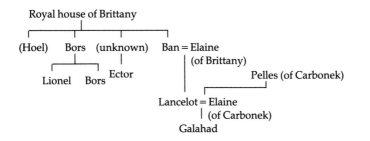

N.B. Some say that Hoel was not Ban's brother but his cousin. Lancelot and his cousins Bors and Lionel were brought up as children by the enchantress Nimue of the Lake (see page 86), and only met Ector for the first time when he and they went to seek their fortunes in Camelot. Ector is no relation of the Ector who brought up the boy Arthur (see page 29).

SOME BOOKS
TO READ

This is a selection of particularly enjoyable novels and story-collections which use these tales. Most libraries should have copies – and browsing through the fiction, myth and folklore sections will lead to many discoveries not mentioned here. Dates and publishers are given for modern writers' works and for recommended translations of older ones: these should be enough to help librarians or booksellers locate them in reference books such as *British Books in Print*.

CHAPTERS 1–3

History of the Kings of Britain by Geoffrey of Monmouth (12th century) is a jolly mixture of fiction and half-remembered historical fact. Geoffrey was fascinated by magic, and his accounts of Merlin, and of the part played by sorcery in Vortigern's reign, are some of the best things in his book; but he had a modern reporter's eye for a juicy story, true or false, and his accounts of the madder British kings are as fascinating as a gossip column. The best translation is by Lewis Thorpe (Penguin, 1966).

CHAPTERS 4, 5, 9, 11, 14, 15

The most famous of all books about King Arthur is *Morte d'Arthur* by Sir Thomas Malory (15th century). While in prison for cattle-rustling, Malory spent his time collecting, translating and expanding every Arthur story he could find, and his book is still vivid, exciting and moving. It is available in the (perfectly comprehensible) English he wrote it in (ed. Michael Senior, Collins, 1980). Of the thousands of later versions, the best are John Steinbeck's *The Acts of King Arthur and his*

Noble Knights (Farrar, Straus and Giroux, New York, 1977), based closely on Malory, and T. S. White's *The Once and Future King* (Collins, 1958), which, by treating the knights and lords of old like people with modern feelings and a modern sense of humour, turns the stories into an exciting (and very funny) modern novel, far better than the childish cartoon-film *The Sword in the Stone* which Walt Disney made of parts of it. The story of Gawain's contest with the huge green man is beautifully told in the 15th-century poem *Sir Gawain and the Green Knight*, little-read but glorious and moving. (A good translation is by J. A. Burrow, Penguin, 1982).

CHAPTERS 6–8, 10, 18–21

The stories in these chapters are told complete, with many other details, in the 15th-century Welsh collection *Mabinogion*. The clearest, most vivid translation is by Gwyn Thomas and Thomas Jones (Golden Cockrel Press, 1948).

CHAPTERS 12 AND 13

Chrétien de Troyes' *The Quest for the Holy Grail* (12th century) is the main source for these stories, and mixes them with gentle discussions of their Christian meaning. Malory adapted parts of the book in his *Morte d'Arthur*, but it's well worth tracking down, and persevering with, Chrétien's original. A good translation is by Pauline Matarasso (Penguin, 1969). (Chrétien also wrote a *Lancelot* and a *Morte d'Arthur*, dealing with the events of Chapters 14 and 15 of this book, but they are far less readable than his Grail-account.) The Grail story is also the basis of Rosemary Sutcliffe's superb novel *The Light Beyond the Forest* (Bodley Head, 1979), whose sequel *The Sword and the Circle* (Bodley Head, 1981) also deals with Arthur and his lords.

CHAPTERS 16 AND 17

The story of Beowulf was first told in an anonymous epic poem of the 10th century; the clearest translation (in prose) is Robert Nye's *Beowulf the Bee-Hunter* (Faber & Faber, 1968), and the translation which gives the best feel of the original poetry is by Michael Alexander (Penguin, 1973). The story of Cuchulain was first translated from the Gaelic by Lady Gregory, and her book *Cuchulain of Muirthemne* (1902; 5th ed.

Colin Smythe Ltd, 1970) is the basis for such lively later versions as Rosemary Sutcliffe's novel *The Hound of Ulster* (Bodley Head, 1963).

CHAPTERS 19–21

Of the thousands of folk-tale collections available, those closest to the original form of the stories include Jeremiah Curtin's *Myths and Folk-tales of Ireland* (1890, republished by Dover in 1975), with some particularly good stories of Finn MacCool, W. B. Yeats' *Fairy and Folk Tales of Ireland* (1888; republished by Colin Smythe Ltd in 1973), and Kathleen Briggs' two-volume *Dictionary of British Folk-tales* (Routledge and Kegan Paul, 1970–1), with its shorter selection *British Folk-tales and Legends: a Sampler* (Routledge and Kegan Paul, 1977). These books, and Andrew Lang's more child-centred *Colour Fairy Books* (originally published by Longman in the 1900s; reprinted by Dover in the 1970s) will tickle the palate of anyone even remotely interested in folk-stories; they are where most modern folk-tale books begin.

INDEX

261